Glories
of
Midnight

A Novel of the Peacock Court

ISBN
978-0-9997603-3-8

August Publishing

First Edition

For Lindsay

Glories of Midnight

A Novel of the Peacock Court
Book Three

E. S. Obern

This is the paradox of trauma: The worst has already happened, so the place of trauma, conversely, becomes a safe place. The limits of pain are known. Tasted, felt, suffered. The boundaries have been marked in the soul. So the sufferer returns to the place of suffering, knowing its limits, having grown into its dimensions. A fish swimming in the poisoned water of its tank. It may have some faint memory of the ocean, but kept in the tank, it learns the invisible boundaries that contain it. It feels safe, drinking its contaminated water. Swimming in its own filth. Thus, the courtesan. Having been raped, having been degraded, having been subjected to gendered oppression day in and day out throughout the entirety of life, the courtesan does not seek freedom. Trauma is a known entity, not a threat. Degradation is a chore to be borne in hopes of reward for having suffered prettily. Oppression is accepted in return for the oppressor's approval. Its least valued member by far, the courtesan does not criticize the Court.

He cannot afford to. What he can afford are the trinkets and emblems of beauty and privilege allotted to his position. That is enough for most. For the Court exists in a precarious balance: too cruel, and it destroys its own members; too lax, and it loses control. So a balance is struck. Here is your position: here is what it takes to keep it, here is what you must suffer, here is what you are given in return. You will always have less power and respect than the women of the Court, the women who run the Empire. But you will always have more than the commoners beneath you. You will have beauty to be envied (until you get old, and then you are tucked away and forgotten, or become a tool to increase the power of the women in your life.) You will have privilege to be enjoyed (decorations, and servants, and conveniences, until you become inconvenient, and then you will have memories of youth.) You will have money and the power that comes with it (for a brief time, until your beauty is no longer a viable commodity, and then you will make do with what little is left.)

But you will always be a lord. Not as good as a Lady, and you can never be a Conventionwoman or a Steward, and whoever heard of a male Empress? But a lord is better than a peasant. And even if some of the female peasants have more power and agency than you, well, they are still peasants. You are a lord. They cannot take that from you. It means something, to be a lord. Grace and status cling to the syllable; the very word is gilded. As long as you hold your position, as long as you cling to what it means to be a lord, and everything that comes with it, you get to stay in your place. It's not such a bad place. You never had a chance of getting the best place, no, but your Lady might, your daughters might, and you can help them. It would be selfish not to. It's not such a bad position, worse than some maybe, but if accept that – if you defend that – you're still better off than most.

This is the deal that is offered to you when you are born a lord in the Empire of Kanai.

You always accept.

But, maybe, some of you remember the ocean. The tank in which they're keeping you is far inland. The water, though contaminated, will not kill you quickly.

Still.

If you leapt far enough, would you reach open water?

-Vin Ayet, Ages, 05.24.1010
"Instruments of Oppression: Trauma"

Part One
The Deal

Chapter One

The Palace rose above him, a single tower eclipsing the sun. Pale rays found glints of gold against the curve of the dome, the fluted hollows of the pillars, the polished mirror of the courtyard across which Luken tread. All white and gold, as if the Palace had been forged from the heat of dawn.

The servant strode ahead of Luken in swift, relentless strides. He struggled to keep pace, the heavy billows of his ando surging in a scarlet wave at his feet as Luken scurried to answer the summons of the Empress.

The courtesan suppressed the urge to vomit up his nerves.

"What did she say she wanted with me?"

The messenger cast him an annoyed glance. "What do you think she wants with you, boy? What does any woman want you for?"

Luken stomped to a halt, his steps echoing into the bright shadows of the ivory vaults above. "Who are you?"

She answered without glancing back, her voice ringing against the stone. "The Steward of the Royal Chambers."

The breath left Luken's body. For the Empress to send not a common messenger, but one of her Stewards... If he had been nervous before, it was nothing to the feeling that wracked his body into stilted strides as he struggled to keep pace with the Steward.

They came, at last, to the heart of the Palace. Here, the ceilings lowered, the harsh white and gold surrendered to a blush of pastel colors and damasks upon the walls and they came, through a heavily armored ring of guards, to the Inner Chambers where the royal family lived. Over an oak door with a polished, bronze knocker, the emblem of a peacock had been carved and painted in the wood of the doorframe. Luken eyed the guards to either side, dressed in pale armor, their faces hidden beneath their helms, a spear in one hand, a sword at their hip, a musket strapped to their backs. The eunuchs who formed the guards of the Inner Chamber. Second only to the Empress's hand-picked private guard, these men were donated to the military at birth, as the unwanted boys of Noble Houses often were, but raised apart, trained from earliest memory to iron and blood and absolute devotion to the royal family.

Luken swallowed as the Steward sifted through the keys on the ring – wider in circumference than her wrist – until she settled on a long, gold key with the symbol of a blue feather wrought at the head, and slipped it into the lock.

They entered upon a private garden, buried in the heart of the Palace. Unroofed, the sky formed a circlet of fading blue high above, as though at the far end of a spyglass. A spiral of ascending pathways led up through the Palace, barred from open air by a lattice of iron lace between them that evoked the latticework through which Empress Aikanzo had first glimpsed her beloved Liliray in his maternal House.

Lilies circled the grass. Jasmine climbed the first few floors of the spyglass garden, shadowing them in a semblance of privacy. A dozen guards in their pale armor stood around the perimeter of the garden, though there were only two entrances; the one through which Luken had emerged, and the far entryway, which sloped up into the spiraling pathway behind the latticework. They kept an eerie stillness, broken only by the Steward's stride through the grass and the murmur of the figures seated at a table on the far side. Between them, pieces of polished stones in many colors spangled a checkered board.

Luken followed, the train of his ando brushing a hint of perfume from the lilies with each silent stride.

The Empress Raisaga, and her daughter, Princess Oan.

Luken folded to his knees and pressed his forehead to the grass, heart pounding in his ears.

"Lord Luken Kenkazu-son, Your Grace," came the Steward's voice, laden with irony.

"Rise, Luken." The Empress's voice, warm and quiet.

As he pulled to his full height, Luken noted the Princess watching him, not a sliver of recognition on her face though he knew her all too well from the party a few years ago at which he had – a chill of memory – met Lady Dare, the Empress's niece. How the circle traced to its end; a snake swallowing itself.

"My Lady Empress," he said softly, bowing his head.

"You may leave us, Oan." The Empress nodded to her Steward, "Fi."

Left alone, the Empress studied him, her

expression one of calm curiosity. "You're a hard man to find, Luken."

Luken blinked. "My Empress had only to send for me, and I would have rushed to attend her."

She chuckled. "Ah, but I would have sent for you sooner, if I had only gotten your name that day in the garden. Do you recall it? Pazu's son had become a little over-impassioned, shall we say, in the rivalries of courtesan life."

Dread sickened his heart. "I pray we did not offend thee-"

He fell silent at the wave of her hand. "I was not offended, Lord Luken. Curious, perhaps. But not offended. Sit."

Gliding through a dream, Luken took the seat lately abandoned by Princess Oan and found himself opposite the Empress of Kanai, not three feet apart. "I had my Steward make inquiries, you know." Her eyes flickered, as though studying each feature of his face. "But 'a beautiful young man with black hair' is a rather poor description to go on when searching the Garden. Rather like trying to find a particularly fine leaf among all the trees in the forest." She cocked an eyebrow. "A daresay there were plenty of volunteers offered when the Abode Masters heard the Empress's Steward was making inquiries."

Despite his nerves, a grin tugged at the corner of Luken's lips as he imagined Amae shoving his way through a crowd of greedy, grasping Masters to thrust his own courtesans in front of the Empress. "I daresay there was."

The Empress reached out an idle hand, placed the tip of her finger upon a blue stone, and watched it glide three places across the board, joining a formation there, like a V of geese in flight. "In the end, the Steward had to find that boy, Ohfene Pazu-son, to get your name."

Luken's eyebrows rose. "Ohfene told you who I was?"

The Empress chuckled. "From the sound of it, I don't think he relished surrendering the information. But it seems he guided my Steward true." Her eyes flashed up to meet his. "And here you are."

Luken made a mental note to tell Isaun that it had been Ohfene who'd been forced to give his name to the Empress; how he must have hated sending a rival to this meeting, but he wouldn't have dared lie to the Empress's Steward. Isaun would love it.

"I am at your service, Your Majesty."

"Indeed. And what services are you equipped to provide to your Empress, I wonder?"

"I dare not describe them in such esteemed company, my Lady."

She laughed then, a full, brilliant laugh. "Ah, but you are just as I was told you'd be. Beautiful, bright, and when the mood strikes, coy as a demon prince." She looked at him then as so many Ladies had looked at Luken before he found himself with a new client. A disorienting moment. Did he dare place the Empress in that same category, even in the privacy of his mind?

Confusion snarled his voice. "Forgive me, my Lady, but I still find myself in the dark."

"No matter, Luken. I desire only the pleasure of your company."

"That I have in ample supply, if indeed it gives

you pleasure."

"It does. But I would rather speak of what you take pleasure in, my young lord."

I don't think you would. Luken's thoughts went reflexively to Jes, and her face flashed before his mind, dark eyes unguarded. Unconsciously, his hand moved to angle a rose-marbled stone across the board at random, swooping the piece to the left-end of a broken crescent Oan had been assembling.

She wanted him coy? Fair enough. That was one role he certainly could play. "If I confess it, you must not put it about."

She looked up, intrigued, and leaned toward him. "You have my word."

He leaned toward her, mirroring her gesture, and the space between them narrowed over the checkered board.

The blush was genuine, if the feeling behind it was not, and Luken knew the rose beneath his pale-blue courtesan's paint only completed the image in her eyes; the shy lordling, a vault of sweetness beneath the sex appeal. "The other courtesans would mock me, but... I am..."

She leaned closer.

"Too much a fan of poetry."

The Empress blinked at him – and burst into laughter. "Ah! Salacious indeed!"

Luken released a silent sigh. He had amused her twice.

A thrill of relief. But is this what she wanted him for, this courtesan banter? Surely the Empress had no need of him for that.

"My Lady Empress." A voice, from the far

entrance. The Steward of the Royal Chambers, Fi, returned with a stern Lady in her mid sixties perhaps, with iron grey hair, a prominent nose, no chin to speak of, and dark eyes that lanced through Luken as if he were only another lily of the garden before settling on the Empress. "The Council of Defense is ready for you, Your Grace."

The Empress stiffened, her tone riming over with a frost Luken had not heard there before. "I daresay I know my schedule, Lady Ekaris, having set it myself. I am not so senile, yet. The Council will begin when I arrive."

A distinctly hostile smile spread over the Lady's dry lips. "Of course, Your Grace. One only imagines how you find the time to defend our Empire with so many pressing concerns demanding your attention." Her gaze lingered on Luken, and he answered it with a *fuck you* smile, as that seemed to have become the fashion of late.

"If you ever looked beyond the end of your musket, I dare say you'd find there are a great many things in this Empire of ours that demand my attention," the Empress said dryly. "Thank you, Lady Ekaris."

The Lady dipped a bow, and turned to leave.

The Empress sighed and flicked her gaze to Luken. "Since the election, some of my Ladies seem to have trouble remembering that the Empire still has an Empress." She shook her head. "Till we meet again, Luken Kenkazu-son."

He slipped from the seat and let the petals of his ando fall around him with silent grace.

"Fi, if you would escort the lord out."

The Steward nodded. "Of course, Your Grace."

Luken strode after her, journeying the passage from chalice of gazes to the sanctum of invisibility. It was a familiar journey, to pass from center of attention to absolute irrelevance in the world of women, often accomplished in the blink of an eye.

Luken's joh rang off the marble, following in Fi's silent panther-stride through the Palace once more. The light faded from the windows, a dull purple drifting into darkness. Around them, white-clad servants transferred embers from lantern to lantern and lifted them on long poles into the rafters, a blazing path spangling the way before them.

"She likes you," Fi said at length.

Luken raised an eyebrow. "Surely the Empress could have any courtesan she wishes, without this preamble."

"Yes," was her only reply.

Stars trembled in the early evening as Luken swept free of the Palace. From this height, the Garden sprawled before them, a quilt of diamond-shaped courtyards burst-through with gold-leafed trees and the colored tiles of the Abodes' slanted roofs. Luken thought he spied the Abode of Scattered Flowers, nestled there, in the heart of the Garden. The sonorous voice of a bell rang out from high above and behind him; evening song, as the Palace beckoned to the night. The bell's tone trembled to silence, and a high clamor kicked up in its wake, silvery and bright as the stars they sang down from the heavens. Luken drew a deep breath, waiting for it – an echo, answering from the city. The Temple of Kuiken and the Temple of

Shayah, twin voices, clear and strong, ringing out from across O-Han's breadth. And then, joining in the song, a light and lovely stream of notes chorused up from the lesser temples scattered across O-Han as the Palace called to the city and the city called to the Palace, and together, they sang in the night. And fell, softly, to silence.

Ah, but he would miss this. Not much else perhaps, when he left Court, but he would miss this.

"Come," the Steward barked, her legs pumping down the steps.

Annoyance flashed as he silked into her shadow. "I can make my way home from here, thank you. Your presence is not required."

She ignored him, taking the lead through the Garden. Luken refused to quicken his stride to meet her. She annoyed him, this one, and if she insisted on leading the way, she would just have to wait for him and to the Seven Hells with politeness. He was done scurrying around after women like a dog at their heels. She stopped once, eighteen paces ahead of him, and waited, radiating irritation as he closed the distance with somewhat more patience than necessary.

The Steward cocked an eyebrow. "You're one of those courtesans that looks sweet, but comes with a bite, I take it. Lucky for you, that's the Empress's type." For the first time, she looked him in the eyes. Hers were large and round; a deep, multifaceted brown, like knotted oak. "Oh yes, I see why she had me running all over the Garden looking for you. Her type, indeed. And young too, but not *too* young. A rare find."

Luken took that moment to delicately clear his

throat. "Doesn't the Empress already have a Consort?"

"Mind your place." Those were the last words she spoke to him until they reached the Abode of Scattered Flowers.

As they entered the courtyard, Luken found the Abode's windows agleam with a soft, amber radiance. The shadowed column of a body, blurred by white curtains, hovered at the window. At the sound of his joh clicking on the tiles, the figure within stirred, and the curtain pulled back to reveal Lifelle's face, all excitement.

No sooner had Luken reached the porch than Lifelle and Dandelion tumbled out the front door, nearly smashing Fi aside with the ferocity that threw the door open.

Lifelle seized his arms. "Did you really meet the Empress?"

"Yes," he breathed, and mewls of excitement met this response.

Luken looked over Lifelle's shoulder and Dandy's shining face. Isaun stood in the center of the Abode's main room, his expression blank.

"Your Abode Master," Fi demanded.

Isaun stared at her for a long moment, his features striking in their cold repose. Then, with indifferent grace, he pivoted and strode from the main room, his ando a river of burgundy, pricked with opals, slithering in his wake.

"What did the Empress say to you?" Dandy's large, dark eyes drank in Luken as if he was a wonder.

"I'll tell you everything in a moment," he whispered, and pushed past them, into the Abode.

Amae, head bowed toward Fi, answered her in low tones. Isaun stood a few paces behind his master, his hands folded before him as he watched the scene play out. Luken tried to catch his eye, to impart with the quirk of a brow or the flash of a grin that he had news for the older courtesan, but Isaun would not look his way.

Fi jerked her head in a nod, then spun on her heel and took her leave, scarcely acknowledging Lifelle and ignoring Dandy entirely as she left the Abode.

This was not the welcome Luken had expected. Amae stood where the Steward had left him, and his hands – Luken realized, eyes going wide – trembled as he knotted them together. Luken waited for the usual snarled commands from the Abode Master, but Amae only nodded vaguely in Luken's direction before shuffling back to his room.

"Sit down, sit down!" Lifelle fluttered. Oblivious to the strange silence that dominated the Abode, Dandy kicked a cushion into place beside the low table and knelt. "Take it from the beginning." Lifelle hefted a pot of tea, a breath of chamomile stoking the air as he poured. "Don't leave out a single detail."

Luken turned, confused. "Isaun–"

"I'm retiring for the evening," Isaun muttered, though it was still quite early. He left in long strides, vanishing into the bedroom the two of them shared.

Slowly, Luken lowered himself to kneel at the table. "Some kind of a day this has been…"

Dandy leaned across the table, the rose-pink sleeves of his ando billowing across the polished oak.

"What does the Empress want with you?"

Luken looked back at him, and sighed. "Hell if I know."

Chapter Two

If Luken had expected that his sudden meeting with the Empress would impact his work going forward, he need not have worried. Aside from Lifelle and Dandy's giddy excitement, the Abode of Scattered Flowers offered no response. A harsh contrast to the flurry of change and preparation that ensued after the beginning of his courtship with Dare. He would have thought that the Empress herself would make a bigger splash than the Empress's niece, but Luken awoke the following morning to a strange silence filling the Abode. Amae was nowhere to be found and not for the first time, Luken wondered where the old man limped off to when he wasn't berating his courtesans or negotiating the value of their flesh with Ladies. Isaun had vanished before Luken rolled out of bed and he painted his face before the mirror, taking longer than usual to blot out the dark crescents beneath his eyes. After all the fighting during the election and the blowout after Hani's victory, he and Isaun had reunited for scarcely more than a moment before the Empress's summons had disrupted them again. *We will never really be friends again,* Luken thought, tracing his lips with scarlet. And then, as he stood and turned for his irlan, *We were never really friends to begin with, though.* Luken sighed, twisting the gold-iridescent irlan across his chest. The name *Isaun* was a knife, one side love, one side hate, meeting at the razor-thin edge.

A green ando today, with a heavy billow patterned with gold and lifted to loop around one side before falling into a fluted cascade behind him, the skirts beneath the same deep green, without gold, and the underskirts a fine ivory sheen, like light rolling over the surface of a white pearl. Luken pulled his hair back so that it twisted into the beginnings of a braid behind his head and fell free down his back. He did cut a fine figure, but there was no joy in it this morning. A taut chill on the air, as if the world stood on the precipice of a storm.

In the main room, Luken found a note, white and folded, waiting for him on the table. He prepared tea and a bowl of fruit in the little corner with the stove that served as their kitchen, then flipped open the note as hot green tea bit his tongue.

You have an appointment tonight with Lady Mian, Third Daughter of the House of Victory Hill. Standard request. Nine o'clock at the Blue Dahlia. The coach will arrive at eight.

Amae's cramped cursive. Luken laid aside the note, and took a long sip. So. They intended to continue as if nothing had happened. Strange, that, but so be it.

Standard request. No fetishes or unusual behaviors to cater to. Luken resented the gratitude that washed through him at the words. He had not worked since before the election results came in, and though in truth it had been only a week or so, it seemed another lifetime. Lady Mian. Hadn't she been one of Lifelle's clients, for a brief time? But of course, now that Lifelle was consumed with Lady Ahn, Amae would have pushed her onto him instead. He was a little surprised Amae hadn't taken the opportunity to start building up Dandy's client list. The young lord was still in training, but wasn't it about time to be sending him out to the Dahlia? Perhaps Amae was waiting for a particular caliber of client. Dandy was the son of High House, after all. Amae would want him to appear exclusive. And Isaun was always busy with his long list of clients and courtships, so that left Luken. He wouldn't complain. A nice, normal job to cleanse his palate after all the upheaval. It was just what he needed.

Left to his own devices, Luken lounged on the veranda in the back garden for the better part of the day reading the book Jes had found for him at the used bookstore they visited, *A Likely Story*. The book, a worn chronicle of Empress's Consorts throughout history, sat propped open on his lap. He was up to the chapter on Lonyelay, a fascinating man who – Luken was surprised to find – had virtually ruled the Empire himself when the Empress of the day, Haitano, was senile and in failing health. He had signed bills into law, presided over meetings of the Convention, and even exiled a Lady of some considerable power who offended him. Despised by the Ladies of the time, faced with constant resistance, and openly mocked by peasants and nobles alike, Lonyelay, nonetheless, had nudged the Empire away from its corrupt bureaucracy, in which nothing could be done without bribing at least one official at every level of government, developed the Empire's first governmental system of relief for the poor, and helped his Empress suppress a revolt and protect the inheritance of her daughter when all of her advisers had urged her to abdicate and flee as O-Han burned around her.

And Luken had never heard of him until now. Strange, how the names of men like Lonyelay were buried by history. All he had accomplished – forgotten and ignored, except for a few pages in an old book that probably no one but Luken would ever read.

Luken sighed, a bleakness descending on him in the wake of his initial surge of admiration. Men's accomplishments were never remembered. Historians – almost all women – simply did not acknowledge or care about men's works in general, but oh, how they protected one another's reputations. How they kept famous the ones most like themselves, hearing only what it pleased them to hear. Ladies rolled their eyes whenever a male historical figure was mentioned, as if it was an unreasonable affront on their time to hear about men doing anything, ever. Any accomplishment was dismissed as a modern fabrication to make boys feel less useless. As if history was an unbreakable vault, containing only women, great women, and men had been mindless objects up until a few decades ago, when they had, apparently, awoken from some primordial slumber to discover speech and thought. As if they had just arrived. As if history could only now begin recording their names, if it wanted to, if they deserved it – if women ever decided to allow it. Which they would not.

And thus, Lonyelay, lost to time.

But Luken would remember.

"There are forces of human existence beyond individual control," Luken murmured, reading aloud from the book; Lonyelay's words, reaching out to graze him with a gentle, electric touch, like the gossamer spiral of a jellyfish's limb, swimming past him in the cold and black depths of the sea. "It can be hard to resist them, harder still to change them, and impossible to control them. But in the end, we all have to decide what we will or will not be part of."

He pushed the book aside and gazed out at the garden, watching the shadows of the clouds ink across the combed sands and a peacock, shod of his great fan of feathers as the summer dwindled, settle himself in the grass beneath the cherry tree, going still.

By the time the coach arrived, Luken had been ready for hours. With restless energy, he yanked the green elaborations of his ando into the seat and gazed out through the slightest sliver of visibility, between the veil over the window and the window-frame, to watch O-Han's familiar squalor and splendor blend into one winding, moonstruck river in the night, all darkness and gold.

At the Blue Dahlia, he was greeted by a servant whose face he had seen a thousand times but whose name he had never known, and escorted to a chamber on the top floor. His joh clicked against the polished wood, the tapestries of famous Ladies and courtesans by turns glorious and despoiled sliding by around him until they halted at a familiar door. A wistful grin twitched at Luken's lips. He knew this room, only too well. At this door, he and Isaun had paused – four? five years ago? – and Isaun had quieted his nerves, telling him he was beautiful. Countless people had told Luken he was beautiful over the years, but it had meant something, coming from Isaun, for the man had only said it once.

In these chambers, he had begun his first night of courtesan's work under the tutelage of Lady Kahr. Lost in memories as he gazed about the room, Luken gave a little jump when the servant turned to him with a chaos of scarlet lace and ribbons in her arms. "The Lady has left instructions that you are to be wearing this, when she arrives."

A soft laugh. "Of course she has."

With an admirable stab at keeping a straight face, the servant asked, "Would you like assistance with putting it on?"

"No," Luken said dryly, "I think I can manage."

"Very good, my lord." She ducked a bow and whisked from the room, leaving Luken to tug off his irlan and slip from his ando into the rasping embrace of the scarlet confection. He laid himself upon the bed, an exquisite gift waiting to be unwrapped.

~

As easy as the slip into sleep, Luken watched the world pass with a kind of mindless acceptance as the carriage rattled along through the streets of O-Han the following morning, bearing him back to the Palace. A stark change from a week or two ago, when he would have been alert for any fresh rumors of the election results for the Convention, or news of Iriko's murder. He ignored the news now. A world in which Hani sat in Eikara's seat on the Convention was not a world he cared to hear from. A sort of dreamy emptiness stretched through him, but he reveled in it; it freed him from caring. The wheels of Empire turned; he merely waited to be crushed beneath them. But if he was to be crushed either way, why should he know the exact hour when the oak and iron would close down over his bones? He'd spent his passion in writing all that had passed for an obituary for Iriko. Even now – the thought drifted like a feather through his mind – that article would be reaching the shelves of the newspaper pushers and journal sellers as *Ages* printed its monthly publication.

With annoyance, he felt the carriage slow as they entered the marketplace. Voices crowded the carriage. They came to a standstill as the driver shouted at someone, her voice pitched in annoyance. Somewhere, a horse brayed; a shriek of laughter, the barking of O-Han's wild dogs. Luken sighed.

Pushing himself upright, Luken tugged his veil over his head so as not to be seen by peasants as he nudged the covering back from the window and peeked outside. Perhaps, if they passed a newspaper seller, he might catch a glimpse of the new *Ages* cover, and see if his article had been published yet. With an indignant heave, the carriage started forward again, forced by foot traffic to crawl along. Luken could have traveled faster if he'd shoved the door open and walked, but of course, he'd not get far dressed as he was. Instead, he watched the stalls on his left side carefully, hoping to pass a book or newspaper seller.

Fruits and vegetables teemed from the stalls, swollen with color. Here, pocket-watches sat beneath glass cases. A toy seller found her stall hemmed in by urchins, watching with large, dark eyes as she painted a wooden horse. A Lady stood before a stall, this one of glossy sweets. Luken knew her at once for what she was; the subtle, tailored cut of her black coat and trousers spelling wealth, even if the guard in the regalia of the House of Emerald Echoes standing at one shoulder didn't give her away.

Memory jolted. A strange and pleasant surge. "Lady Kahr?"

She looked up at the sound of her name, brown eyes coming to rest on the veiled face framed by the carriage window. The carriage jolted to a halt again as they reached the cross-streets and a carriage, cutting east to west, trundled across their path. "Driver, wait here a moment!" Luken called, ignoring the driver's muttered curses and the stamp of the horses, annoyed by the crowds in the market.

"Is that you, Luken?" Lady Kahr approached the carriage, dragging a small child of about three or four years by the hand. He whined as she pulled him away from the sweet-seller, though he already gripped a swirl of blue-and-white candy in one little fist, his fingers sticky and smeared, his teeth stained blue.

"How strange, I was just thinking of you last night at the Dahlia."

The Lady chuckled. "You remember that night, a courtesan like you? How flattering. From what I've heard, you've gotten more than enough work in the meantime to forget about old me."

"Don't be ridiculous, of course I remember you." In truth, she would not have stood out in his memory – but she had been his first.

She waved that away but he could see, from the flush that warmed her cheeks, that she was pleased. Kahr glanced down at the boy that gripped her hand, using the anchor of her weight to swing back and forth on his heel, his large eyes, black and liquid as two dark pearls, wandering the busy marketplace with interest.

"I have my own memento from that night," Kahr gave the hand that held her son's a playful swing, "it would be impossible to forget."

Not comprehending, Luken's gaze followed hers, to the boy. And took in the familiar cast of his features. A dark mirror, reflecting Luken's face back at him through the filter of Kahr's swarthier complexion. A single mole dotted one cheek but otherwise, Luken might have been gazing through a portal back into his own childhood.

A fist, whirling out of empty air to knock him flat on his back, could not have stunned Luken with greater force. The breath abandoned his body. "Oh..."

The boy looked up at him, his expression blank, bored, and he returned to his sweet.

"What- what's his name?"

"Roku. First Son of the House of Emerald Echoes."

He could not comprehend her calm indifference. Did she know what she was telling him? It was as if he had suddenly lost the capacity to understand human speech. A wild, sinking panic. And disbelief at *her* – It was as if she thought it meant nothing to him. As if he should be no more interested in this, this information, what it *implied*, than if she'd remarked on a turn of the weather.

"And he's–" *ours*, "yours?" Perhaps there was some misunderstanding. It could not be what he thought. The boy must be a nephew, a little brother, nothing to do with him–

Lady Kahr chuckled. "A shock, isn't it? I thought, when I came home from the war, that I'd missed my chance for motherhood. It just wasn't in the cards for me. My childbearing years ought to have been over, by then. Imagine my surprise," she gazed down at the boy fondly, "when this one came along. My little miracle."

"*Mama*," he whined, kicking one foot out, the wooden sandal flapping, "I want to *go*."

A searing, tearing panic swelled in Luken's chest, as if trying to burst out and through the irlan, spattering the insides of the carriage with his lungs, his heart, his blood. The same swirling dread that had wracked his mind the night before he left the House of the Golden Sun, the night he'd lain awake every moment and watched the clock tick down the final hours of his existence in the same House as Valor. The night he left his daughter.

The carriage jolted forward.

"Looks like the traffic's clearing up," Kahr said, shading her eyes against the sun.

Luken could not tear his gaze from the boy's face. He struggled to form the words in his mind, *my son*. But they would not come. The feeling, like shadows flickering across the inside of his skull. But the words would not form.

"It was good to see you again." Roku tugged on his mother's hand, straining to pull her along; she stood calmly, smiling down at him. "I'd better be getting this one home." Her gaze flicked up to his. "Good-bye, Luken."

The carriage began a slow roll forward. "Good-bye."

How much time passed, Luken didn't know. It seemed eons rattled by as the carriage bore him north, toward the Palace, but it could not have been long, in truth; when he came to himself, they had come as far as the Ruby District, and the Palace reared above them like a pale mountain in the shadows of morning.

Every time he closed his eyes, the same image, carved beneath his lids: The boy in the marketplace that wore his face.

"Driver!" Luken slammed his hand against the side of the carriage. "Nevermind about the Garden, I need you to take me to an address in Topaz."

Her annoyance bled through the carriage walls. With an impatient sigh, Luken added, "For an additional ten bohda, of course."

At once, the carriage groaned into a long turn, cutting across traffic with a wave of peasants shouting as they scampered from the carriage's path, horses huffing in the mounting heat of the day as the sun climbed free of the clouds' fraying wreath.

Chapter Three

"Rori!" Luken thrust the violet door open and crashed into Rori's apartment in the Topaz District like a tsunami, the turbulent swells of his cerulean ando flaring around him. "I swear I'm going to start screaming and never stop- Oh, hello."

Rori twisted around in the cushy armchair in the living room of his small apartment, his brown eyes wide, almost comical, in his pretty, round face. Across from him, a woman in a tailored jacket and trousers gaped at him, lips parted as though mid-sentence when he'd burst in.

"Oh," it escaped Luken as a mewl. "You have company. Well," he gathered up his silken storm and started toward the apartment's single other room, where Kat and Rori slept, "I'll just wait till you're finished, then. Sorry."

"No matter." The woman rose, smoothing the front of her jacket with a swift flick of the wrists. "We were just about done here, I think. I'll be seeing you, Rori. I see you have," she glanced at Luken, "interesting company to attend to. Oh and," she paused at the door, leaning back in to give Rori's hand a formal shake, "congratulations. And good luck."

"Thank you, Polay."

She pulled the door closed behind her, as Rori turned to him. "What's wrong?"

Luken found himself wringing his hands like a

stage player in some Old Dynasty theater, and forced himself to stillness. "Rori-" he breathed, and then it was too much. He collapsed onto the couch, bent double, sobbing for breath.

"Oh Goddess, Luken, what's the matter?" Rori's hands around his shoulders, Rori's hands smoothing back his hair, Rori's hands pulling him close, cheek to chest, as he struggled for breath.

He swallowed a deep breath and managed, in shards and pieces, to explain.

Rori blinked at him. "I... don't understand. You have a son?"

"Goddess, Rori, he looked just like me, but I didn't recognize him at all until Kahr said- How is that possible? How could I have not known my own child?"

"Luken," warm and sweet as honeyed tea, Rori's voice, but there was a nervous tenor there; a stray leaf of wormwood drifting on the ripples, "Surely you expected this?" Luken's eyes went wide, returning Rori's stare. "I mean, isn't that the nature of your work? You probably have multiple children by now-"

Luken stood, ripping free of Rori's grip. "Don't say that." He paced a crescent around the low table in the middle of the living room and stopped, nowhere to go. "I cannot bear the thought of it."

"I'm confused. Weren't you told on your first day of courtesan training that the whole purpose of this endeavor- I mean what did you think it was all for?"

"You'd think they'd tell a man!" Luken exploded, rounding on Rori. He flinched, and Luken stammered, "I'm sorry, Rori, I shouldn't be taking this out on you. I shouldn't even be here, you're busy. Goddess, when will I stop being such an ass?"

Rori laughed. "It's alright. You're a bit shaken, that's all. I suppose it would be a shock to the system, wouldn't it, going through your normal life from day to day and out of the clear blue sky falls a child."

Luken gave a feeble laugh and collapsed again, a wave of silk settling over his legs. "He had my face, Rori..."

"I know." Rori made his way to the stretch of countertop that divided the kitchen from the livingroom and hefted a teapot over the stove. "Tea? I've got green and chamomile."

"He had my eyes."

"Chamomile then, I think."

Luken buried his face in his hands. The domestic clatter of Rori busying about the kitchen steadied his nerves a bit. "I am such an annoyance to you," he murmured.

Rori clucked his tongue, swishing forward to set a teacup on the table in front of Luken before resuming his place in the cushy armchair.

"Ridiculous. It's no trouble at all." They were quiet, a long moment. Rori sipped at his tea, steam coiling up like a phantom reaching to embrace him. "The trouble, Luken, is that the Empire makes no considerations for men such as you. It is assumed, as it has been for millennia, that men are weak in their emotional capacity compared to women," a sip, "and that the goddesses ordained this arrangement to keep us all in our proper roles, so that the wheels of the Empire may turn smoothly. The mother devoted to her children, the children, in turn, obedient to the mother. And the father, spared the same emotional investment, left to attempt reproduction elsewhere, until his youth and vigor are spent, and there is no longer any need for him. At which point it is deemed decorous that he remove himself from public view, now that his use has expired. The idea that a man might possess the same instinctual, emotional investment in his offspring as the mother is deemed not only redundant, but, in truth, a threat."

Luken shook his head, lifting his teacup in both hands. "As if anyone could mistake me for a threat. Seven Hells."

"Ah, but you are, Luken. If you had legal control of your children, as Kahr or even Lady Dare does, well, I daresay things would be done differently."

"That would never happen. A woman always knows when a child is hers. But the father- A father can never be irrefutably proven. There's always reasonable doubt as to the identity of the father."

"Nonetheless, what if you insisted upon being allowed to raise your children?"

"I would be laughed off the face of the earth."

"What if all men insisted on raising their own children?"

Luken gave a bitter laugh. "I daresay the aristocracy would spend a great deal of time at war with itself, fighting over children and inheritance. It would be chaos. Ladies would be wary of using courtesans then, if that courtesan's House was going to sue for custody of the child."

"Like I said, a threat. Better for men to be told they don't have the same emotional capabilities as women, and relinquish their investment before they even considered making it. All stereotypes exist for a reason. And that reason is virtually always the same – it protects the status quo. And what's good for the status quo is good for those in power. In the Empire, that means Ladies like Kahr. Lady Kahr wasn't being cruel when she told you, so casually, that she'd had a son by you. Undoubtedly, it just never crossed her mind that you would care. She would never have even thought of contacting you with that information, solely for the reason that she had probably never known of a Lady in that position reaching out to inform the father. She has probably never heard of a man protesting his lack of access to his children. Lack of protest is deemed consent." He glanced down at his cup, and took a long sip. "If anything, she would believe it to be a burden to you, that knowledge. It would only confuse and alarm your stunted man-brain to conceptualize the responsibilities and affections represented by an infant. Kahr, like most Ladies, would assume you were happier not knowing for all these years. In her own way, she was being kind." A sip. "All stereotypes cause harm in one way or another, but those who believe them usually do not think so. To them, it is only business as usual. Drink your tea before it gets cold, love."

A bitter laugh. "You always make it scalding hot." But he sipped anyway, flames licking at his lips. "I don't want to have any more. I can't stand the thought of it. Some child, wandering around in the world with my blood in his veins, and I know nothing of him- I don't want it." Voice falling to a murmur, he turned his face to Rori. "What can I do?"

Rori cocked his head. "Well... There are substances a man can take that render him rather less than potent."

"What do you mean? I still have to be able to work."

"Of course. But there is a drug I've heard of that will allow you to continue your courtesan work without causing any pregnancies."

Luken sat bolt upright. "What! How long has that existed?"

"Since the dawn of time, love. It's legal, in some other countries, but of course the Empire considers it immoral. A man controlling his own reproduction is always considered immoral in Kanai."

Rage surged through him, and Luken spat a vile curse. "This Goddess-damned country. Where can I get this drug?"

"I have to warn you, there may be some fairly serious side-effects. You might have a bad reaction."

"What's the worst that could happen?"

"Brain damage. That would be the worst bit." He sipped his tea. "Though there's debate as to how dangerous it actually is. The usual side-effects are nausea and mood-swings."

Luken paused, considering. "I'm willing to risk it. Anything's better than having no control at all over the future of my own reproduction."

"You *could* stop having sex."

Luken held his gaze. "Have you considered just *stopping* being gay?"

Rori smiled. "Ah, no, I don't think I would consider that."

"I'm not going to stop being what I am, either."

Luken sighed. "Sex is part of us. Part of being human. It always has been, it always will be. Some people can abstain, if they like. But as a species, we can't cut out the core." The image of his lover, Jes, flashed in Luken's mind. "For better or for worse, we can't stop being what we are." He shook his head. "Why must there always be people who keep a stalking eye on lovers, adults full-grown and free, enjoying their sexuality, harming no one, wishing only to keep everyone healthy and happy and secure, and think, 'We must do everything we can to hinder and punish those lovers as much as humanly possible, even though it is none of our business'?"

Rori laughed. "That's Kanai in a question, love. But are you sure you'd rather take the pills? It might be better to just," Rori shrugged, "turn a blind eye to the suspiciously *familiar* children of Ladies who've paid your Stud Fee once or twice."

"Rori. I *do not want that*. I don't want the uncertainty, the sense of helplessness."

He sighed. "Do you remember my friend, Kyo?"

"The scary one who lives in the shitty tenement building?"

Rori threw his head back in a peal of laughter. "Yes. Him. Kyo has a friend who sells such things to men. It's not what one would call *legal*, necessarily, but I assure you such things are common."

Luken nodded, though a trickle of anxiety wormed down his throat. "Could you retrieve it for me?"

"Sure. I was going to visit Kyo tomorrow anyway. The next time I see you, I'll have them."

"Thank you. Goddess, Rori, what would I do without you?"

He shrugged one shoulder. "We must look out for one another. I expect you'd do the same for me."

Luken sighed, a sense of calm stretching, tentative, through him. He drew a long draft of tea and rose to return the cup to the countertop. A flash of scarlet, in the corner of his eye. A book, bound in deep-red leather, with the title lettered in gold cursive. *Scarlet and Gold.* Luken drew a sharp breath. "Rori! Is this-?"

He twisted, the book gripped to his chest, and found Rori watching him with a twinkling grin. "Yes. My baby has been released from editing jail, and will finally see the world."

Almost shimmying with excitement, Luken flipped through the gold-edged pages of the novel; he had been the first to read it, when the book had been nothing more than an early version of the manuscript, handwritten and littered with errors, now clean and crisp – like watching a grubby little child mature into a sophisticated young adult in their courtly regalia. "When is it coming out?"

"The end of next month. That woman who left earlier, Polay, is my editor. She dropped off a few copies for me." Rori rose and strode to his side. "You keep this copy."

"Really?"

Rori dragged a pot of ink and a pen from the edge of the table, amid a swarm of loose papers and pencil stubs, and taking the book from Luken, scribbled his name on the first page in long, loopy letters. "There." He handed it back to Luken. "This time you won't have to suffer through my spelling errors."

Luken flipped through it, enraptured. "I am so proud of you, Rori."

Rori collected their teacups and placed them in the sink with a silvery *clink*. "Yes," he said dryly, "almost four years of work, and it shall be read by, well, two people, at least. If I can get Katobi to read it, anyway."

Luken could not pry his eyes from the gold lettering. But later, as he drove home in the carriage with the book cradled in his lap and his eyes closed in rest, all he could see was the boy in the marketplace who wore his face.

Chapter Four

When the second summons came, Luken almost expected it. Fi materialized out of the late-summer haze, pumping up the front steps with her hands in the pockets of her black trousers, and knocked on the door. Luken, adorned that day in a sleek ando of deep purple stitched in a fine weave of gold thread, beneath a tight irlan of shimmering gold and pearl-pink under-skirts, straightened the net of pearls – stark in contrast to his long, black hair – over his head and turned his face in the mirror, watching the chain of pearls around his neck move gently against the silk. He looked particularly elegant that day, and didn't mind at all the faint arching of Fi's eyebrows as he emerged.

"Come, the Empress wants you."

"Good morning to you as well, my Lady Steward."

A muffled grunt as she stalked away. Luken walked at his own pace, letting her speed ahead, pause, look back at him with irritation, stalk off, and pause again as he made his way, once more, into the Inner Palace. He expected a return to the garden near the royal family's chambers, but Fi veered off down a long, shadowed corridor, where a reverent hush filled the air, and though well-kept and clean, the shadow of time stretched long over the bare stones and the twisted, iron limbs of the candelabra that stood guard like sentinels at their posts along either wall.

"Where are we?"

His only answer was the sharp echoes of Fi's footsteps ringing off the stones as they came to a large door of dark, ancient oak. Such doors normally stood sealed, keeping the Palace's secrets to herself. But today, oak and iron had been prised open, the space between a column of shadow, dented by faint, amber illuminance from a distant source. Fi slipped into the dark, and Luken followed.

The room was not so black as he had thought at first, only vast, with a high ceiling, and a sharp contrast to the brightness of the morning behind him, with few torches on the walls, burning behind their black bars. A strange location for a courtship – but of course, that assumed the Empress *was* interested in a courtship, and Luken was not at all certain of what she wanted from him. As his eyes adjusted, he followed Fi's shadow ahead of him, weaving among large tables on which glass shells protected their treasures. There, against the right wall, stood the Empress. One of her eunuch guards stood a few feet off, holding a torch aloft. She looked up at his approach, and he could see the grin that split her features.

"Luken Kenkazu-son."

He dipped a quick bow. "My Lady Empress."

"Come," she angled her body toward him, one hand resting still on the slanted table beside her on which a large and very old-looking book was propped open, "have a look." The glass case around the text had been opened and pushed back. As Luken drew near to her, he found himself gazing down at the antiquated calligraphy of what appeared to be a poem, floating in the fractured style of Rose Age poetry, painted in black ink against a background of faded watercolor clouds. "You had a weakness for such things, I seem to recall."

Luken's breath caught. "Lady Nu's *Upon the Thrashing of the Boughs.* Is this the original text?" He turned to find her watching his face with an amused grin.

"You even know the poem. I thought perhaps you were attempting to be literary as one of those tiresome ploys courtesans use to appear interesting, but you actually know the title. And yes, it is the original text. I daresay the Empress of Kanai need not settle for a forgery."

He gave a giddy bounce on the slant of his joh. "The Rose Poets were my favorite school of poetry. Lady Nu is quite good but-" his gaze raked the row of texts that lined the wall, until, with a strangled mew of delight, "Lady Xansa!" He scurried over, recognizing the image on the cover of the text: a rain-beaten willow. "She's my favorite, I think, of all of them."

"That shrimpy pagan?"

"Ah," he flashed a grin he knew to be playful; easy enough, for he was ecstatic, "you are not E-Karan. You would not understand." At a time when the beliefs of ancient Kanains were viewed as childish and rather barbaric, Lady Xansa had famously drawn from pre-Imperial myth and folklore from her native E-Kara to create a body of work that had immortalized not only the names but also the dark, mythic heartbeat of the ancient woods and rivers, the sacred sense of Time distilled in every sylvan breath, that shaded E-Karan culture before the advent of the Empire and its all-consuming Mother Goddess.

The Empress chuckled. "You know she was a weaselly little woman who stalked a famed courtesan, and, failing to procure his affection, later went after his son."

"Yes, but I can forgive a dead woman her faults. It's the living ones I have trouble with."

The Empress snorted. "I doubt you have trouble with any woman." She rounded on the darkness, and commanded the void, "Open the case for him."

A woman – some sort of grim cross between a librarian and a prison guard – materialized from the gloom with a jangle of keys. Giving a start, Luken inched back for her as she unlocked the case. It swung open without dispelling a single mote of dust, and Luken felt a flicker of admiration. At least she kept her charges in good order, though the sour look on her face as she stepped back for him told Luken exactly what she felt about his presence among her relics.

He raised a hand. "Can I-"

"No," the reliquarian spat.

"Norahn," the Empress said with dry amusement. "Let the boy look at your books."

A strangled expression twisted her features, as if she had been force-fed a lemon. Then, heaving a theatrical sigh, the reliquarian fumbled at a small box on the counter beside her and retrieved a pair of dark gloves. Luken and the Empress exchanged a glance of secret, shared amusement. The reliquarian thrust the gloves at Luken, who slipped them on over his lace gloves and, under Norahn's hawk-like glare, pulled the book into his hands and eased it open.

His gaze fell on the page and a smile found his lips. He knew this one. Lifting his voice to a warm and mellow timber that drifted into the high ceiling, Luken recited the final stanza.

Trample now the darkness,
Shake free the day,
Who will walk with thee, Fatal Beauty
Beneath chains of ivy woven,
O'er moss like phantom flesh
Lain cool and soft?
Who walks with Trinekay, shadow-prince,
When all of light and dark slaughtered
Cry from the blood-
What new dawns to conquer?

He looked up, and his gaze met the Empress's. The book between them, ancient and loric. But her eyes, like metal wire heated in a furnace until it burned glowing scarlet. She drew a deep and silent breath. Luken let his gaze fall, as if considering her or overcome for a moment, then his eyes flashed back up to meet hers, focusing on her with a passion. Isaun had taught him that little trick; the focus, fall, and refocus, of the eye-triangle; Luken used it now on instinct, his courtesan training hewn deep into a receptive mind, but he found it worked well enough. She was still a woman, the Empress.

"No breathing on the book!" Norahn snatched the volume from Luken's hands so quickly he jumped. The moment shattered as, grumbling, the reliquarian returned Lady Xansa's collected works to the case.

The Empress chuckled. "I think perhaps we have overstayed our welcome."

Stripping off the black gloves and handing them

to Norahn, Luken turned to the Empress. "Perhaps a walk in the garden would be a welcome change of pace."

Empress Raisaga took his hand, the brittle pressure of her fingers reminding him, suddenly, of her age.

She led him, not back the way they had come but across the vast hall, to a door that, opened for them by a pair of eunuch guards gliding in front of them, gave way to a sprawl of gardens that wove among tiers of camellias. Just before the door closed behind them, a final litany of mutters hissed from the darkness.

"I think she likes me," Luken said.

The Empress laughed. "You do amuse me, Luken."

"Glad to be of service, Your Grace."

It was a fine morning, warm beneath a light feathering of clouds to the west.

"You hold a love, then, in your heart for old E-Kara?" the Empress asked.

Luken shrugged. "It was a lovely place to grow up. Often, in my dreams, I hear the rush of the wind through the orchards."

"The House of the Pear Blossom," the Empress murmured, contemplative. "They tend to vote Reformist in the Noble Assembly, don't they?"

Luken tensed, at once defensive. "Yes, but my mother is not very political."

She shook her head, and spoke in a quiet voice. "Tell me, then, of E-Kara."

For a time, they wandered in slow strides through the garden, and Luken spoke of E-Kara as he remembered it: the scent of the deep woods, the fruit so ripe upon the bough that it fell to burst against the grass, weeping its juices, the whisper of the river beneath the bridge that carried him home-

"Empress!"

A voice cracked the stillness. Barging from the arched entryway to the Palace, a trio of women stormed towards them. Luken recognized the stern, chinless visage of Lady Ekaris, leading the way. "There you are! We've been looking for you for hours!"

"What a spectacular waste of time," the Empress said idly. "When you could simply have made an appointment with my secretary." Luken took a respectful step backwards, as if bowing out of the conversation. But of course, he need not have bothered; the Ladies took no more notice of him than if he were a beetle dislodged from the grassy lawn they trampled, though Lady Mian, with a jolt of recognition, lingered longer on his face than the others. Luken, recognizing her in turn, blinked – and was back in the Blue Dahlia, pumping into the pale body in front of him, stalks of cellulite gleaming like iridescent scars in the lantern-light up the backs of her thighs as he watched his cock vanish into the slick, dark curls that hid the hot grip of their joining, her squeals of pleasure ringing in his ears – his member, ribboned with a white skein, and back in–

Panic swirled, like a vulture eyeing his memories. *No,* Luken thought as his heart leapt to thunder, as his lungs shrank to nothing. *Not a panic attack, not now. Why?*

But he knew why. Lady Mian had been his

most recent client – suppose he'd gotten her pregnant, like Kahr? And goddesses, it was too late to prevent it if she were–

The woman on Lady Ekaris's left side, who Luken knew only from the sigil woven onto the breast of her navy blue coat – Lady Parnet of the House of Endless Jasmine – said, "The Assembly is to be presented with a bill that would allocate funding away from Imperial Defense toward-" her face colored as she spoke, as if her rage had grown hands to strangle her with, "toward *poverty relief*," spittle flecked her lips with the force required to expel these words from her throat, "in the Desmeran Isles!"

Calmly, the Empress said, "No funding is being taken *away* from Defense, Lady Parnet, only from the increased funding for Defense that you proposed last week. The Empire already spends a ludicrous amount of gold on Defense-"

Lady Mian's eyes widened. "To call any amount of gold spent on Defense *ludicrous*-"

Luken had never imagined Ladies, of any rank, speaking to the Empress in such a manner. But even through his disbelief, he could scarcely tear his eyes from Lady Mian. His hands shook, and he hid them in the sleeves of his ando in a gesture of patience. He maintained a serene expression, despite the coruscated blots of dark light bursting before his eyes as he let the panic roll over him, the despair that he lacked control over his body, that Mian could be pregnant even now-

"Just as the war in Hindigga is drawing to a close," the Empress continued, "and we are taking measures to withdraw our troops from all foreign shores. As I told you then, I will tell you now, there is no cause to increase Defense funding when the Empire will soon be at peace."

With a hateful slip of a grin, Lady Ekaris said, "The Empire's enemies will just give up and slither off, will they? Gu Adaran is still radicalizing our men against us-" Her gaze swiveled to Luken as if he would suddenly devolve into a baboon and hurl himself at her with a screech.

"There hasn't been a sighting of anyone calling themselves that in years-"

"And while we are vulnerable, you will cut our military's hands off just to make it easier for the enemy to do their job-"

The Empress drew herself up. "The Empire," she said with deadly calm, "is vulnerable to no one. Your constituents may believe your fear-mongering, Ekaris, but I do not. *I* am charged with protecting the Empire and have sworn to do that at all costs. And I shall. I, not you, will decide when we are vulnerable."

"So you intend," her voice, cold and soft, as if she spoke to lunatic, "to push this bill through the Assembly?"

"Have I ever withdrawn a proposal, Ekaris?"

"It will not pass the Convention, you may be assured of that, Raisaga!"

Luken tensed at the use of the Empress's first name.

"You dare-" she breathed.

"I dare as much as you." Ekaris's gaze shot to Luken, and narrowed, her lip curling with disgust. "Take it up with my nephew." She turned and strode back into the Palace, the others falling in behind her like the wings of some great bird of prey, folding shut.

The Empress stared after them. "I have not faced disrespect of this nature since-" She shook her head. "I'm sorry you saw that, Luken."

Luken forced himself to draw a deep breath, and willed his heartbeat to slow. "That was deplorable."

"And Lady Mian with them?" Her sneer was its own answer.

Luken, pulling back from the coils of a panic attack, said the first thing that came to his dazed mind. "Lady Mian likes to be fucked from behind with a finger in her ass."

Raisaga blinked at him, then threw her head back in a roar of laughter. "I forget, sometimes, you men see things from a different point of view." She cocked an eyebrow. "I don't suppose Lady Ekaris has ever hired you, has she?"

A faint smile. "I haven't had the pleasure." A moment's hesitation, and then, "My Lady Empress, if you'll forgive my saying so – I know, as a man, it isn't my place – but, to be frank, I do not see why you should tolerate such defiance." She watched him, her expression guarded. "I think that diverting an increase in military funding to poverty relief in the Desmeran Isles is a splendid idea. You had the right of it. You should not let fools bully you into pulling back the proposal."

A weary smile. "Thank you, Luken. And speaking of fools, come," she offered him her arm, "we cannot allow fools to spoil a morning as fine as this."

He would have rather gone home to be alone and breathe easy, but one did not say so to the

Empress. He took her arm and they resumed their walk through the garden, taking jabs at Ekaris and the others, making each other laugh until Luken breathed freely again, the panic dropping to the back of his mind.

As they traced a lazy loop back toward the entrance of the camellia garden, two elderly men, in black wigs and red andos patterned with silver dandelion spores, shuffled past in the opposite direction. Arbiters. Their eyes widened, first in recognition of the Empress, and then at Luken, who blinked back at them in surprise. As denizens of the Hidden Palace, Arbiters were rarely seen in person, though courtesans too often faced the aftermath of their decisions.

After they had swept past, Luken glanced over his shoulder and found the pair of Arbiters goggling at him. He shot them a wink.

Chapter Five

Luken pulled open the mouth of the drawstring bag and gazed down at a hefty well of pills. A white powder frayed from the edges, dusting the purple silk of the coinpurse, embroidered with golden cranes in flight. The pills were the first of two prizes he'd gained from his meeting at *The Royal*, a restaurant in the Sapphire District where he'd bought Rori, and his partner Katobi, dinner.

The second, the new book by Koko, Second Son of the House of the Verdant Fen, sat beside him in back of the carriage as he trundled through lower O-Han. Luken glanced at the book, and his lip twitched into a sneer. *The Irrefutable Science of Sex, Romance, and Gender: How New Data Confirmed What We Already Knew and How You Can Use it to (Finally) Claim the Love Life You're Entitled to!*

Koko's bloated titles had officially grown to fill the entirety of the book's front cover.

"I can't believe I'm going to read this thing," he muttered. But Seito had liked his acerbic take on the other book, and Luken was willing to suffer through the vile little read for the chance to get another review published in *Ages*. Developing his writing, getting his pen name out there – that was how Rori had started his career.

Luken flipped the book open and found himself reading the foreword:

For many years, the women and men of Kanai have been pressured by a societal preference for egalitarian ideals that has robbed us of our natural, Goddess-given roles, and in turn, drained the spice from sex and romance. Ladies walk on eggshells for fear of offending men's new resentment for being treated as men, while men try to act like women and lose big in the course of their inevitable and pathetic failure to do so.

But the science of sex and romance has proven, beyond even a single shadow of a doubt, what common sense has told us for thousands of years: a man's brain, when driven by the need for sex, is no different than an animal of any inferior class, while women are able to retain their reason and select the mate best suited to produce the sort of daughters that will enhance her standing and her House. No doubt there are many of you who are offended by this statement – good. More people in our society need to be offended, and I'm going to do what's good for them, whether they like it or not.

Instead of clutching our pearls at the obvious truth, the time has come to embrace our differences and play our positions. Men, bow to your superiors with grace and a smile, and enjoy the benefits of sex and luxury. Ladies, accept your power, meet and overcome the challenges of men and courtship, and claim the pleasure and status to which you are entitled; be merciless in your appraisal and ruthless in your selections; the fate of the species – and the hard-earned sums in your bank account – depends upon it.

It is through the filter of this proven truth that I have written this book – NOT in deference to the tidal waves of ulterior forces in our society bullying us into treating each other equally.

If the cultural exactness police are going to arrest me for that, fine. Come arrest me. I dare you.

Luken was still laughing when the carriage

pulled up outside Jes's.

He dropped the book and returned his attention to the pills for a final, lingering look at freedom before snapping the drawstring taut and secreting the pills into a pocket sewn into the insides of his ando.

The carriage rolled to a halt. Securing his veil, Luken slipped out and tipped the driver a few extra bohda; technically, he wasn't doing anything wrong, visiting a residence in the city, but it never hurt to have the drivers on your side when you valued discretion. He crossed the sidewalk, buffeted by a snap of cold wind. Autumn's first appearance, still garbed in summer's blue. He ducked into the apartment building, and made his way up to the fifth story, where Lady Eitan rented her rooms.

Luken knocked on the door, feeling a thrill of excitement. Footsteps, on the far side.

Jes opened the door, a weary smile appearing at the sight of him. "I feel like I haven't seen you in ages." She stepped aside.

Luken swept inside and ripped the veil from his face. At once, she stepped into the embrace of his arms and pressed a long kiss to his lips. A knot loosened in his chest, and slipped apart. As though he'd trudged a long way, through the deepening snow, until he no longer felt the cold, and all at once – came home.

"It's so good to see you," he murmured, pulling back from the kiss only to hold her face in his hands, their foreheads pressed together, her eyes – a flecked mahogany, rich and warm – all he could see. His thumb rose to trace the dark half-crescent beneath her left eye, his gaze traveling over her wan features, her hair lank, oily. "But you look tired."

A shattering cry, from the far room. Jes sighed. "Jenh." She slipped from his arms and crossed the apartment's living room, into the adjacent bedroom. Luken waited a moment, followed. Lady Eitan, Jes's mistress, cousin, and best friend, was still recovering from the birth of her second child. The infant boy had been named Iko after a courtesan, Iriko, whose brutal, unsolved murder had fascinated Luken to the point of obsession, before quietly fading from the newspapers and forcing him to make his peace with the subdued horrors of life's long and restless mysteries.

In the bedroom, Eitan lay amid white, rumpled sheets, a quilt thrown over her legs, and quieted the fretful bundle in her arms while her older son screamed, red-faced. "Jenh, hush now," Jes cooed, plucking the boy from his crib. She moved him to the changing table in the corner of the room while Luken sat down on the edge of the bed.

"Hullo, Luken," Eitan said.

In a tentative voice, "Are you well?"

Glassy eyes blinked back at him. "I'll be alright in the end. Just in pain, that's all." She grinned at him, a nub of valerian root wedged between her teeth; she chewed in slow motions as he murmured, "Oh Eitan."

Her eyelids drooped once, flickered open. Gently, Luken eased Iko from her arms and pressed him to his chest as he strode from the bedroom and paced the living room, making quiet, comforting noises to the fussing newborn until Iko fell asleep in his arms. Luken slowed to a halt, looked down at the baby in his arms – and caught his breath. The perfect features, cast in miniature, caught in slumber – tears stung. Needles, digging behind his eyes.

A faint noise. Luken looked up, found Jes at the opening to the bedroom, watching him. She moved aside for him as he crossed into the dimness of Eitan's bedroom. She had drifted off to sleep, her hair a wild, black flame against the pillow. Jehn had settled in his crib. Luken tucked Iko into his bassinet and withdrew from the bedroom, closing the door on darkness and sleep.

Jes cocked her head to the door behind her and he followed her within, to the small, spare room that had formed their lover's lair since Luken had returned to Court.

Luken closed the door behind him. Jes approached him, shrugging out her shirt. Her large breasts came free, pressed against his chest as she slipped a hand behind his head, fingers lost in his long hair, and pulled him down for a lingering kiss.

It was like making love in a dream.

He yanked off his irlan and let the rest collapse in a heap of expensive silks. He stepped free, stumbled, kissed her laughing lips, all while they moved toward the bed. Jes kicked her boots off. Luken took the moment to rip a tangle of silver links from his hair, loosing the intricate bundle atop his head to join the cascade down his back. Jes hopped onto the bed, grinning up at him while Luken pulled her trousers free. He climbed onto the bed to join her, and without speaking a word, they had closed the space between them.

"This never gets old," he murmured.

Jes chuckled, low and soft, then put a finger to his lips. "Hush, don't wake them."

He nipped at her fingertip and grinned as her

hands slipped down his stomach, moving to palm the length of his member, nearly erect already. Long, full strokes. A thumb, lingering hard over the head. Her right hand dipped to cup his balls, giving them a gentle squeeze before taking his now fully erect shaft in both hands and stroking it from base to tip.

"Oh, Goddess," he whispered.

She drew him down, so that he lay over her, whispered "hush," and kissed him. His hair, unbound, tumbled over them both, a silken chaos to match the glide of their tongues. He pulled to the side so that he could feel the fullness of her breasts, never breaking from her lips, then slipped his hand down the curve of her waist, and glided – whisper soft – over her labia. She shivered.

Shiver, soft. Shiver, soft. Soft until it was fierce, frenetic, hard, and with a shudder, she groaned.

"Hush," Luken whispered.

Jes laughed and pulled him atop her, angling his penis into her. Wet and open for him. He bit his lip and started to grind against her, the front of his body rubbing her clit with each motion. The bed creaked gently beneath them, the sound of their quickened breath rasping the air.

She gazed up at him from half-lidded eyes, cheeks flushed. A splendid vision.

Often they would move from this to two or three more positions; tonight, they didn't make it that far. Luken ground hard into her and Jes arched beneath him. He slipped into that fierce, sudden bliss and let it rock through him to the last, to the sweet, final shudder. Til even the dream dissolved.

After, Luken pulled the sheets up over them.

With a ghoulish whisper, his discarded ando slithered off the end of the bed and coiled itself up on the floor. Jes fitted herself to his side, her head resting on his shoulder with familiar weight.

"We should go out into the city tomorrow," Luken murmured, keeping his voice from carrying into the adjacent room. "We always said we were going to go back to that sweet shop. Or we can try the cafe next door, then go back to *A Likely Story*."

"I can't. Eitan needs me here."

"You're going to go crazy, stuck here with two screaming babies all day and a woman who can't get out of bed."

"Luken."

He sighed. "I know. She needs you here. It's getting harder and harder to share you."

She made an effort to keep her tone light. "At least I have one last link to the outside world. What's been going on?"

Luken wavered. Now was the time to tell her about the Empress, about the boy in marketplace, but- "Nothing, really. Just getting back to work. I have a new client."

"Anyone important?"

"You could say that."

"Well I hope she pays well." Jes snuggled into the crook of his shoulder; he felt her warm breath gust his neck. "I've been saving my coins. I'm going to take you out somewhere special for your birthday, just wait."

Luken smiled. "I expect nothing but the best, you know. I want *two* muffins from the cafe for my birthday."

She dug a finger into his ribs. "Normally the cafe would be too good for you, but I have something proper fancy in mind."

She described a restaurant in the Diamond District, but while Jes's warm tones rolled over him, a knot formed in Luken's mind and he tugged at it, to no avail. Why didn't he just tell her about the Empress? About his son? But the moment had passed, and it would ruin this, a moment of stolen comfort, a brief haven in the familiar, the warm, the perfect. There were so few moments like this in life. And she was tired. Why distress her? He'd wait, then, til she wasn't so tired. Til Eitan was better and Jes bore less of the burden of caring for Eitan's sons. She'd take it better then, with a decent night's sleep, and an emotional foundation that hadn't been nibbled at by the termites of stress. Why ruin this?

"You're getting the lobster. I've already decided. You're going to give shellfish a chance, and you're going to like it."

Luken's nose crinkled. "Anything that hideous can't really be trusted."

"And yet you gave me a chance."

A soft laugh. "A moment of weakness. And see where it stuck me- Ow! You're going to have to answer to my next client, when she asks why my ribs are bruised black and blue."

Voice honeyed with drowsiness, Jes murmured, "Shush, don't wake them."

He kissed her brow. "Get some sleep, love."

Drifting, "Just wait til I have you all to myself."

"Jes?"

Her eyes had slipped shut.

~

The seasons seldom overstayed their welcome in O-Han.

When Luken left Jes's place the following morning, clouds inked the sky, a bitter chill slinking into the breeze. Autumn had not fully announced himself yet, but he was getting around to the idea.

Huddled in the back of the carriage, Luken had the driver drop him off at the Garden Gate, in the shadow of the Palace, rather than take him straight to the Abode, and climbed the long flight of stairs into the hall where the Board stood, a massive black obelisk against the far wall. Luken approached, his jaw going slack as he read and reread the symbols on the Board.

Luken, of the Abode of Scattered Flowers. Number Eleven. Stud – 9,000 bohda.

A low whistle behind him. Nikay, a courtesan who shared the Abode of the Midnight Heron with Ohfene, approached in slow strides, morning's light finding low glints of gold in his gliding spill of chestnut hair. "Eleven." His gaze fell to Luken. "I checked the Board the day before yesterday. Weren't you twenty-something?"

Luken struggled to clear his throat. "Twenty, I think."

Four or five other courtesans, who had been striding through the hall on their way through the Palace, slowed, as though sap caught at their joh once they passed the shadow of the Board, and Luken watched their eyes travel from him and Nikay, up to the Board and back before coming to a halt, their expressions blank.

A younger courtesan with auburn hair gawked at the Board, then leveled Luken with an accusatory stare. "What did you do?"

"I- I'm not sure, really."

He'd known, of course, when the Arbiters had seen him with the Empress, that it would affect his rating on the Board. How could it not? But such a jump, over so many established courtesans – all from High Houses – was rare.

No, unheard of.

Other courtesans, passing through to check the Board before breakfast, began to appear in the hall and stopped when they saw the others standing there. "What's going on?" someone asked.

"Bullshit," spat the auburn-haired courtesan. "You must have done something. You've almost breached the Top Ten. No one makes that kind of leap."

Luken flushed. "Ask an Arbiter, then."

Nikay stepped forward, blocking Luken from the view of the gathering courtesans. Murmurs, like doves, filled the dome of the hall. "Come on, let's walk."

Gratitude twisted through him as Nikay escorted Luken from the hall, and they rushed down the steps toward the Garden in hurried silence. At the bottom, Nikay gripped the sleeve of Luken's ando. "It's the Empress, isn't it? Ohfene told me her Steward had asked about you."

Luken nodded, mute.

Nikay gazed at him, then exhaled a long breath. "Goddess-favored, aren't you? First the Empress's niece, then the Empress herself." He shook his head. "Well, who can blame them? I knew, that first day I saw you in Isaun's shadow, you were something else. I guess we've found the Beauty of the Age."

Luken jumped. The Beauty of the Age was a term often used to describe the most compelling, influential, and of course, beautiful, courtesan of a particular generation. Each was said to possess some indefinable quality that made them irresistible to women, but, more than that, they were supposed to embody some virtue or mentality that defined the age in which they lived. Liliray, the Empress's Beloved, had been the Beauty of his Age, without a doubt. A change-maker at the end of the old millennia, a romantic figure, an ideal. Before him, Umewei, the Desmeran courtesan for whom princesses fought; a champion of his people's rights, he'd used his beauty to bridge the contentious gap between the recently-acquired Desmeran Isles and the mainland, standing, even now, as a symbol of peace in Kanai. Generations back, there had been Lord Sanso, the Empress's Consort who rode unveiled through the streets of O-Han, suffering the gaping stares and insults of the shocked peasants in his wild gallop to shame his Empress for the cruel taxes that bled her people dry; faced with the choice of executing her Consort for the embarrassment he'd caused, or ceding to his wishes and lowering taxes, she'd stunned the world by sparing his life and conceding. "After all," the Empress told her resentful Ladies, "one does not slay a white tiger because it took a little swipe at you; if you want something tame, go with a house cat." To this day, the phrase "go with a house cat" was a handy missile to throw at those who couldn't handle a spirited lover, or who threw a fit when an inferior challenged an unreasonable policy.

All so different, but all alike in that their beauty had allowed them to dare what no other man at the time could – and get away with it, too.

The Beauty of the Age.

An old-fashioned notion, but it remained a constant preoccupation among courtesans, even now. What boy, behind his scornful smile, did not secretly dream of being remembered as the next Beauty?

"Don't be stupid," Luken said, breathless. "If anyone's getting that title, it's Aokinay. Or even Isaun. He's a much better courtesan than me."

Nikay shook his head, wearing a rueful grin. "As you say."

They walked beneath the shadow of the arch that divided the Garden and the Palace proper, and along the white-tiled path through the Abodes, the silken trains of their andos whispering behind them.

"Thank you, Nikay, for walking with me."

Nikay shrugged. "No trouble at all. This is where we part." He gestured toward the right-hand path, which spun away into a spiral of courtyards, one of which contained the Abode of the Midnight Heron.

"Nikay-"

He glanced back.

"Please, keep it quiet about the Empress. It may all come to nothing."

Nikay considered him. A long moment, in which Nikay's thoughtful face appeared strangely beautiful, though Luken had always found him rather plain. And then, a rueful smile. "I have to tell Ohfene.

He would never forgive me, otherwise."

"Why are you friends with him, anyway? He's an asshole."

Nikay scoffed. "Why are you friends with Isaun?"

Luken laughed. "Well, that may be less than true these days. But I catch your meaning."

With a sad smile, Nikay strolled away, folding his hands before him.

Luken watched him a moment, then turned, and made his way to the Abode of Scattered Flowers.

~

"What on earth-"

Luken stood in the doorway of the Abode, gazing in at the main room – cloaked from end to end in bouquets of bright, yellow roses. Crowding the table, covering the floor, perched on the windowsill, even jumping up the steps of the stairway to the second story.

It was as if a meadow had invaded their Abode.

In sharp contrast, Isaun stood in the center of the room, his white ando like an icicle jutting from the flowers at his feet. He held a trio of roses in one hand, the other plucking free a petal. His expression, in profile, possessed the cold beauty of some king, sitting on his throne, while offerings were brought before him; pleasing, yes, but no more than he expected and deserved.

Amae huffed in through the open paper door on the other side of the main room, scooped up a bundle of bouquets and, cursing, he stormed out onto the porch and threw the roses into the garden. "Ridiculous," he limped back into the main room, "fucking ridiculous." His black gaze shot up to Luken. "There you are, boy! Help me throw these bloody things out."

Isaun ignored them, smiling coldly at the shiver of the rose as he plucked another petal.

"Who are they from?" Luken asked.

"Lady Romyn," Amae sneered, and seized another pair. Romyn, Second Daughter of the House of the Dragonfly. A feckless, chubby woman whose face possessed a certain lunar quality, in both shape and pallor, as well as its proximity to realities on earth. As a Lady of one of the few High Houses for which Isaun had not yet plied his trade, she made an excellent target. Isaun had fixed on her at the party they'd attended the night the election results came in. Evidently, their courtship had continued.

Luken picked his way through the meadow, holding his skirts up in either hand. "I think she likes you," he said dryly.

Isaun pinched another petal between two long, scarlet nails, and pulled. "What, surprised they aren't for you?" A flash of yellow across his ando, as the petal drifted.

Luken snorted. "Hardly."

Amae huffed back in, spewing curses, and back out.

Luken ignored him and nudged a path for himself toward the bedroom.

A detached voice, at his back. "How was your rendezvous with the Empress?"

Luken looked at Isaun over his shoulder. The lovely features, bent into shadow. A shaft of light from the open door, burnishing the roses in his hands to silent flame.

"Pleasant."

The cold smile sliced wider. Almost imperceptibly, Isaun nodded. As if confirming something to himself. He tore free a petal and Luken saw now the rose clenched in his fist, the center of the trio – whittled down like a skull punched through by a dozen spears.

Another petal fluttered to fall at his feet.

Chapter Six

Hours of furious work had yielded Luken's second review for Seito, the editor at *Ages*. He was not sure she would like it, but he had done his best to remain articulate and logical while skewering every last aspect of Koko's most recent book, the thin, acid-dripping volume.

With a flicker of trepidation in his belly, Luken bound up the review in a packet, sealed it with wax, and sent it off to Seito courtesy of a public messenger, her large, dark eyes going wide at the gold-gleaming bohda Luken dropped into her palm on the porch of the Abode. He watched her scurry off, fearing Seito's response but relieved to have it done.

Still standing on the porch, Luken saw Fi materialize from the lazy warmth of the late summer morning; she passed the messenger without so much as a glance and ambled up to the Abode of Scattered Flowers.

Luken watched her approach. "Steward."

She placed a hand on the railing of the porch steps. "Lord Luken. I've come to meet with you and your Abode Master."

Luken cocked his head. "I don't know that-"

"Luken!" Amae barged from the front door, his grey ando billowing out like fog. "Don't be rude, invite our guest in at once." To Fi, he offered a deep bow.

Luken rolled his eyes and motioned the Steward in ahead of him before following the two into the Abode's main room.

"Tea?" Amae stood over Fi, where she knelt at the table. She jerked her head in a nod and Amae seized the teapot from the table and filled a cup for her. Jasmine perfumed the air with a blossom of steam.

Luken strolled to the table and knelt beside Amae.

Fi's flinty eyes fixed on one man's face, then darted to the other. "May I speak plainly?"

"Please." Amae leaned toward her. "We would appreciate your frankness." Luken watched Amae's eyes glint with greed.

Fi folded her hands on her lap. "The Empress is interested in Luken. Very interested."

Amae grinned, a terrible rictus that consumed the features of his face.

"You are men of the world. You understand such things, I'm sure." Fi stared at the tea, her hand never stirring to raise the cup to her lips. "It is not uncommon for the Empress to take a liking to a comely young courtesan. Such things can be managed quite easily, if each party involved behaves themselves."

"And what if I cannot behave myself?" Luken asked. Amae tensed, as if he was about to shove the table aside and throttle his courtesan, but Luken couldn't resist.

A mirthless grin played at the corner of Fi's mouth. "You would not be the first toy broken and dismissed from the playroom. But you do not strike me as a stupid man, Lord Luken. On the contrary, I rather think the Empress has stumbled across an uncommonly bright plaything on this occasion."

He kept his voice quiet, but his eyes did not leave Fi's. "I am not a plaything."

To Luken's surprise, this assertion was neither challenged nor mocked.

"Indeed. You are intelligent enough to understand the nature of this arrangement. If the Empress chooses you for a dalliance, there is mutual benefit. For all of us. The Empress is a generous woman. You will be given chambers in the Palace, and all your material desires will be granted. Within reason, I should say." Her chin lifted, considering Luken. "There was a courtesan, once, who nagged the Empress to have a castle built for him in the mountains. Seemed to think a stable with fifty white horses and a golden chamber-pot for every bedroom were perfectly reasonable additions, if they were already going to the expense of building a castle. That one didn't last long, as I recall. He took ill, sadly, and decided to retire from the Court."

"What really happened?" Luken asked.

A wry grin. She looked pleased that Luken was keeping up. Undoubtedly, her job had required a great deal of long, tedious explanations to oblivious courtesans over the years. "A letter was sent informing his mother that he had fallen out of favor and she recalled him from Court immediately, with profuse apologies to the Empress. He did not fancy the idea of an early retirement. His screams of protest, when the guards dragged him out of bed and through the corridors, naked, to the carriage outside, woke half the

Palace. Afterward, they said the Main Hall echoed with laughter for days. An exaggeration, of course, though not by much." She sipped at her tea. "It would not do, my Lord, to cause a fuss."

"No." His tone was as dry as hers. "That would not do."

She nodded. "Discretion is a virtue the Palace appreciates. As I said, this can all be arranged in a mutually beneficial fashion. If you please the Empress and do not make unreasonable demands, you will receive benefits unique to your station. In addition to your new chambers and attendants, you will receive a generous stipend, a portion of which, of course, will go to your Master." Amae's hand tightened into a fist beneath the table, straining as if trying to break his own fingers. "Needless to say, if the Empress does take you on, you will drop all of your current clients. I need hardly explain to you why it would be improper for the Empress to share a man with a Lady."

"I understand." *And good riddance to them.*

"Now, your role at the Palace cannot be formally acknowledged. In the past, courtesans in such a position have been referred to as the Empress's concubines, though of course, there is no legal reality to the term. That would be a grave insult to the Empress's Consort, Aokinay, and his House. On the subject of the Royal Consort, you must avoid Lord Aokinay. If he accosts you – yes," she added, in response to the look on Luken's face, "such things have happened before. Aokinay does not appreciate his mistress's, ah, occasional distractions. But if he accosts you, you must not fight back."

"What kind of a rule is that?" Luken spat.

"A serious one, my Lord. Aokinay is the Empress's Consort. Simply put, he is above you. However," her head lifted a fraction, her voice lowered, "if I am being honest with you, the Royal Consort is rather out of favor with the Empress at this time. They quarrel frequently. I do not believe Raisaga has visited the Men's Quarters of the Palace in some time. Quite some time." She flicked a speck of dust from the back of her hand. "It is possible Aokinay may not be Consort forever, if things continue as they are now." She winked at Amae, who looked on the verge of cardiac arrest. No doubt even Amae, with all his greedy ambition, had never dreamed of selling a courtesan to the Empress herself. Procuring a Consort for the Empress. That would be the absolute highest accomplishment for an Abode Master.

Luken was not convinced. "Lord Aokinay's family is one of the most influential Houses in Court politics. His aunt sits on the Convention and the Assembly and is Steward of Imperial Defense. Most likely, she is also the wealthiest member of the Convention. From what I've heard, Lady Ekaris went to great lengths to get her only nephew appointed as Empress's Consort. I doubt the Empress would risk the House of Distant Thunder's fury by supplanting Aokinay for a nobody like me. I'm not even the Son of a High House."

"It is not for you to say what the Empress would or would not do." Her eyes narrowed a fraction. "And since you evidently follow Court politics, you may be interested to know that the Empress grows rather weary of Lady Ekaris's imperious demands on her attention. It may be that the Empress is interested in rebuking the Traditionalist courtiers who, led by Ladies like Ekaris, have been growing in influence for years now, and are beginning to overstep their bounds."

Luken's eyes widened despite himself. "The Empress would depose Aokinay as a rebuke to the House of Distant Thunder?"

"Perhaps. Perhaps not. She did love him once. And their daughter, Princess Sakiran, would be aghast at her father's removal. She dotes on him, you see. Still, it would be useful for the Empress to remind Lady Ekaris who, precisely, leads the Empire. The Traditionalist party has grown overconfident since Hani won the election. This is relevant to our arrangement, Luken, as the position of Empress's Consort is often assumed to be a mark of the Empress's political affiliation. The Royal Consort represents *influence*. In the old days, their sole occupation was to pour their mother's agenda into the Empress's ear."

"What abysmal pillow talk."

Fi chuckled. "Perhaps you could do better. In any event, the political situation at this time is complex. To say the least. Even I do not know who will be Empress's Consort a year from now, and I pride myself on following politics very closely, Lord Luken. Very closely indeed. It may be you. It may be Aokinay. It may be that there will be no Empress's Consort at all. It depends on the message the Empress decides to send. But – and you must forgive me for saying so, my Lord – such matters go well beyond the concerns of men like you. There are issues at stake now that have nothing to do with men."

We are half the population, Luken thought, a cold smile tracing his lips.

"You need only concern yourself with the matter of the arrangement."

"We understand you perfectly." Amae dipped his head ingratiatingly.

Fi's gaze flicked back to Luken.

"Oh yes, Lady Fi, I understand exactly what you mean."

"Good." She sipped her tea. "We are all in agreement, then."

She rose and covered the distance to the door in a few brisk strides. Amae scurried after her, bowing, prattling expressions of gratitude. Her footsteps echoed off the wood of the porch, muted through the door. Amae stood, his hands pressed flat against it. And with a breathless laugh, his back struck the door, and he crumpled to the floor in a froth of pale-grey silk, limbs loose, chest heaving, stern features twisted with delight, with laughter. A wheezing, ugly, broken-glass laugh.

Chapter Seven

This was not the plan.

Luken rode through the city in a daze.

He'd known, of course, that his meetings with the Empress might lead to something but-

Chambers in the Palace. A ridiculously high position on the Board that he did not deserve – and which would only go higher if he accepted the Empress's proposal. A stipend from the Empress. A *generous* stipend, whatever that meant.

This was *not* the plan.

But-

No more clients. No more courtships. No more nights at the Dahlia. Something twisted in Luken's chest, though he did not know its name. Regret? Relief? No more days with Lady Arle, no more nights with Lady Noboro.

Luken withdrew the purse from the pocket within the sleeve of his ando and gazed down at the little white moons, dusted with their grainy powder. No more clients meant no further risk of causing an unwanted pregnancy. All without taking a single pill. Without risking a single symptom. Without fear of being arrested for illegally exercising control of his own reproductive system.

No more children in the marketplace, wearing his face.

A shaky breath, as Luken closed his eyes.

But this was not the plan.

He'd promised Jes. *A few years of work with a good number of clients, and then we'll have enough to start a new life somewhere else, somewhere up north where you're from, somewhere no one knows us, where a bohda goes a long way, longer than it does in the city, and we can live well, the two of us and the family we create, until our days are done.*

That was the plan. That was what he'd promised her when – against all instincts of self-preservation – he'd accepted his role as courtesan, and returned to the Court following that disastrous stint in U-Wen.

And yes, he'd recently received the second installment of his Conjugal Price from Lady Dare. Even now, that gold sat in the Palace Vaults with his name on it, waiting to be retrieved. Waiting for the third installment, at the end of another six months. But it wasn't enough yet.

He couldn't make this choice alone.

Luken slipped out of the carriage almost before it had stopped and tossed a generous tip to the driver. Twin frog faces grinned at him from the statues on either side of the path as Luken strode into the park and stepped out over the water, his joh clunking against the boards of the bridge. In East Park, lakes lay like dark mirrors amid the sprawling lawns and bridges arched from island to island. The islands bore red maples, their leaves twirling to freckle the face of the lake in every gust of wind. A crane, hunched primly in the water, glanced up at the sound of footsteps, and fussed with the great sprawl of his white wings before folding them back in. On the first island, Rori stood with his back to Luken, hands in the pockets of dark brown coat. A stone lion slept at their feet, his paws gathering maple leaves.

Vision hazed by his white veil, Luken rushed to the man's side.

Rori turned. "Strange place, for an emergency meeting."

"I knew it would be quiet here."

Rori cocked his head. "You were right about that." They were alone as far as the eye could see, with the exception of a heavyset woman, strolling across a distant lawn with two children toddling beside her and a dog racing circles around them in the grass. They soon slipped from sight. "Of course," Rori said jovially, "my apartment is also quiet."

"Too far for Jes to walk, and I didn't want her to spend money on a coach."

"Doesn't that Lady pay her anything?"

"She does. But currently the Lady is paying her medical bills after a difficult birth."

"Ah. Well aren't I the asshole today?"

A clatter of footsteps, booming along the boards. Luken twisted, his veil and ando catching the wind in a billow, as Jes raced to meet them, her cheeks flushed pink, her hair wild in the wind. "Luken! What's the matter? What happened?"

He caught her in an embrace.

"It's alright," he assured her.

He set Jes down and she and Rori stood before him, the deep red of the maple leaves twirling down around them as Luken told them everything, from the chance encounter with the Empress when Ohfene had accosted him in the Palace, to Fi's offer that morning, and all that it would mean.

"Luken-" Rori's eyes went wide. "This is incredible! The Empress- Good Goddess, Luken, think of what you could do!" A grin split his lips. "If the Empress had someone like you at her side instead of that Traditionalist wretch Aokinay and the House of Distant Thunder-"

Luken answered with a weak smile, but his gaze skipped to Jes. He studied her tired face, the dark circles beneath her eyes, pale lips a little chapped. A faint vomit stain on her shoulder where the new baby had been sick. She stared back at him, dark eyes dazed with exhaustion. "I don't understand. The Empress wants you to move into the Palace? What would that make you?"

"Well," his gaze jumped nervously between them, "it's an unofficial role, but it comes with a stipend, and I could drop all my other clients." He expected to see relief spark across her features, but Jes just stared back at him.

"And you want this?"

Shouts in the distance, muffled by a gust of wind that sent the leaves scurrying across ripples on the water.

"I- well, it's not like I petitioned for the job. It all just sort of... happened."

"Jes," Rori put in, "this is a once-in-a-lifetime opportunity for Luken. This is just about as high as a courtesan can go-"

Jes did not look away from Luken's face; it was as if Rori had not spoken at all. "And you want this?" she repeated.

Luken swallowed. "Well, it's not as if one can just tell the Empress to go fuck herself."

"How long is this arrangement going to last?"

"I- I don't know." The wind knifed into his voluminous sleeves, reaching his skin. Luken wrapped his arms around his middle.

"Jes," Rori said gently, placing a hand on her shoulder, until finally she looked at him, "you and I both care about Luken. But this, this is bigger than you or I or Luken, this is-"

Her eyes narrowed. "An opportunity to push your politics."

Rori shrugged. "I've never met the Empress. It's Luken's opportunity. To do with as he likes. But to have someone like Luken in a position of influence- such things do not happen every day. You see who has power in this country. Seven Hells, they just swore Hani onto the Convention!" He turned with a pleading look to Luken. "Who knows what good Luken might do if he had the chance!"

Jes shrugged off his hand. "Luken. What does this mean for us?"

Luken laughed weakly. "I'm not going to drop you, if that's what you think." He cocked his head. "If anything, I will be able to see you more. I will only have to deal with the Empress. All the time I would have wasted on clients and courtships is now ours."

He had worried about Jes's reaction, but he had not expected this- this resistance.

"Luken," hard and dead, her voice, "you will be watched more closely than ever. Guards, assistants, a retinue." She shook her head. "If you disappear for even an hour, the Palace will be in an uproar. We'll be lucky to ever see each other!"

Luken drew a frantic breath, his chest tight.

"What do you want me to do? Reject the Empress?"

"Luken, no!" Rori cried. "I'm sorry, Jes, but this is insane!"

Her eyes, wide and brittle as glass spheres, regarded him. *Oh Goddess, I should have told them separately,* Luken realized, too late. It never worked, this merging of the worlds.

He looked back and forth between them. "Jes," he whispered, "we'll find a way."

"You *will* have power, Luken," Rori insisted. "You won't be completely helpless. Perhaps you can even hire Jes into your retinue, she could live in your chambers. That would make it easy-"

Jes rounded on him with a sneer. "They do not hire women into the retinue of a royal," she fished for the right word, and finding none, spat, "boytoy!"

Luken laughed at the absurdity of it. His lover and his best friend, fighting because he had told them that the Empress of Kanai wanted him as her *boytoy.* It was, actually, beyond absurd.

"There are options," Rori said stubbornly. "There have to be." He cast a nervous glance at Luken. "And let's be frank, Luken – do you really have the choice to say no?"

Jes's shoulders sagged. "Luken... I do not understand such things as well as you or Rori perhaps, but..." Tears started in her eyes. "If you do this, it will hurt us."

"Goddess," Luken breathed. He was silent a long moment. A sudden gust of wind tore the maple leaves from the paws of the stone lion, sent them whirling between them. "Jes," he said slowly, guilt and regret tugging back and forth in his chest; starving dogs, fighting over a bone, "you are more important to me than anyone."

Rori closed his eyes and sighed.

"If I can get out of this- I will."

Jes returned his gaze. "Thank you, Luken." A well of sleepless nights and loveless days spilled over in her voice. "I just love you."

"I love you, too."

She pressed forward and lifting his veil, kissed him suddenly, tenderly. For a moment. Instinctively, Luken scanned the lawns, but no eyes rested on them except Rori's.

He gave Luken a rueful grin. "I think you may find the Empress of Kanai is not so easy to walk away from, my friend."

~

Luken dragged himself back to the Abode, feeling as if he had lived an eon since morning.

He'd thought his mind would be quieted after meeting with Rori and Jes, but he was more conflicted than ever. Before the meeting, his mind had been all but made up. Now he had to unmake it, and drag it back the other way. He'd told Jes he'd get out of it, if he could. But could he?

Did he even want to?

"Jes," he sighed. He loved her, and he shared her misgivings, but it would be a lie to say that he was not disappointed in her. Jes's contempt for the Court clouded her judgement. She did not really understand the worth of a man in that position. She underestimated what he could do with that role-

The carriage lilted into the diamond-shaped

courtyard where the Abode of Scattered Flowers awaited him. His ando, the color of blood, fell in a regal sheath down the straight lines of his body as Luken hopped down from the carriage and made his way within. Blessed quiet. Tension melted from his chest. Tugging a skein of diamonds from his braid and shaking his hair into loose splendor down his back, Luken made his way to the bedroom, where- "Oh. I didn't know anyone was home."

Isaun sprawled across his bed, his pale blue ando rumpled across the sheets, the golden under-skirts heaped across his legs like a dragon's hoard, his back against the far wall. A wine glass in one hand, half-empty. A bottle stood on the floor beside the cot, its remains sulking at the bottom. Red stained the whites of his eyes and in the mangled shadows of the window over his shoulder, he looked forty-eight, not twenty-eight. Isaun's side of the room was in a state of chaos and clutter. Except for the miniature portraits of his three daughters, which stood in a neat row in the center of his bedside table, though a thin layer of dust blurred the glass, just slightly.

A smile oozed across Isaun's mouth. "Just me."

A strange sinking, in Luken's stomach. Skin crawling with discomfort, he made his way to the dresser on his side of the room and pushed the door open, his face swinging into view as the mirror on the inside of the door popped into the light. He took up a brush, and stroked his hair smooth.

"Such *long, lovely* hair," Isaun crooned, dragging out the 'o' in the words, bleeding sarcasm. Luken glanced at him through the mirror and watched

Isaun drain his wine glass. A sense of déjà vu came over Luken. "I always told you it was lovely. Your best feature." Purple smeared his teeth. Isaun seized the bottle and emptied it into his glass, tapping rim to rim with a shrill note. "No wonder the Empress wants you."

Luken sighed. "What do you want me to say, Isaun? I'm sorry."

He sneered a hateful smile. "What are you sorry for Luken? That you're younger than me? Prettier than me? Smarter than me? Nicer than me? Is that what you're sorry for, Luken? What do you want *me* to say? That I don't mind watching you surpass me?"

Luken closed his eyes, and let his voice drop to the edge of a whisper. "I'm sorry that I hurt you, in any way."

"For Shayah's sake. Do you even hear yourself? Do you hear how pathetic you sound?"

He turned to face Isaun. The older courtesan sat bolt upright in bed, wine glass atilt, spilling its dark juices over Isaun's fingers, dappling the rumpled sheets.

"Isaun. I didn't ask for this. I'm *sorry* that your ego is bruised. I'm *sorry* that you're jealous of me. I'm *sorry* that you're a twenty-eight year old courtesan whose career is drawing to a close. I'm sorry. Really, I am."

"Fuck you," Isaun snarled. "You don't deserve it!" He hurled his wine glass blindly. It shattered against his dresser, spattering the wood. Glass sang off the floorboards. "It would be me in your place if I wasn't from a Minor House!"

"No," Luken said calmly, "it wouldn't."

Isaun breathed like a wild animal caught in a cage, his eyes rolling to meet Luken's gaze.

"You aren't her type."

Isaun's panting rasped the air; he stared at Luken, wild-eyed. And then a disbelieving breath, a withering chuckle. "Well. I guess that clears that up."

"If it makes you feel any better, it's probably not even happening."

Isaun eyed him, wary. "What does that mean?"

In the strained silence, noises reached them from the main room: the front door opening, footsteps clunking in, muffled voices.

Exhausted, Luken said, "I don't even know if I'm going to go through with it."

"What?" Isaun leaned forward, his tone eager. "Did you displease her?"

Luken turned away with a noise of disgust. "I don't know what I did to you, Isaun. I don't know why you hate me so much."

Isaun rolled his eyes. "Because you say things like *that*, you unimaginable prick."

Luken threw up his hands. "I can't argue with you, Isaun. There's nothing to say. I've tried to be kind to you, but I just can't deal with it anymore."

He strode across the bedroom, stopped at the door. "Oh and by the way, I meant to tell you; Princess Oan is back in town."

His last glimpse before leaving the room was of Isaun's face, blank with shock.

Out in the main room, Lifelle directed two servants in Palace regalia; they bustled in carrying large, lacquered boxes bearing the insignia of the famous ando-maker, Bo Tashe. Dandy trailed in after the others, his eyes lingering on the boxes with the gleam of a young courtesan who had just bought his own andos for the first time.

Annoyance lanced through Luken. Too small, this Abode.

Smash and clatter. Dandy looked up, face blanched. Lifelle jumped. Luken spun.

Isaun frothed from the bedroom corridor, his wine glass rolling off a billow of his ando to shatter against the floor. A long, scarlet tear track wept down the silken length.

"You uppity piece of shit," he snarled.

A servant squeaked in surprise, dropping the box he'd been carrying. A confection of violet and blue velvet spilled at Dandy's feet.

"Enough, Isaun." Luken held up his hands. Isaun drew a ragged breath, his bloodshot eyes boring through Luken's.

And all at once, Luken could see Isaun's future, as clearly as though he was a soothsayer gazing into his chalice: Isaun was living out the last days of his prime. He had a few good months left, during which he would generate a small fortune in Stud Fees as a trained, experienced courtesan. With luck and some good sense, he had perhaps one more Conjugal Leave in store for him before he was too old and the offers stopped coming. His youth and beauty – and with it, the only power he possessed – would slowly, inevitably, disintegrate. Women would laugh at him as he went into hysterics over every wrinkle he awoke to find in the mirror. Then, in a flurry of glamor – one last hurrah – Isaun would retire from the Court with his gathered wealth, and, having nowhere else to go, would rent lavish accomodations in the city. He would never move back in with his large family in the House of the Lily; he despised his five brothers and was ashamed of his parents' lack of ambition or success. It would destroy his pride to live off whatever table-scraps his family could afford to throw him, and Isaun would not allow that. Terrified by the dawning reality of age and irrelevance, Isaun would run through his money in a quick spurt of years, bludgeoning himself with drugs and alcohol and lavish gatherings of Ladies and courtesans as he clung to the remnants of the Court. Striving against the grip of powerlessness in a society where beauty was a man's power, the remainder of his gold would be wasted on shifty doctors and mystical healers in exchange for potions and creams and dangerous surgeries to slice open and rearrange his skin or pierce him with needles and inject him with concoctions of chemicals – all to preserve a fraction of his beauty for another day, another week, another year. Once 'worn out,' he would quickly become a joke to the rest of the city, as so many older courtesans did when they overstayed their welcome. He would begin petitioning for a position as Consort at one of the Houses where he had fathered his children, but a penniless stranger with a reputation for loving wine and himself above all else presented little appeal and the rejections, polite and condescending and ultimately devastating, would come one after another. At last, when his final wealth trickled through his fingers, he would find himself begging the Arbiters to let him move back to Court, where, powerless to do anything else, he would submit to the inevitable, and become an Abode Master. Enlivened by the Court, a little of his old ambition would return, and for the next decade or two he would train some of the fiercest and most successful courtesans of the new generation, surviving off a fraction of their income and mollified by the position of minor authority he occupied. A small amount of power, but better than nothing. Far better. He would be hard on his courtesans, for though he led them to wealth and Status, in truth, he would despise their youth and beauty as he himself passed, finally, into old age and lived out the rest of his days bitter and wistful, knowing that he had once been prized above all others for his beauty. And with that beauty gone, he was no one. Growing ever angrier and lonelier and more pitiful.

The vision spread out before Luken all at once, followed by a terrible sadness. A vision of a powerful personality, in a position of abject powerlessness.

And without power of his own, Luken's fate could be the same.

Luken rebelled against this thought with such forceful disgust that he twisted away from Isaun, storming past Dandy and Lifelle without seeing them.

"Collect my things," he spat at the servants. "I'll be staying in my chambers in the Palace."

But what of the natural order?

Behold the ram, rattling his brains about inside his skull as he jousts with other males in a mindless effort to earn his place as top consort for the females.

Behold the spider, cracking the tiny white film of his egg to enter the magnitude of the world; his life spans a few days, a few weeks, perhaps, if he is lucky, a few months. Little does it matter, so long as he accomplishes the sole purpose of his existence. Courting his Lady Colossus, the smaller male runs the risk of being devoured alive, once his use is finished. But who can deny that the flesh of his body should nourish the young?

Behold the lion, frilled golden for his Ladies' pleasure. The lionesses venture forth to hunt and provide while the male, lingering behind, gathers his bulk to meet the challenge of any other male who ventures too close, rending and roaring, so that he alone may remain as consort among his Ladies.

This is the theory we hear so often when some scientist turns her gaze to the natural world, and returns a philosopher: Who can deny that the natural world echoes and – dare I say – reaffirms, and proves the legitimacy of, the structure of the Empire? Why should we change when Mother Nature herself has given this order to the world? You can see, from this careful selection of examples from the natural world, that gendered oppression is, in fact, only the reality of nature. The earth herself says: mind your Ladies, boys, and die.

Enter the male penguin, waddling and foolish. In spite of the dazzling monotony of white and black, somehow, they choose one another; the female lays her egg and the male, tapping into some root of primordial, penguin paternity, pierces the snowy veil of anonymity to discern their egg from all the others. The females depart in search of food. The males remain, planting their bulk atop the egg in a second gestation, no less desperate than that which came before, for now – bared to the snows of deepest winter – Father Penguin pits the warmth of his body against the world's hostile and indifferent cold for the life of his child. In the ice and snow, they amass; a sea of white and black birds, flightless, soft. Weathering the abysmal snows in a collective misery, hunch-shouldered, frigid, waddling in their slow revolutions as each takes their turn at the center, where the multitude press of bodies – the necessary collective heat of the species – warms the core, and each in slow turns takes his respite from unrelenting winter. Who can say he is not attached to his egg? Warmth demands proximity. Survival demands warmth. Motherhood. Fatherhood. Grandparent, aunt, uncle, sister, brother, cousin, friend, community. The egg cares not. Any warmth will suffice in a chill.

For every peacock there is a penguin. For every 'proven' theory that legitimizes human oppression by turning to the natural world for confirmation, there is an example that contradicts it.

But let us leave aside these juvenile animal metaphors. This play-acting at scientist, this fake impartiality as we pretend to examine the natural world. Shucking it of its complexities to force human society on animal acts. Pretending the latter somehow justifies the logic of the former. The proper development of the male. The proper development of the female. The carefully constructed explanation of our differences. The importance of creating – sorry, responding to – those differences in the course of development. The redundancy of the individual when we can explain away the need for any deviation.

Still, there are those who insist: The final,

demolishing logic of the raw, animal world will obliterate your tender agendas.

So you are told, my Lady. So you believe. Perhaps. Maybe it depends on your favorite animal.

Nonetheless.

If we are to be human then let us, finally, act like it.

-Vin Ayet, Ages, 7.8.1010
"Instruments of Oppression: Metaphor"

Part Two
The Mascot

Chapter Eight

"Oh goodness, you do look lovely." The Empress lifted the white teacup, with its ring of pink roses chasing the rim to her lips, sipped, and returned it to the porcelain saucer with a clink.

Sprawled on the deep-green divan, its velvet luxurious on the backs of Luken's thighs, he masturbated feverishly, the slick click of his hand moving in rapid strokes on his oiled cock. He bit his lip, moaned softly.

"Are you ready to come, darling?"

"Oh yes." He whimpered and wriggled, his ando open and his hair disheveled. Completely undone – as she liked him.

When they'd first started this, Luken had been unbearably shy. But that was the appeal of it. Raisaga liked nothing more than to take a shy young man and coax him, with gentle commands over the course of a tender eternity, until he had dissolved by slow degrees from a proper and intelligent young lord into an abject, squirming rake, sobbing with pleasure. His hair in his face, his paint smeared, eyes peeled large with desperate appeal.

She sipped her tea, watching him.

His balls clenched. "Please," he whispered.

"Very well."

No sooner did she wave her gloved hand than Luken shattered. A single arrow – aflame with scalding, merciless bliss – shot through him. A gasp, and some noise squirreled out of him even he couldn't have identified. Hot semen squirted his stomach, his chest. A ribbon laced his hair. He panted, let the waves roll over him, made it last, ringing out the last drop where it gathered on the tip of his slipping erection like a single, precious pearl.

The Empress laid her saucer on the table, closed the distance between them and pulled the glove from her left hand. As Luken lay panting, melted into the sweat-slicked chaos of his open ando, she gathered the bead of semen on the tip of her finger, gazed at it a moment, then, arching an eyebrow, laid her finger against his lips and pushed it in till he felt the salty sweetness burst on his tongue. Her fingertip traveled the length of his tongue, almost gently, till he felt it push against the back of his throat and gagged with a satisfying squealch, gazing up into her eyes so that she could see their black pools wild with desperate, tender need.

The finger slipped free. Luken sucked in a breath, still panting.

A drowsy, pleasing warmth leadened his limbs. Luken sighed, and gazed up at the Empress with a sweet smile as she wiped her hand with a hankerchief and tugged the glove back on. She winked down at him.

Luken had been wary, of course, about this aspect of things. He'd already moved into his chambers in the Palace before there had been any sexual interaction between them at all, and Luken had feared- If she had favored a sexual activity that he despised, he would have swallowed his pride and put up with it, because he had no choice, but it would have made their arrangement a grueling chore. But after the first time, he knew he had nothing to worry about. Such a relief, to know her inclinations, and know that she could be pleased with what he also – somewhat to his surprise – found pleasing. Luken had not expected such compatibility with a woman four decades his senior, but his brief time in the Palace had already provided enough examples to prove his expectations unfounded.

The first time, Raisaga had all but chased him through his new chambers, articles of his clothing dropping one by one as each new location brought some new little experiment – his jewelry pattering to the ornate rug of the bedroom as, in a quiet, commanding voice, she explained, in intricate detail and mannered terms, exactly what he would be doing to himself and the color rose in his cheeks, demure and pink as a fresh-plucked petal – his irlan, coiled loose in the washroom as he oiled and stroked his cock – the outer robe of his ando flung into a magnificent heap in the hall as she chased him downstairs – his joh kicked off before he knelt in the main room, and she lounged on the divan, slipping open her shirt for him to take her nipples in his mouth, suckling one and the other while she stroked his hair with a strangely intense intimacy – his underskirts lost one by one on their trek through the library, the study, the staircase, as, in each location, the Empress found something new for him to suck into his mouth and shove up his ass – until somehow, the details lost in the drunken haze of dragged-out desire, Luken found himself back in the bedroom, where Raisaga, her voice going whisper-soft the harsher his panting became, had him lay facedown across the luxurious, silken softness of the sheets, and asked, rather politely, that he pump himself against the bed until he came.

"I'm an old woman," Raisaga said conversationally, sitting on the edge of the bed and stroking his damp hair after that first encounter, when he still lay flat against the sheets, his pleasure cooling wet and sticky beneath him as a bead of sweat worked down his cheek and the sound of his breathing rasped his ears. "I need very little for myself. But I still like to watch a man, young and spirited and beautiful, lose himself to ecstasy. Are you satisfied?"

"Yes," he whispered.

Chuckling, she rose, the bed scarcely moving as her slight weight left its frame. "I think this arrangement will work out just fine." The Empress slipped on her coat, grumbling about having to meet with the Steward of Domestic Works. Before she left, she stooped to murmur in his ear, "You were, at every stage, magnificent," and pressed a kiss to the smeared paint of his brow. "Luken Kenkazu-son."

After that, Luken had awaited their trysts with greater anticipation from day to day. The fatal flaw, of course, was that he remained completely dependent on her schedule, which was every bit as busy as one would expect from the most powerful woman in the world, and unpredictable, as a result.

But today it was he who had a prior commitment. With a sigh, Luken slunk from the divan, shrugging off what remained of his soiled ando, and slipped into the washroom. He whisked the semen from his hair as best he could, wetted a comb, and stroked through his tresses before tousling his hair with a towel, and brushing it back.

As he washed off and reapplied his paint, the Empress lingered in the doorway, leaning against the frame and finishing her tea. "It seems you've taken to your new chambers well enough. I trust your expectations have been met?"

"I love having all this space to myself." In four deft strokes, Luken left his lips a rosy pink hue. "It's sort of nice, being surrounded by the rest of the Palace, but still allowed my own place. No one bothers me here. It's wonderful." When the Empress had no need of him, Luken whiled away most of his hours reading and writing or strolling through the gardens, throwing feed to the peacocks and dreaming, lost deep in his mind.

Luken kissed her cheek as he passed her in the doorway and felt her eyes on his naked form as he climbed the steps to his bedroom. There, he changed into an ando of pale rose with a great, gleaming dragon twining its length, the jaws gaped in a roar and the stream of golden scales wrapping his skirts. When Luken reappeared on the landing over the main room, the Empress stood at the base of the staircase. "You were expecting a friend, weren't you?" Luken scurried barefoot down the steps, his joh forgotten in the gleeful informality that came with being master of his own chambers.

"Let's not keep him waiting any longer," the Empress turned to the door, "I should take my leave, anyway."

"Don't make *me* wait so long before your next visit," he chided, smiling.

She kissed his lips at the door. "I'm working on something for you."

"Oh?"

"A treat, the night of the party in West Hall. For both of us."

"I can't wait."

She kissed him again, and he consciously ignored the faint whiff of age.

Her eyes agleam, looking up at him. "Luken Kenkazu-son."

"Raisaga Aikanzo-daughter."

She chuckled, and hands in the pockets of her silver-and-black brocaded coat, she strode from his chambers. The moment her foot touched stone outside his door, a fleet of guards swept in to either side of her and kept pace with silent grace. Watching from the doorway, Luken grinned toothily at Lifelle. His former Abode-mate lurched to his feet from where he had knelt with his forehead pressed to the floor as the Empress passed. He twisted to watch her back as she strode down the stone hallway, beneath a vaulted ceiling that gathered the echoes. Yellow ando flaring around him, Lifelle rushed toward Luken and practically tackled him back into his own chambers, laughing breathlessly.

"That was *the Empress*, Luken! The Empress of Kanai!"

Luken pushed the door shut behind Lifelle. "I'm aware."

"Oh Goddess, were you–?" He cocked his head, eyebrows lifting.

Luken let a smile suffice and with a mad titter of a laugh, Lifelle spun away from him, gazing with wonder at Luken's chambers.

"Sorry to have kept you waiting." Luken made his way to the divan and fell across it, bare feet pressed to soft velvet. "We were a bit preoccupied, when the knock at the door came."

Lifelle's gaze traveled the dome that formed the ceiling of the sitting room, then wandered to the staircase, and the landing there, the bright hallway beyond lined with stained-glass windows that led to his bedroom on the second floor. "Never mind that. I would have waited all day, if I'd known she was with you. I mean, I suspected, from all the guards in the hall – but Goddess, how do you ever get used to it?"

Luken shrugged.

"This place is *enormous*." Lifelle charged into the washroom, looking around. He turned the tap and hopped up and down with a squeal of delight at the beam of water that coiled into the marble basin. "Working pipes! Oh Luken, this is *fine*. Very fine, indeed. Your own washroom!" He spilled back into the main room, cheeks flushed pink beneath his courtesan paint. "And you've eunuch guards at the door! I saw them when I came in, standing all silent and proper. With muskets on their backs and swords on their hips. Too fine." He whisked around the room, the pale yellow silks of his ando flaring as he turned a circle, taking it all in. "Not too shabby, my friend." Lifelle plucked the ornate porcelain vase of blue and white from the table between the divans and admired it a moment.

Luken chuckled, and glanced out at the balcony. "I'm having morning glories planted along the trellis. They're climbing vines. In the summer, I'll look down from the balcony and find a wall of blue-and-violet petals unfolding for the dawn."

Lifelle sighed and collapsed onto the divan opposite Luken. "You were born for this, I think."

"I don't know about that. Every time I wake up in the new bedroom, I feel uneasy, like Fi is about to burst in the front door and tell me a grave mistake has been made and I need to leave at once."

Lifelle kicked his feet over the end of the divan; Luken watched his joh sail in two neat arcs, one to clatter across the polished, hardwood floor, the other to land with a soft thunk on the Bushani rug that carpeted the floor beneath their divans, rich with a design of phoenixes in flight, trailing embers of flame. "It's Aokinay who should be worrying about that, just now. Not you."

Luken shifted. "Don't say that. Aokinay is still the Empress's Consort."

"For now. All the Garden is whispering that Aokinay is out of favor, and you are ascendant."

"All the Garden had better watch its collective tongue, then."

Lifelle stretched, his back arching luxuriously against the deep green velvet of the divan. "Isaun would love this."

Luken snorted and snatched a box from the low table before him, ripping it open to reveal the rows of chocolates and caramels within. He popped one into his mouth. "No he wouldn't. He would only love it if it were him living here, and expect us to be happy for him. You know full well he is anything but happy for me."

Lifelle sighed, gazing up at the dome ceiling.

"Isaun has always been... difficult in that particular way."

"In the way of being a selfish asshole? Yes, he has always been difficult in that particular way."

"Luken," Lifelle chided, glancing at him. Soft brown eyes, rings of honey blond hair spilling across his cheeks. "Isaun loves you."

Luken flicked a caramel back into the box. "Now *that* is a hell of a conclusion to reach at this juncture."

Lifelle propped himself up on one elbow, reached into the proffered box, and flicked a cube of white chocolate between his teeth. "He's always kept you at arm's length. I don't really know why. At first, I think, it's because you were so much younger than me or Isaun. Eight years makes a great difference, at that age. In the early days, you were like a shy kid brother, following us around. But we didn't mind, we wanted you to do well. Then you were gone for three years on Conjugal Leave, but Isaun answered every single one of your letters. Do you know how many people in this world Isaun would bother to answer letters from, Luken? Three or four people, at most, and I daresay half of them are sitting in this room. And then you came home from U-Wen and things were so perfect for awhile. You and Isaun seemed so happy, I thought, 'Finally, this is how things were meant to be.' Then, with the election, well, it became obvious you were on opposite sides, there. And now, with the Empress – you can't imagine the depths of his disappointment, Luken. It's all been so easy for you."

Luken's laughter rang into the chambers, laced with scorn. "If you say so."

Lifelle watched him, his large, brown eyes serious. "Luken. Isaun doesn't know where he's going to live when he retires from Court."

The laughter fell away from Luken's lips. "How is that my fault? He's had so long to figure it out!"

"I think, in the back of his mind, he always expected-"

"For Goddess' sake! Princess Oan never even so much as looked at him! He's still harping on that, after all these years?"

Lifelle shook his head. "But don't you see? There's never been a Lady that Isaun couldn't get before. Once he sets his sights on a client, he always wins them in the end."

"Well it's high time to grow up and realize you can't get everything you want in life."

"*You* can, apparently, and without even trying that hard, really," Lifelle pressed.

Luken sighed. "You can't tell me that there are truly no other prospects. What about Lady Romyn?"

Lifelle rolled his eyes. "That woman. I know she's the Daughter of a High House, but I really think Isaun should have steered clear of that one. Every day, there is some elaborate gift or poem or pleading invitation. I've never seen a more annoying courtship. Isaun answers about one letter in five, but the Lady continues, undeterred."

Luken smiled. "He's her Princess Oan."

Lifelle's head fell back, his laughter ringing up to the dome. "Ah, dear. I think it's time they both gave up."

Luken sobered. "What about the rest of his

clients?"

"Isaun has always had many clients, but none that would offer him a position as Consort when he retires from the Court." His voice fell. "None that love him."

"What about the Houses where he went on Conjugal Leave?"

"The trouble, Luken, is that Isaun – well, he did very well for himself when it came to finding Ladies that were above his station. They paid him well, and at the time, that was all Isaun saw. But now- Well, he is the Son of a Minor House. Most Minor lords Consort at Minor Houses, or not at all. If they're lucky, they Consort at Middling Houses. But it would be a love match. After all, if a Lady is going to take on the expense of maintaining a Consort, she may as well gain a favorable political alliance from his maternal House, correct? But there is no political gain for a Middling or High House in taking on a Minor lord as Consort. Isaun's Ladies did not love him. And if they do not love him, and if there is no political advantage in taking on a Minor lord..." Lifelle spread his hands in a gesture of surrender.

"His daughters may lobby on his behalf. It's not so unusual for a Lady to take on a Consort she does not love at her daughter's insistence."

"His daughters barely know him."

Luken sighed. "What do you want me to do, Lifelle?"

"Invite Isaun here. Make him part of this world. Forgive him."

Luken pulled a chocolate from the box and watched cracks spread across the surface from the soft pressure of his nails, digging in. "I wish Isaun well. I really do. But if he wants my friendship, he has to come to me. I'm not a novice; I don't scurry around behind him, hanging on his every word." He looked up at Lifelle. "I'm not his shadow any more."

Lifelle sighed, and sat up, honey hair spilling across his chest. "Luken, Lady Ahn has offered me a position as Consort at the House of Lush Vale. I've accepted."

Luken froze, the chocolate halfway to his lips. His teeth clinked together. "I see. I- congratulations, Lifelle." He stood, and moved onto the other divan, wrapping his arms around Lifelle. "I'm happy for you. At least one of us will have a happy ending."

Lifelle gave him an odd look. "More than one of us, I hope."

Luken squeezed him, breathing in the faint, flowery scent of his hair. "When are you leaving?"

Lifelle's hand found his. "A few weeks."

Luken gasped. "When were you going to tell me?"

"It only happened the day before yesterday, Luken. You were still moving into the Palace. I couldn't get ahold of you."

Luken stood and paced to the balcony, gazing out on the planter boxes of peonies that brimmed in such delight at his feet. He watched, for a long moment, as they bobbed their heads in the wind. "I only hope she deserves you."

A soft laugh. "The Abode will be quiet. Once Isaun retires, Amae will need a whole new stable."

"What about Dandy?" Luken turned back to Lifelle, and found his shadow falling across the courtesan. "Can you leave before he's completed his training?"

Another odd look. "Luken, Dandy started working a fortnight ago."

"What!"

He crooked a grin. "I don't blame you for not noticing. You've been courting the Empress. Next to that, the mundane affairs of the Scattered Flowers must seem unimportant."

Luken wrung his hands together. "You're making me feel terrible! Of course Dandy's first night is important." He sighed. "I shall have to make it up to him. Who was the client, anyway?"

"Lady Imoh. A younger daughter of the House of Bronze Hills. Nice girl, very sweet and very sweet on Dandy. At this rate, he might beat your record for shortest period of availability between starting work and going on Conjugal Leave to a High House."

"I'm glad to hear it." He moved back to the velvet divan, gazing without appetite at the rumpled box of chocolates, half-spilled from the skins of their papery cups. "Bronze Hills, aren't they-"

"Enormous? Yes. Five Daughters, eighteen cousins, thirty-something secondary cousins. Sprawling compound with multiple mansions being built for the lesser branches of the family. Dandy could have done much worse for his starting courtship."

The word on the tip of his tongue had been *Reformist*, but after a moment's consideration, Luken was glad Lifelle had misunderstood him. Not everything had to be political. Trained to be universally pleasing, most courtesans didn't think like that. Nor had he, until recently.

Guilt trickled like sap through Luken's veins. "So once you leave, it will just be Dandy and Isaun at the Abode."

Lifelle nodded. "And trust me, Amae will be looking to get Isaun out of there as fast as possible, now that his career's on the downturn. Isaun still generates a high income, but not as much as he used to, and without him, it's just Dandy. Amae's going to get a new trio in."

"Our replacements," Luken murmured, not sure how he felt about that. He could almost see them in his mind's eye, the hopeful, fresh-faced virgins who would scutter nervously up to the Abode of Scattered Flowers to begin their training under Amae's baleful eye. And how would Isaun look, there with the new generation and no prospects of his own? Luken sighed. "Isaun will be alone."

"I want things to be right between the two of you, before I leave."

Luken closed his eyes and collapsed across the divan, his face falling into the billows of his ando's sleeve. "Why must you be my conscience, Lifelle?"

Lifelle plucked a caramel from the box and bit into it, tawny skeins wilting from the nub between his fingers.

"Ask, rather, why the two of you must be my headache."

Chapter Nine

Cries of delight rang through West Hall in the light of a thousand candles, the oaken walls aglow with torches, and the massive blue-marble fireplace at the far end of the Hall ablaze and glinting off a dozen crystal chandeliers that hovered like icicles over the heads of the crowd that packed the room, a swirling swarm of Lords and Ladies. Almost all were of High Houses, their retinues in tow. A world from which Luken had mostly been excluded. Until now.

A dozen tables clamored with the sound of dice rolling or the cries of onlookers as a game turned to victory or defeat, as though a gambling hall had been dragged whole into the Palace. Luken itched to try his hand at one of the games; he had more than enough bohda jingling in his coinpurse from the Empress's stipend – which *had* proven to be generous, as promised – just waiting to be gambled.

Ladies and Lords alike parted before Luken as he swept through the Hall, his ando billowing around him; the primary color was a rich green, but delicate pinks, golds, whites, reds, and blues slashed the ando in a controlled chaos, so that with his long train and sleeves that dipped to the floor, Luken all but shimmered as he strode through the crowd.

At his side, the Empress plucked a flute of champagne from the platter of a passing server, and eyed Luken as she slipped the flute into his fingers.

The server – naked, like all of them, except for the black, velvet bow tied around his throat and the other adorning him a little lower down – bowed his head as the Empress selected her own flute from his platter, and vanished the moment she turned from him.

"Is there any color in which you do not look resplendent?"

Luken chuckled. "My Lady Empress, I do believe you are trying to show me off."

"Easy enough to do." She sipped her champagne. "Your beauty begs to be admired."

He fluttered his lashes at her. Breaking into a toothy grin, Raisaga placed a hand on his cheek. "Come find me, in a little while. I'm going to see that your surprise is being prepared."

He kissed the palm of her hand before she slipped away, the crowd parting before her as she took the western door deeper into the Palace.

The crowd swamping the table behind him erupted into cheers and Luken turned to watch Satomi – a bubbly courtesan with a mass of red curls – leap up and down like a child as the dealer pushed a pile of bohda at him. Luken smiled, and slipped away, feeling like a knife as he sluiced through the crowd. Curious eyes trailed him wherever he went, stares lingering on his face.

He almost passed right by them, Isaun and Princess Oan. It was the silver diadem, with the trio of sapphires spangling her brow, that drew his eye. Luken's eyes widened, but he did not approach the table. He and Isaun were not on speaking terms; Isaun's invitation had been the price of persuading Lifelle and Dandy to come. And how could he deny

Lifelle anything, when the man would be gone soon enough?

Isaun's back was turned to him, but Luken could tell from his gestures, from his energy, that he spoke to Princess Oan with enthusiasm. The two sat at the farthest uju table, and when the dealer turned to Isaun, he tossed another bohda on his wager – a small mountain of gold coins gleaming before him – and rolled the dice. Five dice, each a different color, bounced across a table that was blocked off into sections with colors matching the dice. The blue die struck the far side of the table and hopped back to land in the blue square, showing the emblem of a falcon facing upward, and the crowd of onlookers erupted. Luken did not know enough of the game to know if it the roll was good – but the crowd certainly did. Laughing, Oan clapped a hand to Isaun's shoulder, her expression girlish with delight, and the dealer announced, "The table goes to the young lord!" before turning to the Princess.

Oan paused a moment, drinking in the crowd's attention as she sipped her champagne and glanced at Isaun with a playful gleam in her dark brown eyes, before announcing with roguish indifference, "To the Hells, I'll double the round."

Applause roared around them as Isaun leaned in close to her, and Luken just barely caught the words, "We may come to regret that, Princess."

Champagne swirled in her glass. "I have no time for regrets."

"And if my wager is lost…?"

"There are others ways to cover a debt."

The Lady beside Oan – a sloe-eyed woman

who Luken recognized as a friend of the Princess's – gathered the dice in a wooden cup and handed it to Oan. But while the Princess cast her dice, the Lady's dark eyes fixed on Isaun and did not falter.

The center of attention once again, Luken thought, shaking his head. A weary smile on his lips. *Well you have your chance, Isaun. Make it count this time.*

And with that, he moved on.

"Luken!" Lifelle waved to him from the tano table, Dandy beside him resplendent in a pricy ando of voluminous gold and pink silks. Luken met them both with an embrace, and when he pulled away, Lifelle fumbled at the gold coronet, with its splendid ring of pearls, that Luken had slipped from the sleeve of his ando to his housemate's blond locks while Dandy held up the ring on the end of the chain Luken had fastened around his neck so that deep, scarlet glimmers appeared in its ruby.

Lifelle's eyes went wide. "Luken, what–"

"To celebrate your new position as Consort." He turned to Dandy. "And for you, Dandy, to celebrate the end of your training and the beginning of your life as a courtesan."

Dandy stared, wide-eyed, at the ring in his palm. "But I can't accept this, it's far too expensive–"

"Nonsense. You'll look lovely."

"Luken," Lifelle pled, turning the coronet in his hands, "this is too much."

"Lifelle." Luken let his voice fall. "Let me do this for you. Please."

He returned Lifelle's earnest gaze, until the older man sighed and, crooking half a grin at Dandy, slipped the coronet back onto his head. "Well, if I *must*."

"You must." Luken smiled as Dandy tentatively prised the ring from its chain and slipped it onto his finger. "What is the point of good fortune if I cannot share it with friends?"

Dandy gazed up at him, his voice almost a murmur. "I will never be able to pay you back."

"You can do so easily enough, just teach me how to play this game."

"You've never played tano?" Dandy pulled out his chair and offered it to Luken. "Sit down! You can play my hand." He gathered a quartet of cards from the table and handed them to Luken, standing over his shoulder as Luken spread the cards out like the fan of a peacock's feathers. "It's not a bad draw," Dandy whispered in his ear. "Red cards, like these two," roosters preened on the twin cards that Dandy tapped, "always have an odd value less than ten. Blue," he flicked the corner of a card with a trout spinning after its own tail, "always has an even value under five, and yellow," he pointed to Luken's topmost card, which bore a lioness lifting her tawny face as if scanning the grasslands for prey, "can be any even value under ten. Every turn you have to set the value of a card, or return one and draw another. You always have four cards. You want to reach a total of twenty-six before the other three players, but if you go over, you lose. Unless you have a silver or a white card, which can multiply or divide your total. Green are less common, but can duplicate whatever value you have played before."

"Dandy," Luken grumbled, betrayed, "this is math."

Lifelle settled beside him, one finger grazing a pearl on his coronet. "I give up. I've got nothing."

"No!" Dandy cried, "don't give up, you've got a good hand!"

"Mind if I join the table?"

Luken looked up to find Ohfene sidling into the chair opposite Luken on the half-crescent table. Ohfene's housemate – not Nikay, but a pretty blond on the upper-middle tier of the Board – slipped into the empty seat between Ohfene and Lifelle, completing a group of four. Ohfene tossed a fifty bohda note on the table and the others, one by one, matched his bet. Luken felt tension gather like a storm, crisping the air at the table. Only the dealer did not feel the stormwinds, tossing Ohfene and his housemate four cards before calling, "First round!"

Ohfene's warm, chestnut eyes flickered over his hand before he snapped a yellow card – a lioness – sideways. "Eight."

The blond courtesan flipped a red card sideways. "Nine."

The dealer looked at Lifelle who, eyeing Ohfene warily, handed one back to the dealer. "I'll swap."

"I heard you moved into the Palace, Luken," Ohfene spoke as the round came to Luken's turn.

Repressing a sigh, Luken glanced up at him. "Yes, Ohfene."

"Swap one of your red cards," Dandy hissed in his ear. Luken obeyed mechanically; he had already forgotten the rules of the game.

"Well, it's no surprise." Ohfene's turn came back around, and he accepted his new card from the dealer, glancing at it before he laid a green serpent down beside his lioness, "Eight." His gaze lanced up to meet Luken's. "From what I've heard, you follow the Empress about like a puppy."

The blond snorted with laughter. Luken felt Dandy's frame stiffen beside him. Lifelle's eyes narrowed, and he raised his gaze from his cards to stare at Ohfene with a warning look. Not for the first time, Luken was struck by the distinct sensation that everyone at the table knew something he didn't. Some joke, bandied about behind his back. Last time Ohfene had played this game it had been at Dandy's expense, but this time–

A cold smile curled Luken's lip. *Still stings that you brought me to the Empress's attention, doesn't it Ohfene?* "Do they say so? Well, people will enjoy their talk. I rather think it more common that she comes to me, but the Empress will do as she likes."

The blond courtesan flicked a card at the dealer. "Swap."

Lifelle, barely paying attention to the game, glanced from Dandy to Luken and laid down a blue card. "Four, I suppose."

Luken glanced at his own cards. Another blue card sat in the place of the red card he'd traded. "Swap again," Dandy murmured. "The blue." He did, and felt Dandy's silent intake of breath when the new card appeared in his hand, a white tiger, delineated by its black stripes on a background of perfect ivory.

Ohfene spared an annoyed glance at his cards, and played a blue. "Four."

Ohfene was within six points of winning, and Luken had no cards on the table. He surpressed a flash of annoyance with Dandy.

"So you've not been dogging her footsteps? Good to hear."

The blond gave a high, silvery laugh, though Luken could not have guessed what was so funny about that line. Lifelle's scowl deepened.

Luken returned Ohfene's gaze with a frosty smile while the others took their turns.

Dandy nudged him. "Set the red as a nine."

The card slapped the table. "Nine."

"It does give me pause," Ohfene lingered on the last word, while his housemate fought down a sneering grin, "of course," he laid down another blue card as a 'four' with an arched eyebrow, "now that you're running with the big dogs, I must warn you, from the Son of a High House, you do not want to behave," he cocked his head at Luken, his lips fixed in a curve of mirthless condescension, "like a bitch in heat."

Dandy's ringlets brushed Luken's ear; he scarcely heard the young courtesan's whisper over the pounding of his own heart. "Play your yellow as a four."

"What?" Luken hissed back, dropping his gaze from Ohfene's. "That would give me thirteen."

"Trust me."

"He only needs two points, he's going to win on the next turn."

Dandy shook his head. "He can't. You can't play all even numbers or all odd numbers, you have to have at least one of either kind. He needs two points, but he hasn't played an odd number yet."

Luken sighed, and played his lioness. "Four."

Ohfene cocked an eyebrow, and laid down a rooster. "One."

The blond glared at his cards. Luken suspected he would have liked very much to make a particular play, but did not want to step on Ohfene's toes. Well, who could blame him? The blond, like Lifelle, swapped.

A rush of excitement in Dandy's whisper. "The white card."

Luken laid his white tiger down beside the lioness. Side-by-side, they made a handsome couple.

"Twenty-six!" the dealer announced. "We have a winner."

Dandy shook Luken's shoulders, laughing. "White cards double the total value of your other cards."

Surpressing a swell of fear, Luken glanced up and met Ohfene's gaze as the dealer pushed the handful of bills toward Luken. *We should not be enemies,* he wanted to tell the other man, but there was no arguing with the withering contempt in Ohfene's eyes.

"Beginner's luck." Luken shrugged.

"You could call it that," Ohfene said flatly. "But I do wonder how long that luck of yours is going to last." He stepped away from the table, smoothing the skirts of his violet ando. He pivoted, as if to storm away, then froze. Luken's eyes widened. He did not need to follow the older man's gaze to know that Ohfene had spotted Isaun sitting side-by-side with Princess Oan at the uju table. Confusion smoothed his lovely features blank, then rage, even something like betrayal, cracked the marble. Turning the other way, Ohfene swept across the hall, vanishing into the crowd.

Luken sighed with relief as Lifelle and Dandy closed in on him.

"That's one thing I won't miss when I leave Court," Lifelle hissed.

"I'm sorry, Luken, I'm so sorry!" Dandy wailed.

Luken shook his head. "I'm out of the loop."

Lifelle sighed and, leaning close to Luken, murmured, "As usual, Ohfene and his little section of the Garden have been spreading their rumors. It's ridiculous of course, completely childish–"

Luken's stomach dropped. He found a deadened laugh somewhere within himself and unrolled it. "What is it?"

"I don't even know how it started. It's just one of those fabrications that is so bizarre it's either discounted out of hand, or it gains legs and kicks off running–"

"No one actually believes it of course," Dandy piped up. "You'd have to be insane."

"You'd better just spit it out," Luken said.

A blush crept across Lifelle's features. "Something about you having," he waved his hand in the air, as if the right words might be floating around in the ether for him to bump into and pull down, "I don't know, fucked a dog, or whatever."

"What!"

"I know, it's preposterous," Lifelle said at the same time Dandy bleated, "No one believes it!"

Luken's shoulders shook, and laughter bubbled from his lips. "And when did this particular, ah, assignation, occur?"

A weak smile. "From what I can gather," Lifelle arched an eyebrow, "you offered this service to a Lady during that period, for about half a year or so, between your return to Court and the beginning of your courtship with the Empress a few weeks ago."

"A period during which I was working a great deal, and it would be easy to claim that I had done such a thing for the amusement of any number of clients I had at the time." Luken closed his eyes, weary beyond belief. His gaze alighted on his flute of champagne, forgotten on the tano table, and he finished it in one gulp. "It was all going so smoothly. Of course, I am to be punished for my success. Of course, I am to be put in my place for being too fortunate, as if I asked for this. *Of course,* I am to be humiliated for being a man and doing well for myself. And of all the rumors they could have started, it had to be sexually degrading. There was no other way they could have attacked me. It had to be sexual degradation. Of fucking course."

"They are children," Lifelle murmured to him, laying a hand on his arm. "Ignore their antics."

Dandy cocked a brow. "Ohfene actually *would* fuck a dog, if he thought it would get him where you are."

A laugh – a startling, genuine laugh – broke from Luken's lips, unfurling from the core of his body, until Lifelle and Dandy joined in.

"Goddess," Luken seized a champagne flute from a passing server, "I need a drink."

They spent the better part of half an hour swirling through the hall, pausing here and there to watch an interesting turn at one of the games; a jubilant victory, a crushing loss. Luken found he liked watching others play more than he liked trying his own hand at the game, though truly, they should have stopped at each table and let Dandy win the round; he had the mind for it. Just when Luken had almost forgotten his encounter with Ohfene, and the champagne warmed him to contentment, fingers seized around his arm. Luken whipped around to find Fi glaring up at him.

"The Empress's Consort is coming," she hissed. "You need to leave. Now."

A bolt of panic. Luken let himself be hustled from the room, his skirts swishing around them in a soft counterpoint to the ringing echo of the Steward's boots. Out from the hall. A couple, locked in embrace in the hallway, shot apart and bolted at the sight of him. Fi pulled him into a foyer, where a spiral staircase soared to the second floor of the Palace.

Luken's cheeks flushed. One moment, lord of the night.

The next, he fled from the hall like a mouse scurrying from a cat.

Chapter Ten

"There you are!" The Empress's voice rang from atop the spiral staircase. Luken looked up, his heart wild as a hummingbird pillaging the blooms for nectar. Fi, her features set in stone-carved resolution, dragged him to the staircase. Over his shoulder, Luken watched the blurred sliver of the crowd in West Hall disappear as they mounted the second floor. "Another moment, and I would have sent a servant for you."

Winged by a pair of eunuch guards, the Empress withdrew down a shadowed hallway, and Luken followed her into a remote chamber of the Inner Palace.

"I will ensure you are not disturbed," said Fi.

The Empress paused, her hand on the knob of the door, and gave her a wry look. "As ever, you are a treasure, oh Steward of the Royal Chambers."

Fi gave her an ironic bow and took her post opposite the door as the guards gracefully positioned themselves to either side, staring straight ahead.

The Empress glanced at Luken. "Ready for your present?"

Luken grinned, relieved now that they had put distance between themselves and the party, where one too many rivals prowled the chaos amid floating champagne and the rattle of dice. "As I'll ever be, my Lady Empress."

He was not ready.

When Luken slipped inside the chamber, he found it to be a small but well-appointed bedroom, both cozy and elegant, and lit only by the deep, amber glow of the fireplace where flames danced on Luken's left, illuminating the nude limbs of three women and two men who lounged on the large, circular bed, hands traveling idly over one another's bodies, a low murmur of talk dropping to a hush as the door opened, and five pairs of eyes gazed up at Luken with tender hunger. He could only guess that they were near to his age, and each stunning after their own fashion; fair or dark, voluptuous or slim, hair long and sleek or thick with curls.

"Oh…" Luken breathed.

Raisaga gazed up at him, watching his expression with a mischievous eye.

Standing on her tiptoes, the Empress slipped her arms around his neck, and pressed her lips to his. "They're all yours."

"Raisaga," he murmured. He felt a weight tumble against his chest and, in a ghostly reversal of earlier that evening, he looked down to find a diamond between them, gleaming in the amber light of the fireplace; it lay against his chest on the end of a fine, gold chain. Luken drew a breath, torn. Desire, yes, and gratitude that she had gone to this trouble for his pleasure, but also the sinking horror that occurs when safety, security, is ripped away just when it had felt certain. He'd thought he was done with this, the risk of unwanted pregnancy – and darted a glance at the lovelies on the bed, a woman meeting his gaze with open longing in her eyes as the man behind her massaged her shoulders, his member stirring already to a considerable length. And guilt, trickling like ice water down his heating flesh, that he *did* want this, or part of him did, but he didn't really, and how could he say no?

Soft moans and sighs from the bed, a mist creeping in to shroud his thoughts.

Raisaga winked up at him.

The boy in the marketplace. The image of his face, phantom-hovering over the Empress's, jolted Luken out of his shock.

"This is... an exceptional offering." He let his head lilt a little to the side, murmuring in her ear, "But can't I save myself just for you?"

The Empress blinked up at him, taken aback. Flattered, even. For a moment, he thought he'd won. *Go on,* he thought, *tell the others to have at it while we keep to ourselves.*

Then she gave a little shake of her head. "This is a gift for *both* of us, Luken." Her black eyes took on an obsidian gleam, and he knew there would be no compromise. Not with the Empress.

She turned to their guests, lifting the diamond on the tip of one finger. "Whoever earns his load, earns the diamond too." She whispered in Luken's ear, "Give me a show, love."

He felt his irlan tugged loose. Tightness, and falling. Numbing himself to acceptance, Luken stepped out of his ando. The lovelies on the bed bloomed and contracted like a winter blossom, closing and opening to cold and warmth; writhing open, twisting inward. Slowly, Luken peeled off his under-robe and looked back over his bared shoulder to find Raisaga seated in the armchair by the fireplace, gazing at him. An encouraging smile. A log cracked in the fire, a spiral of sparks flitting upward and gone. He turned, releasing the under-robe from his other shoulder.

Naked, the diamond gleamed on his chest. Hair unbound. Desire stirring, in spite of himself. But there was a misery to it – this helplessness. Lust deadened his limbs, hazed his mind; he felt heavy and warm, as if he moved through melting honey, and drank in its sweetness. Was this what it was to be a man? They said women were not so affected by lust. That men alone were the slaves of sex, and no more than animals when Shayah's touch grazed them. And for all that he resented and hated that claim, he felt himself growing hard as two of the women drew him down, their hands caressing his arms, reaching up to grip his shoulders, tangle in his hair.

Ah, but they were lovely. He let himself fall between them, their firm, athletic limbs silk-clad in smooth skin and pushing against him, stroking his chest, trailing down to tease his thighs as lips pressed to his neck on either side. Behind them, the others had hastened onward. Luken let his head fall back and found the third woman, her hair a cascade of fair, Bushani curls, sliding a cock into her mouth while the man behind her knelt to tongue her vulva. The slick sounds of their mouths at work, the soft moans and groans, enflamed Luken's need as much as the delicate touch of both women's fingers, grazing and teasing his erection.

Whoever had chosen this little quintet had done a fine job. Of the two men, one was of a dark complexion, the firelight drawing caramel highlights from his smooth skin, his hair a glorious chaos of curls, his dark eyes half-lidded as the redhaired woman ran her tongue along his cock. The other man, light-skinned, with high cheekbones and pale blue eyes, blazed with a haughty sexuality; a need that knew it would be met, unashamed of its own ferocity. Of the three women, all were lovely, the redhead the most voluptuous, her breasts quivering with each quickened breath. The dark-haired woman who bent to press a tongue between his lips, her petite body no less bold and her desire, when he lifted a hand to her vulva, no less eager. He stroked her vigorously as the hand on his cock pumped him. He gasped for breath as the petite brunette drew away from him, and the blond, fine-featured, her lips and nipples a rosy pink that Luken longed to nibble at, closed the distance, drawing him into another kiss. Even as her lips met his, the brunette swung a leg over his waist and, all at once, she sheathed him, hot and wet, and started riding. The blonde drew away, giving the brunette a sullen look, then turned to smile down at Luken. "I wanted your cock first," she flicked at the diamond on his chest and watched it bounce on the chain, "but I'll settle for your load."

The dark-skinned man wrapped his arms around the brunette's waist and playfully tustled her off Luken's cock. "Don't be selfish, Nilayn." He kissed her and rolled atop her, glancing up at Luken, eyebrow cocked. "You have to share him with the rest of us." With that, he thrust into her, her fingernails scratching eagerly at his back as he pumped her. Nilayn writhed beneath him, arching her back, cursing and gasping with pleasure.

Luken pushed himself back, onto the center of the bed. His head swirled. In the dimness, the Empress watched, her eyes alight in the reflection of the flames. In this brief reprieve, caution rattled in the back of Luken's mind; he had to be careful, there were so many ways this could go wrong.

He should have taken the damn pills, before it was too late.

Luken wrapped his arms around the fair-skinned man and bent him forward, thrust his cock into his ass. Yielding flesh promised they had prepared for this. The fair-skinned man gasped, surprised and delighted, and arched back into Luken. Luken nudged at him with gentle strokes, but the blond would have none of it. He pumped back, rough, the chant of their skin connecting with a rhythmic slap. Luken pumped, a bead of sweat budding on his brow, watching the man's strong back contort before him. He was exquisite, in his manner, but there was no flavor to the encounter, just the mechanical pleasure; Luken had never been able to enjoy a man as he did a woman. Still, at least this was safe.

"Seven Hells," the fair-skinned man breathed. In front of him, the two women had tumbled into an embrace, their tongues dancing, their fingers working inside each other. Luken almost lost it there; on instinct, he yanked back. His courtesan training would not allow him to put on such a poor performance. He couldn't be the first to come. For Goddess' sake, he was trained for this.

The fair-skinned man straightened with a sigh of disappointment, carding fingers through pale, silky locks.

The petite brunette arched her back with a desperate groan. Luken watched, his vision fever-glazed with lust. Well. At least he wasn't the first to come.

"You're not half bad, you know," the fair-skinned man murmured; he had flipped onto his back in front of Luken, giving him a lazy grin as he stroked Luken's cock clean with a damp towel from the basket beside the bed.

"Thanks." He nodded toward the head of the bed. "Now lay back." The blond cocked an eyebrow, but obeyed, leveraging himself back. The blonde woman and the redhead watched him, curious. Numb, hazed over, Luken gently pulled the redhead to him and squeezed the delicious heft of her breasts before whispering, "Do you want to suck his cock?"

She glanced at the fair-skinned man. "If you fuck me from behind, I do."

"You read my mind." She knelt and licked the length of his shaft, from base, across a rather impressive distance, to the tip. Luken spared a moment to watch before turning to the other man; with a grin and a nod toward the headboard, he positioned him beside the blond man. The fair-haired woman, without a moment's hesitation, knelt to take him in her mouth. Luken watched, drunk on the sight of their hips turned up to receive him. To his credit, he resisted a moment. A long moment.

Then he pressed into the redhead, telling himself, *I'm not going to come in her, I'm not going to,* as flame licked at his thoughts. He held her hips with both hands and thrust into her, mounting to a swift rhythm while she sucked the other man's cock, cheeks hollowed with effort, mewling her pleasure as he worked.

When he couldn't take it any more, he pulled back, dimly aware of the brunette watching them, her cheeks flushed pink, her fingers circling her clit as if considering a second orgasm.

Luken moved behind the blonde woman and gripped her hips, angling into her to be greeted by sweet, clenching heat. Perfection.

He went back and forth between them, losing himself in the wild rhythm. Deep, gratifying strokes. Rampant with glory. Until- at the final moment, the unstoppable demand of his body stole his breath- He tore himself away.

Ribbons of ejaculate, thick unspooling, painted the blonde's back in spurts that wracked Luken's body, his whole frame seizing with ecstasy. A spray of drops, pearls of searing pleasure. He fell back on his heels panting, his erection wilting. Through a breathless haze, he reached a hand between the blonde's thighs and stroked her, slick and wanting, until her back arched, her eyes rolling in her head, even as the penis in her hand jut its milky spill over the other man's abdomen.

In the honeyed warmth of his afterglow, Luken heard the others find their pleasure. Distant, like voices through the mist.

Gentle hands, stroking his hair, cupping his face. Luken looked up to find the Empress gazing down into his dazed eyes. She looked pleased, proud even, in some odd way. She pressed a kiss to his lips and, unhooking the clasp from behind his neck, held the diamond aloft. It twirled at the end of its chain, catching glints of amber in the firelight.

"I think we have a winner." She hooked the chain around the blonde woman's neck where she knelt, panting and satisfied. She looked up, finding Luken's eyes on her, and winked. He gave her a tired grin, and watched the diamond twirl to rest between her breasts.

~

In his own chambers, alone, Luken sat before the fireplace; it lacked the heat of the dancing blaze in the private chambers he had so recently abandoned, but he preferred this: the sulking embers, the dim scarlet that bathed his skin, bared to the night beneath the rumpled under-skirts he left undone. What time was it? Soon, he thought, the bells would toll. But perhaps not. He may have missed them during his hours with the Empress, or before that, in the grand merriment of the hall. He waited for the bells, standing as though on the edge of a dark precipice. The dawn would make it clear, should it slip its rosy fingers in through the windows that stood, curtains flung back, to the black face of midnight. Til then, he sat before the fire in the dim shades of his chambers, watching the logs glow from within, basking in their hidden heat. Exhausted.

Shame, the companion that had joined him that night at the lake house and tracked him from U-Wen, had trailed farther behind in recent months. So far behind, in recent days, that Luken had lost sight of it around a curve in the road. So far that even the echo of Shame's footsteps had receded, and he had not heard them above the tread of his own. Luken simmered, angry at his own stupidity. Why had he thought that a few good weeks meant triumph? He felt as though he'd been unmasked as an idiot with half the world watching.

The last chocolate in the box that he'd shared with Lifelle sat on the sidetable cozied against his armchair. His fingers searched the paper cups with mindless intent, scuffling them aside until they stumbled across a stale disc of milk chocolate. He chewed mindlessly.

In the ugly shadows of the fire's dim light, Luken stared down at his body, dissected by the random fall of his under-skirts, and hated it.

This would happen again. He knew that. He'd given in to the Empress's will – *but how could I not?* The feeling seethed against the current of his blood – and in the end, he'd given in to what felt-

Luken sighed, clenching his eyes shut. Even through his eyelids, the firelight glowed. Scarlet after-images, drifting in the dark.

He could not trust himself. Yes, he'd pulled back at the last moment, the crucial moment, but it had been the final possible instant and if that scenario repeated itself, he may not be able to do it again. He could not trust himself to retain control.

And isn't that what the Empress had always said? She liked to see him lose control. He'd thought himself safe with her, an old woman long past childbearing years. But her very interest was that which he feared most.

Luken withdrew his gaze from the flames and surveyed the box of chocolates, now an empty, little paper grave. Idly, he smashed the box aside, letting the loose papers whisper across the floor, under the chair, into the corners. It did not matter. He would wake tomorrow and they would be gone. A cold smile curved Luken's lips; he had servants for that. Good ones. They were like phantoms, coming and going without drawing his attention. It was as if his chambers sustained themselves.

Fingers probing the dim surface of the sidetable, Luken found the little coinpurse and pulled it into his lap. When he'd first moved into his rooms in the Palace, he'd very nearly thrown the pills away. It was a dangerous thing to be caught with, and at the time, he'd been certain the danger had passed. He'd have no need of them. But some compulsion, some lingering distrust of his own good fortune, had stayed his hand.

Now he was relieved he'd kept them.

Luken pressed his fingertips into the coinpurse, and withdrew a single pill, chalky and white. He rolled it between the tips of his fingers. Rori had promised-But in the shadows of night, it seemed unlikely that such a small thing could deliver him from the fate of his body. From what he was.

And what was he, anyway?

A voice hissed at him from the chambers of memory, echoing with contempt. *Poor little rich boy.*

Luken stared. From the white disc, future children in the billions, in the billions upon billions, stared back at him from the realm of possibility where they teemed ad infinitum; an endless crowd of faces moon-white, moon-drifting, gazing at him with his eyes, handsome and stolen, hovering beyond the threshold. All the possibilities; all unwanted, all threatening. And all just possibilities, to which he could say 'no.'

Luken laid the pill on his tongue.

I decide what I am.

He swallowed, and wondered how soon it would take effect. When, precisely, would his body be his own?

Chapter Eleven

The days passed, a handful here, a handful there, until Luken could again descend from the Palace without causing too much suspicion, for the Empress was busy all throughout the day with meetings, and Luken's bodyguard – a duo of silent, eunuch guards – escorted Luken into the city to visit Rori's apartment.

To her credit, Raisaga had been neither shocked nor bothered when he mentioned visiting a commonstock writer friend in the Topaz District. If anything, she accepted this detail as another piece of evidence that Luken's eccentricities were genuine, and not mere affectations meant to make him appear charming or mysterious – a trait she had apparently found annoying in previous lovers, who had tried too hard to cater to her interests in lieu of having their own. Luken walked away from their conversation with the promise of bringing his new guards and the hopeful impression that so long as he did not invoke her generosity too often, Luken would be able to continue visiting Rori without trouble.

So it was that a small gathering had been arranged – and Luken planned to see Jes for the first time since he had become the Empress's concubine. He had sent word discreetly, through Rori, and they had arranged for her to visit him at Rori's apartment. The presence of Rori, as well as his lover Katobi and their friend Kyo, would mask Jes and Luken's relationship. If all fell out as it should, she would arrive not long after him.

It was too dangerous now to meet alone or for Luken to go directly to Jes and Eitan's apartment. The eunuch guards – who served him under the monikers Sami and Cami, though Luken did not believe those to be their real names – escorted him into the city. They might be tight-lipped, but Luken had no doubt that behind their aura of cool disinterest, they watched him with the terrifying intensity of a cat that had cornered a mouse, and only toyed with the idea of letting it go.

But he could not let himself be cowed by them, these tall, lean men with their flawless white coats and trousers, swords at their hips, muskets at their backs. Dark eyes flicking to him, and away, scanning his surroundings with a mixture of haughty calm and icy caution. Luken was strangely fascinated by them; they were not men, according to the standards of the Empire. Nor were they women, nor children, nor peasants, nor outlanders, nor any other category that Kanai would acknowledge; they stood in a world apart. Indeed, they were almost genderless. And yet there was something distinctly male about them, in some manner that Luken struggled to articulate; in Kanai, masculinity meant physicality, and while they were asexual, there was, nonetheless, a spare and hard physicality that distinguished them. A feminine sleekness gave them an air of dependability not often attributed to Kanain men. Yet their competence was beyond question – a fact that sent a shiver down Luken's spine. Nor were they without a certain flair; the image of a strange, half-lidded eye that leaked a single teardrop had been hand-painted in white on the dark hilts of their blades, and their long hair was bound back in a sleek plait that had been wound up and pinned behind their heads. Sami, who always looked annoyed. Cami, who always looked bored. If the pair had been women, Luken might have been just a tad in love with them, but he settled for a shy admiration as the guards swept him up to Rori's apartment in silent grace and posted themselves outside Rori's door, to the consternation of the neighbors who shared the fifth floor of the rickety apartment building.

Despite the unease that had dogged Luken since the night of the party, he entered Rori's apartment upon an explosion of mirth, and felt his spirits lift at once.

Rori hopped up and down behind the couch, Kat and Kyo both laughing.

"The man of the hour! Luken," Rori called as he waved a magazine publication in his hand so quickly that it blurred into a fan of colors, "we were just enjoying the bounty of your labors."

Luken nudged the old, sticky hinges of the door until it slammed shut, and raised an eyebrow. "My review?"

"Even better." Katobi stood at the kitchen counter, dicing carrots to add to a bowl of mixed vegetables beside him, the scent of baking ham flirting with Luken's senses, "Koko's response."

Luken blinked. Even when he'd been at his most vicious, it had not occurred to him that Koko would – or even could – respond to the review. "Koko reads *Ages?*"

Rori chuckled. "Darling. You know Koko doesn't read."

"Someone must have told him." Kyo, sprawled on his back across Rori's couch, sipped deep of the cordial in his hand, his voice rumbling with amusement and more than a touch of intoxication, though it was still early-afternoon. "And he didn't like what he heard."

"These ignorant and prejudiced attacks are only further examples of how good-old fashioned Traditionalist values are being crucified in our society," Rori recited aloud, and glanced up at Luken, eyebrows raised. "*Crucified*, mind you."

Luken chuckled, laying down his things and letting Katobi slip a glass of cordial into his hand. "Imagine being crucified by one bad review of a stupid, sexist book about scamming people into liking you. Who knew I was so powerful?" Luken cozied up on an upholstered chair in the living room, his legs folded beneath him and the glass of cordial perched precariously on the arm of the chair. Only Jes had not yet arrived, and Luken could not keep his gaze from wandering now and again to the door.

Grinning, Rori continued, "You can't say anything any more without offending the sensitive cultural extremists who have targeted me for personal bullying-"

Luken rolled his eyes.

"Forcing one to ask, who is the real victim – those who take offense, or those who are maligned and persecuted for accidentally giving it even though it obviously wasn't my intention, which they should have known, although I stand by what I said and will not back down, in fact, on the contrary, I will go on to add- Mother hold us, how convoluted can you get?" Rori threw the magazine into the air like a piece of confetti. "It goes on and on like that."

The pages fluttered near, and Luken snatched them from the air, flipping the publication over. The cover revealed it as *The Easterner*, a magazine Luken had seen in the marketplaces, sometimes next to *Ages* on the shelf, though he had never bought one. The opinion piece Rori had recited identified Koko as a regular contributer to the magazine as well as the author of – Luken shook his head in disbelief – thirty-six books. The opinion piece had been published, for some reason, alongside articles on the withdrawal of Imperial Forces from Hindigga and the proposals slated to be introduced at the upcoming meeting of the Noble Assembly, as if each piece was equally newsworthy.

Kyo chuckled. "Well done, lad. You really pissed him off."

Luken laid the magazine on the table. "I assure you, I am merely returning the favor."

"Luken has been more than usually triumphant, of late." Rori's eyes sparkled as he withdrew to the nook that served as his kitchen and fixed himself another cordial. Beside him, Kat sprinkled a dash of pepper into the vegetables before plucking a large wooden spoon from the counter to begin mixing them. "The Empress's concubine!" Rori tittered like a schoolgirl.

Luken submitted a shy grin. "You're drunk."

"Only a little." Rori sipped. "Mostly, I'm drunk on excitement. You must tell us everything! I hear you've moved into the Palace."

Luken described the Palatial chambers, his encounters with the Empress, and all that had occurred in the blur of weeks since he'd first been summoned to her side, before coming, finally, to the tangle of passions that had resulted in him beginning the birth control regiment.

"I must thank you again, Kyo, for securing the pills for me. I know they are not easy to get."

Kyo gazed at him. "So you are taking them, after all. No side effects?"

Luken hesitated. His gaze, as he spoke, traveled the dreamy spill of watercolors that adorned Rori's walls, many of them covering cracks. "To be honest, I have felt, I don't know – ill at ease – since I started taking them. Anxious, somehow. Uncomfortable. Like I don't quite fit into my skin any more, and I'm aware of it all the time. Like something's wrong, even though there's no reason to feel that way."

A waterfall, brimming with lotuses, solidified from what Luken had always taken to be the formless spill of airy pastels within the painting beside the door. He blinked, and wondered why he had never seen it before. "It's hard to put it into words. I don't feel right. I get headaches. Stomachaches, like I've been kicked hard in the gut. Waves of nausea overcome me, suddenly and randomly, and then vanish."

Rori and Kyo exchanged an uneasy glance.

"It's a serious hormonal shift," Kyo said. "Your body needs time to adjust."

"And then these side effects will go away?"

"I'm not a doctor, Luken. But you know," he propped himself up on one elbow, "there are other options."

"What do you mean?"

"You could always get a vasectomy."

Rori snorted. "As if it's that easy."

The chopping in the kitchen stopped, replaced by an ominous quiet. "If you want one, you'd better get it quick," Katobi said. "With Traditionalists in power, vasectomies will get more and more difficult and expensive to obtain. We're practically back in the days of not being able to get them at all, except from a dark-money doctor in some dingy back-alley."

"It isn't *that* bad." Rori crossed one leg over the other. "Yet."

"I can't get a vasectomy," Luken protested. "Jes and I are going to have kids." A bitter laugh. "She's the only woman I actually *want* to have kids with." His eyes flicked to the door.

"Well then you'll have to stick with the pills," Kyo said gruffly.

"Have you ever taken them?"

"For years, back when I had a lover. And it's a good thing, too, or I'd have more kids I can't afford. The one is bad enough."

Luken smiled. Kyo had a harsh manner, but Luken knew from Rori that Kyo had devoted his whole life to raising his son on his own, since the mother had died many years ago.

"I can't imagine how it would be if I'd had more kids. I'm strapped as it is."

"Kyo..." Luken cocked his head. "I don't suppose you would accept an," he waved his hand in the air, "indefinite loan? Of a considerable sum?"

Kyo gazed back at him, his eyes hard. "I'm

poor, not desperate. I don't need handouts, I need a good job offer for my son. Supporting two grown men on one salary is no easy thing, in this city. But a good job is hard to come by, for men like us." He shook his head. "Still, you can't solve everything in life by throwing bohda around, Luken."

"That hasn't been my experience."

A wheezy laugh. "Keep your money, concubine. You never know when you might need it." He drained the dregs of his cordial and thrust it at Rori for a refill. "Anyway, if things get much worse in this city, I might just chuck it all away and move to the commune."

"What's a commune?"

"It's a sort of," Rori fished for the right word, and Katobi took over, "experimental society, where the majority of land and property is held by everyone who is part of the commune, and distributed equally, or according to need. We had a few friends who left O-Han years ago to join this commune, the one in the far northeastern edge of the Empire, at the base of the Seven Sisters mountain range. The land is distributed to people who want to live according to the rules of their community, and they're given a small cabin on a plot of land to farm and cultivate. It's a rural community and poor. Hard-living, but very free-thinking. You can live a life there that you can't live in most parts of the Empire." He cast a significant glance at Rori. "We've considered moving there, from time to time. We certainly would not be the only same-sex couple there, we know that for a fact."

Rori sighed. "I'd go in a heartbeat, if it was on the west coast. But Seven Sisters? I'd freeze half the

148

year and smother in pollen the other half."

"And I wouldn't be able to teach there. Not formally." Kat shook his head. "I've spent my entire life fighting my way into academia, I'm not throwing it all out the window to teach adding and subtracting to farmers in some tiny schoolhouse with ants crawling on the floor. Not now. Not after all the years of fighting for a post in an academy."

"You're both too particular," Kyo grumbled. "Fussing about with window decorations while the house is on fire. And what's wrong with Seven Sisters? I hear it's grand, how the mist weaves with the pines up the steep rise and fall of the mountains. They say there are tigers, up in those forests. Now *that* would be something to see."

Rori snorted. "It would be the *last* thing you see. Imagine, living your entire life within ten streets of the same broken-down tenement building where you were born, only to travel hundreds of miles to the Seven Sisters and be mauled to death by a tiger on some frigid northern peak."

"An increasingly appealing option, these days." A beat, and the dry humor slipped from Kyo's voice. Leaving only a somber pall. "I've been depressed, since Eikara lost the election. If the Palace gets any more Traditionalist, I don't know what we'll do."

Luken sipped his cordial. Tentatively, he offered, "Things seem to have leveled out. At least for now. The Empress resents the pushiness of the Traditionalist blockade, as she calls them. Ekaris, Hani, Pazu, Parnet. Those are the main Ladies, but of course, they have many allies in Middling and Minor Houses. Or rather, pawns. But the Empress is resisting their agenda, and that may be enough to keep things in balance."

Rori considered him. "I don't think so, Luken. The Empress may be able to keep them in check for some time, but Traditionalists are merely waiting for something to happen, to tip the scales in favor of action. We are not safe. They have plenty of time."

"You don't think the Empress can stand up to a pack of bullies? She is *the Empress* still, is she not?" Luken said, a little annoyed.

"Of course the Empress holds the majority of power, in... certain aspects of governing the Empire. But gone are the days of Divine Mandate, when the Empress was believed to be the living avatar of the Mother Who Cradles the World. She cannot simply do anything she likes. That is why the Convention and Noble Assembly were created in the first place. They have the power to remove the Empress-"

"Only with a trial-validated cause and a universal vote, which will never happen-"

"And they can enforce their agenda without her permission, if they hold a majority in both legislative bodies."

"Which Traditionalists do, thanks to the idiots who elected Hani and gave them the Convention, as well as the Assembly," Kyo muttered.

"That's true," Luken admitted, sipping his cordial. "But the Empress can regulate and limit their ability to enact and enforce their agenda. If worse comes to worst, the Empress can simply overrule them by invoking the Imperial Mandate. She has *that* Mandate, if not the Divine one."

Rori cocked his head. "Empress Raisaga has never invoked the Imperial Mandate."

"Her mother did," Luken said softly.

With a sad smile, Rori nodded. "To ban foot-fanning, yes. It took an Imperial Mandate to end that atrocious business. But there is a reason Empresses do not like to use it. The Mandate can only be used once in a three year period. Yes, using the Mandate would allow the Empress to completely override the decisions of the Assembly and the Convention, but it would leave her vulnerable. Knowing she cannot use it again, the majority party would use their power to shove as much of their agenda through the system as they could until the end of the three year period, when the Empress could overrule them again. The extreme end of that party's agenda would be forced into legislation. Besides, using the Mandate would turn every Lady against the Empress; they'd be furious at having their designs discarded. It would be like burning down the enemy's crops and salting the earth before trying to plant your own in the same soil. For instance, if the Empress used the Mandate now, when the Traditionalists hold the majority in both the Assembly and the Convention, they could vote to legalize foot-fanning again, and there would be nothing to stop them. Nothing at all."

Luken frowned. "Every member of the Convention would be voted out for allowing such a thing."

The sad smile lingered. "You give the voters too much credit, Luken. Some of them, no doubt, would lose their seats over such an atrocity, but not all. Do you think the kind of people who voted for

Hani over Eikara would balk much at a few boys they don't even know having their feet fanned? Any horror can be normalized, given the time and pressure. And anyway, it would only matter when the next election came around. Til then," Rori spread his hands, "we'd be helpless."

"We are already helpless," Kyo muttered. "More and more, I'm beginning to think there is just no winning with this system. Better to burn it all down and start over."

"No such thing as 'starting over,' I'm afraid," Katobi said. "Everything builds on that which came before. Even that which is rejected is remembered. Nothing is shaped in the void. If my studies of history have taught me nothing else, I've at least learned that much."

"So basically, we're fucked forever?"

A wry grin. "I did not say escape was impossible. There's always the Seven Sisters commune."

Kyo raised his glass in salute. "To the commune. Our last resort, when everything finally goes balls-up here in O-Han."

Luken grinned, joining the others in raising his glass of cordial. "To the commune."

A knock rapped at the door. Luken leapt to his feet. "Jes!"

"Finally, I shall meet the famous Jes," Kyo murmured as Luken scurried past him to the door.

Luken ripped the door open – and startled the chubby messenger on the other side into a jump.

"Oh! Sorry, I was expecting someone else." He turned away, instinctively hiding his face behind his sleeve, as Katobi rushed to the door and traded a few dennys for the envelope in the messenger's hand. Shouldering the door shut, Kat prised open the letter, scanned it, and handed it to Luken.

He accepted it, heart sinking.

Luken-

I won't be able to make it to Rori's apartment. The baby has colic and Eitan is still confined to bed. Give my best to Rori and Katobi.

Slip away and see me when you can.

I miss you, Jes.

If he'd been alone, Luken would have ripped the paper apart and let the pieces lie wherever they drifted, like so much new-fallen snow. Instead, he nodded, refolded the letter, and tucked it into the sleeve of his ando, affecting a casual tone as he told the others, "Jes won't be able to make it. The baby has colic, whatever that is."

"Ah, Luken." Rori laid a hand on his shoulder. "I'm sorry."

Luken shrugged it off. "It's alright."

He'd not seen his lover in weeks, but it was alright.

He was making himself sick with drugs rather than getting the vasectomy that would have solved his problem permanently so that he could have a family with her, just her and no other, but it was alright.

He had everything a man could want. So it was alright.

"Just the boys tonight, then." The others watched him, expressions blank, but he gave them a smile and shrugged. "It's alright."

~

The sun had not yet set when Luken left the apartment, though the moon grazed a tower of the Palace, shedding a mellow glow over its heights; pale, like wax-dripped towers cooled from the melting of the stars. The city sulked in sleepy quiet behind him as the carriage trundled up the path to the Lion Gate, and through. Luken's thoughts whirled; Jes, pills, Rori and Kat, a strange community at the fringe of the Empire in the shadow of the Seven Sisters, angry Kyo alone with his son who was near full-grown and had nowhere to go, Jes, pills…

As they neared the Palace, Luken's unease spiked. Messengers swarmed the front steps of the Southern Door as the carriage drew near. Through the open doors, the Palace looked like a hive of hornets that had been kicked into a rage. Luken tipped the driver in mindless anxiety and lifted the skirts of his ando to climb into the teeming foyer. Ladies stood in clumps, conversing rapidly. A messenger nearly vaulted headlong into Luken and did not even apologize before rushing past him, trampling the skirts of his ando.

"Seven Hells," Luken muttered, tugging the diaphanous material – stained now with a smudged bootprint – out of the way. He grabbed a Lady's arm as she quickened past, "What's going on?"

She tugged her arm from his grip and stormed past, shouting to a servant to pull her carriage around.

One of Luken's guards stepped forward and placed a gentle hand on his shoulder. It was the first time the silent, white-clad eunuch had addressed him, Cami's voice as light and clear as a ringing bell. "My lord, I think you should return to your chambers."

Tension clenching his stomach, Luken mounted the stairs and made his way eastward. He caught snippets of conversation here and there, but could not piece the puzzle together. Words in a foreign tongue – *Builay, Olmpuay* – mingled with panicked questions, *"When?" "Why?"* and, like a punch to the gut, *"How many dead?"*

All the Palace was in turmoil. Ladies in disarray, enraged. Servants and messengers scurrying like mice underfoot. Courtesans, confused and alarmed, abandoning their pleasantries. Luken found himself part of an exodus trickling through the Palace as he joined a stream of men, but while they returned to their Abodes in the Garden, Luken cut north, making his way to his private chambers.

He found a cluster of women in the hall outside. Fi, in the center of them with a scroll clenched in her fist, looked up, her face pale. "There you are! A hell of a time to be wandering about in the city, boy-"

"Will someone please tell me what's happened? I can't-"

She held up a hand, cutting him off with a tone like a swinging blade. "Luken. The Empire has been attacked."

A ringing, in his head. "Attacked?"

"Kanai's embassy in Builay has been under siege by rioting protesters since the death of a provincial leader in the coastal city of Olmpuay, where Kanai's holdings are located. Kanai is being blamed for the provincial leader's assassination, and several of our own people were killed in retaliation."

"I don't understand-" A wave of nausea climbed out of his belly, squeezed his throat, and reached his head with a dizzying blow. "I want to see the Empress."

Fi's lip curled into a sneer. "She has no time for you now. An important Builayn cultural figure is dead. Kanain ambassadors are dead. We may be at war with Builay at any moment."

She spoke, but the words did not penetrate his skull. If only Raisaga would explain the situation to him, then he could understand. Then he would know what to do. "Did she send no word to me?"

Fi's eyes widened. "At a time like this?" Disgusted, she shoved open the door of his chambers and pushed him through with no great excess of gentleness. His guards assumed their usual post to either side of his door. "No," Fi spat, "the Empress did not send you word." A shaky sigh. She tugged her coat down, smoothed it. "But you *did* receive this. I came to deliver it to you earlier, before the news from Builay arrived, but of course, you were not here." Fi shoved the scroll she'd been holding into his hands. "It's a summons from the Empress's Consort. Aokinay demands to see you. Tomorrow morning. Look sharp."

With that, she snapped the door shut behind her. And left Luken alone in his chambers, forgotten in the chaos.

Chapter Twelve

Luken had seen the Empress's Consort only once before in his life. His first year at Court, at the Festival of Flowering Summer. Aokinay had seemed then more beautiful than any earthly man. A god, wandered down from the heavens with clouds beneath his feet.

But that was years ago, and Luken steeled himself to meet the man behind the title.

The Swan Doors swung open, the servants heaving at their silver chains until the momentum of their awful weight broke open. Whatever Luken had expected, it was not this: A sultry pleasure dome, the ceiling half open, like the moon when it is half in light and half in shadow, to the pearly clouds of early autumn. Black branches, wreathed in golden and deep-green leaves, rose to shroud most of the sky, sundering the bright sorrow of the autumnal sun, and shrouding the domed space in a twilit gloom. A path of white tiles fed from the Palace into lawns of grass and rampant peonies, but even in the cracks of the tiles, moss budded. A woodland scent, tasting of childhood and freedom, lingered beneath the perfume of the flowers. In the center of this space was a circular dais, mounted on ten steps of white stone so polished that the structure gleamed in the gloom. A moat encircled the dais, and here and there, turtles stood on the rocks or at the pathway's edge. A soft gulp somewhere as a koi broke the surface. A single white swan drifted on the water, her eyes closed as if in long slumber.

Atop the dais, a gazebo stood, delicate white beams arching to meet at the center. Low voices murmured from the gazebo, and nerves gutted Luken.

With a rumbling purr, a lion paced to the edge of the dais, gazing down at Luken with tawny eyes. Luken drew a sharp breath, and eternity stretched between them, the great cat drawing breaths between open jaws, its white fangs visible, its eyes set upon him. And then, bored, the lion turned and paced back across the dais, the slither and rattle of a chain following the iron collar beneath his golden mane. Luken released a long breath, and commanded his hands to cease their trembling.

A breeze rolled in and Luken shivered, as if he were one of the branches that stirred above him, the leaves whispering to one another. It was a striking venue, he would grant Aokinay that. The beauty and gloom of it, standing all in subtle shades. The unexpectedness of it as well, this strange threshold between nature and woman-made things, buried in the far reaches of the Palace. He knew at once that it was old; it had the feel of the forgotten. Of what was once sacred, and is now broken pillars in the grass, left bare to the skies, the storms.

"Are you afraid of stepping into the light, Luken Kenkazu-son?" A man's voice, from the gazebo; deep, sonorous. "Don't be so skittish. This weak, autumn sunlight won't set that delicate, Ennish skin ablaze. Come forward."

Luken found his head bowing, his shy nature

overcoming him, and forced his chin up. He would not bow to this man. *He is only Ekaris's nephew,* Luken told himself, *and he despises you without an ounce of mercy.*

He strolled along the path and climbed the steps to the gazebo.

The deep murmur of masculine voices receded with each step. And there they were, Aokinay and a small retinue of his lords, sprawled across the divans atop the dais, the shadows of the gazebo's beams slanting across them.

He was beautiful still.

Aokinay, with his long, black hair that fell unbound over his shoulders and down, bridging the space from where he lounged in his elaborate ando of rainbow geometries, to a marble floor so polished he did not care if his hair curled against the flawless white. There was a heaviness to his features that made them striking, a contrast to Luken's delicate symmetry; a passionate, demanding beauty, perfect in its dimensions, tolerating no inadequacies, even within itself. He must have been about forty – old for a man – and a cursory glance at his lords confirmed they were all cut from the same cloth, though of course, none came close to Aokinay, either in beauty or presence. The lion paced between them, rumbling low in its throat, its chain rattling off the marble at their feet. Aokinay's hand lifted, phantom-like amid the vibrant silks, to caress the lion's back in passing. His eyes, though – pale blue, a slant of grey, like the sea after a shower of rain – his eyes never left Luken's face.

He knew at once that the man hated him.

His lords scoffed and glanced at one another.

They did not spare even the slight effort of ironic, mocking politeness.

Ah, but that made it simple, didn't it? Luken squared his shoulders, and bowed to the Empress's Consort. "My lord. It is an honor to be summoned before you."

A titter of laughter shivered from the Consort's retinue. Aokinay arched an eyebrow. "Is it? I should rather think you'd be shitting your silks. Or at the very least," a slow smile, in answer to his lords' laughter, "ashamed of yourself."

Seven Hells. "Ashamed, my lord?"

"Yes, dear." He stroked the lion's mane as it paced between them, snapping its tail back and forth, its energy restless, contagious. "It's what men in your position used to feel, when they sniffed around another man's woman, and were caught at it." He cocked his head, just a fraction. "Shame, it seems, is out of fashion in your generation. You aren't the first to appear before me, immune to it."

"I-" *He will bully you into offering an apology, then use it as a flail against you. There will be no forgiveness, so admit no wrongdoing,* Luken thought urgently. "I suggest you talk to the Empress about that, my lord. I daresay she's her own woman."

Aokinay's eyebrows rose. The laughter died behind him, replaced by an ominous silence. "So that's how it is." He lurched forward, shoulders wracked by a hacking cough. It went on long enough to make Luken uncomfortable. Veins cracked the whites of his eyes when, drawing a ragged breath, Aokinay straightened, glaring at Luken.

Luken gazed back at him; they could raze

cities, those piercing, pale blue eyes. Guilt stabbed his chest, twisted like a bayonet. But he dared not let it show. "I don't know what to say. I respect you, Lord Aokinay-"

"Shut your whore mouth."

"You summoned me for this?" Luken spit, then added, a moment too late, "my lord."

In a whisper, Aokinay bid, "Leave us."

"With pleasure-"

"Not you, idiot." Aokinay rose from the divan, drawing himself to his full height, and strode across the dais, turning his back on Luken as, in a silken flutter, his lords scurried from the dais, and rushed from the dome.

Luken found himself alone with the Empress's Consort. The lion stood beside him, a huge, unsettling presence that panted its subdued ferocity into the air they breathed.

A long pause, as Luken gazed at the Consort's back. And waited.

"I must be losing my touch," Aokinay said airily, and turned, taking mincing steps around the outer circle of the dais, so close to the edge that it made Luken nervous. "Once, I made one of Raisaga's whores so flustered, he burst into tears in less than a minute." He made an airy gesture, as if throwing something away. "That one was easy to get rid of. I don't think Raisaga even missed him." His joh clicked softly against the marble. The lion went to him, but reached the end of its chain, the iron links taut from the stake in the dais's center, and strained a moment before surrendering with a yearning bellow and pacing back, encircling an abandoned divan with its chain.

"Another, I threatened outright. Told him that if he answered the Empress's summons again, I'd have his mother's House demoted from Middling to Minor before he had time to clean the jizz off at the end of Raisaga's next game." He circled behind Luken now, so that Luken had to swivel his body toward him, twisted like a ferret searching for a predator. Aokinay sighed. "Some of them, of course, are much harder to get rid of. I had to slap one, once, when he told me to my face, 'I'm not going anywhere.' I had to slap that one a few times, actually. To his credit," Aokinay arched an eyebrow, "he did stick around almost a whole year before Raisaga got tired of him. That one didn't go easily. But they *do* go, in the end." He glanced at Luken. His expression almost bored beneath his distaste for the younger man. "They do go."

The lion butted its head against Luken's thigh, like a house-cat would rub his ankle in passing. Luken gave a little cry of surprise, but let his hand rest of the lion's head. Soft fur, over the indomitable bone. "Why don't you?"

"Excuse me?"

"Why don't you go? It sounds like a poor deal, being the Empress's Consort."

Aokinay considered him for a long moment.

The blow, when it came, knocked Luken's head back with a snap. Lights burst behind his eyes. Aokinay paced the edge of the dais, drifting away from Luken in small, mincing steps. There was no pain, just the shock of having been struck. And then the moments it took for his brain to catch up. Luken worked his jaw.

"You're not as annoying as some of others," Aokinay admitted. The lion left Luken's side and trailed after its master, orbiting him like a moon around a planet, their orbits close but locked, always in motion but never to touch. "Unfortunately, that means you'll last longer than the others, too." The chain slunk and leapt tight as the lion paced after Aokinay. Bitterness crept into his voice. "Considering where things stand between Raisaga and myself, you may very well last a long time. She's angry with me, you see. I ask too much." He chuckled. "If I ask for the same thing that she receives, I ask too much. If I expect to be treated as an equal, I expect too much. If I want the attention and pleasure that is lavished upon her, I want too much." He paused again at the far end of the dais. "She was never exclusive to me. She made that clear from the very beginning. 'I love you, but it will never be just you.' I laughed it off at the time. Trying to be charming. Trying to be sexy. Trying so hard to make her like me. And she did. We *were* in love – true, passionate, devoted love – for a long time. There were others, of course, pleasure-objects here and there, but," he sighed, "she was *the Empress.* I never would have tolerated it, from another woman. But from the Empress..." He shrugged, gazing up at the open half of the dome, at the delicate opal of the clouded sky. "I told myself: You have her heart. Next to you, the rest are but toys to her. They are nothing. *You* are the Empress's Consort. She only loves *you.* But you know something, Luken? Love fades."

The lion slunk to the center of the dais, and settled its heavy limbs against the marble. It shooks its golden mane, the iron collar visible as the lion lay down its head.

"I'm the only boy in my family. They fed my brothers to the war in Hindigga. Only I was allowed to remain. Only I was deemed pretty enough that I might, some day, catch the eye of the Empress herself. My aunt was very insistent, you see, that her nephew become the Empress's Consort. I was raised to it, since as far back as I can remember. Like a pig raised for market. I *studied* the Empress before I even met her. Spies were employed by the House of Distant Thunder merely to report back with Raisaga's hobbies and preferences in men. I learned this information as if I were a priest and she was my sacred goddess, every word from her lips of divine importance." He sighed. "And now I can barely stand to look at her. Every time she rolls her eyes at me, I almost wring her fucking neck. But I still love her, a little," he added weakly. "That's the worst part. To be only a little in love with a woman you used to be besotted with. We were *torrid*. Have you ever had that kind of passion, Luken?"

Jes's face appeared in his mind's eye. "Yes," he said quietly.

"Really? Ah, but you are young. No doubt you enjoyed some fumbling romance with a young Lady and dreamed yourself in love. It doesn't matter. Either you find lasting love with someone decent when you're young, or you grow old and settle for whatever you can get. It is that way for every man."

Aokinay twisted away from Luken and another fit of violent coughing wracked his frame. A wet, broken roar. When he regained himself, Aokinay dragged the back of his hand across his mouth and Luken caught a glint of scarlet on the white of his lace glove.

He turned to face Luken, cocked his head to the side. The smile that played upon his lovely features was almost sweet. "You may think it is a fine thing, to be the Empress's concubine. The diamonds and riches, the Palatial chambers, the awe and wonder with which others look at you, the respect you receive – even from Ladies – and more than anything, the power. It's intoxicating, is it not? To ask for something and watch others scurry to retrieve it for you. To hold the fate of another person in your hands, and decide if they shall prosper or be destroyed. To force your will upon the world. I used to love it. But like any drug, the edge wears off. You grow accustomed to it. What then, Lord Pear Blossom? What does a man do when his best years are behind him and the one thing he was promised in life, the one thing he ever achieved, the one thing that's supposed to matter – fades before his eyes? What then, Luken?"

"I... don't know."

"No?" The smile turned cruel. "No advice for me then?" He advanced a step. "Then let me give *you* some advice. Don't play this game, Luken. Don't ask for power. Don't try to be her equal. That was my mistake. She fucked other people, so I tried, once or twice, to fuck other people. Ah, she didn't like that. It was well enough for her to have her fun, but she's *the Empress*. I was supposed to be a gem, a trophy. The trophy does not award itself to other women. It belongs to the victor, the powerful one. Why was I not content to belong to my superior? At the time, I burned with the unfairness of it. I rebelled against it. If she could cheat, I should be able to cheat. But it didn't matter. She had that privilege, I did not. That's all there was to it. Life's not fair. We limped along, through all the screaming and weeping and fighting, and told ourselves we had gotten past it. But in the end, she never really forgave me. She didn't have to. I had tried to play her game, and lost. It was never the same after that."

He dragged a hand through his hair. "Just settle, Luken. Settle before you get too old. Don't try to play the Lady's game. Even if all goes well for you, the Empress will take the best years of your life, and let you go, in the end. You'll find yourself alone at the end of your twenties, and who will want you when your looks have faded? What torrid love awaits you then? Once you reach your thirties, no woman will want you. This game of power and privilege will leave you empty; men always lose, when they play that game. Settle for what you have, and try to be content. That's the best a man can do in this world. It isn't fair, but there it is. Settle, and keep your mouth shut."

"Thank you for this advice, Lord Aokinay." He bowed. "May I take my leave?"

The Empress's Consort waved a lofty hand. "I fear we shall see each other again only too soon, Lord Luken."

Luken turned and swept down the steps. He looked back, only once, to find Aokinay still standing upon the dais, alone in his forgotten pleasure dome; beneath the breeze, it rang with the echoes of idyllic bacchanals that had, at last, yielded to this: his loneliness, his restlessness, his bitterness.

Luken strode toward the Swan Door, and did not look back again at the Empress's Consort.

Only one thought ran through his mind: What a pathetic creature.

Chapter Thirteen

"They say there is no love in Scarlet Chambers,
Where my brothers live long days
Kept like embers in the furnace
Waiting to stoke to flame.
Waiting and burning in dull and gentle languor,
Waiting for whoever shall claim me with a coin.
But look beyond the sighing veils,
To your face, like the moon in the sky
Outshining all others, outshining the stars.
I look from the high window and see you
Striding beneath the shadow of the hawk
The long grass licks at your heels,
Lanu. You walk beyond the Scarlet that shrouds me
The walls of gold that secure me,
A treasure, nestled in my chest,
Till you find me, bearing, like a silver tongue,
The key that turns the locks,
And speak the words of longing.
Who says there is no love in Scarlet Chambers?

"Graceful Shayah," murmured Luken. "Not bad for a man who was illiterate the year before. And you wrote that for my grandmother when she was just a client..." He shook his head in wonder, and laid the scrap of poetry back in the box of his grandfather's letters and journals.

A knock at the door.

Luken looked up, annoyed. Since the attack in

Builay, the Empress had been too busy with affairs of state to visit him. Aside from his unpleasant rendezvous with the Royal Consort, Luken had kept to his chambers. Unable to glean any further information on Builay than the precious few details doled out in the newspapers that littered the floor of his livingroom, he had retreated into the shards of the past found in his grandfather's box. He'd tried to divert himself with a few chapters from his book on Empress's Consorts throughout history, but his meeting with Aokinay had soured that prospect, at least for now.

The knock, again.

Who would be bothering him?

An attendant slipped in, so obsequious that Luken, studying his grandfather's writings, did not recognize her until her voice reached his ears.

"My Lady Eitan, Fourth Daughter of the House of the Silent Lake, seeks an audience with her former acquaintance, my Lord Luken."

Luken jolted upright, banging his thigh on the table as he rushed to Jes's side. "Jes-" The word tore the breath from his lungs. For a single moment, brief and bright as a lightning-strike, they were alone. He swept her into his arms, lifting her up. Jes landed light on her feet, taking his face in her hands. At some point, Eitan nudged in, awkward with the weight of a baby tucked in either arm and massive rucksacks hanging from her shoulders to bob around her waist. Her face shone with merriment and for a moment, the brief years of motherhood dropped away, and she looked once again like the fey, ebullient Eitan Luken remembered from his earliest days at Court.

"I take it my request for an audience has been granted?"

"Yes, of course." Luken laughed, and threw the door shut behind her. Now that they were alone, he wrapped his arms around Jes's waist and pressed another kiss to her lips. A proper kiss, tender and lingering.

By the time he surfaced, Eitan had wandered to the far end of the room, gazing up at the dome of the ceiling, at the landing that led to the second story, and his bedchamber. She shrugged her bags off, and they sat like bulging toads beside the fireplace. Jenh crawled on the ornate Bushani rug with a wriggling surge of energy. Iko lay bundled and mercifully quiet in the cradle of his mother's arms. "This place has a second story? Well aren't you fancy now?" A toothy grin lit Eitan's face.

"You're welcome to explore the upstairs, if you like."

Her eyebrows shot up, her grin too amused by half. "Don't mind if I do. And I'll take my time, too." She scooped up Jenh in one arm and skipped upstairs, a tuneless whistle receding down the hallway on the second floor.

Jes rolled her eyes. "This was her idea, you know. She felt bad about keeping the two of us apart. It's not really her fault, though."

Luken blinked, sensing a strange shift. The initial thrill of seeing Jes fizzled and beneath an unfamiliar and unnerving sense of disappointment, he discovered defensiveness. "It's not?"

"That day, when we were supposed to meet at Rori's apartment..." She gazed at him, her dark-brown eyes distant, as if trying to trace the outlines of mountains, so far off as to almost be invisible to the eye.

"There was a time," slowly, softly, "when you would have received that message and rushed to Eitan's apartment. If I couldn't come to you, you would have come to me. If only for a moment. If only to see my face."

A jab of annoyance. "Are you joking? I had to return to the Palace. I'm busy."

"Doing what, fucking the Empress?" If he could barely restrain his annoyance, she could no longer restrain her resentment. It saturated every word.

Luken threw his hands in the air. "Yes, because that's all I do! I have no other plans! That's all I'm good for!"

"I didn't say that," Jes spat. "I would rather you do anything *but* this job, you're the one who insists-"

"You won't complain when this job buys you a house or feeds our children or pays for an early retirement. I can't wait to see if you're still complaining then."

"Because there's no other way to pay for those things? Goddess Luken, I just wanted to see you!"

"I don't have time to chase you around the city! If we arrange a meeting in one place, how am I supposed to know you-" He sighed. "This is ridiculous. We have so little time together, there's no sense in spending it quarreling over nothing."

Her jaw set, stubborn. "It's only *nothing* if I'm upset. If you're hurt, there's an existential misunderstanding afoot, devaluing you."

"The only person devaluing me these days is you, apparently. Everyone else appreciates the potential of my position. You act like the Empress is just another client."

"What has she done for you so far?"

Luken's eyes narrowed. "I must first secure my position."

"You will never finish that task, Luken. Even the Empress's Consort is not secure in his position – thanks to men like you. There's always another man."

The silence unfolded between them, like the wings of a black swan. "I see. So I am fundamentally powerless and replaceable."

A faint widening of her eyes, a hint of regret in her voice. "Not to me, Luken."

"Because you are the only woman in the world who would ever see value in me. Well, thank goodness I found you Jes!" he said sarcastically. "I'd better cling to you, since no one else will ever see any worth in me!"

Jes sighed, shook her head. "I give up. I'm exhausted. I just wanted to see you."

The anger slithered from his body, a python releasing its hold. "I'm sorry, Jes. I'm sorry. I wanted to see you too, but you're so preoccupied with Eitan and her sons, I just thought you had no time for me. It doesn't matter. I'm sorry."

A whistle, twirling through the taut silence. "Excuse me." Eitan stood on the landing, her hand resting on the polished oak of the railing. "This is not the sort of clamor I expected to overhear." Jenh grabbed at her hair with pudgy fists as Eitan cocked her head. "I didn't bring Jes here so the two of you could quarrel."

"Thank you, Eitan," Jes said stiffly.

"Eitan, did you notice the library?" Luken asked pointedly.

"No, but I shall find it this time!" She spun on her heel and vanished back into the shadows of the hallway.

Luken released a shaky sigh. He let his lids slide shut, held the darkness. And looked at Jes.

"What's happened to us?" He reached a hand to cup her cheek. "I miss you."

He watched the ice melt in her eyes. "I miss you too."

With a thrill of victory, Luken bent to kiss her again and felt her lean into him. Hard this time, fierce. His hands slid up her body, rolling in over the curves of her waist to her slim middle and up again, to the fullness of her chest.

"Luken..." Reluctance, like an anchor, dragging the word beneath the waves, to chambers deep and blue and dark.

"It'll be alright," he whispered.

She sighed, regret and longing mingled in her eyes. Jes kissed him, renewed force behind it. Need, intense, almost fearing to be met. Yet reaching anyway.

He met her, eagerly. Ripped her shirt open, cupped the soft fullness of her breasts. She ripped the clasp from his hair, a pearl pinging against the floor as his hair cascaded free. She set to work on his irlan as he pressed a ragged trail of kisses from her lips, her jaw, her throat, and to the joining of her neck and shoulder that made her knees go weak as he suckled on the flesh there, nibbled, drew a moan from her lips.

The irlan dropped and the silken weight of his ando fell open, his erection springing to attention. He dropped to his knees as she shucked her shirt. It fluttered like a dark feather in the corner of his eye as he ripped off her boots and the remainder of her clothes. Breath quickening, Jes planted her hands on the writing desk behind her, against the wall between his green velvet divan and the staircase, and threw a leg over his right shoulder, her thigh pressed down on him as he teased her labia with his tongue. Luken wrapped his arms up and around her legs, her waist, and pressed close to her, sucking her clit between his lips and releasing, sucking and releasing, working the rosy bud with tongue and lips until her panting grew fervent.

"Fuck me," she murmured, a desperate command.

He pushed upright and turned her so that he stood behind her, her hands on the desk, and angled his cock up to rub at the wet lips of her vulva in teasing strokes before pushing up into her, holding her waist in both hands until, with a groan, he was fully sheathed.

Luken let his forehead fall against the crook of her neck, moving inside her with a gentle grinding. She let her head fall back, reaching up to cup his cheek as he kissed her. The moments swirled away into the tenderness of it, the rising, aching need.

Pulling back a little, gathering his breath, Luken quickened the pace of his thrusts. Pumping her from behind. Oh, they would do this again, Luken thought, filing away the position in his mind for future use. He liked this. Jes, braced against him. Thrusting into the tight warmth of her body with abandon. He liked this a *lot*.

Urged by her gasps and moans, Luken built to a wild crescendo – and boiled over. Pleasure took him in its fist and rattled him, shocks of white sparking his vision. In the scouring ecstasy, he heard but did not register the thump of sound at the door.

Luken let his cock ease out of her, a slow, delicious slide.

The door clicked open.

A sudden male voice. "Fuck me forever and a day."

Dazed, Luken glanced toward the door. Isaun stood there, staring back at him, his lovely features blanched with shock.

~

Luken jerked the robes of his ando closed. Jes, wide-eyed and pale, pulled her shirt over her head, yanked on her pants.

"I know you." Isaun's eyes gleamed like green fire, fixed on Jes. "You're-"

"Isaun!"

They all glanced up as Eitan appeared on the landing. Luken could see it – the moment Isaun put it together, glancing from Eitan, back to Jes. "Her attendant."

Dressed now, Jes gave Isaun a sardonic bow. "Lord Isaun."

"I think the two of you should leave," Luken murmured to Jes.

She glanced at him askance. "You sure?"

"Yes." A storm wall mounted, the electric energy of confrontation rising between him and Isaun.

A long look. Then she nodded, and Eitan, her babies still tucked in her arms, clambored down the stairs. The world tilted on its axis. Déjà vu, as Luken recalled a scene, so long ago, playing out so similar to this: Eitan, grinning as she came down the stairs in Isaun's wake, buttoning her shirt, Isaun meeting Amae's baleful stare as Eitan and Jes slipped out the door after their first visit to the Abode, and left the men alone.

The door clicked shut behind them.

Isaun stared at him, green eyes blazing, amusement limning his voice. "Well. That certainly explains some things."

"You don't know anything."

"All those long nights in the city, unexplained absences, mysterious traipsing around." Isaun strolled forward, his strides slow. A cream ando, shot through with darts and filials of golden embroidery, clasped his long legs.

"You can't prove it. It's my word against yours."

"It's obvious, in retrospect. I knew you were up to something. I had my theories but," he glanced around Luken's chambers as he spoke, eyebrows rising, fingers tapping along the back of the burgundy divan, "I must confess, I'm a bit disappointed that it was a woman, after all. I mean, it's always a woman. We men can't help ourselves, it's our irreparable weakness." He shrugged. "Still, I thought you were a bit more interesting than that. But an attendant – *Eitan's attendant.*"

"You're a bitter old courtesan close to retirement. I'll say you're stirring up trouble out of jealousy."

A harsh laugh. "Yes, you could do that I suppose." Isaun shook his head. "How long has this been going on?" His eyes flung wide. "Not before they left on expedition?"

"No," Luken breathed. "Not that long."

"After you returned from Conjugal Leave, then? It doesn't matter." His meandering strides took him to the balcony, and he gazed out through the glass door. A shard of the Palace lawns stretched beneath them, giving way to the white and gold river that formed the Garden, and beyond, the tiled roofs of the city sprawled into the distance. Clouds, rising like smoke to fan into feathered plumes, cast shadows over the earth. "Nice view."

"What are you even doing here, Isaun?"

"I came to apologize, actually." He grinned at Luken over his shoulder. "Lifelle's nagging finally got to me. He wants us to be friends again, now that he's leaving." A theatrical sigh. "He thinks I'll be lonely."

"Well you picked a hell of a time to come visit," Luken spit.

Isaun's broad shoulders shook with silent laughter. "Oh *Luken*. I thought you were such a good boy! It is a bit infuriating, I have to say. All this, and you've been fucking Eitan's attendant. You won the game," he spun to face Luken, ando flaring, "and you didn't play fair!"

"This isn't a game, Isaun."

"I should ruin you," Isaun said idly. "I should tell everyone about your servant girl. It's nothing more than you deserve."

He came quietly to Isaun's side. "Would you really do that to me?"

Isaun shook his head. "You have no idea the kind of things I've done." All mirth gone from his voice, Isaun burst out, "I've let old women *shit* on me, Luken." Hysteria edged his laugh. "For fuck's sake. I've been water-boarded for a Lady's amusement, and told her I felt empowered to have endured it." He shuffled to the balcony, laid his hand on the glass door. "I've been choked, spit on, slapped. I've been whipped, beaten, tied up and forgotten for hours." A shaky laugh.

Luken stared at him, his heartbeat quickening with a panic he couldn't explain. Hardly daring to raise his voice above a whisper, he said, "I thought you liked that kind of thing."

Isaun shrugged. "Some of it. Hells, some of it was even my idea. But not all of it." A pause. "Not all of it."

"Then why'd you take those jobs?"

"Well they don't always tell you beforehand, do they? And it's hard to say 'no' when you're already there, when they've got you alone, when they're paying you and you promised them a good time. You just know some Lady's have a reputation for being wild, and if you have the same reputation, well, it should be a match shouldn't it? But they don't always tell you everything that's going to happen, and if you're high enough you don't care in the moment. It's not until afterward you start to feel..." He shook his head. "I don't know why I'm telling you this." Emotion strained his voice. "I just... I just don't know why it wasn't enough. Why you got all this," he motioned to Luken's chambers, "and I got nothing."

With disbelief, Luken realized there were tears in Isaun's eyes.

"I just don't know why I wasn't ever enough. I did everything that was asked of me. I rose to every occasion. I rejected no one. I pleased everyone. There was no degradation too low. Nothing too dangerous or too painful. Not for me. I was ashamed of nothing. Frightened of nothing. I allowed everything. I fulfilled every fantasy." His fists clenched. "Why wasn't it ever enough?"

"I don't know."

Luken closed the distance between them. They gazed out over the Garden, over the city.

"What a story it would have been..." Isaun murmured. Luken looked up at him. "A boy from a Minor House, the measly Fourth Son, stealing away from home to become a courtesan at thirteen, lying about his age, fighting his way up from nothing. I told you once, how few Sons of Minor Houses break the Top Ten on the Board."

"Five, I think you said."

He nodded. "What a better story it would have been, if I'd been the one... I bet you don't even know your name is Number One on the Board."

"What?"

A dry chuckle. "That's what I thought. You don't even bother to check any more, do you? Princess Tsakara made Sirikaf her Consort, removing his name from the Board. And with you as the Empress's concubine – well, I suppose it was an easy decision for the Arbiters. Number One always goes to some unobtainable princeling who's been set aside by a member of the royal family."

Number One on the Board. That solemn meadow of disbelief flowered in Luken's mind.

"You didn't earn it." Isaun's voice, matter-of-fact. "I want you to know you don't deserve it."

"Of course I don't deserve it, Isaun." He restrained the frustration in his voice. "But neither do you, regardless of how many old women you let shit on you. You earned attention, money, the contempt of your clients, and the confirmation in your psyche that yes, you are worthy of that contempt, and yes, you can survive it, just like you had to the first time, and yes, you numb yourself to it with repeated degradations until you convince yourself that even the first wound mattered little, since you've now survived that same wound so many times. Innured yourself to it, to diminish the pain of the first wound, the one you didn't choose. That's what courtesans learn as they age, isn't it? Yes, you are loathsome and that's why you feel the way you do, that's why these things have happened to you, you've earned it, but you can survive being loathsome, and you can say you're proud to walk the path you've chosen, wounds and all, bowing to the world that wounded you, still hoping you may yet earn its love. But no one earns love. Not really. It's not a payment in exchange for services rendered. You don't have to debase yourself for it. You don't have to play the role they write for you, hoping love is the payment for a good acting job. You are who you are and you meet who you meet. You just get lucky. Or maybe you don't. That's love."

If Isaun understood, or even heard any of this,

he gave no indication. With half-lidded eyes, the courtesan gazed out over the distances. Melancholy heightened the beauty his features, Luken thought. More beautiful now even than his implacable youth.

"I'm not going to tell anyone about her," he said softly.

"You're not?"

Isaun sighed, and lifted his gaze to Luken's face. "No. I should. It burns me up – all this and a mistress, too." He shook his head. "But I'm not going to give you away. Everything that's happened... It doesn't really matter." A wry grin ghosted his lips. "Believe it or not, I am your friend. That's all I came here to say."

Chapter Fourteen

The Empress was troubled.

Her hand, gentle as she stroked Luken's hair, fell often into a thoughtful pause, as though tangled in his silken threads.

A bower of honeysuckle cast them both in spades of shadow where they rested in the gazebo, his head on her lap. Orange blossoms stirred above her head, bright against the iron grey of her hair. A lovely scene, except for the low, sickly murmur in the core of Luken's body. He'd awoken sick, his bedroom tilting on a wave of nausea, and swallowed his pill that morning with the same visceral disgust as a man with food poisoning forced to shovel down the rest of the food that had made him sick.

On the other side of the gazebo, two of the Empress's daughters, the princesses Tsakara and Sakiran, spoke in low murmurs. They did not like him, of course. Luken had anticipated that, and sensed their disdain the moment their mother had introduced him, giving only his name as he bowed before them at the base of the gazebo; they had guessed the rest. Luken did not take offense; they would have disliked any man their mother took as concubine, out of loyalty to their fathers. He accepted their disdain with the calm and pleasant logicality the Empress had come to expect and admire in him. The princesses, in their turn, treated him as if he did not exist, which was well enough; he preferred to listen as the royal family conferred in low tones over the mounting issue of Builay.

"Hani spoke in the Public Square yesterday. She claimed it's our civic duty to declare war with Builay." The narrowing of Tsakara's dark eyes provided the only hint of her disdain. "She called you a coward, Mother."

Raisaga's fingers paused in Luken's hair, then continued their slow strokes.

"We should get out ahead of this," Sakiran chimed. "Don't wait for the Noble Assembly, shut up Hani and the others by acting before they have any more time to make themselves the center of attention. They garner public support by calling out your hesitancy without having to do a damn thing themselves."

A slow, dark chuckle. "So I jump into war with Builay just to steal thunder from loudmouth Traditionalists? I hardly like that solution, daughter."

"This will blow over," Tsakara said with a confidence that soothed even Luken's taut nerves. Relief – that Tsakara was the eldest daughter, the heiress to the throne. Sakiran was likeable and energetic, the Empire's darling, but she did not have the cautious intellect of her mother or elder sister. Aizenten, the second eldest daughter, had relocated to the west coast following long years of hard-drinking and cavorting that had culminated in a public scandal – the details of which Luken was hazy on – and had not returned to the Palace in years. Oan, the quiet one, strolled the garden pathway behind the gazebo with Isaun at her side. Luken had brought Isaun with him, and she had, for once, recognized him from the night of the casino party. The sound of their voices drifted to Luken through the honeysuckle.

Of the four princesses, Tsakara was the most like her mother, and not surprisingly, her response to the mess in Builay was the most similar to the Empress's. "There is still no evidence to support the Builayn claim that Kanai had anything to do with the assassination of that provincial leader in Olmpuay, Balla Sulih. No evidence at all. The locals are keen to blame Kanai because they resent our presence in Builay – but if we respond with military force, we only confirm their claim. We give them what they want. Or at least, what they think they want. In truth, Builay would be devastated in a war with Kanai – why do you think their Elect Prima has apologized so desperately for the attacks on the embassy? She has publically condemned the slaying of our ambassadors. The Elect Prima knows that if Kanain warships arrive on her shores, they will never depart. Builay will become a Kanain Acquisition when the war is done. Anyone in Builay with a brain in their head is aghast at the riots outside our embassy. They are terrified of invoking war with us. As well they should be. Our forces have been honed by a long campaign and hard-won victory in Hindigga. Builay barely has a formal military. Our boys would rip them to shreds."

"And they would bunker down in their deep jungles and ancient mountain strongholds, and the war would drag on for decades," the Empress said. The languid comfort of the afternoon, warmed by the standing torches that ringed the gazebo, and the stroking of the Empress's fingers in his hair, might have lulled Luken to sleep, had he not been rigid with a misery of anticipation. "Should we go to war with Builay, I may well be dead before the Empire again sees peace."

Silence lingered. Luken raised a hand to still the Empress's fingers in his hair, holding them in reassurance. She looked down at him, met his eyes. She smiled, holding his gaze.

"Leave me now, girls. I have been in discussion on these matters with my advisors for days now. I must rest."

Tsakara rose and bowed her head. "As you say, mother."

Sakiran leapt up after her, and jerked in a quick bow. The tramp of the princesses' footsteps shook the wooden steps.

Raisaga sighed, and closed her eyes. "It never ends, Luken."

"You don't want this war, do you?" He sat up, gazing at her.

"No." She looked at him, and asked more softly, "You're twenty, aren't you?"

"Yes, my Lady."

"And the war in Hindigga is only beginning to wind down after, what? Seventeen years?" Her eyes traveled the length of his body, stricken as though by a dart of sorrow. "Mother hold us. You were three years old when the war started." She shook her head. "Now look at you. A man grown, and not known peace in living memory. My daughter Sakiran has not known peace in her lifetime. The Empire has not known peace for most of my reign." A wry laugh. "The historians will write of my blood-lust."

"No." He took her hands in her lap, squeezed them. "It doesn't have to be that way." Luken could not have said why he opposed the prospect of war with Builay. He only knew that he felt a deep and instinctive fear of it, a hovering anxiety that darkened with each day, as the newspapers proclaimed war all but inevitable. "Can you not–" He felt unbearably foolish, but could not hold his tongue. "Can you not just – withdraw the Kanain presence from Builay? I mean, sorry, but do we really need to be bothering with them? It's only a poor little country in a far-flung land. We don't need them."

A pitying smile. Raisaga raised her hand to cup his cheek. "I'm afraid the situation is a little more complicated than that, sweetheart."

"An embargo then, to punish them for the deaths of our ambassadors. But why must we commit ourselves to military action? It will only cost more Kanain lives."

Her hand fell away from his cheek, trailing instead down his jaw, his chest, and falling back into the embrace of his waiting fingers. "I wish more of my advisors saw things as you do." She sighed. "The Assembly and Convention are both stacked with Traditionalists this year, and they are all clamoring for war." A weary smile. "Here's a secret for you, Luken: Traditionalists thrive when the Empire is at war. Fear, blame, a unifying hatred of the outsider – and a promise to viciously protect Kanai from those outsiders – this is the lifeblood of the Traditionalist party. Like vultures, they grow fat when the dead are numerous." Luken's gorge rose as she spoke, the forgotten nausea squeezing a fist into his guts and twisting. "Peace with Hindigga is a fundamental threat to party leaders like Ekaris and Hani; they want war with Builay. Desperately. Reformists garner more support in times of peace. When people feel safe, they are no longer willing to sacrifice equality for the promise of security. When there is no common enemy, the peasants feel no loyalty to the Ladies who hold power over them. When spite and cruelty are frowned upon, rather than tolerated as necessities, there is less patience for the corruption or abuses of the privileged. Peace favors reform. Traditionalists will not maintain a stranglehold on the Palace unless war begins anew."

Luken drew a sharp breath. "Goddess..." Of course. Pieces of the puzzle slipped neatly into place. "Do you think- The provincial leader in Olmpuay-?"

"Was murdered by an assassin hired by a Traditionalist Lady? Oh, almost certainly."

"Raisaga! You must have them arrested!"

The Empress shook her head, wearing a rueful grin. "What, anyone who's ever voted Traditionalist? I'm afraid we require proof before making arrests, Luken. I have investigators looking into the theory, but I do not expect they are likely to find anything. The kind of Lady who would have done such a thing is not the kind of Lady to leave evidence behind. They will have covered their tracks."

Luken found himself on his feet, turning away from her. The honeyed languor of the gardens stretched before him, an impossible contrast to the storm that broke within his mind. "How can you *stand* it, Raisaga? It's fucking maddening!"

"Luken, love. Calm yourself."

A shaky breath trembled from his lips. He

looked down at her. One arm slung over the railing behind the bench, she gazed up at him. Poised on his joh, he loomed over her. Framed by honeysuckle. "You must not resign yourself to this, Raisaga. You must not accept war because it was too hard to fight for peace."

Serene, and cold as iron. "You must not speak to me like that, lad."

Luken blinked, remembering himself. *You are only a concubine, boy.* "Forgive me, I- It only makes me furious, the way they try to bully you."

"I understand, Luken. And your passion is not without merit." She let her head lilt to the side. "You care about politics. A rare trait for your gender, but not necessarily something I would discourage. Hells, we only gave men the right to vote a few decades ago." *You gave us nothing. They fought and bled and starved and protested and screamed themselves hoarse in the streets of O-Han for the right to vote,* he thought, and surpressed the urge to say so. A wave of nausea swirled through his gut. "But if you would learn to play politics, boy, you must learn to play with the same sure hand as a Lady. It does me no good to say, 'Don't accept war.' The only useful advice is a path to peace."

"So, what is the path to peace?" He closed the distance between them. "Do you have a plan? I would help you, if I could."

"You would, wouldn't you? I believe it." Affection softened her gaze. "You really are on my side, aren't you?"

"Of course I am. I would do whatever I could to help you." He resumed his place beside her on the bench, smoothing the powder blue skirts of his ando, pretending that he could not feel the bile rising in his throat. *Damn these pills,* he thought, struggling to smooth his features.

"Perhaps I'll take you up on that offer." She traced his lips with tip of her finger. "But in the meantime," her voice dropped to a whisper, "I feel like I haven't enjoyed you in so long." He parted his lips, let her finger slide in. "I think a night of relaxation would do both of us some good. Something like the other night?" She arched an eyebrow as he tongued her fingertip with a coy circling. "I can invite a few more friends along."

Her finger popped from his mouth; he replaced it with a hesitant smile. "Whatever pleases you, my Lady Empress."

Luken made it back to his chambers before vomiting into the delicate blue and white porcelain vase in his sitting room.

Chapter Fifteen

Rain showered the city the morning Lifelle left the Peacock Court, washing the diamond-shaped courtyards of the Garden to a faint gleam before purling back into sun-mottled clouds, broken through with rays of light and vistas of glowing pearl. The petals of the winter cherry trees, which – guided by generations of the Palace's obsessive gardeners – held their delicate white blossoms into the autumn and bloomed in spectacular fits during the winter, were strewn underfoot, mashed beneath the joh of courtesans huddled in their thick robes against the cold, or floating like forlorn vessels on the sudden lakes forged by the morning's rain.

In the end, there was no great ceremony. Amae notified the Arbiters of the date Lifelle was leaving, and his name was quietly removed from the Board. A contract would be drawn up by Lady Ahn's lawyers acknowledging Lifelle as her Consort and granting him the meager legal protections that came with that position. The contract would be sent to Lifelle's mother for her to review, then sent back for his signature, and the arrangement would be complete. A certified copy would be kept in his mother's vaults, in case Lady Ahn attempted to dissolve the union or dispute the contract in the future. Lifelle was now a protected commodity. At least, as far as such things went in the Empire. It did not mean Ahn could not abuse or abandon him, it just meant she would owe some money if she did. Not enough for Lifelle to live on, and he would be spit on by society for accepting the payment, but better than nothing. Better still if their love lasted, and the union was a happy one. Luken prayed that it would be.

They lingered long in the Abode, kneeling at the table in the main room and drinking their tea, picking at the crumbs of a late breakfast while they waited for the rain to lift. Waited for the sound of the traveling coach. Waited for Lifelle to rise from the table. Luken, who had not returned to the Abode of Scattered Flowers since moving into his chambers in the Palace, found a bittersweet sting to every familiar image, every casual, pleasant remark Lifelle made in an effort to alleviate the melancholy veil that draped the morning.

Yuki scurried about the main room, wagging the puff of his white tail, twining between Lady Ahn's ankles.

Lady Ahn milled about restlessly, as though embarrassed to intrude on Lifelle's final hours in the Abode. Luken watched her, unsmiling. Ahn. The great love of Lifelle's life. Or financial security. Or a good home to grow old in. Or intimacy and affection for the years to come. Whatever she was to him. To Luken, she was a small woman, a few years shy of forty, done with child-bearing but in need, evidently, of a companion to adorn her House in A-Ku, in the western reaches of the continental Empire. Luken could not help but resent her, in the same way, perhaps, that the princesses could not help but resent him.

Amae sipped his tea. If the loss of one of his courtesans bothered him, he gave no indication. A gold ring, set with a large, rose diamond, glittered on his withered finger each time he raised and lowered his teacup. Luken's eyes narrowed. His stipend from the Empress – a portion of which went to his old Abode Master so long as Luken remained on the Board and was therefore considered, technically, a working courtesan – no doubt had paid for that ring.

Enjoy it while it lasts, old man. You'll not see the like of Lifelle or me again, once we're out of your grip.

Finally, Lifelle stood. Lady Ahn turned to him, and some silent communication passed between them. A pang of longing echoed in Luken's chest. He and Jes had once communicated like that, conveying all they needed to in one desperate glance at the House of the Golden Sun...

A bustle of activity burst the awkward silence. Lady Ahn's attendant slung suitcases into the back of a traveling coach while the Lady herself conferred with the driver, rapping out directions in unnecessary detail. Lifelle wandered about his old room, checking for any last items to pack away. There was nothing, of course. He'd been too meticulous. It was Dandy who caused the mess, digging through his own belongings in a frantic search for any stray possession that may have snuck from Lifelle's half of their room to his. Of course, there was nothing. That did not stop them from looking. Dragging out the moment.

Isaun stood motionless in the center of the main room, his expression cold, almost disdainful, but Luken knew him by now: the colder, the more regal he appeared, the more he felt beneath the surface.

And then it was time, and the courtesans stood in front of the porch, gathered together against the cold as a brisk wind brought the trampled cherry blossoms skirling over the courtyard. Their tree beside the Abode added a cascade of pale yellow leafs to be snared in their andos, their hair, as Lifelle embraced each of them in turn. Luken expected, at the last, some final decree of – he didn't know what – friendship, or love, or brotherhood. But when he held Lifelle in his arms, the man pulled away with a sad smile, and said, "I will never know anyone like you again, Luken."

Luken blinked. To that, he had no answer.

It did not seem entirely real, watching Lifelle pile into the coach after Lady Ahn, dragging in the skirts of his modest ando, sun-yellow and bright against the drabness of the day. Yuki leapt up into the carriage, still squirming onto Lifelle's lap as the door swung shut. The driver snapped the reins, and the horses pushed their weight against the braces, and the coach dragged into motion. A taut semi-circle brought them around through the diamond-shaped courtyard. Lifelle leaned out the window, waving farewell, and his smile was glorious.

Luken drew a deep breath, leveled by it. By the knowledge that he would never see that smile again. And he was gone. Lifelle and his Lady, leaving for a new life.

They stood in silence. A crisp breeze cracked the air. Ripples scuttled through the rain-puddles. White petals twirled to fall and drown, like sinking ships.

"Did it have to be so fucking cold today?" Isaun spat, and plowed back into the Abode.

Luken and Dandy shared a look, and followed in slow steps, making their way into the main room.

Amae never rose from the table, though he'd emptied his teacup.

~

Luken lost count of how many fervid notes he'd dashed off, telling Jes he could not meet with her. A dark seed spread roots in his core. His birthday passed, and the Empress's orgy commanded his night, his body, his full attention. Time passed Luken like the water of a swift stream, sliding smoothly over him; he scarcely noticed the quickening current.

In truth, it had been only a few weeks, a month or so, but it seemed both an eon of loneliness, and a timeless whirlwind in which Luken could grasp nothing, for everything whipped past him too quickly.

A sense of dread mounted in him. A reckoning.

The first snow of the year dusted in, early for the season but light, though the skies were somber with a deep and restless grey for days before they broke. The flakes twirled down, muting the world to an ethereal hush. And a fist pounded at the door.

Jes appeared like an army at the gates, the door shoved wide, dragging his eunuch guard, Sami, in behind her. Eitan was a step behind, grinning an awkward, guilty grin. Another guard, Cami, gripped her arm as well, his fingers digging into her bicep, his expression more annoyed than violent; clearly, they did not perceive the two women as a threat to Luken's physical safety. His emotional safety was another matter, though, and the guard gripping Jes glanced up at him with a look that said, *We can't protect you from what's coming on that score, boy.*

Luken sighed. Even now, despite her fury, he was relieved to see her. But there was another part of him that went cold.

"It's alright, Cami, Sami. Please, resume your positions. They can stay."

But Eitan skipped out the door alongside the guards, almost outpacing them. And with a sigh of white coats and the click of the door latching, Luken and Jes were left alone.

She stood, wreathed in fury. Her face pale, dark crescents smudging the skin beneath her warm, brown eyes. Long days trapped indoors had bled her skin wan; he could see the lace of blue veins bulging at her wrists where her fists clenched at her sides. The sudden absence of physical activity had lost her some muscle and gained her some fat. Oh, but she was devastating. It was as if, lost in the strange haze that had clouded his mind across the busy weeks, he'd forgotten quite what she looked like. Like a painting, rain-washed. Retaining its colors, but the forms hazed, bleeding into one another. Now the original picture snapped into focus before him, and Luken ran headlong into a wall of passionate love.

And could tell, from the look in her eyes, that it was too late.

"Jes-" He took a few hesitant steps forward, as one would approach a tiger in the wild – if, indeed, one was foolish enough to do so. "I'm glad you've come. I've missed you."

"No, you haven't," she spat. Luken winced. "I've tried, over and over, to meet with you-"

"I've been busy, Jes." He carded fingers through his hair. "And so tired, lately, I just can't-"

His brain declined to let him finish that sentence.

"Tired. Busy." She repeated his words with no emotion, holding his gaze. Those brown eyes, with their honeyed warmth, now hard and glossed over like petrified wood. Luken struggled to hold her gaze. He should have known this was coming, but he'd been sick so often lately, his mind foggy – how long had it been since he'd seen her face-to-face? The pills, Luken realized with a terrible bolt of bright-white clarity, had misted his mind.

Quietly, he said, "I've not been myself."

A harsh laugh. "I can't disagree with that. I don't recognize this Luken at all. At least the moody, short-tempered Luken at the start of the year was still his quiet, sweet self, for the most part. At least he was around. He cared. He wanted to see me-"

"I still want to see you! I just can't," a wave of frustration crested to swallow him, "*think straight*."

"I told you this would happen." Jes's eyes narrowed. "I told you not to seek this out."

"I didn't *seek it out*," he spit the words, "it happened to me."

"You promised me." Emotion entered her voice for the first time, a sorrowful, accusing tendril that rose to coil through the syllables. "In the park, when I told you this was a terrible idea. When I *told you* we'd never be able to see each other once you were in this position. You promised me you would get out of this if you could."

"If I could," he repeated stubbornly. "And I couldn't. Seven Hells, one does not just say no to the Empress."

"Why not?"

He threw up his hands. "Why not? Goodness, Jes, what a good question! Why not? I don't know, perhaps because she is the most powerful person in the fucking Empire?"

"You are not here against your will. You wanted this Luken. You know you do-"

"I- If only you knew the whole of it. If only you knew the ways in which I am resisting this, for our sake, for us-"

"There is no 'us' these days, Luken. Open your eyes. I haven't seen you in more than a month. I couldn't even contact you on your birthday. You turned twenty-one without me." Her voice wavered, as though tears seethed beneath the surface, but her eyes were dry. "I had plans, remember?"

"I remember." A murmur, almost too soft to hear.

"You're changing." It was strange, how little she moved. "You're becoming her pet. Her creature."

Shame shot through him. "I am not *her pet*. Raisaga is not a monster, she's just a woman, and not a bad one either."

Jes's eyes widened. "Are you actually telling me that you care for her?" She mimicked the name back at him, her lips twisting around a spasm of spite. "Raisaga."

"I care for her as much as I would care for any client that I spent this much time with. I'm not made of stone, Jes. Men do develop affections, in case you hadn't noticed. But I do not love her, if that's what you're afraid of. This arrangement is no different than going on Conjugal Leave with Lady Dare."

"You were not Dare's pet. Physically, perhaps,

you were tethered to her House and financially, she controlled you. But not in your heart, and not in your mind." She stared at him, unblinking. "That's the part I can't figure out. You're so smart, but you're letting the Empress do this to you. You're making a choice-"

Something snapped, there. Quick as lightning and as fierce. "You refuse to even attempt to understand this from my point of view." Luken heard his voice rise, despite himself. "Why am I perpetually surrounded by jealous morons?"

"Because you're the same elitist asshole you've always been, even after all this time."

"Elitist? What the ever-living fuck are you talking about?"

"I have stood, patiently, in the shadows. I have watched you share your time and your body with other women. I have waited for you to come around. To do what you thought was necessary. To make enough money to feel comfortable. And in all that time, it never even occurred to you that leaving the Court was more important than leaving it rich. It never even occurred to you that your little servant woman might not still be waiting for you by the time you were ready to leave. It never even occurred to you to say no to the Empress; that whatever second-hand power she could give you would not be worth having. You took it for granted that wealth was your default state and a normal life was just not acceptable. Not for Lord Luken. Not for the Beauty of the Age!"

Breathless with rage. "You would prefer, then," he struggled to speak, "that I live in a state of constant fear and discomfort and panic? You would prefer that I feel vulnerable for the rest of my life? You would prefer that I feel powerless and small?"

"I would prefer that you learn to live without grandiose wealth, if money is more important to you than me."

"Nothing is more important to me than you, Jes."

"You have not shown that."

He sighed, and buried his face in his hands. All the strength seemed to drain out of him, as if he were a willow, his heavy ando like the wreath of hanging leaves, and all the moisture fled his body, draining out through the roots. Leaving the husk.

In a small voice, he asked, "Can you not imagine, at all, why it would be important to me to feel a measure of security? Can you not imagine why power and wealth feel as necessary to me now as shelter and water? I was not always like this, before U-Wen..."

She softened. "Oh Luken..." A long silence. Luken did not pry his hands from his face; he couldn't stand to look at her. "You're right. I failed to understand it from your point of view." A faint creak, as her weight settled on the chair by the fireplace. "Of course, after what happened to you, you would need to seek security. Or, without that, the trappings of security..."

"And it does not help," he said quietly, "that everything about how men are treated in Kanai only makes me feel more threatened. The election, the denial of political representation, the degrading sex, the lack of control over when I have children or with who, even the attack in Builay..." A shaky sigh. "It makes me feel better, to have a little control. And yes,

I am only the Empress's concubine. I do not think I have power equal to her or her daughters. But I am *valued*. Ladies step out of my path with a respectful nod. The Arbiters who once pinched my flesh and shoved their fingers in my mouth to check that I had good teeth now bow to me and place me at the top of the Board, above all others. I desire gifts for my friends, and the Palace invites a jeweler to my chambers with instructions to give me whatever I want and worry about the bill later. The Royal Consort himself fears I might stick around. I give the Empress of Kanai my opinion. I know it is not much, but it's what I have." He dared to look at Jes. She slouched in the chair by the fireplace, her boneless sprawl a strange contrast to her earlier rigidity. "You understand, don't you Jes?"

"I understand." She gazed, unblinking, into the ash-blacked fireplace, dim now in the middle of the day.

"So..." he approached her in silent strides, hands tangled at his chest in a gesture of prayer, "we're going to be okay?"

"No, Luken."

That knocked the wind out of him. "Why?"

"You don't have time for me. Why drag this out? We're only hurting ourselves." She looked at him. Red rimmed her eyes. "If this is something you have to do, then so be it. If you have to become the Empress's Consort, so be it. If you have to fight for your values, so be it. If you have to feel powerful, so be it. But while you do that, you live in a different world than I do. I can't survive any longer on scraps of affection. I can't live in a state of prolonged starvation.

If I can't have all of you…" She stood, and it seemed to take a very long time: leaning forward, gathering up her limbs, mustering the strength to push upright. "I would rather wait until you can give me everything you have to offer than continue as we are now, stringing each other along, feeding on the scraps, while we slowly grow to resent each other more and more, because neither has enough."

"You're breaking things off with me?"

"I love you, Luken. I used to look at you and think, 'This is what the perfect man looks like.' But since then, I've seen the cracks and dents, the flaws and failings – and believe me when I say they've only made me love you more. But I just can't do this anymore. Not like this. Maybe someday, when you're ready, but not like this. Not now."

At the end of the muskets they wore slung over their backs, Luken's guards Sami and Cami had bayonets, about ten inches in length, of sharp steel that flashed with a brilliant gleam whenever they caught the light. Luken felt now as if both bayonets were savaging his guts with long, ragged strokes, in and out, slicing and stabbing, pushing deep and twisting–

"No," Luken breathed. "No! No!" He heard the screaming, and did not recognize his voice.

Jes took a step toward him, hands outspread. "Luken-"

"You can't! You can't do this to us!" What was he saying? A ringing filled his ears.

"Luken, please-"

"How fucking dare you-"

The Empress stood in the doorway, eyes wide. "What is going on here?"

Luken drew a deep breath, his gaze swiveling from the Empress back to Jes. Her dark brown eyes, staring back into his.

He turned away. "This servant has displeased me."

The Empress glanced at Jes, raising an eyebrow. She did not recognize her, of course, but the Empress would not have recognized any servant. "You're fired. Get out."

Jes darted a glance at Luken. Dark eyes pleading, resentful. Then, in what seemed an unbearably long moment, she turned on her heel and quickened through his chambers, head bowed, and a guard closed the door behind her. Luken labored for breath beneath the tightness of his irlan.

Raisaga approached him. "Are you alright?"

"Perfectly." He squared his shoulders. "I- I simply dislike it when my inferiors fail to render me proper respect."

"Ah, Luken." She cocked her head, a look of understanding suffusing her features. Likely, he was not her first concubine to complain of facing disrespect in his position. She came to his side, and stroked a hand through his hair in comfort. "Do not trouble yourself over the help, lovely."

Chapter Sixteen

Luken kept to his chambers. There seemed no reason to leave. When the Empress wanted him, he was there. His books, his writing. His grandfather's letters and diaries. He wanted nothing else, except freedom from the tired uses of his body. Thus, when he left his chambers for the first time in the weeks following Jes's visit, it was to obtain a vasectomy.

Rori sat across from Luken in the coach, watching him with a wary eye.

"Are you sure you're going to be okay? You can come stay with me and Kat, if you want. I know it's not what you're used to, but the couch isn't so uncomfortable."

"For the last time, Rori, I do not need to stay with you. Besides, don't you think that would raise some eyebrows at the Palace?"

"I just worry about you, these days-"

"There's nothing to worry about!" Luken snapped. His entire being felt like a raw nerve, sinew and skin peeled back in delicate exposure, ready to explode with anguished sensation at the slightest touch.

Rori shifted in his seat. "I don't know, Luken. I think you're depressed."

"Of course I'm depressed! We were supposed to be each other's future! I was going to run away with her!" He slammed a fist against the seat. "I was going to have a fucking family with her!"

Rori shrank back, struggling to keep his livid gaze. In a quiet voice, he ventured, "I think you were depressed before- before what happened with Jes. You were not easy to get ahold of in the weeks leading up to that day, and on the rare occasions when I did see you, it was clear you were distracted and tired. Hollowed out."

Luken released a long sigh. "Well then, I suppose it's a good thing I'm getting this vasectomy. I'm not cut out for birth control."

A bitter laugh. "Yes, I think it's safe to say you had a bad reaction." Silence. "Perhaps this is for the best."

Throughout his body came the tingling numbness of a deep and nameless sorrow. "We were going to have a family. Jes and I."

"Luken," Rori said slowly, "do you want a vasectomy, or not?" He ducked his head out the window before throwing his gaze back to Luken. "You had better make up your mind. We're nearly there."

A tear cut down his cheek. Such a small thing, to scorch his eyes like this. "I want it."

"You're sure?"

Luken swallowed. "Yes. If I can't have children with Jes, then I don't want any more children. There's no reason to endure the risk, and my body despises those pills." He took a deep breath, steady now. "This is for the best."

The clinic huddled between its neighbors, its walls a rain-washed square of dull beige. A small placard on the door identified it as the Public Health and Resources Clinic. Luken, dressed in the peasant's garb he'd borrowed from Rori, instinctively bowed his head so that his curtain of black hair offered his features a brush of secrecy. It didn't really matter; if anyone with Palatial connections recognized him here, his reputation would be annihilated regardless of whether he was dressed as a courtesan or not.

What his guards thought of him, he couldn't guess; Cami and Sami sat in their habitual silence, ignoring Luken's bouts of hysteria. Perhaps it was not the first time they'd followed an Empress's concubine on his little adventures in the city. Indeed, he supposed a doctor's appointment in peasant's garb was dull by their reckoning. He wasn't afraid they would tell anyone; like courtesans, guards counted discretion as a virtue.

Leaving Cami and Sami on the porch, Luken and Rori shuffled into the foyer and mercifully, Rori took the lead.

"Hello, we have an appointment." The woman at the desk gave him a long look, as if taking his measure, before, slowly, passing her gaze to Luken. A slight twitch, at the eye. And a condescending smile.

"Of course. Sign in, love." She pushed the registry at Rori, where he added his name and the time of their arrival.

Luken's gaze darted around the small room, taking in its cheap furniture, its ancient publications with curled corners strewn across the table in the center, the ominous press of the low ceiling. Clenching his fists to keep from fidgeting, Luken took a seat at the end of a line of chairs pushed up against the wall. Rori joined him a moment later. When Luken looked up, the woman at the desk was watching him; her expression hard, her small eyes lit by a bland malice. Luken jumped a little, caught off guard, and she pushed another patronizing smile to her lips before looking away.

They waited for an interminable period. After the hour mark, Rori heaved a sigh and returned to the front desk to exchange a series of truncated murmurs with the receptionist. He returned, shaking his head.

"I think I may have made a mistake," he muttered in Luken's ear.

"What do you mean?"

But Rori only shook his head, and the wait continued. Rori approached the desk twice more before, finally, a tall woman with white hair and a long mouth set between deep lines, appeared in the door behind the desk.

"Vin?"

Rori nudged Luken's ribs, and he leapt to his feet. They'd debated about whether or not to use Luken's real name, but ultimately decided against it; even a doctor's obligated confidentiality was not impenetrable, and rumors had teeth in O-Han. As Luken was reminded, every time the yip or bay of a dog in the distance set his cheeks flaming with embarrassment.

Darting a glance over his shoulder at Rori, Luken followed the doctor into her office. With a note of false levity, she gestured to the chair in front of a wide, oak desk. "Have a seat."

"Okay." Why was he so nervous? A chill suffused the air. Ice-white walls framed the doctor's credentials, twin columns of framed diplomas. Except the last of them, which, Luken noticed, was a quotation from the *Book of Kuiken*, the Mother Goddess. *To hold and to keep is our duty,* read the quotation in elegant calligraphy. *The Mother's strength annihilates all enemies of life.*

There seemed no harm in it, yet Luken's stomach sank as he read the words.

"Vin is it?" She gazed at him across the expanse of her desk, one hand folded neatly over the other on its glossy surface.

Luken swallowed. "Yes."

"Doctor Ence. Alright Vin, you're here today to talk about your concerns regarding reproductive health, correct? Let's discuss your options."

"Okay."

"We want to keep you nice and healthy, yes? Fertility is the cornerstone of male health." Reaching into the bottom drawer of her desk, she came back up with a brightly ghoulish, rubbery model figurine of the mid-section of a man's body, sliced neatly across the loins so that their inner structure was visible, as in the illustrations of dissected bodies in a medical book that Luken would have slammed shut at once.

Mortification trickled down Luken's spine.

"You're in a very special position, young man." Her tone bright and cheery as she jabbed a finger at the rubbery gloss of sperm that filled the model's halved testicles. "You are the sacred vessel of millions and millions of living sperm."

"Lucky me."

Oblivious to his sarcasm, she beamed.

"Exactly! It's a very special position to be in. Countless millions of lives exist inside you, right at this exact moment."

"They feel very crowded, I suppose."

She chuckled, and bent sideways to rummage in a drawer of her desk. An ominously large scalpel was laid on the table, side-by-side with the quivering oblong of a chicken's egg.

Luken blinked as the items emerged. "I- I had made this appointment to inquire about a vasectomy."

Doctor Ence nodded. "You did. Let me describe the process of a vasectomy, and then we can discuss why it is such a dangerous and undesirable option."

"That's not really necessary, I've made up my mind-"

"You see, my boy," she popped the pale rubber from the model's testicles and into the loose sack, inserted the egg, "a vasectomy may seem like the answer to all your problems. It's the logical thing to do, after all." She plucked the scalpel from the table. "Human reproduction is messy. Sex is complicated, and the emotions associated with it can be so difficult. Love dies, relationships end, one in five women experiences a miscarriage in her lifetime, pregnancies pop up, unplanned, and you find yourself with kids you don't want with a lover you haven't loved in a long time, the mother favors her infant over you, you're passed from woman to woman and parenthood interrupts your relationship with every single one. Etcetera, etcetera. It can be demoralizing. And when you consider all the complications that arise, you begin to wonder, why not just give up and take myself out of the game altogether?"

Luken watched her, silent.

"After all," she continued brightly, "instigating a pregnancy can't inconvenience you if you're simply incapable of causing a pregnancy in the first place, right?"

"It isn't really about the inconvenience," Luken said dryly.

"But let's take a look at what you're really giving up," she plowed on, "you see, the male body is designed for the production and expression of sperm. It all begins here," she scraped the scalpel against the shell of the egg in the sad pocket where the testicle would be, "where all your cute little sons and daughters are produced. During sexual intercourse, your children climb all the way up," she scraped the scalpel in a wobbling path up the orange tube that looped back around into the scarlet cords behind the penis, "the vas deferens, into here," she tapped the beginning of the scarlet cord, "the ejaculatory duct, which shoots," Luken winced as she dragged the scalpel tip down the bared length of the uretha, "from the penis, into the vagina, in search of the woman's egg."

Or somewhere else, more often than not, Luken thought.

"However," Doctor Ence's dark eyes swiveled to his, "the vasectomy interrupts this process by, quite literally, severing the vas deferens," she sliced the scalpel across the orange tube with such force that the rubber bent and popped with a breathy *ping*, "which prevents the sperm from reaching the penis, and therefore renders his ejaculate useless, and the man infertile."

Her tone was grave, as if she expected this to

make a great impact on Luken, but he merely blinked back at her. "Yes, that's what I want."

Nostrils flared around a silent breath. "But what becomes of your children?" She reeled back, scalpel flashing in the light, and shot into a backhanded swing. The scalpel burst the egg with impressive force, cracking the shell, showering the desk with yolk. Luken winced, flecks of egg spattering his cheek.

"Seven Hells," he cursed, rubbing at his face with the back of his shirtsleeve; he'd have to wash the thing before returning it to Rori.

Doctor Ence whipped a hankerchief from the pocket of her white coat and slid the scalpel clean in one deft stroke. "When you undergo a vasectomy, your children have nowhere to go. They cannot be released from your body, and are therefore trapped inside your testicles. Building up and building up and building up." A sneer, tugging at the corner of her mouth, disrupted her mask of ironic detachment. "Until, finally, the sperm is swallowed by your body, rather like plankton being absorbed by a sea sponge."

The clock behind her ticked with uncomfortable volume.

"Okay."

"No, it isn't *okay*, dearie, and let me tell you why. Each and every single sperm in your body represents a human life. Just because you cannot see them does not mean they are not real and alive." A dull, red blot began to form in both cheeks as the rage mounted in her voice. "Each and every one deserves the chance to be delivered to its Goddess-given goal – the egg. Each and every single one represents the life of an innocent child that has done nothing wrong and deserves the chance to live in this world. Each and every single one *dies*," spittle from her teeth joined the yolk spatter on table between them, "when it is reabsorbed into your body. By obtaining a vasectomy, you are choosing to end the life of those children before it even *has the chance to begin*."

"So… they aren't alive yet then? I mean, if I'm ending it before it has the chance to begin, then a life hasn't started."

She drew a deep breath, nostrils flaring. "This is no joke, young man. We are talking about the lives of your children." She shook her head. "I don't think you appreciate the gravity of the situation."

"Doctor Ence, I already have at least two children-"

"So that gives you the right to kill others?"

Luken's patience ran thin. "I am not killing anyone. I think you're being a bit extreme."

"Extreme? Let us talk about what is *extreme*, darling. In one moment of inconceivable selfishness, a man chooses a vasectomy, and takes the lives of millions of unborn children merely for the sake of his atrocious and immoral whims. Is that not extreme?"

Luken fought to keep the anger from his voice, though she made no such effort. "There is no such thing as an unborn child. There are quite a few stages between ejaculation and childhood, and a rather important one includes the birth. I thought a doctor would know that."

"Are you a medical expert, boy?" The sneering grin – that same grin Luken recognized from so many women's faces, the moment they showed their true colors – adorned her dry lips now. "Are you?"

"Look, you accept appointments for vasectomies-"

"*Are you?*"

Luken stared at her, egg yolk spattered across the desk between them, and wondered how many men these theatrics had worked on.

"Is there another clinic I should go to?"

"There are no other reproductive health resource clinics in the city. Not for men, anyway. The nearest one is in U-Vo."

Luken's stomach fell. "Six weeks away."

"That's right." Cheerful again, as the cat who'd cornered the mouse.

Betrayal scooped his stomach hollow. Was this what it felt like to be duped by a scam artist? It must be. He felt as if he'd paid for diamonds, only to unwrap his purchases at home and find paste and plastic. Except it was his life, and in place of agency and respect for his autonomy, the world had given him... this.

Luken sighed. "I take it you don't perform vasectomies."

"No, I don't plan on going to everlasting punishment in the Hells when I die. So no, I don't perform vasectomies."

"Fine, but say I'm willing to go to the Hells – where can I find someone who *does* perform vasectomies?"

The ironic mask slipped back into place as she finished wiping her hands with the handkerchief, and began folding it into ever smaller cubes. "There is a specialist who performs the procedure out of the

Supreme Mother Medical Center in the Quartz District. However, the Medical Center absolutely prohibits the performance of such a procedure without a prescription from a qualified doctor who works out of a reproductive health clinic certified to deal with male reproduction."

Luken stared at her. "You, in other words. There's only one clinic in the city, and you're the only doctor who works with male reproduction. You're the only one who can prescribe such a procedure."

Again, that grin. "That's right."

The *tick, tick, tick* of the clock sounded like the clamor of thunder in Luken's brain.

Adopting the cheery tone she had affected when Luken first walked in, Doctor Ence tucked the handkerchief back into the pocket of her coat and folding her hands together on the desk, continued. "I think, my boy, I have failed to impress upon you the seriousness of what it means to obtain a vasectomy. Since you obviously are too selfish to care about your children, we should go over the personal damage you will be doing to yourself if you persist in seeking out this procedure. You want to keep yourself male, after all. There are serious health risks that come with making yourself a eunuch–"

Luken felt as if the inside of his skull was aflame. "That's not what a vasectomy is–"

"Men commonly develop severe health concerns after a vasectomy."

"I was told there are no negative side effects at all–"

She shoved a pamphlet at him, whipping it open to reveal a section entitled *The Consequences*, where crude illustrations of suffering men adorned descriptions of what were, apparently, the "likely consequences" of obtaining a vasectomy. Luken's gaze scanned the page, snagging here and there on "prostrate cancer," "early death," "severe depression," and – for some reason he found this the most belittling – "mental illness."

As always, there was no way a man could veer from the path society demanded of him without his mental state immediately becoming invalid. Nothing he said could be believed. Nothing he wanted could be reasonable. Nothing he thought mattered. It was just the "mental illness" of a stupid whore who insisted on taking his pleasure without bowing to the agenda prescribed for his body – without his permission.

The doctor's voice, detailing each "side effect" in turn, became a low drone in the back of Luken's mind while his heart sped up, his blood racing.

"Doctor," Luken said with deadly calm.

Dark eyes flicked up to meet his gaze.

"I am getting a vasectomy. I do not care how much it costs. I do not care what the waiting period is. I do not care how many side effects you threaten me with. I will not be guilted, shamed, bullied, deceived, pressured, belittled, or otherwise degraded into having any more children that I *do not want.*"

She winced at those last words. "Every baby is a blessing, Vin," she whispered.

"Count your own blessings. Don't presume to count mine."

There were few times in Luken's life when he would have been able to speak to someone like this, especially a woman in a position of authority. Even a year ago, he would not have found the words. But his work as a courtesan had conditioned him to accept embarrassment, and months of arguing his views on gender and culture for *Ages* had left the words blazing like embers in his mind, there to spark and burn whenever he stoked them.

She shook her head, mouth twisted with disgust. "I'm a doctor. It is my duty to warn you that you are mutilating your body."

"Last I checked, vasectomies were still legal in Kanai."

She scoffed. "That may very well change, soon enough. A new generation is rising, and they value life. We-"

Sensing the beginning of a speech, Luken dove in swiftly. "I value life as well. But life starts at birth, when a separate person emerges from their parents. While the seeds of life are still swimming around in my own body, they are still *me*."

"Damn it boy, I'm on your side! I'm trying to keep you safe. You *will* regret this. It's not a matter of if, but when. Such an unnatural procedure goes against the very purpose of the male body. You cannot walk away from such a harrowing procedure – such a blatant rejection of your own existence – without permanent damage to your mental state."

"What do you think I am, a semen-dispensing machine?"

"Don't be juvenile. We are speaking of simple, biological facts. This is your natural purpose. You are what you are, whether you like it or not."

"I am what I am," he repeated with a *fuck you* smile. "And soon, I will be a man with a vasectomy. I will like *that* quite a bit. Are you going to write me a prescription or not?"

They stared at one another. The ticking of the clock, like a drum beating through Luken's brain.

She smiled.

Luken had not felt such a chill race down his spine since his rapist had smiled at him the last time he'd seen her in U-Wen.

"There are laws in place, Luken, to prevent irresponsible, rash, young men from making a life-alterring choice that they will inevitably come to regret."

"Do you really talk like this to everyone, or do I just have one of those faces that says, 'Come push me around, I'm easy'?"

"Nothing can be done on the first appointment. You must return with a character witness who can attest that you are in your right state of mind and not making this choice out of rank insanity and childish irresponsibility–"

"My friend is sitting right outside this door, he can tell you right now that I am perfectly sane."

"The law in this region mandates a waiting period of two weeks, minimum. To give the individual in question time to consider the gravity of his decision, and its effect on future generations – or lack thereof."

"I don't need time, I have already made my decision. I know my own mind, and my mind is made up."

"Speak to my secretary, and make an appointment to return with your character witness."

Luken sighed. "Going to drag this out, are we? Very well, doctor, I'll see you in two weeks."

"I'm booked solid til at least next month."

"*Fuck me*," Luken spit in frustration.

A hateful little sneer curled up at the edge of her mouth. "If those words passed your lips less often, young man, perhaps you'd not be here in the first place."

Luken had never, in twenty-one years of life, come so close to tightening his hands around another person's neck. "If anyone had ever responded positively to those words passing *your* lips, perhaps you'd be less unbearably priggish."

Luken would have liked to see her response to this comment, but the rage that smeared his vision also carried him out the door, into the reception room to reclaim a startled Rori from the cheap chairs against the wall, through the tedious process of booking another appointment in what was, evidently, the world's most elaborately inconvenient schedule, and then out to the street, to await another hired coach.

But once they had shuffled into the coach, Cami and Sami behind him, the rage drained from Luken's body, leaving only a feeling of emptiness.

"Goddess, Luken, I'm so sorry," Rori stammered, "I shouldn't have brought you here!"

Luken held up a hand. "You did not know. And it's the only clinic in the city. I would never blame you."

They trundled toward Rori's apartment.
Despite the intense emotion that had animated Luken minutes before, he struggled now to keep his eyes open.

Exhausted and degraded by the process. Which was, he realized, exactly the intention.

Chapter Seventeen

Having dropped Rori off at his apartment, Luken let his lids slide shut and slumped into the corner of the coach. He traveled back toward the Palace by way of the Ruby District. Tired beyond belief, Luken lingered in the harrowed drowse of one who has just awoken from a nightmare. And so it was, when his eyes lifted and he recognized Amae's stooped form in a dusky orange ando shuffling along the garden path of a house on the side of the street, that he did not immediately accept the evidence of his eyes.

Amae? In a residential neighborhood of the Ruby District?

Luken – fully awake now – yanked back the veil to gaze at Master Amae as he limped up to the front door of the house, painted a cheery sky blue. A box of pansies sat on the windowsill. An older woman, plump, with a pleasant face, opened the door for him. She kissed Amae's cheek, and it was that, more than the absurdity of an Abode Master visiting someone in a lower middle class neighborhood of the Ruby District, that convinced Luken, *That can't be him. I was mistaken after all.*

But as he slipped into the house and reappeared in the kitchen's bay window, a warm glow illuminated Amae's profile in unmistakeable detail.

The woman took his coat. A child of twelve or

so embraced him, waving her hands in animated speech as Amae settled at the kitchen table, a tumult of young people gathered to either side of him, snatching bread from the basket on the table, laughing and taking their seats. The coach pressed forward, Luken's sliver of visibility slipping away. But even in that final image, he could see – just before it vanished behind the lacy sprawl of a curtain – Amae's smiling face surrounded by children who looked like him.

~

If the sighting of Amae in the Ruby District, or the belittling dismissal at the clinic, had not been enough to unsettle Luken that day, the scene he walked into next would have done the job.

He heard their voices before he even reached the hall outside his chambers, where the coffered dome caught the echoes of their words, and whispered them back. Isaun, resplendent in an ando of peonies rising to bloom over a background that contained all the shades of dawn, his hair pinned back into a voluminous tumble, only barely contained by the diamond clasps that glittered against the dark waves – hurried down the length of the hallway in front of Luken. A pale woman with short black hair, who Luken recognized a moment later as Princess Oan's sloe-eyed friend, Lady Weim, kept pace with him, her short legs pumping vigorously to keep her within trampling distance of his ando's skirts as they danced like phantoms over the marble floor.

"When will you be available then? Tomorrow night?" Weim demanded.

"I believe I have an assignation with Lady Romyn tomorrow night. She does keep me busy, I'm afraid."

Luken could hardly believe the frigid tenor of Isaun's voice; Isaun never spoke in that manner to a Lady. To a servant, yes. To a man, perhaps. But to a Lady? Never.

"So the night after, you'll be free," the Lady pressed.

"I-" Exasperation leaked through the pause in Isaun's speech. "Will be at a dinner party in the city that evening. My friend Satomi knows someone who's friends with a famous writer. It should be," Isaun was a good actor, but not that good, as his voice fell flat despite him, "interesting."

Their footsteps clacked to a staccato as their pace spilled them into the circular hall. Luken hurried as much as his joh would allow, trying to catch up. His eunuch guards lengthened their stride and kept pace with him with the effortless grace of men *not* wearing forty pounds of uncomfortable fabric and jewels.

"Then the night *after*," Weim pressed, her tone so rigid even Luken grew annoyed.

There was nowhere left to go. Isaun pounded on the door of Luken's chambers, his face falling as silence met his call. Slowly, he turned. Lady Weim took a step towards him, too close. He towered over her – a foot taller, even without the joh – but somehow she managed to press him, till his tentative step backward brought him almost into the wall. A bulldog, pressing a greyhound. Looking for the throat.

"Hello Isaun," Luken chirped. Relief suffused the older courtesan's face as Luken strode into the hall. He bowed his head. "Lady Weim."

Annoyance snarling her features, the Lady

stepped back. "Lord Luken." They knew each other, vaguely, through association with Princess Oan.

"I was just coming to visit you," Isaun said.

"How lovely." Luken noted the frantic gleam in Isaun's eyes and wondered how he could invite the other courtesan inside without, by the demands of courtesy, extending an invitation to the Lady as well.

As it turned out, Lady Weim saved him the trouble. A sudden, sly grin oiled her lips. "You know Isaun, I think I also received an invitation to that dinner party. Was the writer in question Koko, Second Son of the Verdant Fen?"

Isaun's face fell. "I think it was, actually."

Weim grinned like the cat that caught the mouse. "I'll see you there then."

"I suppose you will."

She nodded to Luken in passing and strode off, the slap of her shiny black boots crisping to echoes in the dome, like icicles in a chill.

Luken unlocked the door to his chambers, feeling as if he'd passed a decade since the last time he'd been here. Cami and Sami took up their familiar posts to either side of the door and Isaun shoved it shut.

"That woman!" he exploded. "She has been hounding me up and down the Palace since the night of the casino party!"

"What does she want?" Luken kicked his joh off and collapsed onto the green velvet divan, aching with exhaustion.

A shaky laugh, rather uncharacteric for Isaun.

"You'd think, at our age, we'd be past these little infatuations, wouldn't you? Evidently not. She's only contacted Amae about fifty times, demanding an appointment."

Luken closed his eyes. He could hear the rhythm of Isaun's footsteps, pacing up and down the floorboards. "Why don't you just take an appointment, then? Such Ladies often lose interest, once their initial curiosity or lust or whatever it is, is sated."

"Obviously I know that," Isaun spat. "And normally, yes, I would just take the appointment. But Lady Weim is Princess Oan's closest friend. You know how Ladies can be with things like that. Once one has used you, the other considers you off-limits. I mean, we're not back in the days of Sanctum Sisters," he said, referring to an archaic concept in which Ladies of great friendship and loyalty to one another decided to join their bloodlines by conceiving at the same time, with the same man. If both pregnancies yielded a girl – the ideal result – the bond between them was considered sacred. Sanctum Sisters were often romanticized in Kanain storytelling as heroines of flawless loyalty and devotion.

Luken pressed the heels of his hands to his eyes, not caring if kohl smudged against his lace gloves. "Does Princess Oan know of Lady Weim's interest?"

The footsteps ceased. "I- I think she does. Or suspects it, at least. More than once Oan has left me alone with Weim."

"Oh Isaun." Luken let his hands fall away from his face. "That is not good." It happened, of course; a Lady of higher station would entertain a courtesan's courtship, only to slowly pass him along to her friend of lower station. If Lady Weim was the one interested in Isaun, not Princess Oan- "Isaun," Luken pushed himself up to a sitting position. "I'm sorry."

"What? Don't apologize to me. I have no intention of settling for Lady Weim."

Lord Aokinay's voice whispered in Luken's ear. *Just settle, Luken. Settle before you get too old... That's the best a man can do in this world. It isn't fair, but there it is. Settle, and keep your mouth shut.*

And a day's worth of rage ruptured Luken's chest. "They are both a waste of your time. Lady Weim," he sneered. "I will tell her myself to stay the fuck away from you, if you like."

He expected Isaun to reject this offer with a haughty wave, but to his surprise, the older courtesan considered him, his expression serious. "You may very well be the only one who could get away with it."

Thinking aloud, Luken said, "Because I am the Empress's concubine. And as a man and your former roommate, this is my purview. I am allowed to be protective, now that I've got my grubby hands on some power. The Empress will think it charming that I'm being over-protective of an old friend. And the Lady will back off. After all," a lazy grin found his lips, "my association with the Empress trumps her association with the Princess."

"Yes," Isaun breathed the word like a sigh of relief. "But there's still the matter of the damned dinner party I said I'd go to."

"Does Satomi really know someone who's friends with Koko, Second Son of the Verdant Fen?"

"Something like that, yes. I'm sure he could procure an invitation for you with no trouble, given your reputation."

A dinner party at Koko's house. The thought filled Luken with instinctive disgust, and yet... He knew who Koko was, yet Koko did not know who he was. Or rather, he knew Luken in the same way that everyone knew him now – as the Empress's concubine. But the man had no way of knowing that Luken was also Vin Ayet, whose cutting reviews of Koko's books – and Koko's increasingly irate responses in *The Easterner* – had become something of a literary duel playing out over the past few months, to the amusement of a growing body of readers. Seito, the editor of *Ages*, the magazine that published Luken's articles and reviews, found the situation hilarious. It was not the first time *Ages* and *The Easterner* had dipped into a rather less than friendly rivalry, but it was the first time that a simple series of book reviews had generated so many new customers for *Ages*. As it turned out, there were quite a few people who enjoyed neither Koko, nor the ideology his books represented, and every time he issued a livid response to a bad review, *Ages'* circulation went up. "Negativity can have such positive results," Seito grinned when Luken had handed in his most recent review. He didn't feel much like grinning these days, but that morning, he'd made an exception.

Still, this might be taking it too far. It was an irrational fear, but what would he do if Koko recognized him somehow?

"I don't know, Isaun."

"*Please.*" His mentor rushed toward him in the loveliest swarm of pastels. "Please, Luken."

Gazing up into Isaun's face, Luken sighed. "I

suppose I may as well, if the Empress has no use for me that evening."

"Thank you, Luken!" Isaun ducked down and pressed a kiss to Luken's forehead.

Luken pushed him away with a playful shove. "I shall probably be free."

"What?" Isaun plopped onto the divan opposite Luken. "No secret rendezvous that night with your servant mistress?"

A knife, punched between Luken's ribs.

"No," he whispered, "we ended things."

"Good," Isaun chirped, oblivious to Luken's mood descending like a black veil. "She was a threat to your position. I'm glad you saw reason."

"Actually, she left me." It ached. In his bones, it ached.

"Oh." Isaun blinked, his surprise genuine. "Well, what do you know? She cared about you."

Luken snorted. "Enough to break up with me."

Isaun let his head tilt. "Enough to do what's best for you."

Chapter Eighteen

Koko's home proved to be a large, somewhat old-fashioned house, whitewashed, with a balcony wrapping around the upper story beneath the lace-trimmed eaves of steep gables. A small pond bubbled with an artificial waterfall over the rocks in the corner of the garden; Luken wandered over to check for koi fish and was not disappointed. A huge golden koi wafted through the rippling darkness, attended by swirls of orange and black-and-white brethren. Luken's ando, he could not help but notice, bore a pleasingly similar shade of orange to some of the koi, a design of white poppies drifting across the skirts as if borne by the wind, with a stately irlan of dark-blue dusted by glimmering powder, its bow tied into an elaborate knot at Luken's back that dripped in twin rivers down to his feet, and long sleeves of a diaphanous material that dipped almost to the stones.

"Let's *go*," Isaun hissed at his back over the crackle of the carriage's wheels against the gravel as their driver pulled away. Luken rejoined Isaun on the main path that led up to the portico.

Isaun knocked on the door, and in the space of a heartbeat, it flew open. The servant's eyes went wide with the expression Luken now knew to associate with being recognized from one of the painted miniatures they sold of his face – dream-soft and sweet, with his long hair falling unbound over his shoulders – around the city. She ducked her head to hide a blush, and ushered them in.

It was by no means the most luxurious house Luken had seen, given his experience with Middling and High Houses, and a certain dowdiness lingered about the porcelain antiques and beaded lantern shades. Nevertheless, it had its elegance beneath a veneer of staid and repressive cleanliness. The walls on the inside of the house were as white as the outside, and the floors a dark, polished wood. The rigid furniture, with all its flat cushioning – as if some determined individual had crushed the comfort from each one in turn – gave the truest indication of the owner's personality as far as Luken could discern.

Voices drifted to them from the other room, punctured by a giggle so loud and ebullient, it could only have come from Satomi. Luken found himself smiling at the sound of it as the servant led them down a short hall, and into the dining room.

A long table filled the center of the room, where ten or so men and women sat. Cases lined one wall, filled with glassware that held nothing but the glimmers of the candlelight. A series of windows dominated the opposite wall, looking out onto a small garden where lavender lined the fence. An eruption of enthusiastic greetings met their approach – none more enthusiastic than Satomi, who all but tackled Luken. A mass of bright red curls filled his vision as the other courtesan embraced him.

"I'm so glad you came!" Satomi squeezed Isaun into an embrace as well.

"Such distinguished friends, Satomi." The voice was deeper than Luken had expected, the man tall, his frame so thin as to almost appear skeletal. A thick, dark mass of hair framed a long face with high cheekbones and a finely crafted nose and chin, though his mouth was too wide and his eyes too far apart. Injections of binu venom had preserved his beauty against wrinkles, at the cost of placing a paralyzed mask of glossed dough where his face had been. It made it difficult to guess at his age, but Luken would have said early forties, his wan yellow ando betraying a fashion no longer popular at Court, though it looked expensive. "I'm glad you could invite them, though I daresay they are used to finer settings than my humble home."

Isaun bowed his head. "Koko, Second Son of the Verdant Fen. We are honored to make your acquaintance."

"And this, of course, is my Lady Tilar." Koko held up a hand, presenting a woman scarcely taller standing than she had been sitting. A weathered, chinless face, marked by beady eyes and a grave expression, surveyed Luken and Isaun with complete disinterest, though she jerked into a cordial bow before resuming her seat.

"Your home is lovely," Luken said, and felt a squirming sensation in his stomach when Koko beamed with pleasure at his comment. *If only you knew who I really was*, Luken thought, amazed by the strangeness of it all.

"Sit, sit," Koko beckoned to them, "we are only waiting for two more now."

Luken and Isaun took the empty seats beside Satomi. Surveying the rest of the table, Luken found a mix of older courtesans and Ladies who may have been Palace officials, by the cut of their coats. Satomi and Koko's mutual friend proved to be Xinsey, a spectacularly beautiful courtesan with fair skin and raven-black hair, who shared an Abode with Satomi. From the recesses of Luken's memory, where the lineages of the Noble Houses were forever engraved thanks to his devoted studies during his early days at Court, it came to him that Xinsey, being the First Son of the House of the Golden Fox, was a paternal cousin of Koko's. *We are all connected somehow.* Distaste twitched at Luken's lip as he realized that, tracing the lineages back far enough, even he and Koko may share a common ancestor, somewhere in the mists of history.

Lady Weim, and a friend who Luken could tell at once had been invited because Xinsey was courting her, appeared to complete the guest list, sitting snug between Xinsey and Koko on the far side of the table. Isaun's hand tightened into a fist in his lap.

Koko rose to pour wine for Luken and Isaun, and as he walked away, Luken leaned into Isaun and muttered behind his sleeve, "I'm going to drink like a fish tonight."

Isaun glanced at Weim before deliberately fixing his attention on his wine glass. "Is there any other way?"

The courtesans clinked their glasses together, and took a long sip.

"Lady Asang was just describing her journey from the House of the Stone Cliffs."

Asang snorted. "Not much to tell, really. It's a dull journey, rained most of the time, turned all the roads to mud and slush. Quite miserable, actually."

Luken leaned forward to gain a better look at the woman. "You're in town for the meeting of the Noble Assembly, Lady Asang?"

She lifted a scornful gaze to meet his. Luken could tell at once the Lady was Satomi's mother. The resemblance was uncanny; she bore his angular, high cheekbones and blue-green eyes, though her face was freckled, sallow, and absolutely mirthless. Her hair was the same shade of flaming red, kept in tight, bouncing curls that might have been humorous on anyone else, but the look in the Lady's eye was enough to kill any laughter at her expense well before it began.

"Indeed." She took a gulp from her wineglass that put his and Isaun's to shame. "I came well ahead of time, though, to see my son." She jerked her head at Satomi, a scarlet curl bouncing. "Normally, I'd try to spend as little time at Court as possible, of course, but I've not seen Tomi in years now."

Koko's eyebrows rose. "Not a fan of the Court, Lady Asang?"

"You could say that." She rolled the stem of the wine glass between her fingertips, watching the wine swirl. "I sent them my son, they sent me back a brain-damaged twit. He'd forget to dress in the morning if a servant didn't chase him around with an ando. And what do I get out of it? Half a dozen grandsons with bouncy red hair? I'm glad they're all boys. Why should any other House get anything useful from me? They took my son. They can enjoy watching the Court ruin their sons too."

The dinner guests sat there, faces blanched, eyes wide.

Satomi tittered and gave his wine an audible slurp. "Oh Mama, the things you say!"

Luken found himself grinning like mad. "Lady Asang, it is *wonderful* to make your acquaintance."

She lifted her gaze to his, her grin wolfish. "And you're the Empress's boy, are you? My Satomi says you're the cleverest courtesan at the Peacock Court."

"A low bar, to be sure," Isaun muttered, eliciting a titter of laughter. His gaze lingered on his wine, electing not to notice Lady Weim staring at him across the table, a frown carving her features, a dark simmer to her eyes.

Luken smiled. "The Empress has been kind to me."

"What a politic answer."

Servants purled from the kitchen, laying plates of chicken breast and toasted almond salad before the diners.

"Speaking of the Court, Luken," Koko leaned across the table. "I'm curious about your perspective, given your *ah*, unique position." Beside him, Lady Tilar rolled her eyes and carved into her chicken breast, her knife scraping the plate. "They say the Court uses men. I think men use the Court." He leaned back with a smug smile, as if awaiting applause for this observation.

Luken pushed a smile to the surface. "Well, Koko, given my *ah*, unique position, I think answering that question would give a bit too much away."

Immune to sarcasm, Koko chuckled. "Good point."

"Beware, Lord Luken," Lady Tilar said around

a mouth of chicken, "Koko will talk your ear off about the Court, now that he's no longer in it."

"Well, darling," with a forced lightness to his voice, Koko looked anywhere but at his Lady, "a man can't help but look back on his glory days. I mean," a tinkling laugh as Koko reached for his wine, "things just aren't quite the same once a man goes from courtesan to Consort, are they?"

"You can say that again," she muttered, fork and knife *clink, clinking* against the plate as she sawed at her chicken.

They hate each other, Luken realized, gaze flicking back and forth between them with interest. Dead smiles, on both faces.

"Speaking of Consorts," Lady Weim lifted her voice above the murmur of the table, black eyes boring into Isaun, "where will you be taking up as Consort, Isaun? I mean, now that you're at retirement age. Have you any offers?" A bitter, bullying plea.

Still not looking at her, Isaun took a long sip before answering. "I have scarcely thought of it, my Lady."

A strained smile. "Perhaps you should."

Isaun's mouth twitched with unspoken words.

"Isaun has no shortage of clients," Luken said. Isaun turned a murderous look on him. Luken ignored him, giving Weim a cold smile. "You know how busy he is, these days."

"Is that right?" Weim asked, flat, and turned back to her companion, engaged in conversation with Xinsey.

"Don't antagonize her," Isaun whispered in Luken's ear, "she'll only retaliate."

"Who cares what she does?" Luken hissed back.

"This chicken is positively delectable," Satomi chirped, oblivious to the cords of tension running taut at the table.

A tug, at Luken's skirts.

He looked down to find a boy of about five years old staring at him. A halo of dark curls framed his head, his large, dark eyes so like Koko's.

"Oh! Hello there," Luken said, awkward with surprise.

The boy lifted up a cameo of Luken's own portrait, gripped in both hands.

"He wants an autograph," Koko said dryly, adding, "although he's supposed to be in bed by now."

Luken took the cameo and the pen the boy poked at him. Smiling shyly, Luken signed the portrait while Koko's chair scraped back and he swept around the table. He handed Koko's son the portrait. The boy gripped the gilded frame to his chest as Koko put a hand on his shoulder and led him away. "Come on, Yaney." He flashed Luken a weary grin. "Back to bed." Luken watched the father and son slip down a long hallway, a strange feeling in his chest. An ache of – what? Envy? Anger? Guilt?

The feeling, confusing and detached, that it was not too late to cancel his next appointment with Doctor Ence.

Luken leaned across the table. "Excuse me, do you have a restroom?"

Lady Tilar jerked a thumb over her shoulder. "Third door on the right."

Luken slipped away from the table, the hallway

a blur around him. Once inside, his back hit the door and he bowed over at the waist. A long breath hissed between his teeth.

"What am I doing here?" he muttered at his reflection in the mirror over the counter.

When he emerged, the murmur of conversation and the light of the dining room shone at the far end of the hallway. A nauseous crawl stirred in his stomach, and Luken jerked away. The sooner he could get off these pills, the better. Luken wandered into the darkness, letting the cool air in the lonelier rooms of the house caress the heat from his face. In the back of his mind, Luken noted a shabbier quality to the more remote rooms, but it barely registered. Walking as though through dense fog, Luken found an office in the back of the house and let himself in. A lone lantern flickered on the desk, a fountain pen seeping a slow, black stain across a loose pile of papers. A spike of hatred dug through Luken's heart, the sensation dulled through the fog. *So, this is where you write your books, is it Koko?*

He came around to the far side of the desk, nudging the chair out of the way with his foot, and spread the pages from the pile, gazing down at a vista of angular script on snow-white. Luken plucked a page at random and lifted it so that the lantern's amber light flickered to illuminate the black scrawl from beneath. He began to read, expecting a hot rush of contempt to wash him clean of all uncertainty but-

Luken read the first few sentences in a rush, then stopped, a crease forming between his brows, went back, and read more slowly, with dawning fascination.

This was not Koko's office. It was Lady Tilar's.

And this was not some rudimentary work from Koko's next manuscript. It was a letter. From Tilar, to Koko.

Koko –

Since you will not heed my plea to end this with dignity, and leave of your own accord, I do not know how else to explain to you what I have already said a thousand times before. You do not listen. And since, when I speak, you hear only what you choose to hear, I am forced to do this in writing, in hopes that you will, finally, understand me.

Luken drew a sharp breath. Heat returned to his cheeks for a different reason. He edged to the door, glanced out, then cautiously eased the door shut. He couldn't have been gone that long, they wouldn't miss him for a few more minutes. He hoped.

Luken quickened to the desk and seized the pages of the letter, shuffling the loose sheafs together, and read.

In startling black and white, Tilar laid out a squalid array of dirty secrets; Luken had never read anything so quickly in his life. His eyes flicked from line to line with rapt wonder: *And do not think me so stupid as to not guess you added the cook's assistant to your list of pathetic affairs. Now you know why the girl was dismissed so quickly. What a feat of whoredom that was. Between the two of us, we got her in and out of a job in less than a fortnight. Rest assured, I have paid you back in full with the gardener's son. Did you know about that one yet?*

"Goddess," Luken whispered, almost giddy with the perverse entertainment scratched in black strokes against the page. But, as the letter continued, his amusement drained away. A darker note entered

238

the narrative, until Luken's heart pounded at the mention of bruises left in flesh and unwanted sons, one after the next, while two strong wills went to war over the fate of the third son; Tilar had wanted to devote the third son to the army, but Koko had refused to let him go – refused his Lady's will – and every day since then had added another battle to that endless war. Every day, for five years.

It sounded as if Tilar had tried to end their relationship many times, but Koko had refused to leave. And, on the single occasion when Koko actually had left, Tilar had begged him to come back – *and Goddess how I regret inviting you back, every damned day of my life I burn with regret.* Koko's Consort contract must be airtight, to allow him that.

There were mentions, here and there, of Koko choosing notoriety over Tilar, and obvious bitterness over Koko's fame and the time he spent writing. *Maybe he actually does write all those books himself,* Luken thought, surprised that Koko had chosen a career over his Lady's regard. But given the state of their relationship, perhaps it was not so surprising. He shuffled through the pages.

It went on and on, an epic of squalor.

But the last page, when Luken reached it, cut off abruptly, with a blot of ink smeared across a half-finished sentence, as if Tilar had abandoned the letter after a sudden interruption, and not been able to return. But there, emblazoned in the bottom corner of the letter, was the seal of the House of the Swift Nimbus: a cloud bent into the wind against a bright blue sky, but underscored with a broad shield, the symbol of Kuiken, the Mother Goddess, which distinguished Tilar's seal from the main branch of her House.

Luken stared at the white of the empty page.

Then he folded up the pages, and tucked them into a pocket in the sleeve of his ando before making his way back to the party.

~

As Luken returned to the dining area, the servants whisked scavenged plates away from the table while the guests rose, drifting to the bar in the adjacent sitting room, where the rattle of a tumbler filled the air. Luken longed to join them, craving a drink to steady his nerves. But as he entered the dining room, he found Lady Weim and her friend lingering beside the table, their heads bent in tense conversation.

Luken sighed. He hated confrontation but it was easier, for some reason, to be brave on Isaun's behalf, than on his own.

"Lady Weim."

Her head jerked toward him, black eyes narrowing.

"I'd like a word with you, if you don't mind."

An acidic grin eased its way across her pale lips. She nodded to her friend, and the Lady trooped past Luken, leaving him alone in the dining room with Lady Weim.

He kept his voice low; unthreatening, but determined. "You know what I am going to say to you. It isn't meant to be, you and Isaun. I must ask that you stop trying to contact him."

Weim stared at him, her gaze flat and unsettling. A dismissal as complete as oblivion. "Noted." She strode away, her shoulder knocking his arm in passing.

Anger whipped through his chest. He pivoted, gripped her arm. She twisted around, teeth bared in a sneer.

"It's enough, Weim. Leave him be."

Her eyes narrowed to slivers. "You think just because you're licking the Empress's cunt you can give me orders? You must be dumber than you look."

Luken's blood rushed, scalding. "Darling, at least I've got a cunt to lick. You're chasing a man who wants nothing to do with you, and I've seen him fuck grandmothers. Let it go, Weim. This is sad."

The air left her lungs in a hiss. "Don't talk to me about what's sad, dog-fucker. I'd have had Isaun a dozen times over by now if he wasn't obsessed with Oan – who will *never*," she bit off the word, "want him."

"Noted," Luken spit back at her. But as she turned her back to him, the rage roared to overcome him. "And don't call me dog-fucker again, asshole. I've never even met your mother, let alone fucked her."

Weim stopped. He saw her shoulders tense, her spine run rigid. In a soft voice, she said, "You think the Empress will protect you. Maybe she will. Or maybe both you and Isaun will regret how you've treated me."

"You're not entitled to anything from him."

"Then he'll get what he gets."

She stormed away from him.

Luken rolled his eyes. It was hardly the first time a jilted client had made vague threats against a courtesan. Usually, it was all just talk. Pointless cruelty, designed to punish and degrade, so that a wounded ego could regain a brittle sense of power. The kind of pathetic nonsense courtesans dealt with every day. But as Luken rejoined Isaun by the bar, an uneasy weight settled in his core, and lingered.

Chapter Nineteen

"What are you going to do?"

Seito returned the letter to the center of the desk between them. Her cat, a longhaired and wonderfully obese tabby, leaped up onto her lap.

Luken chewed his lip. "I don't know. What do you think?"

Seito blew out a long breath, scratching her tabby's chin. The morning light, weakened by a veil of clouds, fell in silvery bars across the breadth of her desk in the *Ages* office building. Rori stood at the window, a faint aura of stolen light illuminating his dark hair.

"The letter bears Lady Tilar's personal seal," Seito said, after a thoughtful pause. "If we publish it in the magazine, they cannot deny its authenticity. The affairs, the unsavory name-calling, Koko threatening Lady Tilar over the third son – all Koko's dirty laundry."

"They could sue," Luken warned.

"Possibly." Seito gave the tabby one last pet as he jumped up onto the surface of the desk and strolled across to sniff at Luken. "But I've been in this business long enough to know my way around a lawsuit. The letter can be authenticated, so a libel charge can't be substantiated. It's only libel if it's not true. They could try to get us on a violation of privacy, but if we redact the names, there's nothing they can do. There was a very similar case, years back, in which a Lady's salacious diary was stolen and published. The thief was fined for stealing, but the heftier lawsuits fell apart. And the letter itself," she held up the pages, "well, I'm happy to repay Lady Tilar three dennys for the cost of the paper and ink."

Unease squirmed in Luken's belly. "You'd be willing to take on a lawsuit over this?"

He was able to pet the tabby twice before the cat bit Luken's finger and jumped down from the desk.

Seito shook her head. "I'd have to discuss it with my colleagues first. But if the names and identifying markers on the seal are redacted, I really don't think they have a case. Kanain laws are fairly loose when it comes to that sort of thing. And we have the right to protect our sources. No one will know it came from you."

Rori's voice drifted to them from the window. "People will know its Koko. The letter mentions his books, his notorious politics... They'll put it together, with or without the names redacted."

"Of course," Seito nodded. Her gaze returned to Luken. "Really Luken, the question is, are you willing to release the document?"

Luken's fingertip traced the fleur-de-lis woven in silver on the jade green of his ando's skirts. "It would devastate Koko's reputation. His entire brand is predicated on the most Traditionalist view of gender." He reached the end of the fleur-de-lis's curved petals, and started again. "All those details about Koko pushing Lady Tilar around over their sons – it defies the very basis of the mother-controlled household. His fans wouldn't like that. Not to mention the hypocrisy of Koko having argued for the dominion and primacy of the mother all these years, and the so-called natural place of the man. The fact that they have three sons to begin with, and Koko wouldn't allow Lady Tilar to do the proper thing and devote the third to the military… No, Traditionalists wouldn't like that at all. The affairs, the physical fights, that's all damning, but the business with the third son: in the mind of a Traditionalist, that's the coup de grace." Luken's gaze traced the jagged handwriting, inscribed like knife-strokes into the pages of the letter. "They don't care if Koko's dishonest, or even a hypocrite, as long as he plays the role they like him to play and says the things they want him to say. But this proves he hasn't been playing by their rules. Once he offends the Traditionalists – instead of offending everyone else on their behalf – they will recoil and lash out ten times worse than anyone else Koko has had to deal with before. When he makes someone else look bad, they applaud. When he makes *them* look bad, they'll scream as if the world is ending in blood and flame. They'll harass him out of O-Han."

Rori turned his back to the window, approaching with the light gilding half his features. "It will be the end of his career."

Seito nodded. "It's up to you, Luken. You brought us the letter. Do you want to release it?"

Luken sighed, and pressed his fingertips to his temples. "Goddess, I don't know. I genuinely believe that Koko's propaganda makes the world a worse place. But… aren't men humiliated enough in our society?" Ohfene's rumors tickled the back of Luken's brain, and a familiar blossom of shame spread its petals. *Dog-fucker,* Weim had hissed. "I don't know if I want to be the cause of more of that."

Rori and Seito traded a look at the edge of his vision.

"If anyone deserves it," Rori murmured, "it's Koko."

"Perhaps."

A heavy *clunk.* Luken jumped, and twisted in his chair. The tabby cat raced away from the bookcase, the tome he had wrestled off the shelf tumbling after him. The fluff that tipped his tail white vanished beneath Seito's desk. Chuckling to himself, Rori moved to push the book back into place. As if woken from a dream, an easy humor warmed Rori's voice once again. "Do you suppose Koko and *The Easterner* would angst over the morality of it if they had one of our secrets to expose?"

Seito snorted. "They'd rip us to shreds in a heartbeat, and do it cackling and praying and patting each other on the back."

Luken sighed. "You're right, of course. You're both right. And even now, Koko is writing more propaganda, preparing more ignorance for the world, all wrapped up in a bow like chocolates in a box. Ready to be swallowed. But," he wavered, as the tabby cat leaped up into Seito's lap again, "I need to think about it."

Seito pushed the letter back towards Luken. "Take your time." She cocked her head. "Just not too long. The truth always comes out eventually. But a good secret can only be sold once."

Chapter Twenty

The secretary's bland, malicious smile and wide, amphibian eyes stared through Luken for so long he began to wonder when she would need to return to the swamp to submerge again beneath the algae-muddled waters and rehydrate for another day of glaring men into nonexistence. Luken sighed, and shifted against the discomfort of the cheap chair. He and Rori had returned to the clinic for his second appointment, but it was Rori who had vanished into the doctor's office on this occasion to attest to Luken's sanity.

I will owe him for the rest of my life, Luken thought. He stared at the wall, ignoring the secretary. He did not doubt this would take an excessively long time.

Murmurs, from down the hall. Shadows swiveled across the beige wall at the far end of the hallway. A voice, a woman's voice, tickled Luken's ear; familiar, though he could not immediately place it. Luken stood, and made his way to the desk. "Excuse me, what's in that room down the hall?"

"That would be Doctor Nalay's office. She specializes in female reproductive resources."

Again, that familiar voice. A murmur, the words too low to hear.

"Thank you." In tentative steps, Luken made his way down the short hallway and found a larger waiting room, sunlight pouring through the twin windows in the far wall. A few women waited here, some with small children seated on their laps or tinkering with the brightly painted blocks and dolls that sprawled across the table in the center. In the nearest chair, a woman in her late twenties with Ennish features of tan skin and dark brown hair and eyes, sat alone with a book open in her lap.

Luken drew a breath. "Kenze?"

She looked up, eyes widening, and cursed under her breath. "Luken? What are you doing here?"

A few women cast curious looks in Luken's direction. He took a seat beside his half-sister, grateful that she had sat at the end of the row so that he could turn his body away from the rest of the room. He wore peasant's garb again, forsaking his courtesan's paint, but the possibility of recognition remained, especially now that his portrait seemed to be sold across half the city; he could not drive through the marketplace without peeking out of his carriage to find little mirrors of himself, gazing back.

"I should ask you that question," he whispered back, "last I checked, you were at the House." He darted a glance over his shoulder, but the other women in the room were preoccupied with their children or their books. "Can you keep a secret?"

She arched an eyebrow. "Who would I tell? The only person I know in O-Han is you."

He whispered, "I'm getting a vasectomy."

"Is that all? I thought you'd picked up syphilis or something. You'd not be the first courtesan to sneak off into the city for a problem the Garden gave you."

He cocked his head. "You're not offended?"

"Over a vasectomy? Please. Think a little higher of your sister, Luken. I'm not living in the Iris Age."

"I'm used to being around people who are... a bit more resistant to the idea."

She shrugged. "But why would you want one? Mother used to read us the letters you wrote to her from U-Wen, after your daughter was born. I got the impression you loved being a father."

Luken grasped after words, and could not find any. His mother had read his letters to his half-sisters? But even more surprising – Kenze had cared enough to take note of that? He'd always thought his half-siblings indifferent to him, even hostile.

"I did love being a father," Luken murmured, "but there is a huge difference between impregnating a woman and being a father. If I can't be a father, I don't want- I don't want my children to grow up without me. I don't want to be used."

"I understand."

You don't, really, Luken thought. But sympathy warmed her gaze, and he was thankful for that.

"But what are you doing here? You could have told your own brother you were visiting O-Han, I would have let you stay with me."

She shook her head. "This isn't a vacation, Luken. I'm here to get an abortion."

Luken blinked, taken aback. Fertility obsessed the Ladies of Kanai to such a degree that abortion, while available, was rare in the Empire. The more children a woman produced, the higher her Acclaim, the greater influence she commanded in her community, the more her authority was trusted, and the more her will was obeyed. The Mother Goddess was the chief deity of the Kanain pantheon for a reason.

"After paying all that money for a courtesan? Why?"

She sighed. "To be frank, Luken, the House is strained to provide a good future for the children it already has."

"No it isn't–" Luken said at once, then, seeing the look on her face, leaned back, glanced around the room, and leaned toward her again. "What are you talking about?"

She shook her head, a grim smile on her lips. "Mother never told you. I suppose she wanted to spare you the distress. It's not your concern, after all." Kenze sighed. "The truth is, Luken, the House of the Pear Blossom is near enough bankrupt."

"No," Luken breathed. "How is that possible?"

"It's been a bad season."

"But next year–"

"It's been quite a few bad seasons, Luken. Poor yields on the orchards, investments going bad." She closed her eyes. "It's not Mother's fault. She led the House to financial prosperity for decades. It's only in the past few years that things started to go badly, but once the ball started rolling downhill, well, it picked up speed. When things go to shit, they go quickly." A bitter laugh. Then, after a pause, "The investments were sound, they shouldn't have gone belly up. The orchards were well tended, they shouldn't have– Well, it doesn't matter. We did everything we could do, but one can't control five years of bad fortune, one after another. The goddesses have their own plans, regardless of ours."

Luken shook his head. "I don't believe it. We can't be broke."

She gave him a wry look. "We? From what I hear, you're doing better than any of us. The Empress's concubine," she said softly, and took up his hand between hers, rolling his diamond ring between her fingers so that it shone in the light, glinting at them.

Luken flushed. "I'll sell my jewelry."

"Don't be stupid." She gave his hand a gentle squeeze. "They belong to you, you earned them."

"Not really."

She ignored that. "I daresay we can provide for ourselves. All the Daughters of the House are going out on expedition or to work. Csin is moving to A-Dul to work in Aunt Tsapa's hospice. Tian is waiting until after she gives birth to meet with that Sworn Sister of hers, Ren, to plan their next expedition. Your brother Kenris is moving back to the Palace to become an Abode Master and generate a little income; I'm told you can make good money at it, if you've got decent courtesans."

Luken laughed; wind howling through a cracked vase. "If you're lucky, yes. But this is crazy." He ripped off the ring and held it up to her. "Take it. Yellow diamonds are rare, you should get good money for it."

"Luken-"

He fiddled at his ears and came away with pearls, gleaming on their thin, silver chains, and pressed them into her hands. She balled her fingers into fists and jerked away from him. "Luken, please-"

"Just take them. I don't need them."

"Luken. The House is 300,000 bohda in debt."

The breath left his body.

She nodded. "I know. But we have a large staff, and they still need to eat, even in lean years. Even when the investments go bad. And that number climbs every day. Selling your earrings isn't going to do anything. That's just a drop in the pail."

"At least take the diamond. I'm pretty sure it's worth a lot."

Kenze chuckled. "You're as stubborn as your father, aren't you?" She held up the diamond. "Got this from the Empress?"

"Yes."

"It might be worth more, for that. Thank you, Luken. I'll sell it before I leave O-Han. It'll be nice to bring some money back to the House, instead of more debt. I'll tell Mother you did this."

"I understand that the House is strained, but do you really want this abortion?"

"It's what's best for the family right now, and for me. Besides, I have my daughter. I have Aifin. I don't care what anyone says, she's all I need." Her eyes flicked up to his face, searching. "Do you really want this vasectomy?"

"Yes."

With a small smile, Kenze laid the back of her hand to his cheek. "I haven't seen you without your courtesan's paint since you were a kid."

"Kenze Kenkazu-daughter?" Doctor Nalay's secretary called from behind her desk.

Kenze stood, and Luken followed suit. "It was good to see you, Luken. This is the last place I thought

I'd run into you, but I'm glad I did."

"The same for me."

She embraced him, and Luken watched his half-sister stride into the doctor's office. A pang of jealousy, that her abortion was treated like what it was: a medical procedure, obtained for an adult with privacy and respect. Meanwhile, he had waited over a month for a chance to have his friend insist on his sanity so that he could continue pleading with a doctor for a vasectomy.

With a sigh, Luken returned to Doctor Ence's waiting room.

When at last the door eased open, Rori emerged, shaken, but not without a wobbling grin to offer Luken.

"Now I know what it's like to be arrested on suspicion of murder," Rori murmured in his ear while they passed each other at the door, and Luken took his place in the doctor's office.

Still hollowed out by what Kenze had told him, Luken barely heard the doctor as she reviewed her interview with Rori. A hum in Luken's skull.

"Are you going to write my prescription now?" he asked, once the droning finally ceased.

"Oh no." A smile. "No."

"Why?"

"The psychological reference is an important part of the process, yes, but by no means the only step. I cannot, in good faith, give you a prescription without first obtaining signed permission from your mother." She slid a piece of paper across the desk.

Deep embarrassment rankled him at the thought of telling his mother he wanted a vasectomy.

"This has nothing to do with my mother."

The doctor cocked her head. "Of course it does. You're killing her grandchildren. She deserves a say in that."

Luken found himself on his feet, though he did not remember standing. "You are falsely accusing me of murder, trying to humiliate me in front of my own mother," he seized the document from the table, unable to even read its black script through the rage that blurred his vision, "trying to bully me into letting your agenda govern my body, and still–" he hissed, watching her face go still, a mask of hostility, "*still* I am getting this fucking vasectomy. One way or another."

He spun on his heel and left the office, slamming the door behind him.

"When is the next available appointment?" he asked the secretary.

With the same dead smile, she calmly flipped through her book, the pen in her left hand tap, tap, tapping against the desk. "Oh, that's gonna be another five weeks at least, sweetheart."

Through gritted teeth, Luken said, "Make the appointment."

~

The eye of the storm. A calmness shiver-shot with chaos before, chaos after. Static expectation, swallowing the last of relief.

Luken felt that eye peel open within him, gazing out at the storm.

Broke. In debt. The House of the Pear Blossom, tilting on the brink.

Even now, part of him did not believe it. Yet...

Details clicked into place, a larger image suddenly becoming clear.

Why had he never questioned his father's hunger for money and fine things, though he lived in a Middling House? His mother was a generous woman, yet her Consorts wore faded andos, struggling against the shabbiness of what was allotted to them. The guesthouse, left to languish in disrepair until Luken had paid for its renovation. Luken had been sent to Court with only one ando to his name, borrowing clothes from Isaun and Lifelle for months after his arrival, until he could afford his own. His sisters had paid the Conjugal Prices for their courtesans from the earnings of their expeditions, but none had stayed on as Consort. Luken had just assumed it was his family's way, a product of his parent's indifference to him. The children, expected to bear those responsibilities, though other Houses sent their boys to Court with a full wardrobe of andos. Luken had been sending his father money from his earnings for years, and not once had it occurred to him that his father never should have asked him for that; it was the Lady of the House's job to provide for her men. He had just assumed it was proper, the children sending their father a fraction of their earnings. He had just assumed, and never asked his mother...

Strange, how a man could get used to anything. Could breath it in until it was so deep in his blood he forgot what it was like to be without it. But it never should have been there to begin with.

The House of the Pear Blossom. Broke.

Luken sighed.

Everything rose only to fall.

Chapter Twenty-One

Luken lifted the small pot from its warmer, and dripped oil on his cock. He stood over the bed, the Empress gazing up at him, her dark eyes alight. He pressed back inside her, the oil slick and hot between them.

"Oh," he breathed, lids fluttering half-shut.

A grin. "Do you love it?"

"Yes." He set to work, shallow strokes that led deeper. "I love it." He moaned the words, let them drip like honey from his lips.

With her thighs parted around him, her bare breasts shivering with each thrust, her eyes half-lidded, luxuriant, the Empress of Kanai was like any other woman. Her tastes simple, when it was just the two of them. "It's so good." Whisper, sweet and strained.

"Mm."

"What feels so good?"

"My cock." Low, desperate.

Contorting to fuck her harder, hair a tawdry tumble over his shoulders, down his back, a diamond hair-clasp fallen askew. Her dark eyes glittered, roaming his body. How she loved to see him in disarray.

Too well-made to squeak, the bed gave a silent shudder with each thrust. Raisaga rode the quake, back lifting from the sprawl of deep purple sheets beneath her. A long, leisurely fuck in the darkness and density of the cavernous bedroom, lit by only a dozen scattered candles.

"I need to come," he whimpered, "oh Goddess, I need-" Ecstasy spasmed up his spine and he lost himself inside her, drawing a sharp breath through clenched teeth.

"Luken," she sighed, watching him with quiet delight.

Panting, he collapsed to his knees before her, like a priest at his devotions, and paid obeisance with lips and tongue. Her fingers knotted in his hair, tugging at the threads until she gasped, and released a long sigh.

A few panting moments.

She never lingered long, Raisaga. The Empress rose and moved to the set of dark blue trousers, white blouse, and coat resting on a hanger within her closet, and slipped from view. She emerged, shrugging into the coat, while Luken lay sprawled across her bed, his black hair a mass beneath his head. Luken loved the way the three-quarters length coat swept to settle over her calves, the final foot of soft velvet woven with a tracery of golden fretwork to highlight the dark blue.

"Are you leaving me already?" He stretched, nothing but luxury to greet his limbs, the hardness of his muscles finding only silken softness.

"Alas, there is still much preparation to be done for the Noble Assembly." She sat at the edge of the bed, gazing down at him.

"You don't sound excited."

Raisaga chuckled. "To welcome nearly a hundred headstrong Ladies, each bearing the grievances and prejudices of her own region to one location so we can all fight over the future of the Empire? No, I'm not particularly excited."

About six months after the election of the Convention, the Ladies of each Noble House in Kanai traveled to the capital to propose, debate, and ultimately vote to approve or reject whatever laws and measures were brought to the table. Typically, the Traditionalists and Reformists each formed their own coalition of Ladies who determined the party's agenda, and formed a slate of proposals to introduce at the Assembly. Luken's only prior experience with the Assembly was watching as a child as his mother left the House and vanished for weeks at a time, not knowing when she would return or why she was gone, for no one had thought to tell him or imagined that he would care. Boys need not trouble themselves about politics.

"It'll be all about Builay this year," the Empress sighed. "That blabbering idiot, Hani, told me as much when she swung by my study to harangue me about it yesterday. It will be the centerpiece of their agenda at this Assembly. The Traditionalist coalition will propose expanding our military presence to Olmpuay, the capital of Builay. Presumably as a peace-keeping force, but inevitably, it will lead to a protracted military suppression of the seditious local populace and, when we have bred enough enemies for ourselves, full blown war and the ultimate absorption of Builay into the Empire when peace comes – ten or twenty years from now, if we're lucky. In the meantime, blowhards like Hani will keep getting elected by trading in nationalist rhetoric and fear-mongering. A neat little strategy, if you care nothing for the lives of our soldiers or the effects of endless war on our people." She shook her head. "I'm getting tired of being the Empress of War. When we began withdrawing troops from Hindigga, I promised the people I'd bring our boys home – not send them to some rocky coast on the far side of the world with rotten fruit broken on the sands beneath strange, wax-leafed trees and monkeys gibbering at them like lunatics in the shadows."

Luken pushed himself upright and slipped from the bed. He went to the closet, gathered up her stockings and shoes, and knelt before her, slipping the stockings over her feet, watching the delicate blue veins that twined the tops of her feet, her ankles, vanish beneath the fabric. His hands gentle. "You, Raisaga, are not the Empress of War. You are the daughter of the great Aikanzo," he slipped the shoe over her foot, "the great Liliray," the second slipped on, "and I am proud to call you my Empress." He looked up at her, and found her gaze tender. "They found a way. We can too."

"Luken." She cupped his face in her hands. "You are worth more to me than silver or gold." The flutter of her lips to his forehead. Luken let his eyes fall shut. It was hard to deny, he savored her affection now more than ever. He'd underestimated how much he would miss this, this easy, loving warmth, without Jes dancing at the border of all his experiences. She'd been right about one thing: he'd taken her for granted. The simple pleasures; her eyes on him, a knowing look that gave them passage into their own little world, the patient warmth of her love.

How fitting, that snow drifted past the windows

now as autumn coiled up and curled into winter's chill.

You could have waited til the spring before leaving me, Jes. He dragged his eyes open.

"Raisaga." Luken nuzzled into her palm, knowing well that Ladies liked it when a courtesan's paint 'accidentally' smudged their hands and necks and clothes – and liked it even more when other Ladies noticed the tell-tale smudge of powder blue. "I do have a favor to ask."

"Oh? And what could you need? Clothes perhaps," she added, glancing down at his body.

Luken chuckled. "I've been thinking things over, talking to some of my friends."

"Mm?"

"I was wondering if perhaps – it's such a small thing, I am embarrassed to request it – it's only that men think of such things, you know."

"What is it?" She stroked a hand through his hair, her gaze soft with affection.

Now or never. "Could you, maybe just, deem waiting periods and maternal permission regulations for vasectomy procedures a violation of reproductive healthcare access laws? Please?"

She blinked. "I-" Raisaga laughed. "What?"

He cocked his head. "It's so degrading, having to ask someone else's permission to not have any more children. Couldn't you just – spare my brothers the trouble?"

"Luken, why are you asking me this?" She chuckled. "I swear, you always say the last damned thing on earth I expected to hear."

"It's just, I've been talking to some of my male

friends, and it's quite a problem, you know, for some men. They think you could just," he snapped his fingers, "make it go away."

A sad smile. "It isn't that simple, Luken. Vasectomy access? That isn't really a priority right now."

Luken rose, and cast about for his under-robe. He found it, an off-white sheen smeared across the far side of the bed, and went to claim it. "Not a priority." He repeated the words with no inflection, and heard a sigh behind him.

"I am trying to keep the nation from war, Luken."

He shrugged into his under-robe. "As I understand it, banning foot-fanning was also not a priority. Not for a long, long time, before your mother got around to it. A lot of people suffered because that was not a priority-"

"Luken-"

He heard the anger coil like a viper in his voice. "But who cares, they were only boys. So it's not a priority."

"A lot of men are going to die in Builay, if I do not stop Ekaris and her crew from sending them to war."

He rounded on her, tying the under-robe at the waist with a tug. "If it's such an inconsequential thing, why can't it be dealt with easily? Just give the word."

How different, her gaze when she looked at him then. It was a wonder how quickly affections fled. But Luken was getting good at chasing them off, these days. "You want me to dredge up that landmine on the eve of the Assembly? Do you want me to lose all good-will among neutral Houses and moderate Traditionalists?"

"Who cares what they think?"

She shook her head. "You don't understand the political situation."

"You don't understand what it feels like to have control of your reproduction taken from you by the same government that is supposed to protect your rights. Raisaga, these indignities occur on your watch. Every single day. It may seem inconsequential to you, but people suffer because they cannot access the services that they have a right to. The services that are meant to be legal in this country, and are instead treated like a shameful crime. I would see my brothers treated with dignity."

"This is what I get for picking a smart one," she muttered, carding fingers through the iron strands of her hair.

Luken's fist clenched. "Next time, go with a housecat," he spat.

She startled, and looked up at him. Laughed gently. "Ah, is that what you think of me? Well, perhaps I deserve that." She stood, and came around to the side of the bed, standing before him. "There would be no *next time*, after you, Luken. Not for me. I'm an old woman. I wanted a comforting companion for my waning years. Something easy and pleasant with someone beautiful and carefree. The trouble is," a grin tugged at her mouth, "I went looking for seaglass, and I tripped over a diamond. Such a rare and splendid find. So beautiful and hard and brittle."

"I am not *brittle*," Luken muttered, but he let her place a hand on his shoulder.

She smiled. "Once you've been given diamonds, you don't settle for sea glass. You are my farewell to the realms of passion and tenderness. My swan song among men. There will be no others, after you. And no, I don't want a housecat. I want my fierce princeling with more brains than half the Assembly put together."

"And twice the Convention, now Hani's dragging their average down."

She chuckled. "Exactly. And I know you want to change things. I respect that. You push me, and perhaps that's good. Empresses become indolent, at my age. History has taught us that. The waning years of an Empress's reign lean into idleness and petulance. You might be just what I need to push me in the right direction. But you are also young and impatient. You expect change to come immediately, merely because I order it. It doesn't work like that. Change takes time."

"How can I trust that the right changes will be made when all the forces at work are pushing in the opposite direction?"

"You keep pushing in the right direction, and know that even if all the world crumbles around you, you will not be held back." Leaning in, the Empress kissed his cheek, and whispered in his ear, "And know that you are not alone." She pulled back, and winked. "I'll see what I can do."

A knock. Luken recognized it at once as Fi's swift, angry fist at the door.

Raisaga stepped back, giving him a final, conciliatory smile. "Come in."

Fi shoved inside, gave the rumpled bed a disgusted glance, and looked up, dark eyes darting between them. "Good, you're both here. You," she pointed at the Empress, "have a meeting with the Palace Steward about preparations for the Noble Assembly and the planning of the Spring Gala in ten minutes, and you," she jabbed a finger at Luken, "I need to speak with."

"Yes, yes," the Empress sighed, tugging her coat straight, "just a moment." She retrieved her crown from its resting place within the velvet-lined box on the desk, and lowering it down over iron locks, the Empress nodded to Luken, and strode from her chambers.

Luken folded his arms at his chest. "What on earth could you have to bother me about?"

Fi grinned, and swung the desk chair around. "Politics, of course." She plopped into the chair, and threw one leg over the other. "What else?"

Luken pulled his matte rose ando from its disheveled cocoon amid the bedsheets. "I have no place in politics, as I have been so recently reminded."

"Your enemies disagree."

Luken cocked an eyebrow. "Enemies?"

"Certain Ladies have begun asking questions about you. Some are merely curious, others cautious about a potential emerging factor. Others, openly suspicious of your influence over the Empress."

A bitter laugh as Luken shook the ando out. "I have no influence over the Empress. She will not do anything I ask."

"Don't be melodramatic. She thinks of you more than you know." A pause, as she considered him. "You're making more than one Lady nervous."

Luken drew the sleeves of his ando over his

arms and shrugged into it, giving Fi a flat look.

"Both too pretty and too clever." An ironic lilt to her lips. "A combination that would make any Lady nervous, but even that they would be willing to forgive if not for the fact that you're very obviously a Reformist, and born of a Reformist House. I've never heard the name Lady Kenkazu spoken so much in all my life."

Luken jumped. "My mother? She's nothing to do with any of this!"

Fi shook her head. "An Empress's Consort is only a mouthpiece of his mother's politics, remember? Sometimes that goes for concubines as well."

Luken scoffed. "Even in this, it is assumed I have no mind of my own."

"Oh, no one doubts what your thoughts are on the matter. Some of them consider you nothing less than an ingenious zealot who has planned this whole affair for Goddess-knows how long. Even that little tussle with Lord Ohfene that brought you to the Empress's attention is now considered staged."

"It's madness."

"It's politics."

"They must leave my mother out of it."

"From their perspective, they can't afford to do that. Lady Kenkazu has become a serious contender in Palace politics all of a sudden, and strategically, they must assume she is both a clever and – because of her debts – desperate enemy that has emerged at the eleventh hour to weaken Traditionalist control of the Palace."

"What did you say? Her debts?"

"You were unaware? That information has

become common knowledge at Court."

"Seven Hells…" A wave of faintness came over him. Luken collapsed onto the bed.

Fi surveyed him, eyes narrow. He yanked his ando tight around him.

"If you cannot handle the position, perhaps you should bow out, and give Aokinay peace of mind." She cocked her head. "He summoned you again the other day, but cancelled the order, feeling nauseous and disoriented. He's been ill lately, and did not want you to see him in a weakened condition."

"And what am I supposed to do with that information?" Luken snapped, hiding a flicker of guilt. "No, I am not forsaking my position. Especially after what the Empress just said to me."

Fi's tone dropped. "What did she tell you?"

Luken tucked a lock of hair behind his ear. "That there would be no others, after me."

"Really?" Fi focused on him with the intensity of a snake watching a mouse. "Interesting."

"In what way?"

A dark smile. "The last time the Empress said that, she was speaking to Aokinay."

Chapter Twenty-Two

Warm and sultry, with fits of storms and few surprises, O-Han rarely suffered more than a few weeks of true cold each year, and then only in the deep of winter. But the wind that howled at the windows, tossing flurries of snow at the Palace, seemed crueler than O-Han's languid wont. Luken could not travel the Palace's long hallways, or venture beneath its vaunted domes, without the sense that beyond stone and snow, a living thing assailed him; a spirit, knit from creaking ceilings, random surges of elemental power buffeting the walls, the dim flickering of light torn through cloud and snow, and the impotent, howling rage of the wind.

Normally Luken would not have stirred from the embrace of his chambers, but the Empress had not called on him for days, and in his listlessness, the solitude that had once been a pleasure, and a relief, slowly molded into loneliness. He found his thoughts turning to wilder nights, jagged with uncertain courtships and brief pleasures between stretches of polite tedium and stomach-turning degradation. At least Isaun and Lifelle had been with him then. Brothers in the night. And Jes- but that was too painful to think of. Whenever her face swam before his vision, a mist of merciful oblivion swelled through his mind, obscuring her.

Strange, how quickly the busy little nights of

youth transformed into a glory age of their own. Memory was a powerful alchemist.

He knew this, of course. Knew it was silly to pine for a time that had passed less than a year ago; a time rife with panic attacks and fits of scalding rage. A time of leering back into the face of contempt with the bravery of the young and wounded. He had not enjoyed those months while they occurred; why now did he feel the need to idealize them? But even the knowledge of what he was doing did not halt its progress.

And so it was that, bored and lonely, Luken left his chambers.

Luken wandered along a lovely set of corridors he had discovered on the north side of the Palace, where the winter light cast a somber mosaic of blue shades through the stained glass windows that lined the northern wall. Courtesans and Ladies bowed to him as he passed. He accepted them with an indifferent nod, knowing they paid their respects to the Empress, not him. He was only an extension of her, a blossom on the stalk. They did not, and never would, respect him as an individual. Cami and Sami shadowed him, so silent he scarcely knew of their presence. They were always with him now, during the day. A dreamy safety that comforted him without infringing on his thoughts.

It was into this contemplative walk that Dandy burst like a drunken hummingbird, stumbling over his robes, a great puff of orange and yellow, dark curls bouncing as his head twisted this way and that. His eyes went wide, landing on Luken, and he stumbled closer. "Luken!"

"Dandy? What's the matter?"

Luken took his arms, steadied the younger man.

Dandy shook his head. "Come see."

"See what? What's the matter?"

Again, Dandy shook his head, curls bouncing madly. He tugged at Luken's arms, pulling him away.

Dandy led him in a swift arc around the Palace's southwest perimeter, babbling between gulps of breath. "I don't know how this could have happened. I mean, Goddess, this much? For what-? It's not *fair*."

Luken gave up trying to interpret Dandy's breathless prattle and clung to his arm, hurrying through the Palace, their joh clacking on the tiles. He'd worn a voluminous ando of pearl-grey clouds and sweeping starlings across a pale blue background, with a tight irlan of startling scarlet in contrast, and regretted it now; lofty and dramatic with slow strides, the weight of it became an anchor the moment he quickened his pace. But as they swept into the southeastern stretch of the Palace, a horrible thought came to Luken, and stole over him with awful certainty.

Sure enough, Dandy led him into the Hall where the Market Board stood. A black obelisk, dominating the far wall. His stomach sank with a horrible, roiling sensation.

Dandy dragged him into the shadow of the Board and pointed, one gloved finger raised toward the top.

Eyes narrowed, Luken's gaze raked the placards of names and numbers. All the courtesans of the Court and the value of their flesh, bundled neatly for all to see. A stab of hatred spiked Luken's chest. He had not bothered to glance at the Board since his own name had been placed at Number One. He'd come once, alone, to gaze at it, to see that it was true – and then never again.

Until now. His own name hovered at One, towering over the rest, just as it had since he'd become the Empress's concubine.

His gaze fell lower, searching. Luken blinked. Where was Isaun's name, tucked snugly at Number Seven, as it had been for almost a year?

"Oh no..."

His chest tightened and tightened, the lower his gaze fell. "Where is-?"

The familiar figures, etched at 120.

Luken read the name on the placard, and then blinked again at the number beside it. 120.

Dandy stood beside him in agonized silence, wringing his hands together. "Those assholes," Dandy hissed, "those miserable assholes. How could they do this?"

From Number Seven, to Number One Hundred and Twenty.

"What on earth happened?" Luken breathed.

Dandy stamped his foot, mindless with anger. "It must be those filthy rumors. Oh but it's obviously not true. Can't the Arbiters see that?"

Luken wrapped his arms around his middle, as if holding himself together by manual force. "What rumors?"

"A friend of mine told me that Ohfene and his crew had put it about that Isaun was having an unregulated affair with Lady Weim."

Lady Weim. Anger and shock in Luken's mind, like a bloated body surfacing over a wrecked ship, drowned and engorged beyond recognition.

"But Ohfene always spreads rumors. He tried it with me just a little while back. People still make yipping and barking noises at my back when I walk by, but the Arbiters didn't lower my name on the Board."

Dandy shook his head. "You're a royal concubine. You have the Empress. Who is there to protect Isaun?"

Luken struggled to reel his thoughts in. He'd always known, of course, that the right rumor at the right time could wreck a courtesan's reputation. Arbiters were a savage lot; they did not wait to see if a courtesan would redeem himself. They just shoved him down the Board until he resigned himself to poor pay and Minor Ladies, or retired from the Court. But a courtesan of Isaun's magnitude? It's not as if he'd fallen from 300 to 400. Isaun had been a mainstay of the Top Ten for years now. He was one of the most famous working courtesans of their time. A fall from seven to 120.

"This is unheard of," he muttered. And then, with a bolt of dread, "Does Isaun know?"

Dandy's gaze drilled into Isaun's placard. "He checks the Board every morning. You know that."

They stood in silence.

Luken released a shaky sigh. "Arbiters hear rumors all the time, but they wouldn't knock a courtesan out of the Top Ten, down over a hundred places, over an idle rumor."

"So you think it's true?"

"Of course it's not true. Isaun would rather slit his wrists than do something that would jeopardize his standing on the Board. Lady Weim just seeks to punish him because she lusted after him, and he rejected her. Still chasing Princess Oan." A bitter grin. "No Lady likes to be passed over for a friend. Even a Princess. Hells, for all we know Princess Oan helped Weim convince the Arbiters."

"But an unregulated affair? Why?" Tears of anger budded in Dandy's eyes. "Why did it have to be that?"

"Why else? To humiliate him. Ambitious Isaun, savvy Isaun – giving it away for free. Thinking he could have it both ways. Thinking he gets to use his body outside of the Court's control and get away with it – only to be told, with vicious and unforgiving shame, that no, no he can't. They would think it very funny. Weim and Ohfene and the rest. Hilarious."

"But what proof could she have if it's not true?"

"I don't know. Perhaps she doesn't need much proof. The Arbiters don't like Isaun. The Son of a Minor House, roosting in the Top Ten. They've only been waiting for a reason to knock him down a peg, and Weim finally gave it them."

Luken drew a long breath to steady himself. "Come, we'd better go to the Abode."

~

Servants shoveled snow from the courtyards, tracing silver veins through the fleshy, fresh-fallen banks. Cami took Luken's arm, offering the support of his lean, muscled limbs, so that he could rush along the icy paths without slipping on his joh. Snowflakes dappled the air, then tapered off with a fitful purl, leaving the sky leaden and unsatisfied.

Luken clutched shivering hands together in the sleeves of his ando, chilled to the bone by the time they neared the diamond-shaped courtyard outside the Abode of Scattered Flowers. And the crowd of courtesans that surrounded it.

Raised voices sounded over the heads of the crowd. The wall of figures, in the lovely shades of their andos, blocked Luken's view of the courtyard. His breath quickened, and he pressed forward.

"Get out of my way!" he shouted.

A few courtesans glanced back at him, looking annoyed, but stepped aside, eyes going wide, once they recognized Luken. With Dandy and the guards behind him, Luken pressed into the courtyard.

It was like a tableau out of some Old Dynasty theater scene. Isaun, on the porch of the Abode, his long hair a dark chaos around him where it had tumbled loose of its arrangement. Lady Romyn, her face twisted with pained sympathy, lurched halfway up the steps, her hand on the railing. Her sister, Lady Jiren, stood on the far side of the courtyard; she'd been pregnant when Luken had last seen her, but now she gripped a small infant to her chest. Jiren watched the scene with wry amusement, ignoring the baby as it hiccupped weak sobs into the air, its pudgy face going pallid in the cold.

In the middle of the courtyard, beautiful and triumphant, stood Ohfene. His smile calm, but eyes agleam as they studied Isaun's distress. Resplendent in crimson, Luken's gaze lingered on Ohfene so long that he almost jumped when he noticed Lady Weim a few paces behind him in a furred cape and grey winter coat. Her features twisted with anger. She did not smile, but there was something almost erotic in the stark satisfaction of her gaze. This, in her mind, was the world being set right.

A chill traced Luken's body. Cami gripped him tighter.

"Are you not pleased, Isaun?" Ohfene lifted his voice so that he could be heard above the slither of wind that stirred the fresh snow to eddies around them. "You are the talk of the Court! This, I thought, is what you always wanted."

Luken was surprised the railing of the porch steps did not crack beneath Isaun's grip.

"You moved a 113 places on the Board in one day!" Ohfene rapped his hands in applause. With a shiver of laughter, more than a few courtesans clapped with him. "Of course," Ohfene spread his hands, "it was *down*, rather than *up*, but no matter. A record is still a record."

More laughter. Luken took a step forward and stopped, yearning an end to this and yet – Why didn't Isaun say anything? Eyes wide, jaw clenched, pale and chaotic, Isaun had the look of a hunted animal, pushed beyond endurance.

"Perhaps," Ohfene continued, glancing 'round as if amused by the crowd he had drawn, "if you apologized to the Court for the shame with which you've tainted it," his tone dripped condescension, "we all might find it in our hearts to pity you. Do you think that would move the Arbiters a little?"

Isaun glared back at him and, slowly, descended the first step. Lady Romyn shuffled aside for him, muttering something plaintive in passing; he ignored her.

"You've lied to the Arbiters, Ohfene. You and that bitter prick over there," Isaun jerked his head at Lady Weim, but did not spare her a glance. "Do you think this won't come back to you?" His voice shook with anger. "If my career is over, so is yours, Ohfene. Lying to the Arbiters is as bad as what you've accused me of – *falsely*, I might add," he spit at the crowd. Green eyes, vivid in the dull winter scene, lanced across the lines of gathered courtesans. "And you all know it. You know me. Maybe you hate me, but you know me." He turned, looking at each of their faces in turn. "You know what kind of courtesan I am. You know I had no *unregulated affair* with Lady Weim. Really," Isaun drew himself up scornfully, "do any of you believe that I – I, of all people – would skip a chance to make money?" Laughter, a few grins. Yes, they knew Isaun. "Trust me, if I were to jump in bed with that one, I would have made her pay for it."

More laughter, murmurs of agreement. Weim snarled with incoherent anger, but Ohfene held up a hand.

He waited until the onlookers quieted, then shrugged. "Men do dumb things when they let emotions override their primary function. Courtesans throw themselves away every day for one stupid reason or another. Is it so hard to believe that after all these years catering to others, you felt yourself entitled to a little something special behind the scenes?" Ohfene shook his head. "No, I don't think you're getting out of this one, Isaun. It's over."

Isaun turned to his rival, a strange expression

on his face. "Ohfene. Why are you doing this?"

Ohfene laughed, a fit of snowflakes twirling down through the air again, catching in hair the rare hue of honeyed amber. "What do you think Isaun? There are a thousand reasons that you deserve this."

Isaun's hands bunched into fists.

Ohfene cocked his head, his fervid gaze never leaving Isaun's face. Almost like lovers, enraptured of one another. "But if you really want to know, Isaun," he stepped forward, light over the silent snow, leaned in, and whispered something in Isaun's ear that made him go pale.

"You," Isaun breathed. Snow fell around them, like a white veil descending. And with no space between one moment and the next, Isaun had drawn back and punched Ohfene with a force that knocked the other man flat into the snow and almost took Isaun down with him. He staggered back like a drunk man, cradling his fist to his chest like the infant cradled to Jiren's breast, working itself into a whining cry as the snow reached them. Casually, Jiren pulled a pocket-watch from her coat and glanced at the time.

Ohfene rolled over onto his side, clutching his face. His scarlet ando pooled like blood in the snow. Gasps, hissed curses, from the crowd. For a nation perpetually at war, the image of violence was rare and strange to most noblemen. They were no strangers to pain when it came to enduring punishment or the sale of certain pleasures, but pain was a thing hidden behind closed doors. Always behind closed doors.

Luken pushed forward, cursing himself. Time to end this. Past time.

As he trudged forward, slowed to a crawl by

the drag of his ando through the snow, many things seemed to happen at once, so that Luken saw them by fragments. Isaun, reeling back, looking around himself with a startled, bestial fear. Lady Weim, surging forward like a breaking wave and screaming at him, spit flecking the snow. Lady Romyn scurrying forward, slipping in the snow, recovering her footing, rushing to Isaun's side. Ohfene, sitting upright, a blanket of snow tarnishing his scarlet ando. Amae, shoving through a wall of observers, shrieking something.

Strange, that no one moved forward to help Ohfene up. Amid the sudden turmoil, Ohfene had become invisible before the crowd. Luken bent to grip Ohfene's arm and pulled him to his feet. A streamer of blood purled down his lovely face, connecting nose to jaw. "Get the hell out of here," Luken hissed, and shoved Ohfene toward the crowd.

He turned to find Isaun fleeing up the steps to the Abode, Romyn at his heels like a simpering puppy. Plucking at the sleeves of his ando, pleading with him. At the door, Isaun whipped around to face her. "Leave me alone! Just leave me the fuck alone!"

Lady Romyn recoiled as if struck. Her sister Jiren laughed, the infant at her chest screeching now.

The crowd broke into chaos, pushed forward, milling back. Growing or dispersing? Luken could not even tell that. He tried to follow Isaun, but Weim blocked his path. She stood at the base of the Abode, screaming, "I warned you!" up at Isaun.

The air ruptured with a thunderous blast. Luken flinched, clutching at his right ear. The eardrum hummed with the force of the sound. He twisted, searching for its source.

Sami stood in the center of the courtyard, wind tugging at his white coat, a trail of smoke uncoiling from the tip of his musket. Silence rang through the snow. "Everyone, return to your Abodes."

With a sullen muttering, the courtesans began to obey, like chastened children.

"One last thing." Ohfene, blood streaming down his face, stood calm and tall in the whirling snow. A hundred faces, mute and blank, turned to regard him. Isaun froze in the threshold of the Abode, looking out framed by shadows. "Now that it's all over, I thought you should know, Isaun. Princess Oan has proposed a Conjugal Leave to me." A dimple appeared along with his gracious smile. "I have, of course, accepted."

Isaun gazed back him, unreadable. After a long silence, Isaun spoke. "Congratulations. The two of you deserve each other."

He slammed the door behind him, and the crowd, with whistles and laughs and unquiet whispers, began to thin.

Chapter Twenty-Three

Luken hurried into the Abode, Dandy close behind him.

"Isaun!"

"No!" Isaun screamed. "Don't say a word to me, Luken! Everybody just fuck off!" He vanished into their old bedroom. Luken stood, heart pounding.

The door flew open again, and Amae limped in, eyes wide, maddened. "Where is he? I'll skin him alive!"

With a jagged gait, Amae rushed across the main room.

"Don't you dare!" Luken rounded on Amae. "Don't you *dare* give him shit over this. Don't speak a single fucking unkind word to him, Amae."

His Master's eyes bulged. Small teeth bared in a snarl. "He is *my* courtesan. You may have slipped my grip, boy, but you were always far luckier than you deserved. Even the Empress's whore can't tell an Abode Master what to do with his own property, and I will do whatever I *please* with Isaun." Spittle flecked his lips.

"Dandy, go to your room."

Dandy, so startled at being spoken to in that way by Luken, blinked at him, and obeyed without question.

Luken glared back at Amae, hatred like a bared blade between them.

"I saw you." The words foamed from Luken's mouth. "I saw you in the Ruby District." With pleasure, Luken watched the color drain from his Master's face as he spoke. "You were going into that little house with the blue door. And the pansies on the windowsill. Ring a bell?"

"You- how could you-"

Luken uttered a cold laugh. "We all have our secrets, don't we Amae? *Never give it away for free.* Isn't that what you told me my first day at Court? Words of wisdom. Keeps a boy out of trouble. Lets him cling to his value. Til he gets old, anyway. Too bad you couldn't follow your own advice. Or did you think you were so old now it didn't matter?"

Luken expected to be slapped for that one. He tensed for the blow. But Amae just stared at him, pale, wide-eyed. Looking rather like a lion whose mane had been shaved. Luken lowered his voice. "All these years, you've peddled young men and boys to the highest bidder. You've pandered to Ladies and kept your fellow men in our places. All in a day's work. I thought that was all you cared about: the money. But all along, you were stuffing your pockets with the wealth of the Court while breaking its precious rules. A woman with no Acclaim. A peasant, in town. You must love her, or you wouldn't risk your position. And all those kids. How many are there, anyway? I counted five through the window."

Amae swallowed, and seemed to dredge the word up from somewhere deep within. "Seven."

"Seven," Luken spat. "Well, you can afford them. Do they know Isaun and I put food on their table? Or do you not talk about work when visiting your peasant mistress?" There was a savage pleasure in saying all the things to Amae that Amae would no doubt have said to him if their positions had been reversed. For so long, he'd lived in fear that his love of Jes would ruin him. The freedom now, the flood of relief, in having these words said aloud and *not to him*. Peasant mistress. *We are too alike, you and I, Amae. Except I won't end up like you.* "I wonder what the Arbiters would do with this information? You can't be demoted on the Board, your name was taken down ages ago. I suppose you'd just be stripped of your lordship and kicked out of the Garden. What an unusual circumstance, they'd have to find us a new Abode Master."

"Stop!" Amae's face twisted as if he'd swallowed poison. "Just... stop." He was silent a moment, reclaiming his breath. "You've made your point. What do you want in exchange for your silence? My percentage of your income?"

"I want what I've always wanted from you, Amae: to be left alone. I never planned on reporting you. I never cared what you did, to be frank. You're just another tiresome old man who sold his life to the Court and never figured out how to buy it back. Except your wrinkled body no longer has any value in the meat market, so you sell young men – vulnerable men, naive men, like I was when I first came to Court – which is much worse, really. You're a barnacle."

A weight lifted from Luken's chest and fluttered free. "If you kick Isaun out of the Abode, if you say or do *anything* to Isaun because of this – even so much as an unkind word uttered in passing – I will tell the Arbiters that you are guilty of exactly what

Isaun has been accused of. Let them do with that what they will."

Amae's pallid face promised no disobedience.

Luken stood, knowing he had nothing else to say to this man, and walked to the door.

"Think you've got it all figured out, don't you boy?"

Luken turned, one hand resting on the lintel. Tears traced ravines down Amae's thick paint. "Think you could have done better with the shit hand I was dealt in life? Think you know everything?"

"Obviously not," Luken resumed his pace, even as he spoke. "I'm still here, aren't I?"

~

Later that day, Luken curled up on the dark green velvet of the divan and tried to focus on Fi's words as she paced about his chambers. He had asked her the day before to set time aside for him, so that he could question her about the Noble Assembly; there was a plan forming in his mind, a way to take action himself rather than waiting on the Empress's convenience, but he did not yet have the particulars.

"The Assembly will begin in a fortnight," Fi explained. "It all comes down to the Ladies of High Houses that have remained neutral. That would be..." Fi paused before the balcony, her arms folded behind her back. "Lady Silan, of the House of Misty Springs." Nikay's mother. "And Lady Asang, of the House of Stone Cliffs."

Stone Cliffs. Didn't he know someone from that House? A jolt of surprise, and Luken laughed out loud. "Satomi."

Fi arched an eyebrow, but Luken turned

toward the balcony, a breeze rolling in through the open doors. The tender vines, rustling on the trellis.

"What are you thinking, boy?" Fi asked. "Countless Ladies have tried over the years to persuade Lady Silan to break her neutrality. Do you really think you are the first person to think of such a thing?" A harsh laugh. "She does not accept meetings. You won't even be able to speak to her, let alone persuade her."

"Nikay and Satomi," Luken mused, ignoring her.

~

A knock at the door. Luken nodded to the servant, who bowed his head and crossed the distance with silent steps, and opened the door for his visitor.

Nikay, adorned in a sleek ando of diaphanous violet and pale yellow layers, his long brown hair held back in a silver clasp of pearls, appeared, and bowed his head as he approached. Luken watched from the divan, his bare feet tucked beneath him.

"My lord."

Luken felt a chilly smile spread his lips. "Am I 'my lord' to you now, Nikay? You met me on my first morning at Court, when I was as helpless as a duckling that had wandered into the Palace."

Nikay chuckled, a little hesitantly, and took a seat on the divan where, not so long ago, Lifelle had sprawled out, laughing and smiling before he told Luken that he was retiring from the Court.

"Thank you for coming. I have some questions I must ask you." He laced his fingers together, gazing at the man across from him. "You know, I suppose, that the Noble Assembly will soon meet. Your mother is the Lady of the House of Misty Springs which, for over a century, has remained a neutral House, declining to take sides in political matters, declining to vote on proposals brought before the Assembly."

Nikay shifted on the divan. "I think you may have the wrong idea, Luken. I am not one to speak of politics–"

Luken cut across him; with Isaun's reputation ruined, the Assembly looming, and Jes gone from his life, he was in no mood to be polite these days. It was time to make things happen. Otherwise, what had been the point of any of this?

"You are the Son of a High House. To say that you are not political is to say that noble blood does not flow in your veins. A lie, we both know." Luken watched Nikay's mouth twist, and force itself smooth again. "The truth is, I like you, Nikay. I want to come to an understanding that will help both of us. You, being the good man that you are, want to advocate on behalf of your mother, and eventually your Lady's, politics. I, as the Empress's concubine, want to advance her agenda and ensure my own position. We all have things that we want, and things that we can offer one another."

Nikay's expression did not alter, but Luken thought he saw curiosity flicker in his gaze. "I'll certainly listen to an offer."

Luken wove his fingers together. "You're going to retire from the Court soon, aren't you? Where are you going as Consort?"

Nikay blinked.

"You've been on Conjugal Leave twice now. The House of the Sunken Star and the House of the

Seashell. Both Middling Houses. Have you gotten an acceptance from either yet?"

Nikay looked back at him, an obsidian gleam entering his gaze. "The Seashell."

"And the Sunken Star?"

A patronizing smile. "Has politely informed me they are full up on Consorts, at the moment."

"Fuck them, then. The Seashell is a good House." Luken paused, considering. "Far though. All the way out on the southeastern coast."

"Yes, that would be the downside. I'd have to travel a great way to visit my family."

Luken nodded, the gears of his mind turning. "You are an only son aren't you, Nikay?"

"My mother birthed four other males, but they were rendered to the military."

"Four others. Why keep you?"

"A soothsayer read the fortunes of each child my mother delivered. We are old-fashioned, in that way, my family." He shrugged. "Only I was predicted to make a good courtesan in the future. The others, my mother was told, would not have the necessary beauty. My mother abided by the sayer's advice."

Luken nodded. Most Noble Houses donoted their excess boys to the military, keeping only those predicted to become beautiful, and therefore valuable in the future. Not all of them, of course. The House of the Pear Blossom had never called upon a soothsayer, not in Luken's generation, but the practice was still considered proper. A House with too many sons was one that had ignored the sayer's advice – to their own dishonor. And if the mother, selfish as she was, struggled to maintain her overabundance of boys, well, that was the judgement of the goddesses, one must suppose.

"Interesting. Alone among five brothers, your mother kept you. She must cherish you."

Again, Nikay shifted on the divan. "We are close, yes. She spoiled me terribly growing up, I will be the first to admit."

Luken could not keep the frost from his smile. "Of course she did." *To make up for sending your brothers to die. Unless – and I must bet everything on the hope that this is not true – she did not care.* "I must speak to your mother, Nikay. There are crucial matters that the two of us must discuss."

Nikay arched an eyebrow. "My mother does not get involved in political affairs. Certaintly not with–" He cut himself off.

"The Empress's whore?"

Nikay sighed. "Do you really think it wise, Luken, for men to get entangled in such matters? My mother's vote has been courted by Ladies on more occasions than I can count, and still, she has remained neutral. I can't imagine what you would say to her–"

"I speak for the Empress. Let your mother decide the value of what I have to say to her. Will you arrange the meeting?" A pause. "Please, Nikay. Do it for the duckling that wandered into the Palace, and was almost trampled underfoot."

Nikay shook his head, a wan smile on his lips. "Oh, you were not trampled. We all thought you would be. You were just so shy, so uncertain, in spite of your beauty." Memory softened his gaze. "I remember when Ohfene first saw you. I had described our meeting to him, and told him that Isaun's new pupil was the most promising young courtesan I'd ever seen – but painfully shy, and so timid. He wanted to see you at once. I pointed you out to him across the distance of the courtyards as you were trailing along one day behind Isaun and a Lady of the Silent Lake. 'Is he not as beautiful as I told you?' I asked Ohfene, but he did not answer, and when I looked at him, there was a strange expression on his face. At last he said, 'But painfully shy. No confidence at all?' 'Yes,' I told him, and he breathed a sigh of relief. He always had that uncanny eye, Ohfene. He knew what he was looking at. I didn't. I could only guess. But in the end, you surprised us all. You surpassed us all."

Luken waited, absorbing these words.

Nikay lifted his gaze, met Luken's eye. "You have a good reason, I suppose, for wanting to speak to my mother?"

"I wouldn't waste your time."

"Very well. I will convince her to see you." Nikay stood. "I must trust that you are whatever Ohfene feared you are, and nothing less."

And with that, they parted. Luken did not stir from his seat on the divan, his bare feet still tucked beneath him, as he dwelled on those words.

Chapter Twenty-Four

You must know that what you ask of me is impossible. It is not a question of whether of not I love thee. We have written the history of our love with one pen in both our hands. What I know, is known by you.

Yet you ask me to forsake my little cocoon for the unknown, with no security, no House, nothing but your promises. I am not a brave man, Lanu. I am a creature of small comforts and closed spaces. It is all I know.

Go on expedition, and return to me. If you become wealthy, all the better. If not – we will both learn the measure of my heart. I assure you, I will be as surprised by the results as you.

Marigold's words ran through Luken's mind, a rhythm stuck in his skull from a morning spent reading through the diaries and fragments in his grandfather's old box.

"Lord Luken?"

He looked up at the sound of the Palace Steward's voice. A large woman, and quite wide about the hips, she had an assistant that scurried everywhere with a chair and a small fold-up table that could spring into action whenever Lady Yua wished. She sat now in the middle of West Hall, where the casino party had been held a few months before. The fold-up table creaked ominously beneath a sprawl of designs for the upcoming Spring Gala, the closing festivities that would come a week after the end of the Noble

Assembly. A final sigh of relief, as winter gave way to spring, the Ladies retired to their Houses for another few years, and the Empire embarked on whatever new path had been set for it.

So it was that Luken found himself gazing down at sketches of elaborate arches, banners, ribbons, and flower arrangements that brimmed with spring colors while snow caked the grounds of the Palace and a bitter wind howled at them whenever a servant pressed in through the slit of the scarce-opened doors.

"Which do you prefer? I am partial to the tulips, myself, but, as you have vetoed them at every opportunity, I suspect you do not approve."

Stirring from his own thoughts, Luken forced himself to focus on the sketches before him. The Steward's assistants crawled around the Hall, taking measurements and notes on the capacity of the space, the height of the ceiling, the lighting.

"I think we can do a bit better than tulips, Lady Steward."

The Empress, finding his study of flower arrangement as amusing as everyone else, had placed Luken in an advisory role for the Spring Gala. So far he had succeeded in arguing the Palace Steward away from the usual tulips and daffodils that had appeared at every Spring Gala for the past forty years. "You won't like it, but the Chief Gardener has promised me hyacinth, starred with yellow cups of winter aconite, bursting from the tables," he gestured toward the doors, "and great arches of creeping phlox in spectrums of white, violet, and purple."

Groaning, the Steward traced a sketch of banners falling in luxuriant arches from the high ceiling. "It'll have to be yellow or white this year, to contrast all your *purples*," she sighed with great dismay.

Luken patted her shoulder. "We will get through this together, Lady Steward."

"Luken," Fi's voice cracked the air like a whip, "you have visitors."

Luken turned, cocking an eyebrow – and saw his parents, standing, a little nervous, in a side door of the Hall, their arms linked, their smiles tentative, as if unsure of finding him here. Or perhaps, of the reception they would receive.

"Mama!" He lifted his robes and scurried toward them as quick as his ando would allow: a padded, pearl-embroidered deep-red affair, with a diaphanous white train that whispered over the marble behind him. An extravagant ando, but he was glad he'd opted for it now. His mother lifted her arms out to him and Luken wrapped her in an embrace, lifting her an inch off the ground and laughing softly at her surprised, "Oh!"

He let her down and stepped back. "I wasn't expecting you yet! You're here for the Assembly?"

She inclined her head. "Yes, but I came early this year to see you."

Luken glanced at his father. They had not parted on the best of terms, when Luken had last visited the House of the Pear Blossom to attend his grandfather's funeral half a year or so ago. Indeed, they'd exchanged no letters at all. Only his sister Tian had written regularly, and her letters dwelled almost exclusively on her advancing pregnancy, her courtesan Tsikoran, and their infant daughter; they contained little, if any, allusions to their father, Amana, who stood stiffly beside his Lady with his hands clasped together at his irlan. He wore an ando of pale yellow swarmed by trefoils of white embroidery. A flicker of resentment. Luken had bought him that ando, over a year ago when he'd stopped at the House after leaving U-Wen.

"Hello, son."

Luken bowed his head. "Father. It's good to see you."

Fi's eyes glittered, darting back and forth between them.

Luken glanced over his shoulder. "Lady Steward, I shall leave it to you." He stepped forward, then paused and looked back. "But no tulips."

She waved him off, shaking her head as she returned to her designs.

Luken led his parents outside, into the pallid sunlight of the winter sky. Snow licked at the flagstones, piled two or three inches high beside the pathway. They hovered a moment, directionless. Why was it so awkward? These people had given him life, and he could not talk to them. Luken suppressed a sigh.

"I moved into the Palace."

Lady Kenkazu nodded. "We heard."

"Would you like to see my chambers?"

"Of course."

Luken turned to lead them along the flagstone path, a glimpse of his father's face in passing revealed his expression to be distant and preoccupied as he surveyed the sliver of Garden grounds down the slope. "How is Tian?" he asked.

"Not long now," his mother said. "We'll have a new grandchild by the time we return to the House, if not already."

And if it's another boy, will you devote him to the military because we can't afford him? Luken thought. "I cannot wait to hear the news. And how was your journey?"

This muttering carried them back to Luken's chambers, where Fi left them. But not before leaning in and whispering in Luken's ear, "You and your father do not like each other."

He frowned. "It's complicated."

"It always is." She shoved her hands in her coat pockets, her footsteps ringing down the hall. Luken watched her, rolled his eyes, and followed his parents into his chambers.

They stood, still arm-in-arm, as if braced against the unknown. His mother and father, dappled by the uncertain light that broke the clouds to fall through the glass doors against the far wall.

"Please, have a seat." Luken gestured to the divans.

The initial spark of excitement at seeing his parents dwindled to a dull dread. Their relationship had always existed in the context of the House of the Pear Blossom, the family home, surrounded by memories and extended kin. Here, they were in his world. They did not know him here. They knew the boy who had grown up at the House. They did not know the Empress's concubine.

"Can I get you anything?" He felt, suddenly, driven to attend to them. "Let me get you something to eat. Are you cold? I'll have a servant build up the fireplace. You must be tired from the journey. Where are you staying while you're in O-Han?"

Lady Kenkazu tilted her head. "We were planning on renting rooms in the city."

"No!" Luken blurted out, and laughed. "You don't have to do that. I have a spare room here, in my chambers. You'll sleep here."

Lady Kenkazu nodded. "Thank you."

A long silence. A shifting of the pearl rays striking across the wall over his parent's heads. Luken looked aside, where a few flakes of snow began their whisper-soft descent. When he looked back, Amana stared at him with those black, rodent eyes that so many people said were a mirror of his own.

A cold smile. "Well," Amana said, "here we are."

~

Sleep came in fits, peopled by strange dreams.

Luken woke with his heart hammering and his eyes peeled wide to blackness, fear racing through his blood.

Such moments had been common when he'd first returned to Court. After the events in U-Wen, that second departure from his maternal House had stirred his trauma from a sluggish malaise of depression to the quivering panic that had shaken his first months back at Court.

How disappointing, that he had not left such things behind. It had seemed like he had, for awhile.

A soft mutter of sound, the creak of a stair down below. Luken lay, a black panic rising over him – until he remembered his parents were in his chambers. Calmed a little, he hid trembling hands in his gloves and slipped into a padded under-robe before edging downstairs. His long black hair fell like a veil over his shoulders and down his back.

Coming to the far end of the hallway, Luken looked out from the landing. A black figure passed the fireplace, tall and grim as a phantom in the glare of the fire's scarlet eye. His father, his head bent over something.

Luken eased down the stairwell with a soft, "Father?"

Amana did not flinch, or even stir, at the sound of Luken's voice. As if this had been an expected meeting.

Faint chimes over the city announced the midnight hour.

"You took Marigold's journals."

Drawing near, Luken heard the shuffle of papers as Amana rooted through the old, wooden box.

"I thought I'd lost them, but you just took them." His back to Luken, he stood framed by the fireplace, limned in amber. Another bell, echoing from the temples in O-Han.

"Sorry. I didn't know you wanted them."

He lifted a scrap from the box, paused, a ghost of ink visible, the paper back-lit to a translucent, scarlet skin in the fire's glow. He let the fragment fall back into the box. "I would have given them to you if you'd asked. All you had to do was ask." He rummaged, raising his voice over the rustle of paper. "You always were secretive, with-holding. Disappearing behind corners. Vanishing to be alone."

You always were drunk, embarrassing. Passing out on divans. Hiding wine stained clothes. Luken let the words simmer in his throat. He was twenty-one years old; Amana had been the same person his entire life. If his father hadn't changed by now, he wasn't going to. What was the point of fighting him?

"But what do I know?" Amana turned and laid the box on the side-table against the armchair where Luken had laid the first pill on his tongue. A final bell shivered to silence over the city. "Whatever it is you do, it works. You have surpassed me in every single way imaginable. The Empress's concubine," he snorted. "Well. That's me beat, isn't it? Talk about the grand finale. What could I say to you after that?"

"It's hardly a competition," Luken murmured. "I didn't do this to spite you."

"No?" Amana strolled to the fire, the front of his body licked crimson by the light. He folded his arms at his chest, the gossamer white of his under-robes falling around him like moth-wings in rest. "I don't suppose you did. Although it feels like it sometimes, you know. Strange; you are so like me, and yet not like me at all."

Luken jolted. Gave a soft laugh. "In what ways are we at all alike?"

A smile sliced sideways, the mask of his profile. "No ambition in you, Luken? No anger? No bitterness? I don't think you get any of that from your mother. Her introversion, maybe. Her intelligence. The rest you get from me."

Luken shrugged his under-robe up, wrapped it tighter around him. "The worst bits, in other words?"

He kept his tone light – or tried to, anyway – but it fell flat, like a toppled obelisk, stone falling to crush the space between them.

The smile hovered in the dark, and did not waver. "It isn't all bad. I gave you my eyes."

Luken fought the rise of a sneer. His eyes. Bistre-black, and rat-like. Is that what women saw when they told him he had beautiful eyes?

"You should sleep, Father. It's been a long journey from E-Kara."

"I'm not that feeble yet." He did not bother to suppress his sneer. Perhaps that was the difference between them.

Amana strode across the room to the darkness that gathered in the corner and kicked the chest that rested there. "I see the final installment of your Conjugal Price arrived."

Luken stared. This third and final installment from his Conjugal Leave with Lady Dare had indeed arrived a fortnight or so ago. Luken had meant to have it delivered to the Palace Vaults, along with the rest of his savings, for safekeeping until his departure. But it didn't seem to matter so much now as it used to, when he'd been with Jes. All that gold. Once, he had been enraged that a courtesan was forced to wait a year after the culmination of his Leave to receive the third payment of his own money. Once, receiving that money had been an imperative, an obsession. Once, it had promised freedom from the Court. Now... Luken had barely responded to the arrival of the chest in his chambers. Just pushed it into the corner. Promised to do something with it, then let it gather dust.

What was he doing?

"What do you want? Gold? Take some," Luken said, tired suddenly. He moved to the armchair and fell into it, surrendering to the embrace of the soft fabric. Quietly, he said, "I know the House is in debt."

Amana went still in the shadows.

After a long moment, he advanced into the ring of firelight. "Tian told you?"

"No. Kenze."

A strange little noise, disgruntled and skeptical. "You talk to your half-siblings?"

"I ran into her in the city."

"Well then, the secret is out. Your mother didn't want to tell you, for some reason. I told her you were in a position to help us now, with the Empress on your side, but she insisted on keeping you in the dark. Didn't want to worry her baby. But now that you know..." He trailed off into thought.

A frown creased Luken's brow. "What is it everyone thinks I have the power to do now that I am the Empress's concubine? She has done nothing for me, except bestow these chambers and trinkets. I have no real power. What do you want from me? Should I ask Raisaga to wave her hand and make your debts evaporate? Everyone thinks I have some kind of power over her. I used to think-" He cut off. And murmured, "I'm no Liliray. No Beauty of the Age. I'm just the Second Son of a Middling House, and a broke one at that. I can't do anything."

He could not see his father's features, but he knew those eyes were on him. "You're less like me than I thought," Amana said eventually. "I would have at least tried."

~

Luken did not sleep again that night.

Laying awake, he thought of his parents. An old scab he'd never stopped picking at.

Early in the morning, with the first breath of dawn in the sky, Luken snuck to his guest bedroom, and woke his mother.

"What is it?" she murmured, dreamy and soft.

"I need your help, Mama."

Chapter Twenty-Five

The note, bearing his mother, Lady Kenkazu's, signature, hovered between Doctor Ence's fingertips. The soft *tick, tick, tick* of the clock filled her office.

Doctor Ence gazed at the permission slip for a long time before, finally, and with great care, laying it down on the desk between them. "I'm afraid I can't accept this. You see," she pointed to an imperceptible flaw, "the signature is smeared. This could be forged. Come back with another one, then. I'm booked solid until next summer, but you can make an appointment." She nodded to the door, but Luken did not budge.

"I thought you might say that." Luken pulled another sealed envelope from his coat. "From my Lady. I think you'll find she has sufficient authority to permit my – what did you call them? – *atrocious and immoral whims?*"

Luken watched her jaw work before she yanked the envelope from his hand, and ripped it open.

Her eyes flicked over it, then, slowly, she drew the note closer, her jaw going slack, the eyebrows rising. "This is…"

"The Empress's seal, yes."

"It can't be- You can't be-" Her eyes darted up to fix him with a hostile gaze. "This isn't real."

"It is, actually. Even you ought to be capable of recognizing the famed peacock seal of the Empress of

Kanai."

She sneered, the note trembling in her hands. "And why would the Empress write express permission for you to receive a vasectomy?"

Luken shrugged. "The Lady will have her concubines. You know how it is. Now." He cocked his head. "My guards are waiting for me outside the clinic. I am done doing things through the proper channels, because – as you have so thoroughly enlightened me, Doctor Ence – the proper channels are all designed to prevent people like me from achieving full agency. So, no more appointments. No more condescending waiting periods. No more scare tactics, no more lies. I am done playing the pretty, polite boy. Would you like to be arrested for defying an express order from the Empress, or would you like to write me my prescription?" He smiled, and added, with a cutting edge, *"Now."*

She glared at him, lips pressed pale and flat, the note now shaking visibly in her hands.

"You are determined to get your way, aren't you?'

Luken sneered right back. "Yes. So stop hindering me, and do your fucking job. Or quit, and let someone else do it."

Her face flushed red, and then, by rapid degrees, the color drained from her cheeks entirely. Hands shaking with rage, Doctor Ence slashed her signature across a prescription pad and threw it at him. "Have fun devouring your children. They'll be reabsorbed back into your body like some grotesque, quivering sea-sponge-"

"Your hatred of my body is well noted, but if

you don't mind, I have an appointment to get to." He paused at the doorway, "And really, dear, it's nothing to do with you at all. So keep your mind off my genitals, and on your own fucking business." He let the door swing shut behind him with a satisfying *bang*.

~

In the end, the process was not nearly so laborious, time-consuming, or excruciating as the lies about it that had been shoved down Luken's throat. He and Rori made their way to the hospital, were directed to the specialist, and presented the prescription. The woman's eyes widened as if she'd been presented with Ushai's Ring of Youth.

"You actually got a prescription for a vasectomy from Doctor Ence? Good Goddess, how on earth did you do that?" She held it up to the light, squinting. "If this is a forgery, it's a damn good one."

"It's no forgery, I'm just well-connected."

"Ah," she nodded, "I suppose that would be the only way, these days."

"I need an appointment immediately."

Her eyebrows rose in faint arches. "This *is* the appointment. We can do this today, if you're ready."

Luken smiled, an orchid of relief unfurling its fuchsia petals in his chest. "I'm ready."

"Very well." She stood. "Let us prepare."

As the specialist made her way to the door, Rori took Luken's hand.

"You're sure about this?" he asked in a murmur. "You're giving up a lot."

"No," Luken said, meeting his warm, brown eyes. "I'm taking control."

~

He ached with dreams, hazed and honeyed; gardens in fragments, blossoms bursting from the dark, voices rising to a hum – the frenetic song of the bees, tumbling in the lavender – and fading without trading a word; until, somewhere beyond, high mountains in crystalline purity, rose from the mists, shrugged on their cloaks of evergreen, rivers falling from the ice, the winter-runoff sloughing white chunks from the snows, falling in frigid streams to join and join and join, until the river met the valley, and the grain, and hands warm and brown that lifted from the sighing fields to caress the warmth-weave of the sun falling from the sky.

"Luken?" Jes's voice, in the morning bright. Sunlight filled the curtains to an alabaster glow. Were they in U-Wen still, in the House of the Golden Sun? Not the city, no; Eitan's apartment had never been this bright. The House of the Pear Blossom, then. His old room, and the murmur of family crawling from the deeper folds of his mind, like honey from the comb. The places they had woken together, in beds that had never belonged to them both. "Luken?"

He woke to the feel of her hand on his face, and the image of her face over his.

Luken blinked. His dreams blazed brighter than reality; Kat and Rori's bedroom stood grey and dim around them. For a moment, Luken struggled to identify the place. The wrongness of it niggled at him, and of Jes being here-

Ah. It always hurt to remember they were not together. Not anymore.

Luken struggled to push himself up onto his elbows. "Jes, what are you doing here?"

"I need to speak to you."

Rori's voice, at the doorway. "If you need to rest, we can put this off."

"No," Luken murmured, his eyes returning to Jes's face. Like a weary traveler reaching home.

"I'll be right outside, if you need me." The door swung shut behind Rori, sealing them into the dim shades of the bedroom.

They had arranged for Luken to recover from his procedure at Rori's place, though the specialist had told him he would need only a few hours of rest before he was fit to be on his feet again. He had received permission from the Empress to spend the night at his writer friend's apartment in the city; she had heard of Rori enough by now not to be surprised by the request. Luken could have returned to his chambers in the Palace, if he'd wished. But in the end he was tired and uncomfortable, if not quite in pain, and loath to be alone.

"I'm sorry to wake you," Jes tucked her hair behind her ear, "but this was the only place I could find you. It's not exactly easy," an awkward smile, "getting hold of you these days."

Sleep faded, ice entered his tone. "What do you want?"

"Look, Luken-" Was she nervous? Luken frowned; nerves never penetrated Jes's stoic reserve. "I know we aren't together anymore, but I thought you'd want to know. I *know* you'd want to know."

A pit formed in Luken's stomach. Or maybe it was the old chasm, cracking further. "What now? What could it possibly be now?"

"I'm pregnant."

Wind through the chasm.

"I want you to know that I don't expect anything from you," she said with a sad smile.

He stared back at her. "You don't expect anything from me." A flicker of anger, stoking to life. "You should. You should expect me to take responsibility for my part. You should expect me to be involved. You should expect something- some contribution, at least." Abruptly, "Are you keeping it?"

"Yes."

A powerful surge of nameless emotion blossomed and swelled and crashed through Luken in a wave. There was a time when this news, delivered from Jes's lips, would have ignited the most breathless excitement, a pure and fathomless joy. Now it was all tainted, all a mess. "I just got a vasectomy," he spat.

Her head lilted, a fraction. "I know. Rori told me."

"Goddess. Fuck me. Why now, Jes? Why *now*?"

Her eyes widened. "You think I planned it this way? None of this has happened the way I wanted. None of it. Not since the first day we met."

Luken rolled over onto his side. "I think I'm going to vomit. And not just because it feels like I was kicked in the balls a few hours ago."

Jes sighed. "I'm sorry, Luken." Her voice went taut, strained. "None of this is right. None of this is how it was supposed to be."

He pressed his eyes closed, buried them against the pillow. "There is no *supposed to* when it comes to this sort of thing. Reproduction is always messy. You might have a miscarriage tomorrow, for all we know. You might give birth and decide you don't want it after all. The baby might live a week and die for some reason that remains unknown even to the doctors. There's never a guarantee."

Her voice reached him in a whisper. "Luken, why are you saying these things to me?"

Tears forced their way out from beneath his stinging lids.

Jes laid a hand on his shoulder. "You will never have to worry about this again. You have that, at least. There's one guarantee."

At some point, the tears melted into laughter. Trembling, silent laughter.

The pillow pattered with tears, a smear of chill wetness against his face. His shoulders shook with silent, helpless laughter. "I'm sure, Jes, you will have a healthy, chubby, baby girl and raise her to be a fine young woman, just like you."

The warmth of her hand, gentle on the back of his. "Actually," she squeezed his fingers, "I'm sort of hoping for a boy."

Let us look at the foundations. You have before you, my Lady Mother, a boy. A healthy, unassuming boy. As a son he is good enough, in his own way, though he carries with him the burdens and attachments of his gender. Not his fault, of course, but there is an expense: the tutelage, the etiquette, the andos that must be purchased for Court, and the eventual cost of resuming his care, should he fail to procure a position as Consort in another Lady's House. Or, having done so, fails to please his mistress, and she seeks a way out of the contract. Chasing him like a shadow, there is always the risk of a financial blow. That was the gamble you accepted when you declined to give him up to the military. But let us put that aside. He is still young. At the moment, he costs you no more than a daughter. And he is good enough, in his way. Just as good – you may even say, in your stubborn, maternal affections – as a daughter.

But, to the point: you have a son.

In the beginning, there is no difficulty. Aside from the obvious structural differences, you find no great division between your male infant and your female infants. He laughs and cries. He learns to crawl and walk. Despite concerns for his inferior language skills, he nonetheless learns to speak. You suspect he may even be cleverer than the average male, and are secretly pleased.

But the years roll on. You either notice – or, should they fail to occur naturally, you begin taking measures to ensure they will be produced – subtle but important distinguishing traits that arise in your boy.

You have been told, and no doubt even found plenty of evidence in your own life, that there are crucial differences between the sexes. You have been told that, for reasons which we can explain to you in a cyclone of details and examples we've selected for you from the natural world (imagine here a *tedious explanation about the natural evolution of gorillas or lions or somewhat, it doesn't matter) that the male brain does not develop an emotional or social capacity equal to that of the female brain. There is a reason that things have always been the way they are. To women, the domains of head and heart: the political, the financial, the familial. To men, the domains of muscle and loins: the farm, the factory, the bedchamber. The fact that one set of domains allows more control over the lives of others in our society is, of course, inconsequential and any complaints to the contrary are to be immediately mocked and dismissed as irrelevant whining.*

So how do you, my Lady Mother, prepare your boy for such a world? To cozen him with affection and attention is unnecessary, possibly even harmful, to his boyish psyche. There is no need to serve him a gallon of love when the boy can swallow only a teaspoon. He grows, living on what you give him. Developing as predicted. You are relieved. They were right after all: he needed only the teaspoon. Too late to consider what may have happened otherwise. He has grown into the fine young man he was always going to become, unless you had done something disastrous. Killed the houseplant by over-watering it. But you did not, so all is well.

There are those who will tell you, of course, that he would have grown otherwise if he had been raised otherwise. That his mind, his heart, his body, are all shaped by his environment. That the much-vaunted differences between son and daughter may become disturbingly narrow if son and daughter are raised alike. Same education, same chores and responsibilities, same values and friends, same choices and opportunities. How dangerous it would be if gender failed to set each of us in our places, and assign labor and value accordingly. What a disservice to your children, if the girl lost respect among her peers for being too boyish. If the boy failed to become desirable to women for being too girlish. Disastrous.

Better to err on the side of caution, and return to the same old standards, right? Mindlessly falling back into the same old stereotypes handed down, generation to generation. Restrictive, perhaps, but safe.

And thus Lady Mother repeats the same old patterns, not because equality is impossible, but because an unequal world demands unequal roles in exchange for its approval, and with its approval – safety. And what mother does not want her children to be safe?

-Vin Ayet, Ages, 6.21.1010
"Instruments of Oppression: Raised to the Standard"

Part Three
The Awakening

Chapter Twenty-Six

Sunlight poured over the balcony, breaking free of the clouds. Lords and Ladies considered the snowfall finished for the year, the courtesans already putting in their orders for lighter, summery andos. Luken counted on nothing these days; he waited, and watched for snow.

As the third bell rang out over the city, a knock sounded.

"Come in," he called, turning to face the door. With the light behind him and a net of pearls falling over his smooth, black hair – so long now that it neared his waist – he knew himself resplendent in an ando of deep, ornate green, the hem trimmed with pearls, a tight, lacy gold and white irlan binding his chest and falling to the floor behind him in a long cascade.

Sami opened the door, and the Lady entered. He watched her advance a pace, look at him, stop, waver, and make the conscious effort to keep walking, her head tucked slightly into that half-resentful, half-wondering look of a Lady forced to acknowledge that a man was almost unbearably lovely – and did not belong to her in the slightest. Luken smiled. He knew people harbored an innate curiosity about the Empress's concubine; a certain sense of wonder, tempered by world-weary skepticism. Everyone wanted to see this man that was lovely enough for the

Empress – and expected, in the end, to be disappointed.

Luken had made certain, this day at least, not to disappoint.

"Lady Silan, I'm so happy you could come." She bowed, and he did not return the gesture. If he was an extension of the Empress, let him act like it. "Please, sit down." He moved to the divan and took a seat, making himself comfortable.

She sat across from him, her posture stiff. "I'm glad to make your acquaintance, Lord Luken. My son has spoken very highly of you."

"Nikay," Luken suffused his voice with fondness, knowing well how Ladies loved to hear their sons praised. "No doubt he has been excessively generous towards me."

A rigid smile. "He always was a kind boy. Found an injured squirrel alongside the road when he was five and insisted on keeping it until it had recovered. The damn thing near-enough tore his room apart when it got loose from its cage. Nikay was just delighted it had recovered enough strength to do so much damage."

Luken laughed softly. "It does sound like him. Lady Silan, there's something I wanted to ask-"

She held up a hand. "I know what you expect to happen here today, Luken."

He cocked his head, suppressing a spike of annoyance at being interrupted. "Oh?"

"You think that you can talk me into changing my vote. I'm sorry to be so abrupt with you, my lord, but I do not wish to waste your time or dash your hopes." She considered him. "It is well-known that the

318

House of the Pear Blossom is a Reformist House, by nature. Unless I miss my guess, you'd like me to side with your mother and other Reformists in voting against the proposed military action in Builay. Is that right?"

"I do not speak for my mother, but yes, that's more or less the gist of it, Lady Silan."

"Then I am sorry to say, I will not be convinced, my lord. The House of Misty Springs is, and always has been, a neutral House."

He smiled. "You are resistant to change, even if it benefits you?"

"Taking a side on such divisive issues does not benefit the Misty Springs."

"Forgive me Lady Silan, but I daresay you may just be wrong about that."

She shook her head. "There is nothing you can offer me. I have my reasons for keeping the Misty Springs neutral." She laced her fingers together and placed her hands on her knee. "I do not know, Lord Luken, if you fully understand the position of the House of Misty Springs."

Patronizing. Luken stared back at her.

"The House of Misty Springs," he said, "is located along the Stone River, midway between the regions controlled by the House of Spiraling Doves – Traditionalists – and the House of the Dreaming Tiger – Reformists. The Houses despise one another with a white-hot passion and have warred over territory in the past. Indeed, I seem to recall from my Imperial History courses that even before the formation of the Houses, the ancestral clans of their bloodlines warred for control of the region. They do not play nice. The

House of Misty Springs, however, plays nice with everyone. The Spiraling Doves trade to you their salt, which you trade, at a great profit, to the Dreaming Tiger and their surrounding territory. The Dreaming Tiger trade you their silk, which you trade, at a great profit, to the Spiraling Doves. You also do a great trade in your own products; foodstuffs from the Lower Valley, copper from your mines in the mountains. Not to mention the trade taxes you impose on your holdings all the way down the Stone River, until the Stone River turns into the Tylisn River, which is controlled by the House of the River Serpent. Ruled, of course, by Lady Pazu, mother of the courtesan Ohfene, to whom Nikay is a loyal friend. An excellent placement. Did you bribe the Arbiters to have your son placed at the Abode of the Midnight Heron, or did the Arbiters do it of their own accord to please you?"

Lady Silan sniffed. "I daresay the House of Misty Springs still commands some respect at the Palace. I have never bothered to bribe a single soul in my life, let alone a man."

"They did it to please you, then. Very gratifying. And not surprising. The House of Misty Springs has done well for itself in trade, certainly. Fought your way up from a Minor House, seven hundred years ago, to a large and wealthy High House. Very impressive. But, you are forced to remain politically neutral, for fear of harming your position between the Houses Spiraling Doves and Dreaming Tiger. Is that not an accurate summation, Lady Silan?"

She stared at him, mildly annoyed. "I see the rumors about you have not been exaggerated, Lord

Luken. You do have a brain somewhere in that pretty head after all. Enough to understand the Misty Springs' predicament. Enough to understand that if I vote against the upcoming war, as you would have me do, I may as well declare myself a Reformist then and there. Which," her chin tilted back, "I am not. It is not merely for economic gain that the Misty Springs remains neutral. We are true moderates. Always have been. We do not get involved in the squabbling of the two parties. There is no point."

"So you would like to see the Empire go to war with Builay?"

"I did not say that."

"Then the time has come to choose. No one stands neutral when their country is at war. With respect, my Lady, in a time of political upheaval such as this, there really is no such thing as a 'true moderate.' Neutrality is also a stance, when the two ends of the spectrum represent such different, and such basic, values as *war* and *peace*. Those who will not stand for peace are choosing war. It is as simple as that."

She bristled. "Am I to be lectured on politics by a concubine?"

"I have the Empress's ear," he said simply, and was only a little surprised when the Lady fell silent. To wield such power, with so few words, despite his gender... Was this what it felt like to be a woman?

"Given where matters stand, I have an offer for you Lady Silan, if you will indulge me."

"That is the only reason Nikay was able to convince me to come here."

He gazed out the window. "Let me lay my

cards on the table then: I am interested in preventing war with Builay. In this, I express the Empress's interests as well. The Empire has been too long at war." He allowed the silence to linger, then turned his gaze to Silan. "Nikay tells me you gave the army four sons. I wonder how many survived the war in Hindigga."

Her eyes bulged. "You dare–"

"Now your final son, Nikay, is soon to retire from Court and has only one position on offer: the House of the Seashell."

A vein in Lady Silan's temple seemed to have become more visible as Luken spoke, like a baited serpent, arching up. He pressed.

"That's a considerable journey, from the Seashell to the Misty Springs."

"This- this is not how one conducts politics, Lord Luken."

"Alas, I am not a politician. I am only the Empress's concubine. But what if I could offer your son a position as Consort at a more, shall we say, *fitting* House? Perhaps the House of the Dreaming Tiger? The Lady of the House has a daughter; the heiress, Lady Tsana, who is thirty-six years old and has no Consort. The Dreaming Tiger is, of course, a High House, whereas the Houses where Nikay went on Leave were both Middling Houses, and far from home. If Nikay were to become Tsana's Consort at the Dreaming Tiger, he would live less than two day's journey from the Misty Springs. He could visit you many times a year, whereas if Nikay goes to the Seashell, well..." Luken shrugged; they both knew it was not realistic for a Consort to simply pack up his andos and traverse the breadth of the continental Empire from south to north whenever he chose. "Perhaps you'll see him again, some day."

Lady Silan frowned. "You are not of the House of the Dreaming Tiger. By what authority do you offer Nikay a position there?"

"I have a connection," Luken said breezily. Tsikoran, Luken's sister's courtesan, had assured Luken via their recent correspondence that the Dreaming Tiger would be only too pleased to draw an ally away from the Spiraling Doves; indeed, it had been Tsikoran's idea to contact his sister Tsana, who had confirmed that she was not opposed to taking on a Consort, if he was tall and attractive and well-mannered and would not embarrass her political ambitions – all of which, Luken had assured Tsikoran in his letters, described Nikay perfectly. That he was the Son of a High House and represented the coveted influence of the Misty Springs would suit Tsana only too well. It was, all things considered, a rather ingenious pairing. Luken could not deny it: he was pleased with himself that it had all fallen out so well. Who said men were useless in politics? It was all courtesans and Consorts, forming these bridges from House to House. "Allow me to confer with Lady Tsana. She is, I assure you, an excellent choice for any lord and currently in the market for a Consort." Luken arched an eyebrow. "I daresay Nikay is as good a candidate as anyone. Wouldn't you agree?"

Silan scoffed. "Nikay would make an excellent Consort to any Lady lucky enough to have him."

"I agree. So let's say I can position Nikay at the House of the Dreaming Tiger-"

"It would be a fine thing, to have Nikay living nearby, at a High House, and to see him treated well. But the Dreaming Tiger is notoriously a Reformist House."

Luken held up a hand. "Let's be clear: this is not an appeal to take on a political cause or to join an alliance. This is a deal."

Lady Silan crossed one leg over the other, but said nothing. Considering him.

Good, she's listening. "The Empress, currently, is indifferent to you. Your political neutrality has resulted in a perceived irrelevance when, in truth, the Misty Springs should be considered one of the most important Houses." It never hurt to coax out a Lady's ego a little. "If you support the Empress in this issue, not only will it ingratiate you to her, but your newfound favor with the Empress can be a boon in other ways. Currently, the taxes that the House of Misty Springs is permitted to impose on transit across the Stone River is fixed. That roof can be raised, if the Empress wills it."

The Lady arched an eyebrow. "This, I suppose, is to make up for the income I would lose on my dealings with the Spiraling Doves if they refuse to trade with the Misty Springs as a result of my voting with the Reformists in the next Assembly?"

"Precisely." Luken played his final card. "To be frank, the Empress does not wish to be remembered by history as a warmonger. She believes it is time for peace. She is prepared to enforce that belief.

Lady Silan's eyes widened slightly. "Do you mean to imply that the Empress will use an Imperial Mandate to overrule the Assembly and the

Convention both, to avoid war with Builay?"

Luken hesitated. No, Raisaga had not said that. She did not want another war, but she had not promised to declare an Imperial Mandate to avoid one, either. It was risky. If he were to be caught lying about the Empress's intentions to a Lady- Well, her previous concubine's disgraceful exit would soon be forgotten, compared to what would be done to him.

Fuck it. "The Empress will do what she must."

Silan stared at him. Hard, cutting. "I must have it from your own lips."

In the end, it was easy. Five years as a courtesan had prepared him to lie straight to a Lady's face as nothing else could. "The Empress is prepared to override both the Assembly and the Convention, if necessary. She does not wish to. It would cause unnecessary conflict and resistance from the Traditionalists. But she will, if she has to."

Lady Silan let out a long breath. "I see. Thank you for telling me this, Lord Luken." She paused a moment, her cheek wimpling as she chewed the inside of her mouth. "So if I vote along Reformist lines on this issue, I anger the House of Spiraling Doves, perhaps losing their trade for many years to come. But I gain standing with the Empress, a good position for my son, and the ability to impose higher trade and transit taxes on the Stone River."

"That is the long and short of it, yes."

She sighed. "I almost wish you did not present such a good deal, Lord Luken. I do not like getting involved..." A distant look entered her eyes. "But I do not wish for more war." A long pause. Luken knew she thought of her sons. The ones she had given up because it was proper and moral and good for the Empire. The ones she had never known. If any still lived. If any were coming home from Hindigga. If any would know peace in their lifetime. "It is enough."

Luken waited.

Lady Silan met his gaze. "Very well, Lord Luken. You have won me over."

"It's nothing to do with me. You have won yourself a good deal and peace for the Empire."

She shook her head. "Even with the vote of the Misty Springs, and my Middling and Minor Houses – who, yes, I shall order to vote against the war – it would still only be a tie in the Assembly. Unless you can turn one of the Traditionalists, which I can assure you, you will not do, or convince the House of the Stone Cliffs to vote Reformist." She gave him a skeptical look. "Lady Asang is the most stubborn spit-fire in the Empire. I don't envy your chances of that, Luken. And if the Assembly ties, well, the issue will go to the Convention. And the Convention is now mostly Traditionalist, thanks to Hani's victory in last year's election. They will absolutely vote in favor of invading Builay."

"I'm aware," Luken said softly. "Leave Lady Asang to me."

Chapter Twenty-Seven

Luken passed beneath the Board on his way through the cavernous hall, and paused, the echo of his footsteps falling silent. His name, at the top of the column. A hateful blessing. He scanned the ranks of men. Isaun, 330.

Luken sighed. The brawl with Ohfene in the Garden had lost Isaun another hundred places on the Board overnight. Every day since then, he'd slipped another five to ten places. The message was clear: *You're done. Get out.* A shameful end to one of the most illustrious courtesan careers in living memory. It still made Luken sick whenever he thought about it.

So far, Isaun had not obeyed, but Luken didn't know how much longer the situation could continue. Every day, Isaun kept to his room in the Abode, like a creature hiding in its den. And every day, the courtesans gathered around the Board like vultures at a fat corpse, tittering at their good fortune as they watched his name sink and sink. He'd heard from Dandy that some Abodes now had running bets on how low Isaun's name would fall before he abandoned Court.

"He's bound to go before it hits 400, right?" a young courtesan asked his friend, their heads bent close together, twin smirks on their lips. Neither could have been older than seventeen. "I mean, he wouldn't let it get that pathetic, would he?"

"As pathetic as mean-spirited gossip?" Luken asked, sweeping through the hall.

The two turned toward him with haughty scorn – then, recognizing the Empress's concubine, bowed low with mews of surprise and scurried from the hall.

Luken strode down from the southern Palace entrance, making for the Peahen Pavilion. He passed the little bench where he and Tian had met every morning during their first brief episode at Court, and through the arch, down the winding path, and into the grassy lawns beneath the shadows of the great oaks. A blanket of snow still lay across the grounds, though the bitter chill had lifted and small patches of green peered through the white as O-Han shrugged off his winter coat.

Technically, men were not permitted to enter the Pavilion unescorted, but it would not have mattered for Luken. Cami and Sami, striding silently behind him, formed the only escort he needed as he made his way to the Diamond Manor, where Lady Asang was staying while visiting the Palace.

Satomi, with heavy coaching, had overcome his distracted nature long enough to secure a meeting between his mother and Luken, though the Lady had flat-out refused to stir from the Manor.

He found her on the portico in back of the Diamond Manor, sprawled on a seat there, her cup of coffee steaming on the circular table to her left, her long legs stretched out in front of her, one crossed over the other. An ancient oak dominated the back garden, the great crown of its boughs dappling half the portico with dancing shadows. Satomi sat on a swinging bench that hung from the wooden beams above them and waved to Luken as he made his way up the steps.

Luken bowed his head. "Lady Asang. Satomi."

She nodded. "Good to see you again, Luken. You're here about the Assembly."

Luken froze midway through pulling out a chair at the table. Recovering, he offered a pretty smile. "Am I so obvious?"

Asang arched an eyebrow. "I hardly think it was the pleasure of my company that drew you."

He took a seat. "You sell yourself short."

"Save your politicking, concubine. My mind is made up."

Luken stiffened. "I see. And may I ask what, exactly, is on your mind?"

She took a long sip of coffee, though it must have been boiling hot. The steam purled around her tight, red curls.

"I prefer not to say. After all," she lifted her eyes to the boughs of the oak, "I might change my mind. I don't like to be bound. By anything. But let me ask *you* a question, Luken. You don't like the Court, do you?"

"What gave you that idea, Lady Asang?"

"General rumor-mongering," she said bluntly. "Dissatisfied little slut, the Traditionalists call you, when they come a-knocking on my door." A smile spread her lips when she saw the look on his face. "Oh yes, you're hardly my first visitor since I've been at Court. Pazu, Ekaris, Hani, even Kanay and Joasa," she mentioned two leaders of the Reformist coalition. "I've got suitors aplenty." Asang sipped her coffee. "Though I admit, none quite so pretty as you."

"And what do they offer you in exchange for

your vote?"

"Money, men, land. All the usual shit. But I've got plenty of money, too much land, and no need for another man."

"They did not stir you, then."

A wry smile. "Not quite. So what are you here to bribe me with, Luken Kenkazu-son? I need nothing, but I'd love to hear what a royal concubine thinks will change my mind."

Luken wavered. This was not at all how he'd expected things to go. "In truth, Lady Asang, I can offer you nothing." She cocked her head. "But you are right, I do not like the Court. I do not like how things are done here. I do not like how courtesans are treated." His gaze darted to Satomi, who swung back and forth on the bench, humming to himself.

Lady Asang followed his gaze. "I'm taking him with me, you know. Satomi's courtesan days are done. We're going home. As soon as the Assembly's over."

Luken nodded. "I will miss him." They let the quiet linger, dappled by changeling shadows as the oak branches stirred in the wind. "You do not like the Court either. You said as much, at the dinner party. What if I told you that voting against the war was the easiest way to piss off the most people in power right now at Court?"

Lady Asang grinned. "It's a pleasant thought, isn't it?" She drained the last of her coffee. "Satomi has told me about you, Luken. You've been kind to him. Encouraged him to sign up for classes, taken Flower Arrangement with him. As if that wasn't an enormous waste of time. Kind, though. My poor, idiot son deserves a little kindness. He used to be quite clever you know, before the drugs and drinking and the concussion." She sighed. "I'm getting soft in my old age. I've heard having sons does that to you. Well." Asang met his gaze. "The Stone Cliffs doesn't typically get involved in politics. We were queens, before we were Ladies – a long time ago, before our little queendom in the north was drawn into the Empire. We are Kanain now, through and through, but the House of Stone Cliffs never relinquished her independent spirit. And never will, while I am Lady. That is why we remain neutral in affairs of the Palace. But I must tell you, Luken, I am sick to death of the Court's bullshit."

"That, Lady Asang, makes two of us."

She smiled, and gazed at her son. "Let us be glad, then, that this business is nearly over."

Chapter Twenty-Eight

Luken strolled beneath the shades of the oaks and the sprawling lawns, making his way free of the Peahen Pavilion and out onto the Palace grounds. Despite the lingering chill in the air, a gentle light warmed the snow to glistening banks whenever the pale orb wandered free of the haze of clouds. Luken let his footsteps take him the long way around, having no desire to reach the lonely shadows of his chambers just yet, not when the feeble sunlight that warmed the air had left it pleasant and crisp for the first time in long, cold weeks. His path took him close to the outer ring of the Palace grounds, where the wall loomed high overhead, barring the city from view. A tower rose from the wall in the distance on his left side, where a retinue of guards watched over the gates. Luken had ridden through those gates often enough, as business at the Dahlia had taken him in and out of the city.

Warmed by a cloak of nostalgia, Luken was almost unsurprised to hear his own name shouted at him across the distance, from the other side of the gate, where his thoughts already dwelled. It was only when the harsh bark of the voice echoed a second time that Luken startled, and quickened forward to find – of all people – Kyo standing behind the black iron bars, waving at him frantically.

"Kyo?" He stepped forward.

An annoyed guard glanced back at him,

recognizing, if not his face, at least the pair of white-clad eunuch guards that flanked Luken. "Lord Luken, this one says he knows you. Been perched outside the gates all day, demanding to see you." He cocked an eyebrow. "Made quite a nuisance of himself, actually." The guard hefted his polestaff with more than a little enthusiasm. "Shall we dispose of him for you?"

"No," Luken rushed to the gate, where Kyo gripped the bars with calloused fingers. "I will see him."

Kyo swore under his breath. "I didn't think I'd catch you. I've been standing here all morning and yesterday too, trying to see you. Hailing every carriage that rolled by. Of course the fucking guards won't let me in, but I didn't know what else to do."

Dread seized Luken's core, a chilly clench. "What happened? What now?"

A rolled and folded sheaf of paper poked through the bars. "*The Easterner*," Kyo said. "You have to read what Koko wrote about Rori in his review of *Scarlet and Gold*."

Luken stared at the magazine. "You sought me at the Palace for this?"

"Luken," Kyo's voice held a note of pleading that Luken had never heard before. "This is serious."

Luken met his eyes, squinting against the sunlight. Without a word, Luken opened the magazine to the page Kyo had marked. He scanned the first few paragraphs of the review, which contained a brief reference to Eru Taler, the pen name Rori was using for this project, and a summary of the book's contents, followed by a searing review driven by exactly the degree of vitriol Luken would have expected Koko to dish out to a book like *Scarlet and Gold*. But after the first few paragraphs, the tone of the review abruptly changed. Koko abandoned the review format with a casual, *But that, Dear Reader, is not the real story. Let me tell you something far more interesting.* Luken's heart sank. He swallowed, despite the tightness of his throat, and read on.

Eru Taler is a pen name, and the man behind it is no newcomer to O-Han's literary scene. How do I know this? That tale, Reader, would form a novel in and of itself, and one far better than Scarlet and Gold, *at that. Suffice to say that following a history of observation of certain publications in O-Han – notably, a Reformist rag titled* Ages, *which some of you may know from the particular care and attention it pays to my humble works – and a series of fortunate inquiries, my research team has been able to deduce that the name 'Eru Taler,' linked to* Scarlet and Gold *publisher,* Century Press, *and Century's editor, Rin Haru, is likewise connected to the author Jiro Ankade, who has worked with Rin Haru over the course of their career. Fans will recognize the name as a popular mainstay of the romance genre, but may be surprised to find that like Eru Taler, Jiro Ankade is a pen name. A cursory review of* Century's *financial files reveal a man named 'Roane Siu' as the beneficiary of profits for the sale of both* Scarlet and Gold, *as well as the entirety of Jiro Ankade's catalog.* "Oh Goddess," Luken breathed. "No..."

Kyo shook his head. "It gets worse."

But wait, Dear Reader. I did not write this article for the dull purpose of revealing the true name of some second-rate romance writer whose beat-up paperbacks line the shelves at your local used bookstore. What we discovered next is far more interesting than that.

Roane Siu did not begin his career as novelist Jiro Ankade. Prior to deciding that he would like to actually make money with his writing, Siu contributed pieces to none other than Ages, *the aforementioned Reformist publication based here in O-Han, which he published under his real name. While it would be entertaining to regale you with the juvenile thoughts and opinions of a young Roane Siu, the pieces Siu contributed to the magazine are more interesting in the connection that they establish between Siu and the publisher. In the past year,* Ages *has published a number of articles attributed to name 'Vin Ayet.'*

If it was possible to survive the complete halting of the heart, Luken managed it then. Even his eyes seemed to have fallen lifeless, fixed to the name on the page. His pen name.

The pieces – or whatever you want to call them – published under the name Vin Ayet have consisted of an esoteric rambling loosely focused on the topic of gender through a predictable lens of Equalist zeal – we are talking about Ages *after all, folks – that began last year with a bizarre homage to the slain courtesan, Iriko Sensa-son, and deviated into a series of attacks on my own catalog of work, punctured by vacuous ruminations better suited to frantic whispers in the padded rooms of an asylum than the pages of a well-circulated magazine. What does this have to do with Roane Siu? Patience, Reader, I am coming to the point.*

Further investigation of the name Vin Ayet, predictably, reveals: absolutely nothing. Why? Because – are we sensing a pattern here? – like Eru Taler and Jiro Ankade, Vin Ayet is a pen name. Admittedly, it cannot be proven that Roane Siu is also Vin Ayet, but all the connections would lead one in that direction: the association with Ages *and its editor, Seito Bakomo, the obsession with gender politics and cultural rectitude, the pretentious and accusatory style of 'observation' regarding Kanai's dearly held and cherished beliefs. It is all there, folks.*

The question now becomes: Who is Roane Siu? Aside from a sad little man who chooses to hide behind a wall of pen names while launching inflammatory rhetoric at the good people of O-Han, that is.

To have a team of researchers at your disposal is such a fine thing, Dear Reader.

Weeks of investigation into the shadowy figure behind these pen names reveal the portrait of a privileged boy, the son of a judge and a minor courtesan; a spoiled aristocrat who toyed with big ideas, caroused with artists and courtesans alike in his early years before his dangerous rhetoric resulted in Siu being banned from Palace functions, and coming to roost, ultimately, in the Topaz District here in O-Han. And through it all, he remained suspiciously devoid of any romantic attachments.

Or did he?

While investigators could find no association between Siu and any women, there is this: a squalid apartment in a crowded tenement building in the Topaz District with two names on the lease. Roane Siu and Katobi Casun, a Professor of – restrain your laughter – Men's History, at the Academy of O-Han.

The two men have evidently shared this apartment – a one-bedroom apartment, by the way – for nine years.

Now, it would be considered libel to accuse Siu and Casun outright of the crime of sodomy. And I will not write that the two men are homosexual. I will not write that, friends. Homosexuality is, after all, a crime and a guilty verdict may be punished with fifteen-twenty years of imprisonment. And while I'm sure that just about any prison cell in Kanai would be an improvement on the hell-hole that is the Topaz District, I will not have it on my conscience that I was responsible for sending anyone there.

Luken's hands shook as he lowered the battered magazine. "He thinks Rori is Vin Ayet. Fuck me. He's going to destroy Rori's life for what – my reviews in *Ages*?"

Kyo shook his head, his face framed by the black bars of the gate. "If only I could get my hands around that vindictive prick's neck."

A blossom of guilt unfolded its black petals in Luken's chest, aching and tentative. The one blossom. And then the meadow. And then the valley. And then the countryside, surging black and blossoming.

"This is all my fault."

"Don't flatter yourself, kiddo. I'd say Koko did more than a bit of the heavy-lifting on this one."

"Does Rori know yet?"

"Luken." Kyo looked at him, jaw clenched. "Rori and Kat were arrested on suspicion of criminal sodomy this morning."

~

"Get your fucking hands off me, I need to speak to her now!" Luken shoved a guard away from him, breaking his grip.

"My lord, please, you can't just–"

Luken thrust the door open with his shoulder and plowed past the guards. They didn't dare manhandle him – not while he had the Empress's favor – but swept in after him, keeping pace like circus tigers mirroring a man's stride past their cage.

The Empress glanced up at him, eyebrows

arched, a pen in one hand poised over a document, as if interrupted mid-sentence. She leaned back in her seat, and laid the pen aside. Whatever she gleaned from his face, it was enough. Fi stood frozen at one end of the broad, mahogany desk. Glancing at her Steward, the Empress said, "Everyone, please step outside." A smile, half-wearied, half-amused. "It seems my young friend here would like a word with me."

The guards and a mousy scribe in the corner turned toward the door, but Fi gripped his arm in passing. "What are you doing?" she hissed.

Luken shook his head; he had no time for her scolding. He'd ruined everything with his amateurish fumbling at a life outside the Palace, and now two innocent people suffered for his mistakes.

The door slammed behind her, leaving Luken alone with the Empress.

"Well lad, let's hear it."

His lips parted – and tears started in Luken's eyes. A sob strangled her name. "Raisaga."

Her eyes widened. "Oh love, is it that serious?"

And then it came over him like a flood. With halting, breathless sobs, Luken stammered a messy explanation. The Empress listened, sympathetic and attentive. But when he had finished, a puzzled expression lingered on Raisaga's features.

"So this friend of yours, Rori, really is a homosexual?"

"I- Does it matter?"

She sighed, steepling her fingers together, elbows on the desk. "Sodomy is, technically, still illegal."

He stared at her. "Well then you'd better chuck me in prison as well. Or do you not recall some of the things I've done for your viewing pleasure?"

A thin smile. "That's different, love."

"Because it's for a woman's amusement?"

"Basically. I mean, we know you're not really homosexual. Don't look at me like that, Luken. I don't hate homosexuals." She sighed. "It's an archaic law, but not easy to change. You may have a more, ah, urban view of the issue, but you must understand, Luken, most Kanain citizens still support the enforcement of sodomy laws."

"Because they're ignorant assholes! Rori and Kat should not have to suffer for other people's ignorance. They've done nothing wrong!"

"I can't change the law just because this time, it happens to affect your friends."

Rage pulsed in Luken's temples with a gathering headache; he fought to keep his voice level. "You have no idea what Rori has done for me over the years, Raisaga. If you care for me at all, you should appreciate that Rori has gone out of his way to help me more than any other person alive."

Raisaga gazed back at him. "What would you have me do?"

"Pardon them. You have that power."

"If I pardon your friends, it's as good as giving my sanction to homosexuality. Judges across Kanai could use my pardon as precedent for leniency in sodomy cases. My approval would be seen as a tacit endorsement of decriminalizing homosexuality."

"Good! That's exactly what you should do!"

She sighed. "This really isn't a good time to

take a stand on the gay issue, Luken."

"Just like it wasn't the time to take a stand on the vasectomy suppression issue, either. It seems like it's never a good time to take a stand, is it?"

"Seven Hells," Raisaga muttered under her breath, pushing away from the desk. She stood, one hand gripping the back of her chair as she turned from him and gazed from the latticed window behind the desk. "I wrote a letter of permission for your vasectomy myself, even though you were not initially upfront about wanting the procedure yourself."

His voice fell, low and warm. "And I have thanked you for that profusely." Luken drew a deep breath, steadying himself. "I have no qualms with the way you have treated me, Raisaga. You have been nothing but kind to me, and I thank you. But there are other lives at stake. I respect you, Rai, but I would respect you more if you cared about the lives of men you don't happen to be fucking."

Silence, ringing through the air.

He'd gone too far. A sickly dread filled Luken.

And then, her shoulders shaking softly, the Empress laughed. Just a moment, and the laughter sighed away. "You know, they say women tend to end up with men who remind them of their own fathers."

"Liliray," Luken whispered.

"Yes. Sometimes you remind me of him with startling clarity." A heavy sigh. "They mean a great deal to you, don't they?"

"If Rori and Kat are imprisoned, I will not be able to stand it. I just can't."

"They may be found innocent."

"You know they won't be. Koko told all of O-

Han they've been living in sin for nine years. Witnesses will be brought in; the neighbors, the landlady. They'll be convicted. Then what will you do?"

The Empress turned. In silent steps, she reached him. Placed a hand on his shoulder. Gazed up into his eyes. A phantom of his troubled face, reflected in her irises.

"I will pardon your friends."

The breath left Luken's body. Relief left him trembling.

"Thank you, Raisaga." He kissed her. With feeling.

She chuckled, pulling away with a grin. "I should have known you would get me into trouble."

~

Luken left the Empress's office infinitely more calm than he had arrived – and, perhaps in answer to that kiss, with the insinuation that she would summon him to her chambers that evening – but as he strode down the hallway, the reality of the situation returned to him.

Even if pardoned, Rori and Katobi's problems would not vanish. Koko had exposed them to all of O-Han. And oh, how O-Han loved its scandals. Within days, gossip about the article's contents would pass like a lightning bolt from one end of the city to the other. The Academy would not allow Katobi to continue teaching – a lifetime of fighting his way into female-dominated academia, wasted in the span of a breath. Rori's pen names were blown, sales would be affected. They would be recognized all over O-Han, especially once the newspapers picked up on the story.

Where could they go? Where would they live?

The horrible realization dyed Luken's mind; Rori and Katobi could not remain in O-Han. The life they had built here had been taken from them.

As he walked, Luken's hand clenched into a fist. Koko.

Footsteps behind him, ringing off the floorboards of the lonely corridor. "Luken!"

He turned to find Fi stomping toward him, shadows skipping across her features in the dimness of the hallway. "Just what were you thinking back there? Throwing a fit in front of the Empress, interrupting her work, barging past her guards. I thought you had more sense than that. Are you *trying* to lose your position as concubine?"

"It doesn't concern you, Fi." He turned and continued walking, but Fi jogged to his side, and kept pace.

"Oh, I think it does. For weeks, I've been lobbying for you, and you just turned around and proved yourself unfit."

"Unfit? What for?"

"To be the Empress's Consort, you moron."

Luken struggled to put his thoughts in order. There was just too much going on. "I don't understand."

"Luken." Fi crossed her arms, looking up at him. "Lord Aokinay is unwell. His health took a turn for the worse earlier this year, and he has not fully recovered, in spite of the doctors' interventions. He's decided to return to his maternal home, the House of Distant Thunder, for rest and respite in the countryside." She cocked her head. "Read between the lines. Aokinay will not be returning. The temporary leave of absence will eventually become permanent, and he will quietly slip away from public consciousness, just like Misene, the Empress's Consort before him."

Luken was surprised by the stab of guilt he felt at these words. He'd left his one and only meeting with Aokinay feeling nothing but contempt for the man.

"I didn't realize his relationship with the Empress had grown so distant."

"It was only a matter of time. They've been growing apart for years, but it took the past few months to finally convince Aokinay that things would never return to the way they had been."

"What changed his mind?"

"The illness excuse is not entirely a fabrication." Their footsteps took them down a series of stairs, into the Southern Hall, where the portraits of by-gone Empress's glowered their disapproval at them in passing. "Aokinay truly has been feeling unwell. Losing weight, hair thinning, general weakness and headaches; a host of minor ills. There was one evening, though, when he collapsed in his chambers. His servants called for the Empress, but she was busy that evening with you. I believe that was the turning point. The next morning, he wrote to his mother."

Luken whistled; it echoed faintly in the dome above them. "He must *hate* me."

"Beyond all reason, yes. But in truth, Luken, I believe this would have happened with or without you. Collapse was imminent. You just delivered a swift kick to one of the last support beams."

Luken sighed. "Still, I do not feel good about his departure."

"Don't you?" She cocked an eyebrow as they swept past the portrait of Empress Rozankin, her beefy features plainly unamused. "This greatly increases your odds of becoming Empress's Consort – or at least, it did before you threw that little hissy fit back there. I made your case to the Empress on the very premise that you were a levelheaded and accomodating young man not given to such theatrics. Thank you for making me look like an asshole."

"You hardly need my help on that score, but you're welcome. Why do you want me to become the Empress's Consort anyway?"

Fi frowned, as if it was not in her nature to release compliments from her lips. "You've been a good influence on her. There's a lightness to the Empress now that I have not seen in many years. More than that, she pushes her position more in political negotiations. Only yesterday, the Empress forced Hani to drop her most extreme policies from the Traditionalist coalition's proposal to the Assembly, or their time to make their case before the other Ladies would be cut to almost nothing. They acceded, with more than a little grumbling. It was lovely to see her shut Hani down, full stop. Too long, Raisaga has played the mediator between Reformists and Traditionalists. It's good to see her fighting back. She credits her 'new conscience' for this change. And unlike Aokinay, your family is not pushy and manipulative." *You don't know my father,* Luken thought. "Your relationship with the Empress is not a calculated political ploy designed to push your family's agenda at Court. And more than that, Raisaga adores you. Do you know how often she has spoken to me of you in the past few months? The Empress does not go on and on like that about her concubines. Promoting you to Empress's Consort makes sense, so long as you behave yourself."

They reached his chambers; Fi halted at the door, forcing him to pause with his hand on the doorknob. "If all goes according to plan, the Empress will announce you as her new Consort at the Spring Gala. Try not to ruin everything before then, and your future is set."

~

Inside his chambers, Luken stood for a long moment. Motionless, and silent.

In slow steps, almost like a sleepwalker, he made his way upstairs and rifled through his drawers until, beneath a copy of *Flights of Midnight*, he pulled out an envelope, and shucked the loose pages of a letter from the white sheath. Lady Tilar's letter to Koko.

"One good turn deserves another, Koko. You aren't the only one who can play this game."

He returned the pages to their envelope, and included a note to Seito with a single line in black ink.

End the fucker.

Chapter Twenty-Nine

The day of the Assembly dawned bright and clear. Ladies poured into the Assembly Hall, in the northern end of the Palace's heart. Black-clad in coats and trousers, each with the insignia of their House sewn on the left breast of their coats, the Ladies took their seats among the staggered tiers that formed the circular amphitheater. They were seated based on the positions of their Houses, the Lady of each region's High House foremost on her platform, and the Middling and Minor Houses fanning out behind her.

Mahogany floorboards, polished to a dark sheen, formed the floor and walls, and climbed into the shadows of the vaulted ceiling. Streamers of golden light slipped from a line of tall, narrow windows just beneath the beams of the ceiling, though the hall itself cradled profound shadows. Candles blazed in their own glimmering assembly around the hall, baking the mahogany to hints of russet. An aisle divided the circle of seating platforms into two halves. At the far end of the Hall, the Empress's throne stood tall and somber upon a raised dais.

Balconies lined the walls, and here, important observers were granted reserved seating. There had never been a doubt in Luken's mind that he would attend the Assembly, but he was surprised to discover that Fi had reserved him the balcony normally occupied by the Empress's Consort. A bold move. She had as good as declared him the imminent Consort, and many Ladies, arriving in the Hall, glanced up to find, not Aokinay, but the Empress's mysterious young concubine, occupying his place. Traditionalist Ladies openly sneered at him, shaking their heads in disgust. Lady Ekaris pinned him with a murderous glare from across the span of the Hall, but he ignored her, and waved to his mother, Lady Kenkazu, as she took her seat behind Lady Kanay, of the House of the Gossamer Moth, the High House of Luken's native E-Kara region. She smiled up at him, and waved back.

Luken resigned himself to a long wait as the Ladies took their seats, until at last the Assembly Hall had filled. The Empress entered, and the Ladies stood in unison as she strode down the center of the aisle, her cloak of royal blue swept in the motion of her stride, still swift and strong despite her age. Luken watched, pride blooming in his chest. And sorrow, regret. Jes's face, flashing white-bright against the dimness of the Hall.

Empress Raisaga climbed the dais, and reached her throne before turning to face the Assembly. A hush fell over the Hall, and for a long moment, despite the great gathering of women from all across the Empire, there was absolute attention and silence.

"Ladies of Kanai, be welcome."

As one, they bowed, and resumed their seats.

"We are here today," Raisaga continued, "to bring forth proposals in earnestness and good faith, for the benefit and improvement of the women and men who depend upon us, and for the glory of the Empire. Many of you have journeyed far, for long and wearisome weeks. Some have crossed dangerous paths and braved uncertain waters. All have left their loved ones behind for this momentous occasion. But each of you must know that you vote not only for yourself, but for all who depend upon us. I trust," her gaze moved across the circle of the hall with the warning of a hawk surveying prey, "that you shall all vote as your conscience bids you, for the good of Kanai." She took her seat upon the throne, and Luken joined in a brief round of applause.

The Steward of Political Dispensement rose and announced the debate portion of the Assembly. Each coalition would have the opportunity to describe the policies they proposed to the Assembly, and defend their merits.

"Pointless," Luken hissed under his breath, but strove not to look bored as the Reformist coalition rose to present their proposal. He saw little point in debating; everyone gathered here already knew the issues they were voting on, and who they stood with or against. Their minds were made up before the debate began.

The Reformist coalition, led by Lady Kanay, did an admirable job of presenting a reasonable agenda for the coming years before turning to the crucial issue: Builay. She argued vehemently against military intervention in Builay, pointing out that it was certain to lead to further war, just when Kanai was most eager for peace. The debate portion of their presentation was contentious enough to make Luken's gut clench, especially with Hani's jeering aggression and stupid questions dominating much of the debate.

The Traditionalist coalition, by contrast, did not bother with the question portion of the presentation. Led by Lady Ekaris, they yelled about Builay for almost an hour, then abruptly sat down.

Luken rolled his eyes.

"Thank you, Ladies," the Empress said dryly. "We will begin a vote of each proposal brought before the Assembly today."

Luken resisted the urge to rip his hair out, thread by thread, as the rounds of voting commenced. His legs ached to walk. He forced himself to be still.

At last, the Empress announced, "We will now vote on the proposed military intervention in Builay. Let us begin with the A-Region. Lady Left Wren, you may vote."

And so it began. The Ladies voted, one by one. Each according to their Houses, their alliances.

Strange, how many faces he recognized. These were not phantoms, pulling the strings of the Empire. These were women he knew.

Lady Kahr, the mother of his son, who remained neutral.

Lady Yinskay, Dandy's mother, who voted against the war.

Lady Jiren, Romyn's sister, who voted in favor of the war.

Lady Dare. Luken's eyes fastened on her, and his lungs could not catch enough air. Dark spots wimpled his vision, the stranglehold of a panic attack crawling down his throat.

Luken forced himself to look away, to fix his gaze on a single bar of the railing of his balcony. No. He would not panic over Lady Dare. What power did she have over his heart? Over his mind? His body? None. Luken stared at the bar, nothing but the bar.

Concentrated on his breathing. U-Wen had no power over him any more. None.

Can you remember all their names? All your clients, one by one. Luken fumbled for their names as black stars swarmed his eyes. Starting with Kahr, and on, one by one, over the months, over the years, he remembered them all, and as Luken recalled each one, he found the syllables of their names solidifying in his mind as the dark stars faded. Until he reached Mian, and finally, Raisaga.

He gazed at Lady Dare, his heartbeat slowing, his vision clear. She glanced up and met his gaze. Blinked. Gave a tentative, almost hopeful, wave. He looked away, and did not look back.

Luken's gaze found Lady Silan among the tiers of seated Ladies, and Lady Asang, toward the bottom right of the far side of the Hall.

It all came down to this.

"Lady Vonli. Please give us your vote on behalf of the House of the Lily."

She stood, a woman in middle-age, with brown skin tanned darker by many days beneath the sun, and her hair, a scraggly wave of dark brown, falling to the nape of her neck. Isaun's mother. If there was ever a son who favored his mother less, Luken had not met them. Where Isaun was striking, his mother had a wiry, forgettable aspect that Luken found an immediate dislike for. There was an apathetic look about her, like an oca addict who has played slave to their drug for so long that they no longer even feel pleasure in the high. "The Lily," thick with a Ysmyn accent, she dripped her words like honey, "declines to vote."

She was forgotten the moment she sat back down, but Luken's gaze lingered on her face long after the Empress moved on, registering the votes of a dozen more Houses until-

"Lady Kenkazu."

With a surge of pride, Luken watched his mother vote against the war, standing with her in that moment with every fiber of his being.

And soon enough: "Lady Silan. How does the House of Misty Springs vote?"

A pause, in which a bubble of conversation rose through the Assembly, filling the hall with a dull murmur. The Misty Springs had declined to vote for so long, no doubt the other Ladies barely waited for the answer. Across the aisle, Luken watched Ekaris murmur something in Hani's ear; her belly heaved with laughter.

Lady Silan stood, and lifted her chin. "The House of Misty Springs votes," her eyes raked the crowd, found Luken's, held a moment, and swiveled to the Empress, "against the proposal."

For a long moment, no one reacted. The murmur of conversation continued, broke off into stunned silence, then rose again with a sudden, heightened pitch. *"What did she say?" "Against?" "I can't have heard her right."*

Luken watched the Lady of Great Falls whip around in her seat to hiss, "You said they would decline to vote!" at the Lady of Ivory Road, who stammered something incoherent. Below Luken's balcony, an ominous voice – laced with admiration – muttered, "Someone finally got to the Misty Springs."

"Quiet!" the Empress lifted her voice. "I will

have quiet in the Hall."

Lady Silan took her seat, gazing downward as if there were nothing more interesting for her to do at that moment than contemplate the embroidery on the back of her gloves.

The murmurs fell away. Smiling, the Empress turned her gaze to Lady Silan. "Thank you, Lady Misty Springs. Your vote is registered. Lady Jade Mountain, do you vote for or against the proposal?"

With distaste, Luken watched Lifelle's mother vote for the war, but the tone in the Hall had shifted; even as she cast her vote, Lady Boaya looked distracted, and more than a few Traditionalists bowed their heads together, conferring in rapid whispers.

More murmurs from below Luken, as the voting continued.

"A tie," someone muttered in disbelief. "The vote will go to the Convention."

"Not if the Stone Cliffs vote."

"The Stone Cliffs never vote. They're neutral."

"So were the Misty Springs, remember?"

It went on, the Hall tense, waiting. More than a few Ladies did the math in their heads and looked to Lady Asang. But the Lady of the Stone Cliffs gave nothing away, her expression detached, wry. She seemed to enjoy the distressed attentions of the Hall, but there was no guessing her thoughts.

Luken found his mother's gaze in the crowd and held it, a long, shared moment.

As last, the Empress turned her gaze to Lady Asang. "Lady Stone Cliffs. Last but certaintly not least. We find ourselves at an impasse. So. Do you vote for or against this measure?"

Lady Asang did not even rise from her seat. She lounged, eyes half-lidded, red hair a flame in the dimness of the hall. And a slow, hateful smile slid across her lips. "Against."

The uproar was immediate.

Voices – angry, stunned, jubilant – erupted all at once. Lady Silan winked at Luken, grinned at the Lady of the House of the Dreaming Tiger – where her son would soon live – and strode from the hall without a word. The Lady of the Gossamer Moth stood in disbelief as the Lady of Bronze Hills climbed over two rows of seating to embrace her. A Desmeran Lady from the House of Waving Fronds cackled and lifted her hands in a gesture of thanksgiving to the gods of her Isle, ignoring the glares of the Ladies around her. Some of the Minor Ladies rushed to attend their furious High Ladies, others merely shrugged and spread their hands. Luken watched, delighted, as Ekaris turned and snapped at her attendants, who flinched back into the shadows. Beside her, Lady Mian looked pale, almost faint. Hani, red-faced, stormed from the hall, bellowing at a trio of Minor Ladies, who scampered from her path.

The Empress held up a hand. Like a difficult client, silence was long in coming, but come it did, in the end. Only then, into the shaken Hall, did the Empress speak. "Ladies of the Noble Assembly, the proposal has failed. The Empire will not send troops to Builay, nor begin any martial activities there. The issue," she smiled, her gaze finding Luken in the balcony, "is settled."

Chapter Thirty

Luken rushed to embrace his mother as Ladies streamed from the Assembly Hall.

"You did it!" he cried.

Lady Kenkazu returned his embrace and pressed a kiss to his forehead. Luken swallowed the urge to weep. It worked. He'd desired something significant, he'd worked toward it, he'd politicked and negotiated and pushed – and it worked.

There would be no war with Builay.

He had achieved a work worthy of Lonyelay, even Liliray.

And felt... disappointed.

Relieved, yes, to see it proven that he had some agency in this world, but...

He had expected something grander. Some choir of glory singing within him.

This was not even an echo of the glory he'd found in Jes's arms on those forbidden midnights when he'd still known her love.

"I'm going to find Amana and tell him the good news," Kenkazu said.

"I'll meet you back in my chambers," Luken said with a soft smile. He went to find the Empress and their meeting on the dais of the throne was brief and ebullient, but Raisaga was soon swept away by her Stewards, for the Assembly was only the beginning of their work.

Alone, Luken made his way from the Hall, but he did not make it far before a shiver of commotion traveled through the loose crowd of dispersing Ladies and their attendants. With a swivel of déjà vu, Luken quickened his gait. *What now?*

South, along busy corridors. Whispers slithered through the air. The pull of the crowd drew Luken toward the Garden. He passed the hall of the Market Board and instinctively searched out Isaun's name – fallen to 363 – before spilling out onto the steps that gazed down on the long road of white tiles that led to the South Gate, a set of stark towers that rose from the white wall encircling the Palace grounds, barricading them from the city beyond.

Luken broke from the Palace into wind and noise.

And the strangest spectacle greeted his gaze.

A confetti of colorful scraps danced through the air. Silk and satin fabric fluttered in brilliant tufts. A chaotic crowd of young courtesans scooped scraps off the ground, ripping pearls and lace from chintz and velvet. Older courtesans ranged the broad sweep of stairs and the courtyard, like lovely sentinels paying silent guard to the scene that played out before them. In the center of the crowd, a tall courtesan with long waves of dark hair, dressed in an exquisite and voluminous ando of deep scarlet, strode forward, tossing out handful of the slips of cloth here and there, until he found the basket on his left arm empty, and tossed it at random into the crowd. A tongue of forest green fabric fluttered to Luken's feet. Quirking an eyebrow, he bent down to retrieve the scrap and felt the unmistakable texture of an ando. Dozens of andos, cut to shreds and fed to the wind. The vast sweep of the courtyard beneath the Palace steps, all colored and cluttered by hundreds, thousands, of the colorful pieces. A storm of shredded andos. Luken marveled. A fortune, mangled and cast away.

The courtesan at the center of this chaos turned, and even before Luken saw his face, he knew it was Isaun. Grinning and beautiful and destructive.

He let a bottle of wine drop from his hand. It hit the ground, cracked, and Isaun kicked it aside, a froth of royal purple bubbling from the cracks in the glass, like blood from opened veins.

"Well everyone, it's been lovely!" Isaun shouted to the crowd. "But I really must be going now! One doesn't overstay their welcome at the party – we all learned that first day of etiquette training, didn't we?"

Drunk. Lavishly drunk. Obscenely drunk. Drunk as only Isaun could be – crude and extravagant at once.

"Oh Goddess," Luken muttered, horror-stricken, and clattered down the steps. He shoved men aside, fighting his way to the front. "Isaun! Isaun!"

The older courtesan caught him around the waist and pressed a long kiss to Luken's lips.

Wolf whistles and startled shrieks rang in Luken's ears.

He pulled away to find Isaun grinning at him, green eyes dancing with mirth. "Glad you could make it out, Luken. It wouldn't be the same without you here."

"*What* wouldn't be the same?"

But Isaun had already turned from him and

strode towards the large traveling coach Luken glimpsed through the crowd; it pulled to a halt at the edge of the courtyard. The door swung open to reveal Lady Romyn, who beamed at Isaun and waved like a puppy wagging its tail.

"She paid his Conjugal Price." Luken turned to find Dandy at his side, the young courtesan's face a mingled expression of wry worry and tentative relief. "His full Price, the number given for Isaun when he was still Number Seven on the Board."

"But- why? His name plummeted, she didn't have to pay full Price."

Dandy shrugged. "She wanted to. Showed up outside the Abode yesterday with a chest full of gold. Amae just about collapsed. He didn't think he'd be able to *give* Isaun away with his number cascading down the Board, let alone get full Price for him." Dandy tucked a stray curl behind his ear. "I never understood why Amae didn't just kick him out of the Abode when Isaun was first disgraced. He clearly wanted to, but for some reason, he never did. Never spoke to Isaun at all, actually. It was almost like he was afraid to. It's a good thing he didn't though, or Isaun couldn't have accepted Romyn's proposal. It's just so unlike Amae though, I wonder why he didn't get rid of Isaun?"

Because I would have outed him for his secret family, and ended his career, Luken thought dryly.

Only then did it hit Luken. "Isaun's leaving."

A sad smile, as Dandy nodded and made an airy gesture toward the crowd around them. "He would have had to go anyway. Ohfene and Weim saw to that. This was his way of, I don't know, leaving on his own terms, I suppose. Leaving with pride, instead of being shamed off the Board by the Arbiters."

The breath abandoned Luken's body. He had never been at Court without Isaun before. Hells, could there even be a Peacock Court without Isaun of the Scattered Flowers?

"But Lady Romyn?"

"She loves him," Dandy said quietly.

"Goddess." Luken shook his head. Reaching the coach with a drunken wobble, Isaun wrapped his arms around Lady Romyn and, despite her less than slender build, lifted her clean off the ground in his embrace. Swung aloft above the heads of the crowd, Romyn dissolved into a breathless giggle. "What a couple of idiots."

Dandy chuckled. "Why not Lady Romyn? She wanted him at his height, and at his worst. That's got to count for something, I suppose."

Apparently it did. Isaun might have been close to utter disgrace, but he was still a courtesan, and the law of the Peacock Court stated that any noblewoman could buy the Conjugal Rights of any consenting courtesan, no matter how laughably low his Stud Fee had fallen.

Lady Romyn piled into the carriage. Her sister, Lady Jiren, watched from the interior with a scornful grin, her infant cradled in the arms of a servant beside her. Jiren tapped a red pen against her knee in impatience as Romyn, grinning widely, plopped down into the opposite seat.

Isaun made to join her, then leapt up onto the rim of the coach's entrance, holding onto the top of the open door with one hand as he addressed the crowd.

"That's it for me, friends! The House of the Dragonfly awaits! It's been an honor and a privilege, and all that horseshit. Just remember, next time you get fabulously drunk on good red wine, raise a glass to lucky Number Seven. That will *always* be my number, and the Board be damned." Luken found himself grinning like mad as shouts of approval rang from the gathered courtesans. Bittersweet to the point of anguish, this sudden swan song. Isaun raised a finger. "Oh, and if you happen to see Ohfene anywhere around here, just shoot him a wink and give him a little message for me: 'You never would have been so lucky.' Can you do that for me, boys?"

"Yes!" a dozen voices cried in response.

"Wonderful." Green eyes rose to survey the Palace. A lingering look. Isaun released a breath, and gazed back down at them. Then grinned, gave a final bow, and waved to the courtesans gathered before him. "Well Peacock Court, I'll take my leave then. Thank you, and go fuck yourselves."

A cheer swept the crowd, full of laughter and applause.

Isaun found Luken's face in the crowd, and with one last smile, ducked into the coach and slammed the door behind him.

~

At dawn, on a nameless day. No crowds, no riots, no public outcry. Safe and anonymous, that was how Luken intended to see this done.

The two prisoners emerged from the shadows of the gate. The prison rose behind them, a rotten tooth of grey stone fallen across the southern reach of the city, beneath the poor and industrial neighborhoods. A bad part of town for the Empress's concubine to find himself in, but worse for any who troubled him. A dozen Royal Guards, their stainless white coats gleaming in the pallid dawn, lined the path between the prison gate and Luken's carriage as Rori and Kat shuffled toward him. Worry and fatigue etched new lines on their faces, but they stood side-by-side and arm-in-arm and smiled when they saw him. Thin, tired smiles.

The prison guards grimaced at them from the gate and the windows of the tower, their faces twisted with disdain. Luken smiled back at them innocently, and ripped prey from their gnarled talons. And there was nothing at all they could do about it, glower as they might, for the Empress had given her word. A Royal Pardon, signed by Empress Raisaga herself.

There would be no time for backlash; Rori and Kat would be halfway across the Empire by the time the pardon was announced to the public.

Luken embraced them, folding Rori into his arms, then Katobi.

"Didn't I tell you becoming the Empress's concubine would have its advantages?" Rori said dryly.

A flutter of helpless laughter. "You always did know best," Luken murmured. "Come, let's get you into the carriage."

They slid inside, the Royal Guards shutting the door behind them and escorting the carriage on its drive across the lower span of O-Han, to the west gate.

"This is it, then?" Kat asked woodenly. A beam of dawn found his face as he gazed out at the city passing them by.

"Yes. I've arranged traveling accommodations along the West Way until E-Hin. Here's some money." Luken handed them an envelope. Kat took it and let it rest in his lap, not even bothering to check its contents. Either they trusted he would see them provided for, or were still in too much shock from the whole ordeal to react to anything that happened now. "Where will you go after that?"

"A-Zu," Rori said at once. "Where my sister lives. A small city by the sea, scarcely more than a town, but there's a school there. Maybe Kat can get a job. And my sister can help protect us, she's influential in the area. A judge."

Luken nodded. Where else was there to go?

Kat's gaze never left the streets of O-Han, but his voice reached Luken, hollow and dark. "And Koko?"

A bittersweet smile. "Seito published the letter. Quite the stir it's caused. Koko tried to issue a response in *The Easterner* denying everything, but Lady Tilar's given a dozen interviews to various publications, confirming the story. I don't think she cares if it makes her look bad, she just wants to see Koko humiliated. He left their home, apparently. Took his sons with him. His fans didn't like that. Saw it as 'stealing' the children from their rightful owner. Lady Tilar is the head of the household, after all," he said sarcastically. "That's the trouble with making a career on the argument that it's perfectly fine for one gender to have more power than the other – when you try to take your power back, you've already made the case that you don't have a right to it. Men like Koko never expect to live according to their own words. Now he has no choice. No Lady, no fans, no career, no power. Nothing but his own words, all turned back against him."

Kat nodded. "He's done, then?"

"I think so. *The Easterner* published an article denouncing him. His fans are disgusted with him. The Traditionalists who once used him as a quote machine are now saying they never liked him that much anyway."

Rori sighed. "Not once, in a million years, did I imagine things would end like this. I never wanted to ruin his reputation."

Kat shrugged. "I'm having trouble feeling much pity, at the moment. He tried to destroy our lives. He took our careers from us, he took our home. He took O-Han."

They watched the city pass around them. The cracked streets of Topaz, the chattering expanses of the marketplace, the lavish blossoms of Orchid Street and all its stately pleasure houses. The shadow of the Creatrix, falling over awakening streets as dawn stole over the city. Their city. For a little while longer, anyway.

They reached the wall, where the traveling coach waited for them.

A surge of fear overtook Luken. For a moment, he almost didn't let them go. "Where will you live?"

Rori looked at him. "We'll stay with my sister until we can find a house to buy."

"Can you afford that?"

A ghost of a smile. "Actually, we can. My editor wrote to me in prison. Since Koko's review, *Scarlet and Gold* has been leaping off the shelves. Ghoulish curiosity, for the most part. But there's been positive attention and support, as well." He cocked his head, and a hint of the old humor, the old Rori, kindled in his warm, brown eyes. "Thanks to Koko, *Scarlet and Gold* is set to become my best-selling book to date."

Luken laughed. An unburdened and carefree laugh, for the first time in weeks. "This fucking city."

Rori hopped down from the carriage and Kat followed with a somber smile. "It's almost a shame to leave it."

~

In the dimness of his chambers, sat the chest of gold. A third of the price for which he had been sold to Lady Dare, and given three years of his life to U-Wen. The third installment of his Conjugal Price. A large chest, locked and incredibly heavy, crouched in the corner of the room. Easy to miss. Almost a piece of the furniture at this point. Returning to his chambers, Luken's eye nearly slid right past it. He'd already learned to see it as inconsequential, a part of the background, like the set of the play at the theater he'd attended with his parents the night before; the last evening of their visit to O-Han.

They were at brunch now, a lovely restaurant in the Sapphire District that specialized in Desmeran cuisine. Luken would have gone with them, especially now that they were all celebrating the birth of Tian's second child – the news of which had arrived yesterday afternoon – but Luken had fabricated a prior engagement with the Empress so that he could steal away to escort Kat and Rori from prison.

It was a boy. Akari. A shiver of unease had traveled the family when Luken, reading Tian's letter aloud to his parents, had reached the announcement of the infant's name and gender. A situation made even more awkward by the fact that Lady Kenkazu did not know Luken was aware of the family's financial situation, or the strain another boy might put on the House. They were all forced to affect a cheerful demeanor, pretending to be unconcerned, while weighing grim figures in their minds. Typically, in such situations, the boy would be devoted to the military. Tian was, after all, only Kenkazu's Fourth Daughter. Her children were already low-ranking in the House, and two of her elder sisters already had boys. Akari may have been Tian's first son, but to the House, he was the proverbial third boy, and therefore useless beyond useless. Destined for the Weeping Mother, as Cami and Sami would have said.

But Tian didn't want to give him up. Of course she didn't. Like Eitan, Tian was the type to keep all her children, no matter how it affected the rest of the family. And the House would fall farther into debt.

Eventually, the debtors would come demanding their due. The House's finery would be sold piece by piece, its property sold off parcel by parcel. In time, the House itself would be sold, and the Pear Blossom would be demoted to a Minor House and resettled on a smaller property. It was likely that a financially prosperous Minor House would be promoted to a Middling House so that the number of Houses remained stable. Perhaps the Swift Nimbus, or the Jasper. The Ladies of Minor Houses waited their entire lives for such a rare opportunity.

But they would not get it this time. Not from Luken's family.

These thoughts chased themselves through Luken's mind as he stood motionless in the main room of his chambers, considering the chest in the corner.

His parents discovered him, still standing there, when they returned from brunch.

"Mother," he turned towards them, "can I speak to you on the balcony?"

Amana gave him a wry look. No doubt he'd guessed the topic of their conversation. "I'll finish packing, love." He kissed Kenkazu's cheek and quickened to the staircase.

Luken led his mother out onto the balcony, and slid the glass door shut behind them. The Garden stretched below in a great white crescent that reached the wall. The dark peaks of tiled roofs hinted at the city beyond. The ink-blot shapes of cloud-shadows traveled over the earth, slow and weighty as whales traversing the depths of the sea. A cool breeze rolled in, caressing Luken's face.

Luken placed his hands on the railing of the balcony. The vines of his morning glories had never fully recovered from the winter cold; dry and tawny-pale, they tangled their thin fingers through the trellis below. But Luken had hope that in time, they might still bloom.

Lady Kenkazu shoved her hands into the pockets of her navy blue coat. "Is something wrong?"

Luken swallowed. He'd never been good at these kinds of conversations. But then again, neither had she. Hadn't someone told him once that he'd inherited the best from both his parents? These days, he rather thought he embodied the worst of them.

"I know the House of the Pear Blossom is broke, Mother."

She stiffened, and swore under her breath. "Amana."

"No, he didn't tell me. It doesn't matter how I know. Listen, I'm giving you the rest of my Conjugal Price."

She shook her head angrily. "No, you're not."

"Yes, I am."

"You're my *son*. What kind of Lady has to turn to her own son for a loan?"

"It's not a loan. Call it whatever you want. A gift, a payment. A return on your investment for raising me to be a courtesan rather than devoting me to the army. It doesn't matter. You're 300,000 in debt, right? The remainder of my Conjugal Price will cover that. This will give you the chance to start over, start clean."

"Those are your savings, Luken. To provide for you when you retire from courtesan work."

"Mother." He waited until she looked at him. "Very soon, I will no longer be a courtesan."

Kenkazu met his gaze. She drew a deep breath, understanding blooming through her. Whistling through her teeth, she turned away. The wind tossed the short threads of iron back from her face. "We did hear that Lord Aokinay no longer occupied the Palace. Amana thought, maybe..."

Luken allowed himself a grim smile. "So you see, I no longer need the money. Take it."

Kenkazu hesitated. He sensed her weakening.

"300,000?"

"Yes. I'd have to pull the second installment of my Conjugal Price from the Palace Vaults, but yes."

Finally, she shook her head. "It's just too much money, Luken. I have my pride."

"You have *grandchildren*," he said softly, but with emphasis. She winced. "Think of Akari. Newborn, just starting out in life. Give him a fresh start. A fair chance. Don't we all deserve that?"

Her grip tightened on the railing. "Why do you want this so badly, Luken?"

"Because we are family."

"You're no longer a member of the House of the Pear Blossom. The Ladies of the House must maintain it. It's not your responsibility."

"I have chosen my responsibilities. I am choosing family."

"Why?"

A soft laugh. He spread his arms, as if to embrace the sweep of the earth before them, the Garden laid out in all its beauty. "What else is there? Gems and wine? Who cares?" He shook his head. "I know I am only a spoiled little boy who has never had to labor for anything or risk life and limb, either to birth new life, or to maintain it. But I have worked and suffered, in my own way. I am trying, in my own way. I have so little agency." A note of pleading entered his voice. "Let me do this, Mother. Don't tell me I cannot make my choice."

A long sigh. Another muttered curse.

And then, to Luken's shock, tears started in her eyes.

"Mama, don't-"

"Luken." Turning to him, she took his face in both hands. "You are- Seven Hells. I am so proud of you."

Tears stung at his eyes now. *"Mama."* Tears spilled down his cheeks, unveiling ribbons of bare skin through his courtesan's paint. "Stop."

There was, through it all, a sense of unbearable parting. He had declared his unbreakable loyalty to the family, even as he felt himself severed from it forever. His life, inextricably separate from theirs. And yet, in some fashion, did he not always walk the hallways of the House of the Pear Blossom? Did the echo of his boyish laughter not ring eternal in the orchards where he and Tian had played out their childhood? Was he not always with her, and she with him, even should the whole of the Empire stand between them?

Lady Kenkazu embraced him, and they stood like that, together on the balcony, for a long time.

So long that Amana yanked the door aside, his features annoyed, impatient. He took one look at them, scoffed, and said, "So, we're taking the money. Thank Goddess."

Kenkazu pulled away with a breathless laugh, but turning to Amana, she grew stern. "Amana," she waved him over. "We are about to leave O-Han and will not be returning, probably for a long time. Come say a proper goodbye to your son."

Black, rat-like eyes darted to Luken. "Goodbye."

"Amana." Kenkazu's voice quieted, went cold. "Tell your son you love him."

Amana blinked, stared at her. Then, without looking at Luken, he shrugged. "Of course I love him.

He's my son."

He vanished back into Luken's chambers, where their traveling cases awaited them.

Luken stared into the dimness of his chambers. He'd waited his entire life to hear his father speak those words and now that he'd heard them, he didn't know how to feel.

It was not until he bid his parents farewell and watched their traveling coach clatter down the white road, toward the Palace gates, that Luken felt a powerful and joyous acceptance overwhelm him.

Chapter Thirty-One

"Are you positively *sure* about this?"

Bo Tashe stood in Luken's chambers, limp with astonishment. The loose robes of Luken's powder blue ando – his first ando, his only possession when he'd come to Court – hung in the retired courtesan's hands, a sprawl of pale blue silk.

Luken, seated in his plush chair with his feet up on a side-table, smiled at Bo Tashe. "I'm sure."

Bo Tashe shook his head. "This will not go over well, my lord. I've seen some bold fashion choices from Royal concubines and high-profile courtesans in my day, but this, *this*." The ando-maker broke off, bewildered.

"Trust me." As he spoke, Luken riffled through the box of his grandfather's papers. He'd read almost the entirety of the journals, gazed long on the sketches and doodles, and made his way through the hundreds of scraps that littered the boxes, pulling them up one by one. Some compulsion moved him; he would read all of Marigold's writings, and carry the words with him.

Bo Tashe sighed. "It's just such a waste."

"Thank you, Bo," Luken said with patience, dropping another scrap back into the box and picking up the old journal. "Please return when you've fashioned the ando to my wishes. I must have it by the day of the Spring Gala."

The ando-maker regarded him, then dipped into a dramatic bow, his free hand tracing a flourish. "As you wish, my lord."

Bo Tashe took his leave, a flurry of assistants fluttering around him. When the door swung shut behind them, Luken's attention returned to the journal in his hand, and his gaze fell on unfamiliar lines; he'd reached the final entry.

Luken traced the words, once. He felt his chest rise and fall more sharply, his heart quickened. "Oh, Marigold…"

He read the entry again, a sacred weight settling over his heart.

"We are all alike," he whispered to the dead. "Generation after generation, we are alike."

Luken sighed, and pushed Marigold's box aside. He'd read the last of it.

Luken gazed into the grand dimness of his chambers, the shadows that traced the corners up into the dome.

He'd made his choice.

He reached for the knife that sat beside Marigold's box on the side-table, and raised it to regard the blade.

He'd made his choice.

~

The Spring Gala.

The evening bloomed warm and burnished by starlight. A docile breeze played with the long, colorful skirts of the courtesans' andos as they streamed into West Hall, where the Gala would be held. Ladies strode beside them, in their tailored coats and trousers, black and grey and navy blue. Petals of jasmine dappled the path beneath their feet. An archway of creeping phlox framed the entrance, and a brilliant scene of violet and white shades decked the vast Hall within. Fountains of champagne giggled here and there, and vast tables lined one wall, each laden with a feast. Cages of snow-white doves sat a-twitter, waiting to be released at the stroke of midnight to welcome in the spring.

Of the hundreds of occupants that milled to fill the Hall, High Houses formed the majority, and a few of the favored Middling Houses. The House of the Pear Blossom had received an invitation in deference to the royal concubine's family, but the Lady Kenkazu preferred to hasten home to meet her new grandchild rather than linger in the city. The Empress's concubine, when he arrived, would arrive alone.

But not yet.

The guests gathered in the Hall, a thousand lanterns blazing golden so that the women and men stood illumed as though in the light of the day. Outside, stars drifted out of the darkness; a clear and cloudless night. Within, a clamor of conversation filled the Hall, bubbles of mirth rising into the air.

A note of expectation filtered through the crowd. Rumor, like a hummingbird, flitted from mouth to mouth, as though from blossom to blossom, quick and nectar-sweet. The soft drone spoke of a new Royal Consort to be announced that night by the Empress. Disapproval and support flickered here and there, but it was curiosity that took the night. Curiosity, and expectation; waiting to see the Empress, waiting to see if a new Consort would be announced. And where was the Empress's concubine?

As the night wafted by, that question appeared with greater and greater frequency.

As the Gala was in full swing, the Empress arrived. Trumpeted and hailed, she strode across the Hall in a tailored suit of pure white, a long white cape flowing behind her. She took her place in a seat upon the raised dais at the north end of the hall, looking out over the highest members of her Court.

More whispers. Where was her concubine? Why had he not arrived with her? When would the announcement come?

A dramatic entrance then, murmured some with a roll of the eyes, or a trace of excitement.

Fi, the Steward of the Royal Chambers, was glimpsed striding through the Hall with a restless gait before coming to the Empress's side, bending her head to murmur in her ear.

The wait continued, until the hour before midnight.

A new figure appeared in the archway of the entrance. Heads turned, eyes widened. Stilted murmurs.

There, in the entrance to West Hall, stood the antitheses of a courtesan. Ando black as a raven. Hair chopped short like a woman's. The flesh of his face bared, no paint.

Silence spread through the Hall.

~

Luken smiled at the stunned faces.

He started forward, his stride graceful, the black ando a silken dream around him. The air tickled his neck; how strange it felt, for the first time in memory, not to have that long veil of hair draped over him.

But it was time for a change.

The eyes of the crowd followed him, silence trailing in his wake. Luken fixed a straight path to the raised dais at the far end of the Hall, where the Empress stared at him, confusion on her face, and then, a careful mask of ice.

The Hall was glorious, his hyacinths thrust from the tables, fresh and beautiful. Luken's heart ached to see it. He was glad he'd helped plan the Spring Gala; it looked like a good party, though he himself would not enjoy it.

Lords and Ladies gaped at him. Whispers, like a swarm of hornets, buzzed to break the silence.

The Princesses Tsakara, Sakiran, and Oan with Ohfene beside her, stood together staring at him. A flute cracked and spurt champagne across Ohfene's clenched fist.

Fi stood beside the Empress, her lips parted, fury in her eyes. Ah, he knew she'd be angry. She'd lobbied for him. She'd liked him, in her own coarse manner.

It was not without guilt that he met the Court like this, but beyond the guilt, beyond the fear, beyond the shyness, an overwhelming sense of liberation obliterated all shadows.

Luken stopped at the base of the dais, and inclined his head. "My Lady Empress."

Raisaga stared back at him. "Hello Luken." She stood. "Perhaps we should step outside." She cocked her head. "It looks like you have something to say."

"I do, actually."

They left the Hall, a clamor of voices rising up behind them. Raisaga strode through a side archway. Luken followed her, but paused on the threshold, and gazed back at the men and women of the Court. He bared his teeth in a grin, and waved goodbye.

Chapter Thirty-Two

Almost midnight, and still warm in the garden.

Shrugging off winter's chill with roguish scorn, O-Han swaggered back to his sultry warmth with no hesitation.

Luken followed the Empress a short distance, into a small rose garden. The moon burnished all to a pale silver, yet Luken thought he could have picked the red roses from the pink, the yellow from the white. A lantern, hanging from a branch of the lone oak that tangled his roots into the grassy hillock at the center of the garden, shed a pool of pale yellow light across the path; it was here the Empress stopped, and turned to her concubine.

She regarded him, and Luken realized he would miss her. Her staid presence, quiet and yet so confident; her dignified manner, her wry humor; the arching of an eyebrow at just the right moment. She would be the only client Luken had ever worked with that he would miss.

Raisaga gestured toward his ando, her gaze flicking up to his shorn-off hair. "This isn't strictly proper, but I feel like I have to ask..."

"Yes?"

"Have you perhaps gone insane in the twenty-four hours since I last saw you?"

"I have not."

"So there's an explanation for this, ah,

transformation?"

Luken spread his arms, the black fan of his sleeves like the sprawl of a great crow's wings. "You may consider this my formal resignation from courtesan work."

She nodded. "And a public rejection, of what it means to be a courtesan. An insult to the beauty ideals of the Court."

"Yes." He added in a softer voice, "But not a rejection of you, Raisaga."

"No? I am the Empress. It is my Court." A rueful grin. "It does not make me look particularly good that my concubine is publicly mocking the very idea of being a courtesan."

"You inherited the Court from numerous generations of Empresses before you, just as we have both inherited the idea of the courtesan from countless generations before us. We did not make it what it is, but we are making it that which the next generation will inherit. We all must decide, in the end, what we will and will not be a part of."

"So this a public statement you're making?"

"More of a personal one. Perhaps a bit of both." Luken shook his head. "I am not suited to be your concubine, Raisaga. I could never be what you wanted of me."

"You realize I was going to make you my Consort," she said tentatively. "Aokinay has retired to his maternal House. I am prepared to commit to you. It would have been announced tonight." A sad smile. "The offer is still on the table. You would be the most powerful man in Kanai. The most powerful man in the world, in truth."

A bittersweet pang. "I know, I-" He took a breath to steady himself. "I won't lie to you, Raisaga, I was tempted by the possibility. There is a part of me that still craves that power. The ability to set the course of the Empire. To seek vengeance on those I despise, to protect my friends from harm, to force Kanai to progress..." He shook his head. "I have tried my hand at politicking, and known failure and success. I could have been good at it, I think, with a few more years to grow into the role. In another life, I could see myself being quite happy as your Consort. I have always needed a purpose beyond the life of a courtesan, and the power to pursue that purpose. Being your Consort... It would have been a magnificent dream."

She watched him, her dark eyes warm with affection. That stung. She did care for him, he believed that. Luken let his lids fall shut. It *was* a dream that he forsook.

But a man had to wake up sometime, and live his life.

"Why not, then?" came the murmur of her voice.

Luken opened his eyes. "There is another woman."

"Ah." The Empress nodded, looking away. "I see. That would do it, then."

"I'm sorry, Raisaga. I loved her before I ever met you. Before I even dreamed of meeting you. I could never have given you my heart, it had already been given."

"And you're giving up all this?" She gestured to the Palace; it loomed over them, a towering shadow.

The moon lifted from the highest tower, its pale eye piercing the heights. "She must be some woman."

"She is." Luken could not fight the smile from his lips. "Goddess, she is." He sobbed a laugh. "She's pregnant, just now. We're going to start a family."

The Empress smiled. "I'm happy for you." She stared across the gathered roses, their petals bared to the moon. The corner of her mouth twisted. "A man's never rejected me before. I admit, it is not a pleasant sensation."

"I daresay you need not fear that it will happen again."

A shaky laugh. "Easy for you to say. For the first time in my adult life, I have neither Consort nor concubine." In a more serious tone, she asked, "Are you sure about this, Luken? You realize that if you change your mind and return, it is likely I will have moved on."

"Oh, I know you will," Luken said dryly. "But I am sure. It was always going to be Jes."

"When did you know?" she asked with a curiosity so innocent that for a moment, she seemed much younger than she was, and Luken realized, in a bolt of clarity, that she had never been able to tell when a man might have been the one for her. She had never had to choose. With power came possibility, and with so many options, she had never devoted herself to just one. Why pick one, when you might miss out on so many others? There was no need for the Empress to limit herself to one man, or even a small selection of men, like Luken's mother and her Consorts. There was always someone younger, happier, more attractive. And what good was a man anyway if he was not young and vital? The comfort that came with long years of loyalty and trust had never existed for her. Love was always passionate, but never assured. Companionship was always on offer, but performed, never lived. In that moment, Luken pitied her.

And with that realization, Luken felt free for the first time, for he did not envy her in the slightest. Not then, not any more.

"When did I know that I would forsake the Palace for Jes? The moment she told me she was pregnant. I knew. I still had business to settle with the Court before I could leave, but even then, I knew. In truth, I've always known."

She nodded. "You always were a bit different, Luken. I've been disappointed by plenty of men, but I should have known you would be the first to break my heart."

Luken returned a sad smile. Let her think this was heartbreak. She would never know. "I'm sorry."

She held up a hand. "Don't apologize. You were," she grinned that brash grin, "at every stage, magnificent."

For a moment, Luken could not speak. Then he murmured, "I should take my leave."

"Before you go, there's something you should know." The Empress tucked her hands into her pockets. "I was going to tell you this later, but given the circumstances, I suppose it's now or never." Looking away from the roses, she returned her gaze to his. "I've decided to issue an Imperial Mandate."

Luken's back snapped upright. "What?"

She nodded. "The Order of Non-Interference to Reproductive Healthcare Access. It will, henceforth, be illegal to hinder or sabotage the efforts of a citizen of Kanai to access legal reproductive healthcare, either by physical force, physical restraint, deception, coercion, harassment, bait-and-switch tactics, blockading, blackmail, obstructive waiting periods, obstructive parameters or qualifications, intimidating, threatening, harassing or otherwise preventing a medical professional from performing such work, destruction of medical facilities or instruments, administering propaganda to the public with the intent to hinder or deceive, or by any other means interfering with an individual's ability to act on their right to reproductive autonomy and agency, etc. etc. etc. on pain of arrest and imprisonment for a period not to fall below or exceed ten to fifteen years for the violation of said Mandate. In other words," she cocked her head, "mind your own business, and stop bothering my boys about getting a fucking vasectomy."

"Raisaga... I don't know what to say. Thank you." He seized her hand and squeezed it. "Thank you, thank you, thank you."

She chuckled. "I thought you'd like that." The Empress gazed up at the gleam of the moon behind the Palace. "I've entered the twilight years of my reign. A new era of peace and prosperity, I hope. It's time for a little progress. My mother understood that, although she needed guidance from my father to figure it out. Just as he needed her respect and support to become the icon that he became. It's time I lived up to my parents' legacy."

"It will make many people angry."

She laughed. "Of course it will. But my mother was bold in outlawing foot fanning, and she did that for my father and my brother, rest his soul. Who am I, if I cannot stand free of my mother's shadow? I have a son as well. He should not have to die in a botched vasectomy, as my brother died in a botched foot fanning, before there is progress on this issue."

Without a word, Luken flew into her arms, squeezing her to his chest with a mew of excitement. "Raisaga!"

She laughed. "Alright boy, enough. I'm still an old woman, remember?"

Luken set her down, breathless with joy.

But then it was time.

He swallowed. "I have a carriage waiting on the south end of the Palace."

"Ah. I didn't even ask you where you were going."

"There's a little commune up north, near Seven Sisters. My friend Kyo and his son just moved there. Plus Jes was born up north; she reckons it's time to return." He shrugged. "Seems as good a place as any to start a new life."

"The Seven Sisters commune?" Raisaga shook her head. "You don't do anything by half measures, do you, boy? A bunch of socialist farmers out in the rugged wilds. I can't imagine anything less courtly or aristocratic. Are you sure?"

"I could use a little change. Besides," his gaze turned to the stars, "I was promised mist and pines."

"Well, it will certainly be a new life," she said dryly. "I wish you well of it. Come, let me walk you to your carriage."

In companionable silence, Luken and Raisaga made their way in a long arc across the southeastern exterior of the Palace, walking beneath the stars. They passed the exterior of the hall where the Market Board stood, but did not enter, nor was Luken curious to glance at it, though it occurred to him that his name would soon be taken down. It seemed fitting. Lifelle and Isaun were already gone, not to mention Nikay and Satomi. Even Ohfene would soon depart to begin his Conjugal Leave with Princess Oan. He scarcely knew any courtesans any more. Amae had a new trio of boys to train up at the Abode of Scattered Flowers, but Luken had not met any of them. A new generation had replaced them, with all the ruthless speed one could only expect from the Peacock Court, where men were disposable and beauty was a commodity with a short expiration date. And yet, Luken could not shake the feeling that he'd come out on top somehow. Beaten the system.

Maybe it was just the delusional thought of a shy boy leaving the life he'd never been suited for in the first place.

Or maybe it was true.

Either way, the gentle breeze of the night felt glorious as he entered the starlit courtyard that led to the South Gate. A carriage waited there, shadowed and silvery in the moonlight. And beside it, a single figure. Jes.

Aside from the curve of her middle, she looked much the same as she had when they'd first met at Court, all those years ago. She smiled when she saw him, and waved. A white blossom spread its virgin petals in Luken's chest.

He made his way to Jes's side, and felt the press of her pregnant stomach against him as they embraced. He released her with a sigh, but there would be time enough to enjoy the embrace of one another's arms when they had left O-Han.

That precious commodity that they had never really had before, through all the secrecy and stolen encounters – for once and for all, there would be time.

"Ready to go?" she asked.

"You have no idea."

But as he turned to speak a final farewell to Raisaga, a familiar voice and one he really should have remembered by now, rang out across the moonlit courtyard. "Luken!"

Dandy bounded down the steps, stumbled on his joh, and rushed toward them, stopping to jerk a hasty bow to the Empress when he glimpsed her standing to one side, hands in her pockets as she watched him rush over.

And all at once, the most perfect and beautiful idea sparked in Luken's mind. The closing of the circle.

"Raisaga," he said, "let me introduce you to my good friend, Dandy. We're much alike, he and I, except that he is younger than me, and much more pleasant."

She cocked an eyebrow. "Is that right?"

"Luken, you're not really leaving are you?" Dandy arrived in a swirl of scarlet silk, breathing hard from his chase through the Palace.

A sad smile. "I'm afraid I am, Dandy." Luken stepped forward to embrace him. "I will miss you." He whispered in the younger man's ear, "Keep fighting the good fight."

Doe-like eyes blinked at him in confusion.

"Why are you doing this? Why now? I don't understand."

"I'm afraid it's a long story, and one I don't have time for just now. I'll write to you on the road, and explain the whole tale. Until then, just know that I am going to be happy. And I want you to be as well."

Luken gave him a reassuring smile, and gestured to Raisaga.

"Dandy, you have not had the pleasure of meeting the Empress yet, have you?"

"I- well no, I haven't." He bowed again, bearing a shy smile. Raisaga regarded him with interest.

Luken felt Jes at his side, her arm wrapping around his waist.

"We should be going. We've a long way to go, before the sun rises. Dandy," the young courtesan pried his wide eyes from the Empress's face, "you will always be my friend. Raisaga," he said quietly, "you will always be my Lady Empress."

She smiled. "And you will always be the one that got away, Luken Kenkazu-son." She considered Jes. "I hope you are worthy of him."

Jes held her gaze, and Luken wondered if there had ever before, in the history of the Empire, been a moment like this: a servant and an Empress and the lover they shared, while the moon shed equal light on them all. "I shall try, every day of my life, to be so."

Luken wrapped his arms around her waist. "Me too," he whispered.

Jes leaned forward to kiss his cheek. "Shall we?"

"After you."

Jes climbed into the carriage while Luken waved farewell to Dandy and Raisaga, then climbed in after her and thrust back the veil from the window. No need to hide his face anymore. That was for noblemen.

As the carriage began to pull away, Luken looked back to see Dandy and Raisaga, two shadows alone in the moonlit courtyard, already turned toward one another in conversation. Luken grinned to himself. Dandy would make a better Royal Consort than Luken ever would; he was kind, as well as clever, and he did not bear Luken's wounds, Luken's anger. He would pick up the threads Luken had abandoned, and weave them to new and better designs.

When they had slipped from view, and the South Gate clattered shut behind the carriage, Luken turned from the window.

"I grew up in the north," Jes said, one hand resting on her growing middle, "but it feels like a long time since I've breathed that crystalline air. Do you think you'll mind it? It'll be very different than all this."

"I don't care where we go, as long as we go together."

Jes smiled. A full, lovely smile, and Luken felt his heart swell within him, spilling over and out to lace into the world.

The light of the stars and moon lit their path north, to a new and strange wilderness. Just as they reached the city wall and broke through, clattering out onto open land, their eyes met, and the bells in the temples and their towers, piercing the skies of O-Han, tolled midnight.

Likely I will regret it, in time. But if I chose otherwise, I would regret it at once, and certainly. In the end, choose love. Though it tear you open and obliterate the boundaries, choose love. Though it cost you that which you were trained like a dog to hunt all your life, only to veer off path at the last, choose love. Though it is hard, the hardest thing in the world, it should also be the easiest, the easiest and the only. How could it be otherwise? Choose love.

—Journal of Marigold, First Son of the House of the Silver Minnow
Final entry.

Epilogue

"...so everything was perfect, and then they all died." The boy announced, looking up from the paper clenched taut between his chubby fists.

"Thank you, Ollan, that was wonderful." Luken reached out a hand to accept the boy's story, a packet of rumpled papers bearing large, childish writing that came marginally closer to legibility with each passing day. "A little morbid, perhaps, there at the end. But a valiant effort." It was better than Luken could have done, at his age. And worlds away from what any of them had been capable of when their parents – peasants mostly, and the occasional upper-class oddball like himself living in the commune – had sent their children with one bohda each to pay their new teacher and more than one eyebrow raised in skeptical curiosity, to the grassy hollow between the barley fields and the forest, before the school house had even been built. People had doubted then, that reading and writing should really be necessary for children of the commune, especially in this rural corner at the ends of the Empire, in the shadow of the northern mountains. But as more and more peasants had come to Luken in the cabin he shared with Jes and their twins in their early years there, asking him to translate this or that for them or write down this or that request or business contract or deed of ownership to deal with those beyond the limits of their humble commune, eventually they decided that the value of having a literate member of the family spoke for itself. Since then, Luken's classes had never been empty. It had taken nineteen years, but he finally had a class that was equal; five boys, five girls, their faces tanned and freckled by the sun.

He added Ollan's story to the pile on his desk as the boy scurried back to his seat, the floorboards of the little schoolhouse squeaking beneath his feet. Luken hid a grin. "Thank you for reading your stories, children, I know you worked hard on them. I think," he stood, stretching a little as he assumed his aristocratic height – an exotic oddity, in these parts – "we are all eager to enjoy what's left of the sunshine." A silent flurry of excitement shot through the classroom as the children anticipated his next words. "Let's end here, for today. Good work on your assignments, everyone, you are all progressing–" Even before the last few words, they were up, tumbling out the front door, the wind rushing in to tug at the precarious order of the papers he'd collected. Chuckling, Luken tucked the stack of stories into a leather satchel and slung it over one shoulder.

Making his way around the simple square of the one-room schoolhouse, Luken yanked the windows closed, nudged the chairs beneath their desks with his foot, rescued a lost spider from the floorboards and restored it to freedom on the railing of the porch in front of the schoolhouse, then turned to slip the key into the lock, feeling as much as hearing the familiar click of another day done, and turned toward home.

A moment, taking in the lovely sweep of the

world around him.

And every day this beauty, drinking in the echoes. A reverent silence within him, Luken's gaze traveled the ancient crags of the mountains, the rise of the grass-covered hills, the fine twist and stand of the white tree in the distance, who bore a heavy crown of leaves crisped to yellow with autumn's weight. Behind him, over the little peak of the schoolhouse, the earth slipped into the shadows of the pines that heaved upon the mountains where the North began. A fierce cry rebounded off the slopes and echoed; a tiger's cry, in the wilds beyond home. Mist, a gossamer breath, lingered in the hollow between two of the Seven Sisters, the mountains divided by a river whose whispering voice could almost be heard, somewhere beyond the barley. Luken's soul sighed.

A clap of laughter down the road drew him back down to earth, and Luken stepped to the edge of the schoolhouse's little porch and hopped down the steps.

He relished in the movement, the clumsy rush of it as his feet pounded down the wooden steps to find the dirt path soft beneath them.

There was a time when he would have angled himself down those steps with care, lifting the edges of his robes. His body still remembered the weight of the ando. Even now, his shoulders rose on impulse to heft the embrace of an irlan that wasn't there. His feet rolled to find the angle of the joh and smoothed flat against the earth instead. His head shook to settle a length of hair that should have reached his waist, though he felt the ends brush his shoulders. Part of him would always remember. Too deep in his blood, those courtesan years. Some of the people that dwelt here in the commune still teased him for his soft, graceful gait, his rigid posture, the lift of his chin, the way he drew up all his height like a thundercloud gathering in wings of rain before the storm. Well, that too was part of him, even if the years had been long in passing and bittersweet in memory. That too was part of him.

Luken began his way home, treading the long loop of dirt path that led from the schoolhouse, around the barley field, and through a copse of trees to the far side, where his cabin nestled amid the birches. The house was seldom empty when Luken arrived. His son, Lumay, would have returned by now from his apprenticeship among the printers in I-Bo, his fingers stained with ink from loading the presses with the copper placards, each letter arranged just so. Lumay loved the order of it, loved to click each copper square into place, building the sentences one by one, tracing their lambent ridges in the morning light before turning to the ink. Or it would be his twin sister, Eilane, leading the donkey home from the riverbank with clay bobbing on its back, wrapped in a tousle of cloth, to her work-shed and the potter's wheel and the kiln and the thousand pots and vases and vessels that waited, glazed to green and grey and gold beneath the watchful warmth of her eyes.

Jes had a longer way home. She was always the last of them. Last, and long awaited. It was no short ride, her journey from the House of the Towering Oak where she worked as the Lady's steward, across the river and the valley, home to the cabin. A long journey to make five times a week, but the money was good and they needed it. Even with most of his novels now published and the bohda per child he got for each class, the entire sum of Luken's income amounted to little more each year than he might have made in one night as a courtesan. He wouldn't have gone back, though. Not for anything. The wealth of a courtesan had been nice, while it lasted, but dignity was without price and the Court would not have allowed him to have both. He'd made his choice. This was better.

He liked his work, and so did Jes. She would arrive with the last light of the sun, the dappled mare tossing her pale mane in the dust of the road, and her face turned toward him as Luken appeared in the doorway to welcome her home, his waiting for that day done.

Drinking in the echoes.

He only made it a few paces toward home before a voice broke his thoughts.

"Wait!"

Luken turned, blinking at the shadow that peeled from the side of the schoolhouse and jogged after him, a few paces, before slowing to a halt before him, searching Luken's face. Searching with a strange hunger, as if Luken's expression hid traces of salvation.

Luken cocked his head. "Can I help you?"

The stranger stepped closer. Cleared their throat. Their eyes, a lovely, liquid black, looked back and forth between his. "Luken Kenkazu-son?"

An eerie thrill shot through Luken's chest, like a shooting star. No one called him by that name, anymore. Kenkazu-son.

"Yes," he said softly, eyes narrowing as he

looked closer at the stranger's face. At the familiar, black eyes that greeted him as if from a mirror. At the black hair, silken straight, that framed their fair features; the troubled mouth, with the pert arch of the upper lip. Not so different from his son's, not so different from his daughter's.

"Oh..." The breath fled his body, all at once. His eyes widened.

The stranger stepped forward, still searching Luken's face with a desperate intensity. "Do you know me?"

Tears slit Luken's eyes, an emotion more powerful than anything he had felt in years trembling through is body. For he did. He did know them. In his flesh, his blood, his heart, with all the force of time and sudden, indomitable love. "Yes."

Intense emotion twisted their fair features. Despite their fine clothes, dust marred the coat, their gaze weary and ragged from the road. They spoke almost through gritted teeth.

"I've waited a long time and come a great way to find you."

Luken nodded, his jaw burning with pain as he clenched. But when he spoke, it was no more than a whisper. "Of course you have."

A sob wracked their body.

"It's alright," Luken said. "You're here now. You made it." Luken opened his arms and the stranger stepped forward. With his whole being, Luken folded in to embrace them. This stranger, his child, shuddered, returning his embrace. "I'm here."

The World of Kanai

Dramatis Personae

Ahn: First Daughter of the House of Lush Vale, a Middling House on the west coast of the Empire in the Annish region, or A-Region; in love with Lifelle.

Amae: The Master of the Abode of Scattered Flowers. A former courtesan, Amae transitioned to the position of Master after aging out of courtesan work. Second Son of the Sapphire Caves, a Minor House in the Mid-Northwest of the Empire. An ambitious Master, Amae has worked to build the reputation of the Abode in hopes of attaining a stable of High House courtesans; Dandelion, Second Son of the Dawn's Hollow, represents the first acquisition from this strata, though Isaun has been by far his most lucrative courtesan, and Luken, having gone on Conjugal Leave with the Empress's niece, represents his most successful courtesan. Little is known about Amae's history or personal life, but his devotion to his work is unquestioned.

Amana: The Second Consort of the House of the Pear Blossom, father of Luken and Tian. Formerly a courtesan of middling success at Court and the Third Son of the House of Whispering Willows. The youngest of five children borne by Lady Lanu, of the

House of Blooming Riversides and the courtesan, Marigold, and the last now living.

Aokinay: The current Empress's Consort, First Son of the House of Distant Thunder. The Second of Raisaga's Consorts, preceded by Misene. Father of the youngest princess, Sakiran.

Arle: Third Daughter of the House of the Golden Fox, currently dwelling in O-Han. A former client of Luken's.

Asang: The Lady of the House of Stone Cliffs, a High House. Mother of three children, including her eldest, Satomi, a reasonably successful courtesan. Asang resents the Court, as she considers it responsible for the brain damage Satomi endured there.

Birin: The proprietor of The Blue Dahlia, a famous Pillow House, or Pleasure House, in the capital city of O-Han, a frequent venue of high price courtesans. The Blue Dahlia is the favored Pillow House of the Abode of Scattered Flowers.

Cami: A eunuch guard who serves in the Inner Chambers of the Palace. Cami frequently attends Luken and guards his chambers. Formerly a soldier who served in Hindigga.

Dandelion: Second Son of the House of Dawn's Hollow, now of the Abode of Scattered Flowers. "Dandy" is currently being mentored by the courtesan Lifelle, with the expectation of soon beginning work as a courtesan.

Eitan: Fourth Daughter of the House of the Silent Lake. A second cousin of Jesheray. Mother of sons, Jenh and Iko.

Ekaris: First Daughter of the House of Distant Thunder, Steward of Defense, and a prominent member of both the Convention of Representatives and the Noble Assembly, Ekaris is a well-known and powerful Traditionalist politician. Her nephew, Lord Aokinay, is the current Empress's Consort.

Ence: A physician at the Public Health and Resources Clinic in O-Han, which specializes in reproductive healthcare, though not always with the intention of administering it.

Fi Tenh-daughter: The Steward of the Inner Chambers, Fi is a court official appointed by the Empress to govern the affairs of the "Inner Chambers," giving her authority over the administration of the royal family's private chambers. Though Fi herself is asexual, her job often involves serving as mediator to royal Consorts and concubines.

Hani, Daram: First Daughter of the House of the Cerulean Phoenix, a High House descended from Hani, a daughter of the First Empress, and a distant relative of the current Empress. The Hani family is a large, old, wealthy and Acclaimed clan, though in recent decades they are known more for the scandals of their living heiresses and heirs than the accomplishments of their ancestors. Daram Hani recently defeated Soma Eikara to win a position on the Convention.

Iriko: First Son of the House of the Tea Leaf, a High House. Recently the victim of a brutal murder. The case is currently unsolved.

Isaun: Fourth Son of the House of the Lily, now of the Abode of Scattered Flowers. Currently Number Seven on the Market Board of Courtesans. Twenty-eight years of age at the beginning of this tale, father of three known daughters. Isaun's ambition has carried him from humble origins to the forefront of men at Court. He longs to rise farther still, into the arms of a princess. Isaun was Luken's mentor when the younger courtesan first arrived at Court.

Jesheray "Jes": A daughter of the House of the Silent Lake, Jes is part of a lower branch of the family, and is not a Lady, but grew up in the House, where she became close friends with her cousin, Lady Eitan, whom she now serves as an attendant. Jes met Luken when he first arrived at Court, about four and a half years prior to the beginning of this tale, and reunited with him later, when Luken was on Conjugal Leave at the House of the Golden Sun with Lady Dare, a paternal cousin of Eitan's. While staying at the Golden Sun, Jes and Luken began an illicit affair.

Jiren: First Daughter of the House of the Dragonfly, sister of Lady Romyn.

Katobi: The professor of Men's History at the Academy of O-Han. "Kat" is Rori's lover and the couple has lived together in a small apartment in the Topaz District for about nine years. Bias against men in academia remains aggressive and extensive, leaving Katobi one of only a small handful of men who have ever taught at the Academy. A friend of Luken's.

Kenkazu: The Lady of the House of the Pear Blossom. Luken and Tian's mother by her Second Consort, Amana. She has four older children by her First Consort, Sirane.

Kenris: First Son of the House of the Pear Blossom. A courtesan staying with Lady Iku of the House of Honey Hives, where the couple has two young sons. A half brother of Luken. Son of Lady Kenkazu and her First Consort, Sirane.

Kenze: Third Daughter of the House of the Pear Blossom, daughter of Lady Kenkazu and First Consort, Sirane. Luken's half-sister, with whom he has not had much contact in recent years.

Lifelle: First Son of the House of the Jade Mountain, a Middling House located in a region south of O-Han, the capital city of Kanai. Blessed with a mild, pleasant personality, Lifelle has achieved a modest career at Court, but longs to retire to the stability of a Consort position with a respectable Lady. Aged twenty-nine at the start of the novel.

Liliray: A former Empress's Consort. Father of the current Empress, Raisaga. Notably, Liliray was the last Empress's Consort to possess fanned feet, the brutal practice of mutilating the feet of a young boy to appear spread out like a fan. This beauty standard was favored in Kanai for centuries, but outlawed by Empress Aikanzo after the death of her son in a botched foot fanning, though pressure to ban the practice had been building for decades. Liliray also famously ended the practice of keeping Harems, favored by Empresses since the beginning of the Empire. The love affair between Liliray and Aikanzo has become legend, though in recent years, some Traditionalists have tainted Liliray's legacy, painting him as a meddling extremist who destroyed traditional gender roles in the Empire and caused great societal damage, the echoes of which are still being felt. Others consider Liliray a romantic hero who helped guide the Empress to end the cruelty of foot fanning and made men more visible in the political and cultural sphere of the Empire.

Lonyelay: Royal Consort to Empress Eizanfe

in the fifth century of the Old Dynasty. Though his legacy has faded into obscurity, Lonyelay was a controversial and powerful Consort during his time and is sometimes cited by Equalists as an early example of male capacity for leadership in the political realm. Though popular in her youth, Eizanfe deteriorated rapidly in her twilight years, allowing Lonyelay to effectively rule the Empire in her name for a period of almost twenty years, though he is said to have worked closely with Eizanfe even before her decline into poor health and, eventually, senility. Where his legacy does endure, he is best known as an advocate for the poor, the disabled, and an early icon of male suffrage, though mention of his name in modern years is often countered by a sneering reminder that his reforms primarily benefited urban centers, rather than rural areas or the Desmeran Isles.

Luken: Second Son of the House of the Pear Blossom, a Middling House located in central Kanai, near the heartland of the Empire. Now a courtesan of the Peacock Court, of the Abode of Scattered Flowers. Twenty years of age at the beginning of this tale, Luken returned six months previous from a three year stay in the region of U-Wen, where he served as concubine to the Empress's niece, Lady Dare, and produced a much-desired heiress for the House. Deeply devoted to his daughter, Luken would have given up everything to remain in U-Wen, if it were not the site of a great trauma in his life. Still recovering from this trauma, Luken has returned to Court hoping to capitalize on his beauty to such effect that he and Jes will achieve lifelong financial independence and the freedom this will grant.

Lumay: Formerly a promising courtesan from a Middling House, Lumay was disgraced years ago
when he was discovered having an illicit relationship with a woman of low class and no Acclaim. Now a prostitute in O-Han, notorious for his use of oca, a powerful but addictive intoxicant.

Marigold: First Son of the House of the Silver Minnow, now Lord Marigold, residing at the House of the Pear Blossom. Amana's father, Luken and Tian's grandfather. Former Consort of the late Lady Lanu.

Mian: A Lady of the House of Victory Hill, a Middling House. A former client of Lifelle's, one-time client of Luken's. Allied politically with Lady Ekaris's Traditionalist coalition.

Nikay: First Son of the House of Misty Springs, now of the Abode of the Midnight Heron, roommate and friend of Ohfene. A high-ranked courtesan with a winsome disposition.

Noboro: A Lady of the House of Bronze Hills, a High House in a lush agricultural and fishing region. A cousin of the presiding Lady of the House. A client of Luken's.

Oan: The Third Daughter of the reigning Empress Raisaga. A princess of Kanai. Isaun and Ohfene have both sought her affections for years, but not yet managed to secure them.

Ohfene: First Son of the House of the River Serpent, now of the Abode of the Midnight Heron. Abodemate of Nikay. The River Serpent is a High House located in north-central Kanai, and one of the elder Houses of the Empire, descended from an ally of the First Empress. Ohfene's mother, Lady Pazu, is a Traditionalist politician. Ohfene and Isaun have a long-standing rivalry, though its origins are not well known.

Raisaga: Reigning Empress of the Empire of Kanai. Currently sixty years of age. Daughter of Empress Aikanzo and the famous Consort, Liliray. Mother of the Princesses Tsakara, Aizenten, Oan, Sakiran and Prince Lisein.

Romyn: Second Daughter of the House of the Dragonfly, a High House. A devoted client of Isaun's.

Rori: A writer from an upper-middle class background who lives in the Topaz District of O-Han. He lives with his male lover, Katobi, though societal taboos against homosexuality force them to keep their relationship secret. Rori publishes under the female pen name, Jiro Ankade.

Sami: A eunuch guard who serves in the Inner Chambers of the Palace. Sami frequently attends Luken and guards his chambers. Formerly a soldier who served in Hindigga.

Satomi: First Son of the House of the Stone Cliffs, a High House in the far Northeast. Son of Lady Asang. Satomi is a beautiful, redheaded courtesan of Bushan descent. Years of drug abuse, and a head injury incurred on a drunken night in the Palace, altered Satomi's personality, spoiling his previously normal intelligence and leaving him with a childlike demeanor. Satomi is a friend of Luken's and fathered a son with one of Luken's half-sisters, Lady Csin.

Seito: Founder and editor of *Ages*, a magazine published in O-Han, comprised mainly of literary reviews, original fiction, and opinion pieces related to current events, with distinct Reformist leanings. Seito has published work from both Rori and Luken.

Silan: The Lady of the House of Misty Springs, a High House. Mother of Nikay, a successful courtesan.

Tian: Fourth Daughter of the House of the Pear Blossom. Luken's sister, Amana and Kenkazu's daughter. Having returned from expedition with a respectable degree of wealth and Acclaim, she now lives at the House with her courtesan, Tsikoran, and daughter Radin. Prior to arriving at Court, Tian and Luken were close friends, but have grown apart as the demands of the Empire set them on different paths.

Tilar: A Lady of the House of the Swift Nimbus, second cousin to the Lady of that House, which resides in the Y-Region, in the south of the Empire. The scion of a metallurgic processing factory in the Iron District, Tilar resides in O-Han, with her Consort, the writer Koko, and their three sons.

Tsikoran: First Son of the House of the Dreaming Tiger. Currently on Conjugal Leave with Tian. Father of Radin. Formerly Number Nine on the Board, now retired from the Court.

Vinayet: First Son of the House of Aspen Creek, a Minor House in the north of the Empire. The son of Amana and Lady Ede. Luken's half-brother. The two have never met, but Luken has borrowed his half brother's name for use as a pen name.

Xinsey: First Son of the House of the Golden Fox, a Middling House in the A-Region under the governance of the local High House, the Spiraling Doves. A courtesan of the Peacock Court, Xinsey shares an Abode with Satomi.

Yuki: A small white dog owned by Lifelle.

Bloodlines

House of the Pear Blossom

Kenkazu (The Lady) + First Consort (Sirane) = Akane (f), Kenris (m), Csin (f), Kenze (f)

Kenkazu + Second Consort (Amana) = Tian (f), Luken (m)

Akane (The Lady to Be) + A courtesan (Mirabe) = Kenda (f)

Akane + A courtesan (Farian) = Liamore (m)

Kenris (First Son, on Conjugal Leave) + Iku (Second Daughter of the House of Honey Hives) = Miku (m), Noa (m)

Csin (Second Daughter) + A courtesan (Satomi) = Sakio (m)

Kenze (Third Daughter) + A courtesan (Kokosi) = Aifin (f)

Tian (Fourth Daughter) + A courtesan (Tsikoran) = Radin (f), Akari (m)

Luken + Dare (First Daughter of the House of the Golden Sun) = Valor (f)

Luken + Kahr (First Daughter of the House of Emerald Echoes) = Roku (m)

The Royal Family: House of the Peacock

Aikanzo (former Empress) + former Empress's Consort (Liliray) = Raisaga (f), Rakayo (f), (exiled to a guarded island in former Desmera after failed coup attempting to wrest power from twin sister) Aifilian (f), Airaya (m) (died young due to infection incurred during foot fanning)

        Raisaga (Empress) + First Consort (Misene) = Tsakara (f), Aizenten (f), Oan (f), Lisein (m)

        Raisaga (Empress) + Second Consort (Aokinay) = Sakiran

        Tsakara (Heiress Apparent) + A courtesan (Sirikaf) = Tsakahn (f), Marikay (m), Eonin (m)

        Aizenten + A courtesan (Meril) = Raikaya (m)

        Aizenten + A courtesan (Orikan) = Raisoma (m)

        Aizenten + A courtesan (Peony) = Rainon (f)

        Aifilian (Third Daughter) + A courtesan (Bonsanay) = Dare (f), Hiro (f)

        Aifilian (Third Daughter) + A courtesan (Tennet) = Jinat (m), Xane (f)

House of the Golden Sun

Dare (The Lady) + a courtesan (Asos) = Ami (m)

        Dare + A courtesan (Atakay) = Aili (m)

        Dare + A courtesan (Luken) = Valor (f)

Hiro (Second Daughter) + a courtesan (Oni) = Hiran (f)

Xane (Third Daughter) = Xilee "Lee" (f), Tyane (f), Darsan (f), Sarine (m), Sien (m), Erelies (m)

Jinat (First Son)

Currency

The Empire's currency is the bohda. Bohda consist of a gold coin, stamped with the image of the current Empress's visage at the time of the bohda's creation. Older bohdas, bearing the images of bygone Empresses, are frequently collected by Ladies; the more distant in history the Empress, the more valuable the bohda to collectors, though their official value is held static in the market.

A cule is equal to ½ of a bohda and consists of a silver coin 2/3 the size of a bohda.

A denny is equal to 1/100 of a bohda and consists of a copper coin ½ the size of a bohda.

Paper currency also exists to represent quantities of bohda at 10, 20, 30, etc. through 100, and 500, 1000, 5000, 10,000, and 50,000.

Time

Lengths of time in the Kanain calendar – 28 days per month; 12 months per year, in addition to a fourteen day holiday period bridging the old year to the new year; 350 days per year. The first day of the year is also the first day of Spring.

Days of the Week: There are seven days in a week, four weeks in a month. Each day represents one of the seven Sacred Symbols associated with the primary Goddess, the Mother-and-Daughter, of the now-dominant Han religion.

Day One – Mother's Morn/Eve
Day Two – Daughter's Morn/Eve
Day Three – Peahen's Morn/Eve
Day Four – Raven's Morn/Eve
Day Five – Moon's Morn/Eve
Day Six – Shield's Morn/Eve
Day Seven – Maple's Morn/Eve

Months of the Year:
Spring: O-Sen, O-Mer, O-Tu
Summer: U-Roan, U-Baro, U-Iso
Fall: E-Losu, E-Haram, E-Temen
Winter: A-Bi, A-Gan, A-My

History

The Empire of Kanai was founded a millennia ago, when the rudimentary noble class of the E-So region absorbed the neighboring region, then called Juniop, renamed E-Si. The foremost Lady of E-So, Enkahna Mis, declared herself Empress Kanai, and began expanding her empire to either coast via a relentless combination of military aggression, expanding trade routes, economic influence, and cunning diplomacy. The Era of Expansion continued for three centuries as the Empire absorbed the lesser territories to the east and west. This ended the most aggressive period of expansion, but the Empire continued to push its border north, into the less-populated hills and mountains, and south, into the rural regions and hamlets. The southwest was the last corner of the mainland continent to be integrated, and famously waged a savage resistance to the Empire. The Y-Region, on the coast, was absorbed, liberated, and reabsorbed, no less than four times over a period of 160 years. The Empire widened its borders across the Barsenij Sea and began establishing colonies on two continents over the following century, while opening expansive trade routes across twenty countries.

At the turn of the millennia, Kanai encompasses a third of the known world, and trades with or possesses colonies throughout over half the world.

The Military of Kanai

In its vastness, might, and cultural and economic influence, the Empire of Kanai is unmatched. While economic influence is the preferred method of contact with other nations, trade with foreign powers often results in exploitation of native resources and labor, leading to division among the populace and, ultimately, defiance to a Kanain presence in that region, often resulting in the deployment of a martial force. Often, the purpose of this military presence begins as a protective measure and evolves into full-blown war. The culprit behind these evolving tensions depends on who is asked; Kanain merchants and Ladies will point to hostility among lower-class members of the local populace who resent the wealth enjoyed by upper-class natives as a result of foreign trade. Lower-class members of the local populace will point to Kanain intruders as the cause of division and disruption in the region. Upper-class members of the local populace, made rich by foreign trade, typically attempt to control the remainder of the population for fear that failure to do so will result in Kanain interference that will expand until Imperial acquisition of the region becomes inevitable. This has been the cycle of foreign relations for Kanai for centuries, until their sphere of influence has grown to include much of the known world. Regardless of who is asked, all would agree that once the sails of Kanain warships appear on the horizon, the matter is more or less settled, for the advent of

Kanain soldiers is, more often than not, a life-long commitment.

Kanai's military structure is unique; they do not recruit adult men or women. In fact, they do not recruit at all. While adults can volunteer at a later date, most soldiers are "devoted" to the army as infants. Working class Kanain citizens and serfs often devote male children to the army because they cannot afford the financial burden of keeping them. However, Noble Houses also commonly devote their sons. The reasons for this are more complicated, though finances may also play a role. Minor Houses often devote the majority of their sons, simply to avoid the high costs of raising a lord for Court, which is often an expensive process, especially if the mother attempts to have the boy tutored or outfitted with a wardrobe of andos prior to his Ascension to Court, thereby increasing his chances of kicking off a successful career. In such Houses, only the most promising boys – those deemed likely to earn a return on their mother's investment – are kept.

Shame is another major factor in the devotion of boys to the military. While fertility and high birth rates are prized in the Empire, the curse of excessive sons is an ever-present threat. The social stigma surrounding the proverbial "excess of sons" is high, especially in more traditional regions of the Empire. It is not uncommon, in such regions, to find that a Noble House boasts a plethora of female children, cousins, and tertiary relations, but one Consort, and perhaps one or two young lords. More than two sons per Noble House would be looked at askance in most regions of the Empire. Generously, a third or fourth son might provoke a shake of the head, an indulgent laugh, as if to say, "What bad luck, there. But your mother couldn't help but keep you, bless her heart." Less generously, the mother would be deemed selfish, even sullied, by the failure to devote these additional sons to the military, while the other Ladies of the House would lose Acclaim in society at large as a result of what would be perceived as a moral failure, or an inability to be properly strict with the indulgent mother.

As a result of these societal pressures, many male infants are devoted to the military each year by the Noble Houses, and are typically collected by the mysterious Grey Hoods, an organization within the Kanain military consisting of women who not only retrieve boys for devotion, but bring them to the camps that will form their childhood homes, and nurse them through their early years, until they are old enough to join the First Barracks.

Once taken by the Grey Hoods, boys are stripped of their name and rank. Some mothers comfort themselves by hiding tokens and symbols in their son's blankets, often with a romantic notion that the boy will cling to this talisman throughout his childhood and the rigors of his training before, somehow, making his way back to his mother many years later, preferably with glory and some riches from their victories in conflicts abroad. In reality, the Grey Hoods add these talismans to the walls of their own housing in the Grey Barracks of each camp, where they form quite the collection, and tell each boy – when they inevitably ask where they came from – the same story: they were brought to the camp on a rainy night by a pauper woman, who wished only for food in her son's mouth and a roof over his head. In this way, princes and peasants serve side-by-side in the Kanain army, their origins shrouded in the same twilight of uncertainty. The famous Pauper in the Rain story has taken on such legendary weight in the Kanain military that images of such a woman – barefoot, thin, her hooded head bent beneath the rain – started to appear on murals in military bases across the Five Continents while her symbol, a raindrop falling from a half-lidded eye, also called the Weeping Eye, has become the unofficial symbol of Kanain soldiers, who jokingly acknowledge her as their universal mother – the more religiously-inclined soldiers conflating her with the Mother Goddess of the Han tradition – and are wont to leave her Eye carved or painted across the temple walls and crooked trees and stones of distant shores. In this way, the Weeping Eye has appeared all across the world, and birthed its own legends among the indigenous peoples who witness it appear in the wake of war, like embers left scattered from the flames of battle.

Because Kanain soldiers are typically raised as soldiers from infancy, their training begins early, and they know no other life. Their education consists only of military strategy, weaponry, and intensive physical conditioning. Obedience is their religion, loyalty is their common bond. They are brothers in one collective family. The Grey Hoods and female commanding officers are their mothers and elder sisters.

High-ranking orders in the military are always reserved for Ladies educated in the Academies of

Kanai; this includes ship captains, martial engineers, siege technicians, explosives experts, chemical warfare scientists, etc. Any position which requires above-average education or authority can only be applied for by a woman. Men, however, can move up in the ranks based on service history, sometimes achieving authority that may even surpass a Lady's in some circumstances.

To avoid troublesome activities, all soldiers are eunuchs, and the procedure of becoming such is treated with great ceremony and celebration in the army. It is considered a fundamental rite of passage, and the culmination of years of fierce training before the final coming-of-age procedure, at which point the boy is now considered a soldier proper, and may join his brothers in the glorious ranks of manhood. Masculinity is understood differently in the army than the remainder of Kanain society, and Ladies who take martial jobs are trained on the subject of proper conduct with male soldiers, as opposed to the peasants and lords they are accustomed to. "These are not courtesans," is the first lesson, and a hard one for some Ladies. A culture of fraternity and sisterhood is encouraged in the military, but the first and final virtue is loyalty to Kanai, which is prized at all times, above all else. Masculinity in the Kanain army is presented as a form of casual cheerfulness in the face of danger and hardship, and a "good man" is one who shoulders the heaviest burden with a smile, protects his brothers, honors his mothers, laughs at death, but holds in his heart a kind of grave and beautiful fatalism by which all life is considered short and brutal, but duties achieved in Mother Kanai's name will buy your passage home. *Home*, to the orphan soldiers of Kanai, represents a sort of mythic site of the mind; interwoven with and yet always beyond the literal Kanai of this world, the Kanai of the *homeland* is larger than life, a sort of ever-present after-life that is never far away, difficult to define and yet marked by a sense of absolute belonging and completion, to which a soldier will be welcomed, when his duties to Kanai are fulfilled.

The Noble Houses

The Empire of Kanai is governed by a matriarchal system of aristocracy. The Empress forms the center of the Empire, though in the past two hundred years, her power has been limited to a certain extent by the growing influence of the elected Convention of Representatives, and the Noble Assembly. The Empress is considered the legal owner of the land and resources contained within the Empire. The land is subdivided and managed by the Noble Houses, who utilize the land to generate wealth, which in turn is used to enforce the law within their territories. The earliest Houses were granted to Empress Kanai's closest allies, and female kin. The land was divided among them, and these later became the High Houses. The Middling Houses are comprised of a combination of lesser rulers who accepted the reign of the Empire. Minor Houses were awarded to allies of the Empress's supporters.

Most Noble Houses are now related to one another by blood, as well as by trade and fealty, as the chief method of securing an alliance in the first centuries of the Empire was the trading of sons as reproductive entities between Ladies. The sons became consorts in the Houses of their mother's allies, and were required to produce a daughter in order to fulfill the terms of the contract agreed upon between the Ladies. This ritualistic exchange forms the primordial origin of the modern courtesan system. After the daughter had been produced, the consorts were released from the terms of the contract and were allowed to return to their mother's Houses. However, many of these men chose to stay in their new Households and preside as the Lord of the House, producing more children with their Lady and raising their sons to be proper lords, laying the groundwork for what later became the Consort system.

The Noble Houses of Kanai are comprised according to three tiers: eighteen High Houses, thirty Middling Houses, and sixty Minor Houses. For the first seven centuries of Kanai's existence, the Empire was divided into ten regions, but the widening horizons of the Empire eventually demanded a restructuring. The Empire was divided into fifteen regions, one in the control of each of the fifteen High Houses that existed at the time. Since Year 732, three Middling Houses have been promoted to High Houses, resulting in eighteen High Houses for the fifteen regions. Each region also contains two Middling Houses and four Minor Houses.

Representatives of the Noble Houses form the members of the Noble Assembly, which, along with the democratically elected members of the Convention, form a system of checks and balances that control the rule of law in Kanai. Theoretically, the Empress possesses veto power on all issues, but there are limited circumstances in which the Convention and Assembly can countermand her decisions, typically by blocking funding from their regions. The Empress's power can only be repealed if she is declared unfit to rule by nine-tenths of both representative bodies, a situation that has occurred only once in the history of the Empire, when Empress

Saisome was declared unfit to rule by reason of insanity, and, lacking any daughters, the young Empress's throne passed to her niece, Empress Kome.

The Names of Noble Houses

The High Houses of Kanai: The Golden Sun, The Dreaming Tiger, The Obsidian Moon, The Dragonfly, The Gossamer Moth, The Misty Springs, The River Serpent, Endless Jasmine, The Stone Cliffs, Spiraling Doves, Bronze Hills, Effulgent Mist, The Cerulean Phoenix, The Star Glade, Dawn's Hollow, The Tea Leaf, Distant Thunder, The Peacock (Empress's Household)

Middling Houses: The Pear Blossom, The Jade Mountain, The Silent Lake, The Plum Tree, The Apricot Orchard, Emerald Echoes, The White Doe, The Roseate Tortoise, The Honey Hives, Morning Glories, The Silver Shield, The Swift Nimbus, The Golden Fox, Victory Hill, The Green Sea, The Towering Oak, Great Falls, The Gravid Mare, Abundant Fields, The Fecund Woods, The Lush Vale, The Plenteous Orchard, The Left Wren, The Black Bear, The Sunken Star, Grey Mount, The Bluejay, The Seashell, Full Sails, Ivory Road

Minor Houses of Note: The Lily, The Silver Minnow, The Sapphire Caves, The Gentle Rain, The Whispering Willows, Blooming Riversides, Aspen Creek, Waving Fronds, The Jasper, etc.

Political Affiliations* of the High and Middling Houses**

Traditionalist High Houses: The Cerulean Phoenix, The River Serpent, Distant Thunder, The Golden Sun, The Obsidian Moon, The Dragonfly, Endless Jasmine, Spiraling Doves

Reformist High Houses: The Dreaming Tiger, The Gossamer Moth, The Star Glade, Dawn's Hollow, The Tea Leaf, Bronze Hills, Effulgent Mist (an inconsistent ally, the High Lady sometimes votes with Traditionalists on specific issues)

Politically-neutral High Houses: The Misty Springs, The Stone Cliffs

Traditionalist Middling Houses: The Jade Mountain, The Roseate Tortoise, The Golden Fox, The Lush Vale, The Plenteous Orchard, Ivory Road, Victory Hill, Great Falls, The Swift Nimbus, Abundant Fields, The Fecund Woods

Reformist Middling Houses: The Pear Blossom, The Honey Hives, The Towering Oak, The Seashell, Full Sails, The Bluejay, The Green Sea, The White Doe, Morning Glories, The Left Wren, Grey Mount, The Gravid Mare, The Silver Shield

Politically-neutral Middling Houses: The Silent Lake, The Plum Tree, The Apricot Orchard, The Black Bear, The Sunken Star, Emerald Echoes

*Note: Political affiliations typically clump into specific regions; the O-Region and U-Region on the east coast run Traditionalist, while the I-Region in the north and A-Region on the west coast vote Reformist. The chaotic Y-Region, in the southwest, largely trends Reformist though it also possesses one of the largest Traditionalist High Houses. In the middle of the Empire, the E-Region is split with the larger northern area voting Traditionalist and the south voting Reformist; the Desmeran Islands, though considered part of the Traditionalist O-Region, have voted Reformist with stunning consistency since their forced acquisition into the Empire about two hundred years ago.

**Note: Minor Houses typically vote in accordance with the High Houses of their regions, for fear of losing trade and local influence if they run contrary to their High Ladies, with the notable exception of the doughty little House of Bright Lightning, which famously votes Reformist, to the continual annoyance of their High House, the extremely Traditionalist Distant Thunder.